For Barbara —

TOMB
❧ of the ❧
QUEEN

Enjoy the magic!

NEW YORK TIMES BESTSELLING AUTHOR
JOSS WALKER

**TWO
TALES**
PRESS

PRAISE FOR THE NOVELS OF
J.T. ELLISON

"Mesmerizing...a compulsively readable tale."
—**Publishers Weekly, starred review on Her Dark Lies**

"Exceptional...Ellison's best work to date."
—**Publishers Weekly, starred review on Lie To Me**

"Outstanding...Ellison is at the top of her game."
—**Publishers Weekly, starred review on Tear Me Apart**

"Shocking suspense, compelling characters and
fascinating forensic details. When it comes to fast-paced
thrillers, J.T. Ellison always has her game on."
—**Lisa Gardner, #1 New York Times Bestselling
Author of Before She Disappeared**

"Wonderful ... a one-more-chapter,
don't-eat-dinner, stay-up-late sensation."
—**Lee Child, #1 New York Times Bestselling
Author of the Jack Reacher series on Lie To Me**

"What J.T. Ellison has done with the city in her award-winning
Taylor Jackson books is magnificent... Lovers of mystery and sus-
pense fiction could not ask for more."
—**Bookreporter**

"Crime fiction has a new name to watch."
—**John Connolly, international bestselling
author of the Charlie Parker series**

"Tightly plotted and often surprising,
this story drew me in and wouldn't let go. A gem!"
—**Keri Rojas, Cornerstone Cottage Kids, Hampton, on
A Deeper Darkness, the May 2012 Indie Next Pick**

PRAISE FOR THE NOVELS OF
ALISHA KLAPHEKE

§⊩ ✦ ⊣⟨§

Praise for the *Kingdoms of Lore* series

"Strong heroines. Swoon-worthy heroes. And banter for days. She weaves magic into every word." **—Melissa Wright, international bestselling author of the *Frey series***

"Whenever jumping into one of her books, I always know the world building is going to be on point."
—Emma Hamm, *USA Today* bestselling author of *Heart of the Fae* and *Of Goblins and Gold*

"Humorous, adventurous, breathtaking world building, and romantic tension that perfectly finds the balance between steamy and sweet. Her writing is gorgeous."
—Sylvia Mercedes, international bestselling author of *The Moonfire Bride* and the *Venatrix Chronicles*

"Sparks fly from page one! Five stars all the way!"
—Tara Grayce, international bestselling author of the *Elven Alliance* series

§⊩ ✦ ⊣⟨§

Praise for the *Queens of Steel and Starlight* series

"The worldbuilding is beautifully detailed and the characters are amazing!" **—*Two Chicks on Books Blog***

"A spellbinding tale of adventure, the perfect amount of romance, and characters so fleshed out they feel real. You'll devour this addictively immersive and unique fantasy world."
—Audrey Grey, *USA Today* bestselling author of the *Kingdom of Runes* series

ALSO BY J.T. ELLISON

ALSO BY ALISHA KLAPHEKE

QUEENS OF STEEL AND STARLIGHT SERIES
WATERS OF SALT AND SIN
FEVER OF SUN AND SOUL
PLAINS OF SAND AND STEEL
FOREST OF SILVER AND SECRETS
RUNE KINGDOM

THE EDINBURGH SEER TRILOGY
THE EDINBURGH SEER
THE EDINBURGH HEIR
THE EDINBURGH FATE

DRAGONS RISING SERIES
FATE OF DRAGONS
BAND OF BREAKERS
QUEEN OF SEAS
SWORD OF OAK
MAGIC OF LORE

KINGDOMS OF LORE SERIES
ENCHANTING THE ELVEN MAGE
ENCHANTING THE FAE PRINCE
ENCHANTING THE DRAGON LORD
ENCHANTING THE SIREN KING

YEW QUEEN SERIES, WRITING AS EVE A. HUNT
FAE CURSE
FAE WORLD
FAE SPELL

DEDICATION

For all the girls who are coming into their powers,
and the extraordinary women they will become.

TOMB OF THE QUEEN

ISBN: 978-1-948967-34-1

For more works by J.T. Ellison, visit TwoTalesPress.com or JTEllison.com

TWO
TALES
PRESS

PART ONE

"I cannot go on playing like that woman
That had but the cold blood of the sea in her veins."

–Deirdre, William Butler Yeats

CHAPTER ONE

Nashville, Tennessee
Now

This meeting was never going to end.

Jayne focused hard on her boss, willing the head librarian to just stop talking. She imagined the woman's lips becoming a zipper and pulling the tab closed from across the room. Nothing. Willed the lights to go off, to no avail. Muttered some words in Latin that roughly translated to *may you be spirited away by gentle dogs*, and yet the woman kept prattling on.

Sadly, unlike the worlds in Jayne's beloved fantasy novels, this one had no such thing as magic. That fact wouldn't stop Jayne from longing for it.

She checked the time on her beat-up phone, the Vandy Research Department's logo superimposed over a shot of Hogwarts blinking across the screen. Nearly six. If they didn't wrap this meeting soon, she was definitely going to be late for dinner with her sister.

"Tomorrow," Eleanor droned on, "Jayne will collate the Latin American poetry and keep tabs on the research room as needed. The rest of you…"

Jayne's phone lit up with a text.

Running late, will see you at 6:30, kk?

A smile pulled at Jayne's lips. Sofia always ran a little behind schedule. Normally it drove her crazy, but tonight, it was a relief. Jayne hated being late almost as much as she hated nights without dessert.

Sounds good, she replied.

"Miss Thorne?"

Jayne's head snapped up. Eleanor was staring at her. "Yes?"

"Do you have somewhere you need to be?"

"Um…yes? No. No, I'm fine."

Eleanor cleared her throat and dropped her glasses, which swung across her chest on a gold chain. "If Miss Thorne can't keep her attention on her work any longer, it seems I've kept you all too long. See you tomorrow."

Finally.

Avoiding a one-on-one with her boss, Jayne followed the rest of the staff into the corridor. If she slipped down to the vault right now and checked the location of the Latin American poems, she'd have a head start on tomorrow's work. She had thirty minutes. She could do this. The bar where she was meeting Sofia was right down the sidewalk.

While everyone else said their good nights, Jayne went to her small office beside the registration desk and stripped out of her cardigan.

"I'll lock up," she called to the vault manager, who waved, relieved to be able to sneak out herself.

Jayne retrieved a book cart, then walked through the reading room to the elevator. When the doors opened, she inserted her key to access the vault level.

The silence afforded by the vault's thick, partially underground walls brought a smile to Jayne's lips. If all the world could enjoy such quiet. At least once in a while. She loved a good night out with live music, but silence was her preference, especially when books were involved.

In the vault, rare books were shelved to the right, and manuscripts, mostly contained in gray boxes, lived on the left. The hush of paper was her only companion today. Slipping down the stacks, Jayne found the three editions of the poetry manuscript and carefully brought them to the table in the center of the room.

This workstation was always a mess. Today someone had left behind a huge, brass microscope and five stacks of papers other staff members were in the middle of cataloguing. Would it kill them to put their work away at night? It was almost as if they enjoyed torturing her, she who put stock in neatness. She had her mother to blame for that trait, she supposed. "Neatness begets order," she would say, staring into Jayne and Sofia's bedroom and shaking her head at the chaos. Always Sofia's. Never Jayne's.

Sighing loudly, though no one was around to hear her, Jayne shook her head and gently cleared a space. The edition at the top of her own stack was nothing more than simple text on parchment. Jayne's studies in Greek and Latin weren't very helpful with this language, nor was her experience studying Irish mythology, but, happily, she spoke decent Spanish and could therefore muddle out most of what was written. Most. Some of the lines were in a dialect spoken by African slaves and she had no idea what was being said.

A tiny, ungrateful part of her wished once again that she'd

nabbed that position at the Library of Trinity College in Dublin, where the Book of Leinster resided. She'd written her thesis comparing the manuscript's version of the old Irish *Cattle Raid of Cooley* with the *Iliad*. But of course, she was just starting out on this bookish career. Maybe someday she'd get the chance to fully immerse herself into Irish mythology and slake her ever-present thirst for more knowledge about the great books of that culture.

Lining up the three editions of the Latin American poems side by side, she studied them for visual differences, looking for an extra paragraph or an obvious additional page.

When she picked up the fourth page of the first edition, a strange hum vibrated through her fingers. Her head began to swim, and something about the feeling was oddly familiar. Comforting. Then the spots started.

She yanked her hand away from the parchment. Oh no. Not now. She had too much to do to be felled. Her ocular migraines were rare, but bothersome enough to ruin her for a few hours.

The black spots morphed into spinning green circles, then combined into a river of stars that felt like it flowed from her neck, down her arm, to the tips of her fingers. As her doctor recommended, she did her square breathing through the episode until the circles and stars stopped spinning, then popped a tablet of ergotamine under her tongue. She always had a pack in her pocket, just in case. Within moments, the headache began to recede.

"Oookay." She'd had these weird migraines as long as she could remember, but seeing shapes was something new. A chill traveled down her back as she curled her tingling fingers. As quickly as the headache had come on, it was now gone, leaving behind only a faint echo of pain.

"Might be time to go for that drink, Jayne."

She set the poetry back in its place, ready for the morning, then gathered her things and left the library.

The headlights coming down the road wouldn't let her stop thinking about those strange circles and stars. It had to be a migraine thing, but she should check with her doctor tomorrow, just in case something else was going on.

"Hey!" Sofia spotted Jayne hurrying down the street and started to wave. At the door to the bar, Sofia hugged her, then pulled back and studied her face. "You look worn out."

"Nice to see you, too." Jayne followed Sofia inside and they found spots at the bar.

"No, you're gorgeous as always, but you look pale."

Something was definitely off, but Jayne didn't want to bring it up. Sofia would freak out. "I'm just a little tired. Headache earlier. It's all good. How was your day?"

"You know."

Jayne did know. Today was the anniversary of their parents' death. Hence, dinner.

No matter what city they'd moved to recently, no matter what demands on their personal lives, Jayne and Sofia always celebrated the sad anniversary the same way—a dinner full of remembrances. As they grew older, dinner was thankfully accompanied by drinks. The dirtiest of martinis for Jayne, lemon drops for Sofia. Instead of recounting the horror of the way their parents died, they shared stories, confessions, secrets, memories.

Jayne ordered a burger, fries, and for good measure, two pieces of pie. She could already tell it was that kind of night.

"And I'll take the Caesar salad," Sofia said to the bartender before turning to face Jayne, a sad smile on her pink-slicked lips. "Remember when Dad took us to the lake, and you fell out of the boat and nearly drowned?"

"How could I remember that, Sofia? I was two. What about that time Spots dragged the cheesecake off the counter and ate the entire thing? I actually helped him. It was my birthday, after all. My rules."

"You loved that dog."

"He was the best."

They talked and ate. Lamented their orphanhood. Toasted their sisterhood. Promised to always stand by each other's side, just as they did every year on this night.

Untangling a piece of dark hair from her glasses, Jayne stared out the bar's floor-to-ceiling windows onto busy Twenty-First Avenue, headlights streaming through the night past the Vanderbilt students' stomping grounds. They were in an expensive restaurant, as befitted a celebration of life. So expensive Jayne was planning to use the quarterly coupon she received as an employee of the university to pay for dinner. She'd chosen this spot because she knew Sofia would love it.

It was all so normal. As normal as two girls who'd lost their parents, two girls who'd moved every few months growing up, who'd cleaved together and supported one another above all else could be.

And yet, tonight was different. It felt...wrong, somehow. Something was off, and Jayne couldn't put her finger on it.

A shiver rode down her back, and she scraped up another bite of caramel apple pie to chase away the feeling.

And then the television burst into flames.

Not the TV itself. The man on the screen. He was engulfed in flames. Jayne's stomach turned and twisted in sync with the dancing fire. Orange arms of light reached away from his ruined body and twisted into black smoke. Behind the news reporter, the fire popped.

Transfixed, Jayne squirmed in her seat. She could almost feel the heat searing her own flesh, bubbling the skin, eating away at tendon and muscle. Fighting the urge to run, she gripped the bar top and dug her nails into the wood's heavily shellacked surface. Fire was the one constant in Jayne's nightmares. Sofia's, too. She was deathly afraid of fire. For good reason.

Flames. Death. Bodies burning…

Stop it, she told herself sternly. She'd promised herself she wouldn't talk about this tonight.

The man on the TV burned and burned. The flames danced over what was now a charred corpse. The reporter didn't seem nearly as upset as she should've been. At last, two police officers moved the news crew away from the site, saying something about dental records and informing the family.

Jayne sighed and looked away. This wasn't her tragedy. Not this time. No more tragedies for her.

Things had been going pretty well, actually. She loved Nashville. She'd nabbed the amazing gig at Vanderbilt Library's Public Services and Reference Department a month earlier. When she was hired to work with everything from rare books about the history of Vanderbilt itself to fascinating Afro-Cuban manuscripts, she nearly broke her arm trying to do a celebratory cartwheel. The work was fascinating. And the books? Every day was nerd heaven, what she'd always wanted.

But the flames…

Sofia's voice was soft in her ear. "Hey. Wanna split?"

Jayne forced her gaze back to her older sister, then pushed her plates closer to the bartender, just wanting something to do with her shaking hands. "I'm okay. Poor bastard. Who would do that to themselves? That's the third burning this week alone. They're saying it's organized. Like some sort of cult. What sort of message are they trying to get across?" Maybe she did need to think about it. Maybe she was being a coward. Maybe they did need to leave.

"I don't know. A terrible one? Let's go, Jayne." Sofia drained the last of her lemon drop and looked toward the exit. "Seriously, we should get home."

Jayne sighed. Sofia always took off at the slightest hint of discomfort. And she never explained why. Jayne had tried to pry a reasonable worry out of her sister time and time again, but Sofia's fears were vague. *You never know who might be watching. We've come so far, lived when we should've died. You don't understand the world, Jayne. There are people out there who don't have our best interests at heart.*

Her sister was always running. They'd moved at least three times a year until Jayne was in high school. Sofia was eleven years older and had done a good job being Jayne's parent. But as Jayne grew up, she began to notice the depth of Sofia's paranoia, how she constantly watched over their shoulders as if the past might chase them down and eat them whole.

Jayne had tried to get Sofia to see a therapist, but she'd refused.

Jayne stiffened her back and signaled to the bartender for another martini, then turned her attention to the TV. "We should watch the rest of the news. It's good to be informed. I hate it, but we can't put our heads in the sand, Sofia." She tried to give her sister an encouraging pat, but Sofia was pulling away, shrinking back from a man who had approached while they were transfixed with the news story.

"Hello, ladies." A tourist in a cowboy hat grinned at them. He was a bit older than the guys Sofia usually liked, but not bad looking. "Bought you another of what you were having." He handed Jayne another martini.

Oh. He was handing it to Jayne. This was new. Sofia was all curves and lips. Usually the guys ignored super-nerd Jayne.

"Uh. Thanks," she said, accepting the drink, her tongue

numb with nerves. She turned to watch Sofia work her man magic. Sofia always had the best lines to give back to dudes who hit on her. But instead of playfully teasing the guy, Sofia's eyes hardened.

"We were just leaving," she snapped at him. She plucked the drink from Jayne's hand, slammed it on the bar top, then pulled Jayne off her stool and toward the door.

The guy shrugged and walked off muttering.

"Sofia. Seriously. You have to chill. He was just hitting on us." Sofia usually loved flirting. What had the guy done to inflame her paranoia? Was it the burning man on the TV? That actually made sense. The reminder of how their parents had died clawed at Jayne's chest. Of course the scene would do the same to her sister.

"Haven't I kept you safe all these years?" Sofia whispered, fingers digging into Jayne's arm, her thumb pressing into the freckle they used to pretend would allow them to communicate. A ridiculous thing to pretend, but it had seemed like magic as a kid. Jayne had always been obsessed with the idea of the supernatural—probably why she read so many fantasy novels. The time when she and Sofia had read *The Fellowship of the Ring* out loud together was one of her treasured memories.

Jayne hugged her. "You have. And I had a great childhood thanks to you. But now we're okay. Right? We're adults. I have a solid job. You're enjoying the restaurant, aren't you?" Sofia had taken a management position at Ruth's Chris Steak House, a laudable gig here in downtown Nashville.

"I am. But I don't know how long we can stay here. In Nashville, I mean, not just this restaurant. Please. Let's go." Sofia's big eyes searched the bar until she locked her gaze on the cowboy hat guy, who'd taken a seat by the back door. Purple circles still ringed Sofia's eyes, evidence of the cancer she'd fought off twice now. Two years ago, Jayne had nearly lost her. It was part of the reason she'd agreed to move to Nashville—some of the best cancer hospitals in the world were here. Just in case it came back.

"If you want to leave, I'm down. But hey, I'll be honest with you." Jayne hesitated, knowing this next statement would seem impossible to Sofia. She hadn't wanted the evening to go this way. "If you decide to move again, I'm not going. I'm staying in Nashville, unless I get a bigger opportunity. I want a career now, Sofia. Not constant relocation just for the sake of running from our tragedy." She said the last bit softly, trying to ease the blow of the truth.

Sofia jerked her gaze to Jayne's face. "We're staying together. Not up for discussion."

"I'm not a child. I haven't been one for a long time now. If you feel the need to keep moving, that's fine. But I will stay or go depending on my position at the library."

Jayne's phone buzzed as she followed Sofia out of the bar.

"Who's messaging you?" Sofia asked sharply.

"I would love to say it's a tall, dark, and dreamy from the stacks, but no. It's my boss telling me to check my inbox. I'm starting a big project tomorrow with some new manuscripts, so she's leaving me more instructions."

Sofia grinned. It looked forced, but she was likely trying to extend the olive branch. "I can't believe you like that place. You work with a bunch of old ladies."

"Old ladies are badass. They know all the things, and no one can control them."

Sofia laughed, and the sound lifted Jayne's mind away from the tragedy they'd seen on the news and from the weird way her sister had treated the cowboy. The tension between them eased a bit, but Jayne knew there was more of a fight to come. When

Sofia left Nashville, Jayne would not be going with her.

They walked to the parking lot. "Who are the emails usually from?" Sofia asked.

"Most are independent scholars, but a good handful come from overseas faculty and grad students who want me to research vault items for their various projects."

"Outstandingly boring. Perfect. Maybe we should stay here for a while longer."

Sofia drove Jayne back to her apartment. It was the first time they'd ever lived separately. Jayne had insisted on it. Sofia had taken a quieter apartment outside the city. She needed more green around her than Jayne did.

Jayne opened the car door.

"Remember to set your security alarm," Sofia said, patting Jayne on the leg.

"Of course. Although I have no idea who I'm worrying about. This place is filled with people even more nerdy than me. The entire complex is probably rewatching *Game of Thrones* and playing Scrabble."

Sofia chuckled. "Again, outstandingly boring. Have fun in the stacks tomorrow, sis."

"I don't work in the stacks, you know—"

"Oh, sorry. Enjoy the ancient and crotchety section where no one goes except you."

"And some other members on staff. And the occasional grad student. Or a researcher. But they do *not* get to touch anything."

"You are a total nerd nightmare."

Jayne pinched Sofia's arm gently. "Jerk."

"Hmm, what is a good nerd insult? Ooh, I know. You are such a *Slytherin*." Sofia looked very impressed with herself as she rubbed the spot where Jayne had pinched her.

"No, dear sister. Slytherins can be noble. A better slam would be calling me a Wickham."

"Who is he in *Harry Potter?*"

"He is in *Pride and Prejudice.*"

"I can't keep up with all of dorkdom, sis."

Laughing, Jayne waved as Sofia drove off.

Jayne started up the stairs, trying to forget about the stars she'd seen in the vault and the horrible TV report and the weird reaction Sofia had to the good-looking cowboy.

It didn't work.

CHAPTER TWO

TCO Headquarters
Washington, DC

When the lights clicked off in Jayne Thorne's humble apartment, TCO Officer Ruger Stern called his boss.

"Nothing," he said, rubbing a big hand against his temple. He downed his coffee, the black liquid scorching his throat and waking him up. Hopefully, it would get rid of this headache. He adjusted the encrypted phone at his ear, turning it on speaker so it wasn't broadcasting noise straight into his brain.

"Nothing?"

"No. I've been watching for days now. There's nothing to indicate Jayne Thorne is anything but a bookish young woman who likes a good dirty martini. She is nowhere on the register, and she's well beyond the age of maturity. If she had any kind of magic, it would have manifested by now. We would know if she were strong. I don't know what they want with her."

Amanda Newport, his superior and head of the Torrent Control Organization, exhaled, her annoyed breath loud over the speaker. She had the patience of a rookie quarterback, especially when she sensed someone might be contravening her orders. "Not everyone's magic rises at the same time. You know that. Jayne Thorne must be powerful if the Kingdom is talking about her. They have operatives in Nashville as we speak. And you know they don't waste time chasing dead ends."

Wincing at her reference to the last trainee he'd lost to the Kingdom's machinations, Ruger tried to push from his mind the image of the young man's nonmagical family lying in pools of blood.

"I'm telling you. This is a simple young woman living a simple life. There is nothing special about her."

He didn't need to add the rest, that the terror organization only went after Adepts who could help them pull magic from the Torrent, and killed any Adept who wouldn't help them with their plans to enslave the nonmagic population in order to return the world to a more primitive state. *Closer to natural magic, my ass,* Ruger thought, gritting his teeth.

"I disagree."

"Amanda, I sensed exactly zero magic coming off the girl. Who do you think is trailing her?"

Sometimes Amanda didn't give him as many details as he'd like, but tonight she ponied up. "There was chatter about someone named Jimmy and an unnamed bartender near Vanderbilt University where the Thorne woman works. If our intel is correct, they tried to drug her tonight. We don't know whether they meant to incapacitate, kidnap, or kill. No matter, Ruger, I want her. She needs our protection."

"I don't like this, Amanda. It smells off. Why are *we* just now hearing about this potential Adept if she was already on the

Kingdom's list?"

That's what was bothering him, he realized. The moment an Adept showed magical ability, the TCO was all over it. They had plenty of operatives in place who could sense a new Adept's first access to the Torrent, to the dimension that held magic.

As far as he knew, no one was sensing anything about the sweet little Nashville librarian.

"I understand your reticence. But she's a librarian. Even without magic, she might be exactly who we need. We're in trouble, Ruger. The Kingdom grows stronger by the day. We can't let them win. And if they're seeking the grimoires..." Her professional tone slipped, and Ruger recalled the night they were snowed in at Boston's Logan International, the night they shared a few too many tequilas and the heartbreak that came with the unique world and classified information they had access to. He'd seen a little too deeply into his boss's mind, and though he tried not to let it affect him, he couldn't help it. Amanda had such darkness, such sadness, in her. She felt so responsible for every death, every mistake. He hated to disappoint her, ever.

"You really think the Kingdom are chasing the grimoires' trail?" He pressed his fingers against his closed eyelids, the headache growing. "The story has no backup. We've never seen a thing to prove it's true. And why now?"

"But what if it is true? What if they have identified their locations? Even with only one, the power they could wield will tip the scales in this war. We must find them first, Ruger. This directive is coming from the top."

Ruger shot the rest of his coffee. "The top" was the non-magical head of the CIA. The TCO was a small, quiet, and little-known branch of that monster organization. Only the top and his direct report knew of the organization's existence. No one else in the government was aware of them. And Ruger wanted to keep it that way. If the Kingdom gained access to the grimoires, the whole world would find out about the TCO, and the magic they'd tried to contain for centuries.

That is, if the grimoires had the power the legends claimed they did. According to the lore, the five grimoires, hidden in historical texts, could raise dead Masters—the most powerful magicians to exist.

With power like that on their side, the Kingdom would be unstoppable.

The TCO had to get to these books first, and Ruger's division, the Library, would need to lead that investigation and retrieval.

Come to think of it, a human librarian might not be the worst idea.

"If it's true, we might be screwed."

"Ever the optimist. I trust you, Ruger. You can ferret out this information. Find her. Talk to her. See what she knows, and what she doesn't." Amanda's voice sounded younger now, and he could imagine her tucking a lock of coppery hair behind her ear and touching the necklace her husband had given her on their fifteenth anniversary. A Kingdom operative had killed the man ten years ago, but she never once removed that necklace or the wedding ring. Nor had she dated. She was very alone, and while it made her a good officer, it also made her a sharp and sometimes difficult friend.

Ruger blinked, trying to shove away the headache so he could focus on what Amanda had brought up, the story about the necromancers' spells.

Too bad they had absolutely no idea where to start.

Maybe this young woman knew more than she realized. Regardless, if the Kingdom was after her, he had to see what he could do to help, because Jayne Thorne's world was about to go up in flames.

"Fine. I'll go to Nashville."

"Good. And Ruger?"

"Yes, Amanda?"

"Go now."

CHAPTER THREE

Since the move to Nashville, Fridays had become Jayne's complete and total favorite day.

And no, it was not because it was the start of a weekend. It was the Friday work hours she adored. Long, and quiet. She got more work done on Fridays than the rest of the week combined. As such, she had a ritual. Two cups of tea rather than one. A stack of pancakes the size of her head. And a wonderful day alone in Special Collections to focus on her assigned projects. During the week, grad students would be working in the reading room with its Chihuly glass sculpture and the windows that let in a very tinted edition of sunlight from the terrace, and her fellow librarians would be scooting around, joking and laughing. But Fridays didn't see many researchers and only permitted the occasional meeting.

No one wanted to work on Fridays.

No one but Jayne.

This morning, fighting down the teensiest of headaches from

her debauchery with Sofia the night before, she set to the task she started the evening before, collating every edition of a set of poems written by a slave in Latin America during the eighteenth century. A student at Berkeley was researching the topic and needed a hand. She had to figure out which editions had missing or additional pages, scan those, then send them off to the student.

In the silence of the vault, she found the poems she'd prepped yesterday. She refused to worry about the shapes she'd seen and the possibility of an ocular migraine. This would be a lovely day. Other than the remnants of last night's drinks, she felt just fine.

But she did decide to use gloves this time.

Vanderbilt, like most modern American libraries, didn't encourage staff or students to use gloves anymore—they only led to more page tearing. Jayne defied her bosses and went to the mostly empty box on the wall, chose a set of smalls, broke them out of the plastic and slipped them on.

"There. Going back in. You are mine, weird manuscript."

She turned to make sure no one had come into the vault after her. It would not be fabulous to have the other staff see her freaking out about nothing during her very first month on the job, not to mention talking to herself. Well, maybe they'd gotten used to that.

After using the back of her hand to push her glasses higher on her nose, she pulled the manuscript closer and started over. Her fingers touched the words…

It happened again. Stars, and shapes, and this time, a sense of purpose. Of power. Of pain.

When she came back to herself, she realized she'd ripped off the glove and had her palm flat on the page. She yanked her hand away, and a chill like cold water flowed down her body.

Her scalp. Neck. All the way to her toes inside her vintage mules. A scent—something like roses and woodsmoke—curled through the air to overwhelm the more familiar smells. What in the world?

She was breathing too quickly, couldn't get a full breath. Her vision blurred again, and tiny lights, lime and grass green, floated around her face in a scattered array of stars. Pressing her palms against her thighs, she took three very slow, deep breaths. The bizarre hum in her fingers was nothing to worry about. She'd probably just pinched a nerve trying to read in an awkward position last night. It was already fading. But the stars floating around her head? They weren't in her line of vision—not internal, an effect of her own brain. She clutched the edge of the table. The stars circled her like birds. What. The. Heck?

As a librarian, she was also essentially a scientist, albeit one who trained with paper and binding instead of test tubes and lab rats. Scientists were honor-bound to re-create their experiments to prove their theses, right? Only through trial and error could she figure this out.

She reached for the page, and as her thumb brushed the ancient calligraphy, the lights spun gracefully around her head. She assessed her body carefully. That strange coldness slid through her, making her remarkably alert. Was she going to pass out? Should she call for help? No. She was fine. If seeing a river of stars flowing around her head could be called fine. But she wasn't dizzy anymore. She wasn't sliding off her stool onto the cold floor.

It was...glorious, really. Almost as if she had control of the magnificent swirl.

Heart pounding in her ears, Jayne finally let her curiosity defeat her fear. She reached for those tiny specks of light.

They threw her into another world.

The lights expanded to fill her field of vision, and Jayne tried to rationalize what was happening. Nothing lay behind them or beside. She glanced at her feet. Nothing below her either, just this fantastic, and altogether frightening, river of light.

Okay. Break it down.

Green spots, check. River of stars, check. All had happened before. River of light? This was new. And she was standing in this...plane, that's the only word she could think of. The plane that existed somewhere inside the Vanderbilt vault that was a river of light.

"Yep, you've gone 'round the bend, sister."

At the words, her body tensed and sweat bloomed along her back. Before she could form another thought, the stars fled, and the walls of the library's very tangible vault reappeared.

Jayne fell hard to the ground with an audible *oof.*

She got to her knees, glancing around. Had she fainted? No. It was as if the river of light had kicked her out when she doubted that it was real. Like it was...alive, in some way. Cognizant. Sentient.

The manuscript was still on the table, acting like it hadn't done a thing. She felt betrayed.

Books, you have always been so good to me!

Sucking air, she ran the past five minutes through her brain. What she'd done. What she'd seen. *Scientist, remember? Repeat the findings, and take notes, this time.* Getting to her feet, she hurried to read the words she'd touched.

...ver el torrente...

"To see the torrent." What was the torrent?

A cough made Jayne leap like she'd never leapt before. She cried out in fright, almost amused at the shrill "eeeee" she made. Almost.

A dark-skinned man as old as her father would have been

if he were still alive stood on the far side of the vault. A very, very large man, with a face that had been through too much, judging from the scar running down the side of his wide, crooked nose and the two shiny patches of skin on his jaw and cheek that showed evidence of serious burns above his tightly trimmed black beard. Along with a tidy leather satchel slung over one shoulder, he wore an immaculate suit, and for that reason alone, she didn't immediately get into her fighting stance or simply flee. Men in suits didn't usually accost librarians. Did they? Maybe she was wrong. She raised her shaking hands, but kept them open instead of making fists, her kickboxing training flashing through her head.

Push kick to throw off his balance on approach. Flying knee to the face.

What if he too was a hallucination? She decided to play along, to humor her hallucination.

"What are you doing here? You aren't allowed." Her trembling fingers lifted the edge of her laminated ID. "You need one of these to get in here."

The man didn't smile. "Jayne Thorne. Will you come with me? I'm with the US government, and I'd like to buy you a cup of coffee."

Yep, she was definitely passed out and dreaming. Next there would be little green men to go along with the stars. Sofia was going to have a field day with this.

But she kept playing along. "You're with the government?"

He nodded. "My name is Ruger Stern. This is a matter of urgency. I have spoken with one of your fellow staff members to ensure you won't be bothered about leaving during your workday. So, coffee?"

Jayne was still reeling about what she'd seen. She couldn't take another surprise. Who was this guy and how the heck was he in the vault?

"How did you get down here without a key?"

A brief smile flashed across the craggy face. "In my line of work, there are very few keys I can't manage to get my hands on."

Jayne didn't like the sound of that. "Oh."

"It is very important that we speak, Jayne, and quickly. Please, will you come with me? If you don't like coffee, tea. Water. Maybe a dirty martini? It's five o'clock somewhere."

He was talking like she was a toddler, and she felt about as reasonable as one at the moment. Kicking her feet and demanding to know what had just happened didn't seem too far-fetched. Did this man know somehow? Was that why he was here? She wanted to ask him, she wanted to scream, but all that came out of her mouth was "Tea?"

"Whatever you wish."

She didn't start toward the door just yet. If he was with the government and wanted to speak to her, it had to be because she'd done something wrong. She could talk her way out of this, surely.

"Is this…is this about me touching the manuscript? I followed all the protocols. I know what I'm doing. I love poetry. I respect books!"

"No need to yell."

"Sorry." Had he seen the strange stars? She had the overwhelming urge to ask him even though he would probably just think she was cracked. Did the government take crazy people away? Yes, they did.

"Jayne. Truly. We're running out of time."

Her throat felt dry and swollen. What could she do? Say no? That would be rude. Besides, he was from the government. Was she even allowed to say no?

"Am I allowed to say no?"

"Yes."

"I'll go."

"All right, then."

He led the way out of the vault. She locked the door, then accompanied him up the elevator and outside onto Twenty-First Avenue. No one in the library looked their way. Strange.

Next door to Mellow Mushroom, they stopped at a caffeine cart, where he ordered black coffee for himself and asked what she would like. She ordered chamomile. This was a time for calming beverages, not more caffeine.

They walked under a magnolia, then past a sycamore whose leaves were turning brown a bit too early. A beat-up Honda zipped by. A Prius. Two Teslas in a row. A roaring motorcycle, followed by three very annoyed-looking joggers. A typical Vanderbilt afternoon.

They found a bench.

"All right, strange man from my hallucination named Ruger Stern. Talk."

"We would like to recruit you," the man said, unfazed by her blabbering. "For the Agency."

The Agency. Beads of sweat rose on her upper lip. "The CIA? That agency?" she whispered, eyeing a family wearing Vandy sweatshirts.

"Yes."

She started to laugh, hysterical. "No way. This can't be happening."

The giant man lowered his sunglasses and watched the road. He was just so big. Like a dark-skinned, middle-aged version of The Mountain from *Game of Thrones* if The Mountain was a handsome Black man with a trim goatee and a five-thousand-dollar suit. Really, her entire head could fit into his palm.

"I'm not sure I'm really the spy type, sir. I'm a bit clumsy, and I am terrible at secrets. I can't be in the...in the Agency. I'm just...I'm Agnes Jayne Thorne, book nerd. I don't know a thing about politics or international security."

It was his turn to stifle a laugh. "We have a position open in the Library, a research division in the Torrent Control Organization."

The world blurred around them as his words sunk in. "The CIA has librarians?"

"Yes, we do. Worldwide," the man said. "Your position with the Agency would involve libraries. And books. Ancient books. You do know a thing or two about those topics." He smiled. "We believe you would be perfect for the job."

She had to wipe the drool from her mouth. Not because of the man—he was twice her age—but because of the books. Libraries around the world? Secret spy government libraries? She could find out so many things. Roswell. Area 51. The genesis of *Sharknado*. A sudden thought pierced through the insanity, and her breath caught. Would she get the chance to be in the same room with the Book of Leinster? To finally study the book she'd pored over digitally for so long?

But this was the real CIA. No way. Insanity. She pinched herself to wake up, but nothing happened. She was awake. She was having this conversation. She'd been seeing stars for two days. *Okay. Roll with it, Jayne.*

"What could possibly happen in a library that would require the CIA?"

Ruger raised a heavy eyebrow, and she nodded. "Of course. Silly of me. It's a secret."

She took a deep sip of the tea, scorching her mouth, but she swallowed, not wanting to look like an idiot. Ruger the CIA man just watched, that eyebrow hiked.

Why was he here? Why did they really want her? Was she *that* good at her job? Had Eleanor recommended her or something? No way. Not this quickly. She'd barely been in the position for a month. Maybe this was about the stars, after all. She had to ask, but how? How could she couch the question in a way that seemed not crazy, just in case it hadn't even happened and/or he had no idea what she was talking about?

"Wait," a deep, mildly concerned voice called.

Jayne realized she'd stood and was walking. She did that sometimes when her mind went on overdrive. She had to move, or she'd explode. The CIA man caught up.

"Jayne—"

"How did you find me, anyway?" she asked. "I haven't applied for any government positions. Did Vanderbilt submit my name or something?"

The side of Ruger's lips lifted. "I can't give you details until you decide to join us. If you are interested..." He pulled a giant packet of paper and a business card out of his satchel and handed them over. "Fill this out, and bring them, and yourself, to this address, tonight. At midnight." He pointed at the black lettering on the card.

The packet weighed about eleventy billion pounds. "Midnight? That's so cliché."

"We try." A grin pulled at his mouth. "Don't be late. And Jayne? Best not mention this to anyone. Oh, and watch your back." With a nod, Ruger ducked into the shade of the trees. And in a feat of impossibility, he disappeared behind a half-wall, leaving Jayne standing open-mouthed and even more confused.

Oh-ho, hallucination man. Like I'd be dumb enough to tell anyone.

They'd take me straight to the eighth floor of the hospital across the street.

But the package he'd handed over was heavy in her hands. Was this a part of the hallucination?

She had seen stars, and a river of light. A man had appeared. He'd offered her a job with the CIA, then disappeared into a hedge. Four bizarre happenings in less than an hour. They had to be connected somehow.

Watch my back. Great. Like she needed more paranoid people in her life.

Her tea was finally at a consumable temperature. Holding the packet and card to her chest, she sipped and drew in the floral scent to calm her nerves and stop her hands from shaking.

When she felt like she could keep it together, she headed back to the library. CIA or not, those Latin American texts weren't going to scan themselves.

CHAPTER FOUR

Jayne went home early, citing a headache, ignoring the kind look of concern from Eleanor. She sat on her couch with the last bottle of wine she'd bought to share with Sofia and perused the elephant-sized questionnaire the man had given to her. The questions were numerous and strange. Some were basic, qualification stuff—high school, college courses, job history—but others were outlandish: *Have you ever dreamed of going to space? Could you live alone in a lighthouse for an extended period of time? Are you frightened of animals with wings?*

Personality questions, obviously. She answered as honestly as she could—space would be cool; lighthouse must come with properly stocked bookshelves; the only flying things she feared were angry dragons, but birds and bats and dragonflies were fine by her.

The clock on her mantel ticked. She took a break, poured a fresh glass of wine, and tried not to think about what Sofia would say to all of this. Her sister would completely freak. She'd insist they move again, that this was some sort of trap, that someone had drugged Jayne in the library, that *they were coming*. Jayne sighed. The Bordeaux slid down her throat easier than the memories of today's shenanigans. *Note to self. Make appointment with Dr. Mortimer.* Maybe he could scan her brain.

She downed the rest of the glass and raised her favorite pen to answer question number 232. *Do you believe in unicorns?*

Seriously, CIA? And what had the man meant by the Torrent Control Organization? What was the torrent, and why did it require a research division run by librarians?

There was no chance she was actually going to become a CIA officer, but she had a feeling Ruger might be her best chance at finding out what had happened in the library. She would string him along and answer their questions, then wait for the right moment to ask about the river of stars. The words from the manuscript came back to her.

...*ver el torrente*... *To see the torrent*...

She closed her eyes, remembering the place full of green lights and starry emptiness. When she'd fallen into...whatever that was, the river of light, of stars, she'd felt fear, for sure, but also something else. Familiarity. A sensation in her fingertips and heart that the other place was real, and right. Which was just impossible.

And...cue the seriously creepy déjà vu. That was enough for now. She needed a break.

Giving up on the packet for the moment, she picked up her battered and beloved copy of Robin Hobb's *Assassin's Apprentice*. She tried to lose herself in the world of the Six Duchies, but the words merely streamed over her brain like water over rocks.

Throat tight, she went to the kitchen for some ice water. Her dinner dishes sat in the sink. Her mind was in such a twist she hadn't even cleaned up. Unheard of. The microwave clock glowed at her. Only an hour until midnight. She never stayed up this late. Normally, it was dinner at 6:30 p.m., clean the kitchen, iron tomorrow's clothes (her favorite chore), and book and bed by 9 p.m. on the dot. Sofia always said *Nothing good happens after ten.* Jayne figured, why push it?

Well, Jayne, you are either starting down the road to being a wine-guz-zling slattern or you are planning on meeting The Mountain *for a quick chat about joining the Central Intelligence Agency. Which is it?*

The glimmer of stars in her peripheral vision made the decision for her. *Not again…*

She set the wineglass beside her dirty plate, popped a pill to keep the migraine at bay, and rushed through the rest of the packet. When she finished, it was time to go. She grabbed her keys off the hook by the door.

There was no way she could join the CIA—no matter how radically awesome that book gig sounded—but maybe this Ruger fellow could tell her something about what she'd experienced. After all, if the CIA didn't know about it, who would?

⊱⊷ ✦ ⊶⊰

A jazz band that sounded like a garbage truck running over numerous geese attacked Jayne's ears as she entered the bar indicated on Ruger's CIA calling card.

She found the huge officer at a table in the back. He smiled when he saw her, or was that a grimace? She couldn't tell. He was so serious. A woman in her early 50s with copper-colored hair sat beside him, mouth pinched. Ruger rose and shook Jayne's hand; the woman only sat, glaring almost curiously, arms crossed.

"Agnes," Ruger said, his palm warm. "So glad you decided to meet us."

Heat spread up Jayne's neck, and memories of long-ago playground taunting filled her head.

"No. Not Agnes. Never again, or I'm out of here." Gods, how she hated her real first name. Hideous. Even when she was young, Sofia had supported Jayne's desire to steer clear of the moniker.

"Pardon me," Ruger said, raising an eyebrow. "Jayne. This is Amanda Newport."

The woman's polite smile was there and gone faster than Vandy's best sprinter. "Come with us, please," Amanda said, leaving the table in one graceful move.

Great, now Jayne was being kidnapped. Or perhaps she already had Stockholm syndrome, because she followed compliantly as the two officers walked her through the bar's back door, across the cracked asphalt parking lot, then up a set of metal stairs leading into what appeared to be a really crappy motel. They entered room 244. It was less than delightful.

"Nice digs," Jayne said, allowing fear to color her words with snark.

Amanda switched on the TV and a rerun of *Friends* started to blare. "Cover noise," she explained, which explained nothing.

Cover noise? Why was Amanda waving her hands in the air? Was the air around her...shimmering?

Jayne shook her head. She was seeing things again.

They took seats around a battered table topped with questionable laminate disguised as wood. There was just enough room for the three of them to squeeze in next to the double beds. Now that they were all seated and being serenaded by "Smelly Cat" and shimmering air, Amanda relaxed enough to at least stick out her hand. "It is nice to meet you, Jayne."

Jayne set her packet on the table. "Yeah, you too. Listen, the only reason I'm here is because I had a very weird experience today." *Way to go the subtle route, me.*

Ruger said, "We know."

Jayne froze. "You do?"

The two officers exchanged a glance, then Ruger said, "I'd like Amanda to hear everything in your own words. If you would, Jayne, please tell us what happened today."

There was something about him that made Jayne want to trust that sharing her story wasn't going to get her in trouble or kicked out of consideration. He reminded her of her father, she realized. Only vague memories of her father sifted through Jayne's mind now and then. Soft, brown eyes. A deep, gruff voice with a singular kindness threaded into its gravelly tone. Jayne was quite good at reading people, and she would have bet her collector's edition of Tolkien's complete works that Ruger was good people.

Heart beating at a quick clip, she gave in to Ruger's request and explained all to Amanda.

"I thought I was having an ocular migraine. But the book..."

They inclined their heads politely as she explained about the medieval book and the green cosmos into which she'd been pitched.

The officers weren't surprised. And that surprised the hell out of Jayne.

Amanda—touching the strange necklace hanging around her neck—nodded curtly, looking vaguely excited. Ruger just smiled.

The. Heck?

"Jayne. This is why you need to work with us," Ruger said.

Jayne clenched her fists in an attempt to keep her voice from heading into some crazed, wineglass-breaking octave. "So you know what that was? You honestly know what happened to me? I'm not actually going bananas?"

"We know exactly what you went through." Amanda's eyes shuttered halfway as she ran a fingertip over her necklace. The gold piece of jewelry was made of three triangles set across one another like a Venn diagram. Touching this talisman of hers made her shoulders drop but also brought the flame of courage into her eyes. "But we aren't going to talk until you sign this." She pushed a sheet of paper across the wooden table.

It was a strict nondisclosure agreement. By signing, Jayne was promising never to reveal the conversation she was about to have. Okay. If this meant she could get some answers...

She signed her name with a flourish.

"And now this," Amanda said, pushing a second set of papers her way.

These spoke about joining the CIA. It was similar to her employment paperwork for the Vanderbilt Library, but with a few rather significant differences.

One, it mentioned death.

Her own.

Two, the form talked about extreme secrecy and classified material.

Three, it mentioned the Torrent Control Organization branch and the Library, their research division.

"I can't ask a single question about anything before signing this?" she asked.

Ruger and Amanda traded a look, and Jayne suddenly felt twelve instead of twenty-three. But that was stupid. This was crazy. This was the freaking CIA. This was a time for any and all questions, damn it.

"Ask your questions quickly, and we will see," Ruger said.

Jayne gave them a flat stare, refusing to be cowed. "If I join... you, I will travel to libraries around the world and do what, exactly? Can you tell me about the actual job?" Was she actually considering this? *No. No, you're not, Jayne. You're here for answers. That's all.*

Ruger leaned on his forearms, his face close to hers. "You will have access to every book, that we know of, on the entire planet. Every scroll. Every manuscript. Every single written record the human race has produced and saved in its museums, collections, and libraries from Egypt to Ireland to the far reaches of the Arctic Circle."

Jayne's stomach flipped. Every book. Every. Book. Even the Book of Leinster. Her fingers tingled. "And I'll be doing research."

"Yes." Amanda said. "Among other things."

"I won't have to, like, kill anyone, right?" Gals named Agnes Jayne didn't go around becoming government assassins. Librarians, yes. Killers? Hardly.

Ruger shook his head. "Jayne. If you don't want to sign, we won't force you. You want answers, answers we're willing to give. I understand this is difficult for you. You're naturally curious, you've had a scare, and suddenly, the CIA is knocking on your door. But we won't coddle you. Make your decision." He looked as though he half wished she'd deny them.

Amanda crossed her arms on her chest and acted like the giant questionnaire Jayne had set on the table wasn't even there. She looked like she was ready to leave. She looked...disappointed. The sadness in her eyes reminded her of the way Sofia looked when they talked about their mom and dad.

"Well, if that's all..." Ruger motioned toward the door.

Jayne was about to lose the chance at finding out what that beautiful, scary, oddly familiar plane of green stars was, as well as a job that involved every single book on the planet. Her heart tapped against her chest as if saying *Helloooo. You can't just go back to regular life without some answers, without at least seeing where this goes. C'mon, Jayne!* She pressed her fingers against her temples, torn.

This job would surely get her into trouble.

It might mess up everything she'd worked for.

But after seeing Sofia nearly die two years ago, Jayne had a different view on life. You had to grab it by the balls, or it might just pass you up. She held the form high.

"'All we have to decide is what to do with the time that is given us,'" she said, quoting Gandalf.

Ruger gave her a puzzled look, and Amanda just stared. Guess they weren't big Lord of the Rings fans.

Throttle back the nerddom, Jayne. "I mean, all right. Yes. I'll join the CIA."

Jayne snatched up Amanda's blue pen and scratched her name on the signature line at the bottom of the second, smaller packet. What would Sofia say when Jayne told her about getting a new job?

Shoving aside worry about Sofia's response, Jayne pressed the form and the packet she'd completed into Ruger's large hands. "When do I report and where?"

He and Amanda traded a look that she could swear was tinged with…relief.

"Tomorrow morning. This address." Amanda handed Jayne another business card. "If your answers"—she waved the packet—"fit the bill, and the wards let you in, we will begin training immediately. This job has been open for a long, long time, Jayne. Work is piling up."

"I understand. What are the wards?"

Amanda ignored the question. "Jayne, this goes without saying, but in case you didn't read the fine print, I will reiterate: Do not tell *anyone*, not even your sister. If pressed, simply say you've taken a position with the Federal Library and Information Network, which operates worldwide, and leave it at that. That will be your cover, anyway."

"And my current position?"

"We will take care of that."

Jayne's hands went cold. She rubbed them together and tried to muster her courage. She hated lying, but if the lie protected books, then surely it was justified. It wouldn't be easy to sell this lie to Sofia, though. She knew Jayne through and through.

"Um, before you go…what *did* happen to me?"

This time, it was Amanda who smiled, and the transformation made her luminous. "Magic, Jayne. It was magic."

CHAPTER FIVE

"Magic," Jayne said. "Like wave-a-magic-wand magic."

Amanda sniffed. "Yes. Without the wand, naturally. Wands are the stuff of fiction."

"Did I hit my head when I fell? I mean, I love fantasy as much as the next girl, but—"

Amanda tossed her a last grin and disappeared.

"What?" Jayne whipped her head toward Ruger. He stared impassively. "Um…"

"Tomorrow, Jayne. All will be revealed. I only ask that you trust me. Trust *us*. And you don't talk to anyone else about what happened today. This is of great importance."

"Let me guess. There are bad guys out there who would like to recruit me, too. The anti-CIA or something?"

"Yes, there are. It's not a joke, Jayne. Magic is real. It's been asleep for a long time, a very long time. What happened today… We think it's waking up. We think *you* woke it up."

"Me. Agnes Jayne Thorne, book nerd, turned on the magic

in the world. You might need help."

His face moved into an approximation of a smile. "Jayne, I do need help. I need *your* help, specifically. Very badly. But I can't tell you anything more until we've processed your paperwork. So go home. Have a glass of wine. Pack a bag. Tell your sister you'll be out of touch for a few days. And don't talk to any strangers. I'll see you in the morning."

"You know, technically, you are a stranger, Ruger."

"I am very strange," he said, a sad chuckle coming from him. "But I believe in you, Jayne. I think you're the key to"—he waved his hands in the air, and she saw that strange shimmer again, small sparks of green and gold—"all of this."

And, like Amanda before him, he took a step into the shimmering air and was gone.

"Why not?" Jayne said aloud, and took a step after him.

But it was like walking into an invisible wall. She fell back. Her nose was scraped, and she'd stubbed her toe; it was throbbing like she'd dropped a brick on it.

At least your hallucinations have rules, Jayne. Go home. Pack a bag. Wait to wake up. Because apparently, you've just signed on to join the CIA.

The bar's overhead lights flashed as she walked back through the door.

The cowboy guy from last night at the Vandy bar sat on a stool beside a table under a Coors Light sign. It was odd that he'd ended up here. It was such a different sort of joint.

"Whoa," he said, smiling kindly. "I saw you yesterday, didn't I?"

"Yeah. Weird." Jayne wanted to get out of there, but she hated being rude to people. Plus, Sofia was the paranoid one, not her. She actually gave people the benefit of the doubt.

"Must be fate," he said. "Hey, it's last call." He jabbed a finger at the bartender, who was drying a large wineglass. "Want anything?"

She did, badly, but decided getting home and horizontal was paramount. She was exhausted.

"No, thank you."

"Are you sure? It's on me." He had a nice smile. And nice arms. Was that a tattoo on his bicep? Sofia might have actually been good with this. Tattooed bad boys were her weakness.

Jayne shrugged. *If I can turn on magic, I can have a drink with a cute boy.* "All right. Why not? Dirty martini, three olives."

"My kind of girl."

The bartender set to work as she watched, absently, thinking about Amanda's and Ruger's parlor trick of disappearing into thin air. That's what it had to be, a trick of the light. There was no such thing as magic.

"Better not let Tinkerbell hear you say that. She'll lose her wings."

The bartender was standing across from her now, the drink in his hand.

"Sorry. I was thinking aloud. Working on a play. Running dialogue."

Man, Jayne, when did you become such a world-class liar?

"Excellent. I'm at Watkins—are you a student there?"

"No, I'm a librarian."

"A sexy librarian," he said with a wink. She rolled her eyes and put the drink to her lips. The scent of juniper and something else, something sharp and uncanny, burned her nose. For some reason, it made her heartbeat start to gallop. "What sort of gin did you use in this?"

"Taste it and see. It's special. I don't give it to just anyone."

The bartender leaned closer. He was flirting, absolutely, but something in her primordial mind rejected this when she saw his glance flick to the right. She followed his eyes. Another man was sitting two seats away, watching her intently. He had red hair and freckles, and his eyes were the color of flames. He made her think of the burning man from the television. Something about him felt wrong. Suddenly she felt boxed in by the cowboy, the bartender—all of it.

Ruger's voice rang in her mind. "Didn't I tell you not to talk to strangers?" She heard him as clearly as if he'd been sitting right next to her, lips an inch from her ear.

She set the martini on the cowboy's table. Gin splashed over the edge and pooled beside the cowboy's hand. "On second thought, it's late and I need to get up early. And there's my friend. Have a good night."

Jayne attached herself to a young woman walking by who'd clearly just left the bathroom, looping an arm through hers. "There you are, I've been looking all over for you. Let's get out of here."

The girl played along, thankfully, until they were outside on the patio.

"Thanks so much," Jayne said. "I got a weird feeling from those two."

"Anytime, sister. We have to stick together." With a wave, she headed toward the parking lot, and Jayne trotted off in the opposite direction, looking over her shoulder every few moments until she was on her street, and in her apartment. Breath heaving, she bolted the door and leaned back against it.

She'd never, ever felt unsafe in a bar like that before. She couldn't get over the look the bartender had exchanged with the man with the red hair. Like they were just waiting for her to take a drink. Had they put something in it?

Weird. Weird, weird, weird.

She put a chair against the door, wedging it under the knob—

you're being an idiot, Jayne Thorne, Ruger and Amanda can appear at will, what makes you think the bad guys can't, too?—but the move made her feel a little bit better. She got ready for bed.

Magic.

What if it were true? Would she have a superpower? What would she want that to be? Flying? X-ray vision? No, what would be the best ever? The ability to read and comprehend at speed. Jayne Thorne, the Speed-Reading Librarian. Maybe they would give her a cape with a big L on it.

With a snort of laughter, she finished brushing her teeth. She slipped between the cool sheets and turned on her reading light. She wouldn't be able to concentrate, but she would try to read. Sofia had given her a werewolf romance novel, not her usual fare.

The book fell open to the third chapter, and Jayne started reading. Her mind whirled around while she tried to focus on werewolf Jake and his biceps and oddly incredible eyesight and how main character and badass Jasmyn wasn't putting up with his alpha-males-only thing.

"Good for you, Jasmyn," Jayne said to the book. "Alpha females for the win. You can both be strong. You show him how it's done."

But her heart wasn't in it. She switched off the light.

The streetlamp bled through Jayne's blue curtains and cast a pattern of squares over her ceiling. It looked a lot like what she'd seen in the library—that starry place.

She was no idiot. She'd never touched a drug in her life, either. It *had* happened.

And there was a good chance the Agency would be the place to find the answer.

She rolled onto her side and put her earplugs in so the neighbor's very sweet but very annoying hound dog didn't wake her up at 3:00 a.m., and started to plan.

Okay, this was what she would do.

Assuming she could get through the wards, she would go to the next meeting with Ruger and Amanda and make them explain everything about the green lights, and magic, and the man with flames in his eyes. And then she would quit. They couldn't force her. She'd probably fail the training that would surely follow her admittance and get kicked out, anyway.

Her brass clock chimed the hour. She watched the second hand click and knew she wouldn't want to get kicked out of a job that led her around the world to study ancient texts. Now that she knew that kind of job was a possibility, she couldn't go back to this room and the Vandy vault and the same books over and over again. The life she had now was great, but it was a lightbulb compared to the sun. Tea from the Keurig versus a steaming pot at the Ritz in London.

She thought about the stars, thought about the river of light. If she squinted, she could almost see them, hovering above her. But trying simply made her head hurt. Forcing her eyes shut against the pattern on the ceiling, she tried to sleep.

CHAPTER SIX

The man in the cowboy hat and the bartender sat in the back of the bar, the lights dimmed, a laptop open between them and the red-haired man. A blown-up black-and-white image of Jayne Thorne took up the screen. She was looking over her shoulder, a confused smile on her lips, completely unaware of the camera.

"Man, you blew it. You had her, and you blew it."

The man in the cowboy hat, whose name was Jimmy, leaned over the bar top and tossed the remnants of the spiked martini down the drain. He faced the red-haired man.

"I tried, Aaró."

"Next time, try harder." Aaró turned to the bartender. "What did you put in it, anyway?"

"Essence of henbane. Just enough to make her compliant. You said you wanted to be able to talk to her."

"She smelled it."

"No way."

"Yes way. I felt her reaction. That was too sloppy. Try again tomorrow. I don't care how. We need her, Jimmy. We need her very badly."

"I don't know what the big deal is. She's just a girl."

Something passed across Aaró's eyes, and Jimmy knew he was about to get a partial truth. "Did you not feel the shift today? The surge of energy just before those assholes from the TCO appeared? They sensed it, too, and came running. If they want her, I want her. And I found her first."

Aaró had. Somehow knowing the woman was important, he'd ordered Jimmy to go after this woman before the shift. "I'll do what I can," Jimmy said. "I gotta jam, it's late."

The bartender put his wallet in his back pocket. "Me too."

"Leave me your key," Aaró said. "I'll lock up."

Jimmy could tell his bartender friend wanted to argue, but Jimmy gave a tiny shake of the head. Aaró wasn't the kind of guy you argued with. The bartender took the key off the ring and tossed it.

"Tomorrow. Bring her to me," Aaró said. "Or don't bother coming back."

Jimmy nodded once, tersely, and walked out, the bartender on his heels.

As soon as the front door shut, the air around Aaró began to coruscate.

"Merda!" He threw up a shield just in time to block a surge of power from three TCO officers who appeared from the back room.

He leapt to his feet, throwing power into the shield behind him, running hard toward the back door and the wide window. Working spells under his breath, sweat forming on his brow from the strain, he shattered the glass with a flick of his fingers and jumped out of the window frame onto the street. The pounding of three sets of feet behind him drove him harder. He could not be taken. Not now. They were so close to finding the first clue in the necromantic works, to the beginning of a whole new reality.

He drew on the energy of the world around him, anything alive he could see, sucking it into his being. The ends of his fingers began to warm, and he ignored the sensation. But ahead, a dark shadow stood, impassive, unmoving, blocking his egress from the street.

Ruger.

Aaró cursed, grinding his teeth as the ambient power from the trees fought against him. He used to be able to wink and create a breeze, now it took all of his energy to put together a shield.

Magic might be waking up, but it wasn't fully back yet. That was why his people kept immolating themselves. They'd been trying to access the power and couldn't. But with Jayne...

"Stop!" Ruger called, but Aaró kept running, his hands wide, scorching the trees along the street as he ran toward Ruger, head down now, a bull charging a matador, the scent of fire strong in his nose.

Aaró couldn't be taken. He knew this. He had to trust Jimmy to get the girl, to fulfill the quest Aaró had given him. To stop her from joining with Ruger and the TCO.

He stopped, ten feet shy of Ruger, let the heat of creating the shield fill him.

Ruger put up a hand to block the heat. "Aaró, it doesn't have to be this way."

"I agree. It doesn't."

"Turn off the heat, you're going to immolate yourself."

"Am I?" Aaró could sense the remaining TCO officers creeping up behind him. "It doesn't matter anymore. Your new girl won't make a damn bit of difference. You will still be weak, and we will still be strong."

Ruger didn't say a word, just thrust out his hand, palm up. Aaró was shocked by the punch, shocked by the power he felt. There had been nothing like this in decades. Not since…

"No!" he screamed, but it was too late. The fire started at his feet and surrounded him a heartbeat later. He fought it; it was impossible to think this was it, he was done for, at the hands of Ruger. At the hands of a TCO librarian. It was a humiliation.

But Aaró burned.

⟨»— ✦ —«⟩

Ruger watched Aaró disintegrate, waiting until the ashes dropped to the ground and cooled before bringing in the retrieval team. It was an old habit, born of superstition. The older Adepts demanded that the ashes of powerful magicians be handled carefully. Ruger had never seen an instance when anything amiss occurred with regard to ashes, but policy was policy.

His mobile rang. Amanda.

"I can hardly believe your luck, Ruger. Aaró himself goes for our new Adept? Tell me you've got him."

"In a way. He burned."

Amanda's quick intake of breath was worth the price of admission. Aaró's mentor was her husband's killer. "Did you—"

"He started it."

"Well. Well, well, well. I don't know what's better about today, Aaró off the table, or Jayne's answers to the question-naire. Do you realize she actually answered everything? All one thousand questions?"

"I'm not surprised. She's thorough."

"Ruger."

He stilled, her voice a red flag. "What is it?"

"Jayne's thesis centered around the Book of Leinster."

"Irish mythology." Members of the TCO who believed the story of the necromantic grimoires pointed to old Irish manuscripts as a starting point.

"Exactly."

Ruger swore. "This could be real after all, Amanda. I can't…"

"I know. We have to follow her lead. She might be the answer to everything."

"If she is, you're right, she does need protection."

Amanda's smile came through the phone. "I'm glad you finally understand my position. We can't have Aaró's followers putting two and two together. Get her in here. We need her on our team, trained and ready to fight. Word will spread quickly enough. If Aaró was sniffing around, I suspect everyone felt the bolt when she touched the book. She is beyond powerful, and the grimoires are already calling her. Magic is unfurling again, Ruger. You can feel it, can't you?"

"Yes, ma'am," Ruger replied, swiping an errant dusting of ash off his jacket. "I'll have her in DC by lunchtime, latest. You know how many questions she asks."

"See that you do. Gag her if it will speed things up. Good night."

Ruger looked around one last time. Nothing to be done about the burns on the trees, though he whispered his apologies and blessings to them, and the branches waved slightly in the wind. They would recover, the damage was superficial. Lucky. Ruger had seen Aaró take down a forest once before. But that was when magic was still pouring through the world, unchecked, unharnessed. Before it had been used up by the last Master, burned into nothingness by her evil.

He nodded to the remaining TCO officers, who melted into the darkness, then he took off, whistling, toward Jayne's apartment. He would keep watch, just in case, so there were no more attempts on her life before he had her fully under the Agency's protection.

Jayne Thorne. Who would have thought a meek, quiet chipmunk of a librarian would have the power to save the world?

CHAPTER SEVEN

Jayne didn't sleep. She finally gave up around and hauled out her suitcase, packed all the clean clothes she had, not sure exactly what a CIA librarian was supposed to wear, and a few of her favorite books. She took a long, steaming-hot shower, just in case she was assigned someplace cold, washed her hair, shaved her legs. It was like getting ready for a date, she supposed, only she was going to get lucky with some seriously old books.

Finally, it was time. She unplugged all her appliances and turned down the heat, locked the door, and pretended she wasn't putting off talking to Sofia, that it was all part of her plan. She'd texted her sister back last night—a simple *Sorry, I can't talk. I'm super tired from work.* Sofia had sent a smiley face and all was well. For now.

The address on Ruger's card led Jayne to Music Row, to a black door set into a building that used to be a studio but now looked closed for good. She knocked twice and the door swung open.

A man in a trim blue suit smiled. A gold pin with a scroll "T" held his tie in place. "Hello. Come this way, please."

A massive baby grand piano stood in the foyer. The long hallway was carpeted in red and black, and the place smelled like any office—paper, ink, coffee, plastic, and someone's perfume. *Nothing strange yet,* Jayne thought as she tried not to be disappointed. A tiny part of her wished Dumbledore had welcomed her in or that the ceiling above her now held floating candles. She silently chastised herself for being a complete moron.

The man led her into a room, and Ruger stood to greet her. He seemed quite happy to see her.

"Good morning, Jayne. Everything okay? No more incidents?"

"No. It's…I'm fine."

"Good. Excellent. Will you please have a seat?" Ruger gestured to a wooden chair beside a desk. "We need to do some testing on you."

Jayne noticed there was a screen on the wall, very high definition, and it showed Amanda seated at a desk, frowning. Jayne couldn't tell if she was in the next room or very far away.

"Good morning, Amanda."

She didn't respond, only nodded.

Jayne's eyes turned toward a strange-looking machine hooked to a laptop. While Ruger played around with the machine, Amanda sat and stared. Jayne had only ever felt this lacking in front of her elementary school principal when she'd read fifty-nine books the summer between third and fourth grade, instead of the sixty she'd promised.

"I'd like to know why you approached me." Jayne wasn't sure she was allowed to ask questions, but the worst that could happen was they'd refuse to answer.

"Let's get you hooked up, and then we'll fill you in on some things." Ruger wrapped a soft fabric cuff around Jayne's arm. He clipped a pulse rate monitor onto the tip of her index finger.

"Is this a lie detector?"

"Mmmm, of a sort. Most lie detectors can only register yes or no answers, using your physiological responses. This is a bit different. More…comprehensive, shall we say. What we establish this morning is the baseline we will use to determine your well-being throughout your tenure with the agency. Now, tell us your name."

"Agnes Jayne Thorne."

The question was followed by a mundane list of what she usually bought at the grocery store (but sometimes she went to the Chinese grocery and went wild with squid and jackfruit that she had no idea how to prepare and ended up throwing out when they spoiled) and how many boyfriends she'd had (two, and they weren't really worth mentioning).

Then Amanda asked a long string of questions about Jayne's early life, starting with a doozy.

"Tell us what happened to your parents. Ruth and Henry Thorne."

Jayne took a deep breath. Talking about them always hurt, even now. "There's not much to tell. I was little when they died, so I'm going on what my older sister, Sofia, told me. My parents went to their longtime friend Saul's place near Yosemite to do some hiking. A wildfire rampaged through the area. It took authorities what felt like forever to finally inform us that they were assumed dead."

"And then?"

"And then…they were gone. The state declared them dead after five years of not finding their bodies." Jayne numbly recalled the facts and spit them out like they didn't belong to her. "And yes, growing up after their deaths, I suffered through an emotional roller coaster that included being horribly sad, bored being stuck with only my overprotective sister who insisted we move all the time, and lonely because no other kids or teens were interested in books quite the way I was. So I turned to books, which have never betrayed me."

"But your relationship with your sister is strong?" Amanda's normally curt tone had softened, and Jayne wondered if she might have lost someone in her own life.

"Incredibly. She is both sister and mother to me. It's complicated." Understatement of the century. It felt as though there were two Sofias, one who freaked out over everything and bossed Jayne around like an overprotective mother hen, and a second who wanted to flirt with guys and joke about them with her little sister. Two people in the same body. Jayne loved them both for different reasons.

"I think I understand more now why you are so perfectly suited for this position." No pity laced Amanda's words, only an odd sort of understanding.

Ruger cleared his throat, and Jayne knew something bigger was on the horizon.

"All right. We have our baseline. Have you ever worked for a foreign government?"

Jayne actually laughed. "Um. No."

"Just answer the question, please." Amanda's mouth grew so pinched Jayne worried it might disappear completely into her face. *Why so serious,* she wanted to ask, in a freaky Heath Ledger Joker voice, but she suspected that wouldn't go over well.

"No. I have not worked for a foreign government."

"Have you ever been convicted of a felony?"

"No."

The list went on and on until Jayne's head was pounding, and she certainly wasn't laughing anymore.

Ruger's gaze met hers. "What happened when you touched the Latin American spell in the vault?"

Jayne froze. Her hands grew slick with sweat. "I…uh…" She'd wanted to ask about everything, but now that the moment was here, the whole experience seemed insane, like some juvenile daydream. They'd kick her out before she got hired.

Amanda was scribbling notes with her spidery fingers. "Please answer the question."

"I accidentally touched the… Wait. What did you call it?"

Ruger frowned. "A spell."

Jayne's heart stuttered. "I don't think it is. I've read about folk magic and more-modern versions of the occult, have seen grimoires. And I've read Harry Potter multiple times. This was simply a poem."

Ruger's eyebrows lifted in amusement. "Jayne. You of all people know that words are magic. To the naked, untrained eye, perhaps it was a poem. But to an Adept, it was a spell."

"What is an Adept?"

"Jayne, just answer the question," Amanda said, clearly getting annoyed.

"The words made my fingers buzz." Jayne knew it sounded crazy, but once she started talking, she couldn't stop. "When I touched it the second time, even though I had gloves on, I saw lights. They were like stars. Green. Glowing. They moved like a slow river. The ground disappeared, and a bizarre odor swam around me. If you don't want to hire me, now, fine, but please explain what happened to me. For my own sanity. It'll be your good deed for the day."

Ruger almost smiled. "I can't tell you anything until we examine the results of today's testing."

Jayne's anger bubbled under her skin, but she breathed slowly, cooling down. "Fine. What's next? Test my urine? Make me say the Pledge backward?"

Amanda slammed her notes onto the table, making Jayne jump. "If you don't take this seriously, you won't be permitted to aid your country or help us keep the world safe from those who would love to see millions die. This is no joke, Agnes."

Jayne felt a flash of heat inside her. "Call me Agnes again, and I'm out of here. My name is Jayne."

Amanda glared, then the screen on the wall went black. Jayne heard a door slam.

Ruger looked down at his hands, resting on the table. They were big as dinner plates. "I'm sorry about her." He unhooked Jayne from the machine, then led her out of the room. "But she isn't wrong. This is a serious thing, us coming to you. The experience you had—well, without proper training, it's going to become quite a problem for you in the future. And we aren't the only ones interested in your talents. We are, however, the only good guys involved."

"Last night—"

"You don't have to worry about that. I've taken care of your bartender and his friend. They won't be bothering you again. I can't promise others will be as polite."

Score one for my instincts. "I knew something was wrong with them. But... 'Taken care of'? What do you mean? Did you... eliminate them? Beat them up? Send them to a Turkish prison?"

Ruger's face was hard. "It doesn't matter. You want to do this, Jayne. I can see it in your face. You want this as much as we want you. You are special, that's for sure. I can train you. I can show you just how powerful you can be. But you're going to have to trust me."

"You're being so damn cryptic," Jayne replied. "I don't even know what skills you're talking about. How am I supposed to swear I'll lie to my sister if I don't even know for sure what I'm lying about or for? I just need...details."

Ruger blew out a breath. "Wait here." He pointed at the leather couch. "I'll get your results and then we'll talk."

Nodding, Jayne sat on the couch, but the moment Ruger disappeared through the door, she was up and pacing. She chewed a nail.

This was all just so crazy.

But they hadn't acted surprised when she talked about the green lights. They knew all about it. And what was that about an Adept and spells? Jayne plopped onto the couch to rub her temples. *Just think about pie. And Jake the romantic werewolf. And how fall is the best time of year. And how good books smell. Happy. Positive. Good things. You can handle this. Somehow.*

A very sterile-looking black-and-white clock hung over the archway Ruger had gone through. Jayne watched forty-five minutes tick by, her brain on overload.

She wondered what Sofia had been doing the last forty-five minutes. Was it something she loved to do? Or had her health scare not affected her as much as the event now influenced Jayne? Jayne felt every second of every day since Sofia's frightening diagnosis. Even when the doctors declared her as clear, Jayne couldn't stop glancing at her phone to check the time. If she told Sofia, her sister would shake her head, grab Jayne into a hug, and tell her to quit being so neurotic. Then Jayne would attempt to explain that her preoccupation with time passing wasn't actually a sign of being neurotic if one studied the true meaning of the term and—

"Jayne?" Ruger held a green folder. She had no idea how long he'd been standing there, watching her stare at the clock like a simpleton.

She stood, swallowing her nerves. "Yes."

"We have your baseline. You've passed. If you are willing,

we'd like to get you onboarded immediately."

Jayne shook her head just like the Sofia in her imagination had. "I just hope you aren't mistaken about me."

"So are we."

"Then yes, Ruger. I'll join the CIA."

Ruger actually smiled. It made his granite face almost handsome. "Good. We'll get you right into training. Bring your bag."

"Where are we going?"

"DC."

"Now?"

"Right now."

"But, I have to talk to Sofia, the library… I'll need to—"

"Jayne. Listen to me. We can deal with all of this on the road. We've just received some important information. It's time for you to help save the world. Assuming you're up for it?"

Jayne shot him a grin. "Bring it on, Ruger."

CHAPTER EIGHT

Dublin, Ireland

In a sweat-stained martial arts gym on a quiet Dublin side street, Cillian Pine tugged off his boxing gloves and checked his encrypted phone. He'd joined the Kingdom because they were actually trying to do something to save Ireland, to get rid of the wasteful idiots who flooded his homeland. But damn if they didn't seem to ask some inane question every time he had a moment to work the heavy bag alone at his gym.

The voicemail his Kingdom group leader had left was terse as usual. "A woman will arrive in Dublin soon. Are you willing to track her? Her name is Jayne Thorne, and we have reason to believe she has a journal with valuable information in her possession. If you are committed, find her and get that journal before other parties discover her. With your confirmation response, we will send pertinent intel for your tracking purposes."

A quick grin of satisfaction flashed across Cillian's lips. Sure, he had the blue eyes and defined features of a spoiled movie star, but he hadn't earned those attributes. He prided himself on the tracking skills he'd worked on since he was a young teen. He studied people and could make solid guesses on where they would go, how they would move, where they lived and ate and partied. The Kingdom didn't see him as a pretty boy. They appreciated his acquired skills.

And the Kingdom paid his lease each month, so all his martial arts students' payments went to new equipment, nights at the pub with his mates, and to fund trips to the countryside where he helped plant trees to reforest barren areas with other new Kingdom members. They were an intense bunch—incredibly different from his mates—but they had their heads on straight, and he liked spending time with people who had more brains than brawn every once in a while.

He sent a thumbs-up emoji alongside a nose, his confirmation code, then the phone buzzed as it automatically erased the voicemail about this Jayne Thorne. He started to set the phone down and go back to the bag—the Kingdom rarely doled out information very quickly—but it dinged with a new voicemail notification.

"Jayne Thorne. Twenty-three-year-old female. Brown hair. Blue eyes. Approximately five feet five inches tall. Will most likely take a position at Trinity Library. Dangerous."

Cillian memorized the information, then deleted the description. He strapped on his gloves and walked to the heavy bags. As he worked a double-jab, low-cross combo, he imagined what she might look like. A tingle of something strange passed through him, a sensation akin to apprehension. He shook it off and hit the bag harder. The Kingdom had adopted Cillian, acting so much more like a support than his worthless drunk of a father ever did, and he wouldn't fail them. If she had lived, had survived that awful gale off the coast, his mother would be so proud to see him now, working with a powerful, secret organization that wanted good for the world.

Dangerous. He scoffed, hitting the bag again and again, powerful punches that rocked deep to the core.

How dangerous could a twenty-three-year-old librarian possibly be?

CHAPTER NINE

Sweating a bit, Jayne trailed Ruger down the hall, up a set of stairs, through a big steel door, then down another long hallway. Because of her kickboxing training, she was in good shape, but it felt like they'd been walking forever. They emerged at last into a brightly lit, marble-floored, windowless hall that looked shockingly similar to pretty much every movie set she'd ever seen depicting the CIA's headquarters in Langley, Virginia. This instinct was further affirmed when she saw the CIA logo on the frosted glass door to her left. As she passed, she heard a deep, angry roar.

"Umm, Ruger? What was that?"

"Class four dragon."

"Are you kidding me?"

He glanced back at her. "Yes, Jayne. We can't fit dragons in this building. That was most likely some sort of recording. Maybe they're watching *Godzilla vs. Kong* on their coffee break."

"Good to know there will be coffee breaks. Wait. Did we

walk to DC?"

Ruger nodded. "Yes."

"No way."

"Yes way. The steel door was what we call a portal. Amanda created it for us. Much easier than flying places. Much more environmentally friendly, too."

"So the CIA is offsetting their carbon imprint by putting portals all over the world? Cool!"

"Not all over the world. Remember, Jayne, magic as we know it hasn't been working...properly for many, many years."

"Okay, right. Got it."

They entered the umpteenth door on the left—thankfully it wasn't roaring at her—and stepped into a large room with black-painted walls. He set the green folder on a table, then shut the door. Ruger's eyes were big and sincere as a Labrador's, but they also held a spark of something definitively more German shepherd.

"I took care of them," he'd said of the men at the bar. *"They won't bother you again."*

He had protected her. It felt nice, knowing someone had her back. Outside of Sofia, naturally.

"Today we'll do an introduction, but your real work will begin when you head to the CIA's TCO training facility in Quantico. We'll go this afternoon. You'll be off the grid there, so you'll need to call your sister before we leave and tell her you're taking a government library position. If she asks for more, you'll be in Washington, DC for the immediate future."

"Oh, she'll ask for more. She's very overprotective, my sister. I at least have to tell her how to reach me."

"We'll give you a number today for your sister to call. She'll reach your secretary, who will tell her you'll call back at a better time. You'll receive her messages, I promise. Just don't mention

Virginia at all. Or the TCO. We have a lot of secrets, Jayne. We keep them for good reason."

"I get a secretary?"

"Yep."

"Cool. Got it. Will I be stationed in Washington? Is that my new home base?"

"Sometimes. Are you ready to learn about what you saw back in the library?"

About damn time. "Very much so."

Ruger sat in one of the two chairs at the table and gestured for her to join him. He crossed his arms and leaned back.

"Have you ever considered the possibility that the world is different from what you believe it is?"

His question was worded like a cheesy line from one of Sofia's favorite sci-fi movies, but the grave tone of his voice turned it into something far more serious.

"I don't know how to answer that," Jayne said honestly. "I would certainly like it to be. I've read a thousand books that capitalize on the thought. But that it might be real? I'd say that's a little crazy."

"Fair enough. What do you really think happened in the library when you touched those pages? An exceptionally intense migraine?"

"Or a stroke."

"Maybe it was something...more." He leaned forward on the table, his eyes intense.

Jayne's hands began to tingle. "Amanda said it was magic. But really, come on. We all know there's no such thing as magic. Since this is the CIA, I assume you've managed to harness some sort of cool alien physics that give you light-years of advantage over other governments. Right?"

At the look on his face, Jayne wasn't sure she wanted to know the truth. She was content with the explanation that their ability to portal was a scientific advancement that hadn't been shared with the public yet. But Ruger ruined all of that.

"Nope. It's magic. A poorer version of what it can be, but magic nonetheless."

"Umm...do you need to lie down, Ruger?"

"Listen. Magic used to be all around us. It was in the air, easily accessed. Our kind thrived. And then, the unthinkable happened. It's just the stuff of legend now, but a terrible spell was put on our land, and the magic we enjoyed was taken away, harnessed into a single, almost inaccessible spot. A few people over the years have figured out how to access it, but for the most part, magic as we all knew it has been...throttled. It hasn't died, but it's been inaccessible. Follow me?"

"Oh, sure," Jayne said, trying to rein in the disbelief in her tone, and failing.

"The stars you saw when you were in the library are a part of what we call the Torrent." He tapped his chest. "Hence, Torrent Control Organization. The Torrent is the dimension where magic now lives. It's where power that once flowed freely across the world now thrives, in its own perfect, encapsulated environment. Only a few people can access it. We can, to an extent, obviously, but we have resources others do not." He swiped a hand in the air, and she saw the river of light again. Just as quickly, it disappeared.

No way.

Not a chance.

"Amanda wasn't kidding when she said magic was real? Like, *real* real?"

Was he saying she *had* seen those strange stars and she *had* been thrown into another world by touching the book's writings? Her mind warred with itself. What Ruger was saying seemed impossible, but really, the whole experience from that moment on had blown Jayne's perspective wide open. She'd seen it with her own eyes. And yet... she was a rational scientist, and rational scientists didn't believe in magic.

"Don't you believe me?" Ruger said. "Even after what you've seen? I walked into your vault, Jayne. How else could I have done that if not magic?"

"Well, most people simply take the elevator, so that's a strong possibility," she said, and Ruger rolled his eyes.

"Jayne. Let go of these preconceived notions. Allow the truth in. Magic is real."

He was rather good at appearing and disappearing at will, she'd give him that. "I don't know. This is all nutso. I mean, I want to believe you, but the rational part of me says this is all a silly dream and I'm going to wake up with a serious hangover."

He stood up. "I suppose I can simply show you your first spell. That will get us on the road more quickly."

She felt as though the floor had dropped away. Her first spell?

Ruger rolled his sleeves up and closed his eyes. That odd scent, similar to the one she'd noticed in the library, drifted through the air. It wasn't exactly the same as the roses and woodsmoke. The scent was more like turned earth, reminding Jayne of working in the garden during summer.

Raising his hands, Ruger dipped his head like he was concentrating very hard. His palms almost seemed to flicker with light the color of sun-washed grass, but the luminescence was gone before she could be sure. He opened his eyes, but kept his hands lifted at chest level.

"The first spell you need to learn is a Block. Protection 101. Come on. Get up. Try to hit me."

"You sure? I hit a lot harder than you might guess." She grinned with all her teeth.

He smiled. "Yes."

Now this was something she was comfortable with. Jayne had been in training for years, fighting opponents faster than Ruger most likely was and stronger than him, too. Kickboxing was second nature to her.

She opened her hand and threw a palm strike toward Ruger's chin, but her hand slammed into an invisible barrier. The impact shivered up her arm, and the room tilted.

"Impressive," she stuttered. But it was more…worse than when she'd walked into the wall trying to follow Ruger yesterday. Her head was swimming, she was going to pass out. Pulling her glasses off, she bent, her hands going to her knees.

"Are you okay?" Ruger's voice was deep and calming.

"I will be. It's just…"

"It's a lot. I know. I remember my first day. Take deep breaths."

She obeyed, then stood, feeling less like puking. A win. "Do you have to hold your hands up to keep the spell working?" She used the edge of her shirt to clean her lenses before putting her glasses back on.

"Not if your will is strong enough. Only those born with the ability to access the Torrent can even try spells. You were born with that skill. As was I. It's no different than being born with blue eyes or high cholesterol. It's in the genes, and only activated in some. Everyone who has the ability to access the Torrent is called an Adept. We can take small spells from the Torrent if our drive or will is strong."

"Can I reach in there right now and get a spell for creating a million dollars?" Jayne started to laugh at herself, joking to keep the situation from being overwhelming, but then a thought hit her like a round kick to the head. What if she could reach into the Torrent and retrieve magic that would cure Sofia once and for all?

"Technically, yes. You could rob a bank just as easily. Drink this." Ruger handed her a water bottle labeled with a dizzying array of numbers and symbols. "It has electrolytes and extra B by the buttload. You don't look so great."

Jayne took the bottle but didn't open it. "Can I access magic that would heal someone?" Her voice sounded years younger than she was.

Ruger glanced at the green file. Because of the research the Agency had done on her, Ruger must have known she was asking about her sister and cancer. Kindness must have kept him from saying it outright.

"Sadly, no. There isn't an Adept out there who can heal such an illness. Too complicated. It may be the skill of some forgotten Master, but I haven't even read any legends about someone powerful enough to do that. This is why you must learn to defend yourself. If you get hurt, you'll have to heal naturally, and that takes time we don't have."

She gave him a sad smile. "Well, it was worth asking."

Ruger nodded. "I would have doubted your heart if you hadn't. Now, let's move forward. It's your turn to access the Torrent. You don't need a spell book to do it. You can move into the flow of magic with only your own concentration. Close your eyes and think about the Torrent. The lights. The scent. The floating feeling. Next, imagine a Block, an invisible shield around your entire body."

"This is a lot to think about all at once." She set the unopened bottle Ruger had given her on the table.

"You can do it, Jayne."

She shut her eyes and pictured the pinpricks of light, the space under her feet where a floor should have been, and the mind-blowing space in the Torrent. How good it had felt. Her nails dug into her palms as she fought fear of the unknown as well as fear of failure. In her mind's eye, she saw the faint shadow of a box, like one of those telephone booths in London, all around her.

The scent of magic curled into her nose.

"You're doing it, Jayne," Ruger whispered.

In her imagining, she looked down. There was nothing holding her up, just like before. But now, now that she was headed to that place on purpose, it became too much. Her eyes flew open to show Ruger's bunched forehead and concerned gaze. Her back was wet with sweat. "I can't."

"You can. Drink." He handed her the bottle she'd set down.

The liquid tasted a bit metallic, but it wasn't bad. Kind of like a blend of Red Bull and a mai tai. Okay, yeah, it was actually pretty horrible. Why didn't they have wine? Or chocolate? This was like battling Dementors, yes?

When she finished the water, she tried to access the Torrent again. Again, she chickened out.

This went on for what felt like hours.

Finally, Ruger helped her to a wooden chair carved with symbols and leaf shapes. "Rest here while I order us some food, then we'll try again."

"What if I never manage to access it properly again? Can't I just try a spell book or whatever? I am a visual learner, after all. Books are my jam."

"I have no doubt you'll manage it, Jayne. You are meant for this job. It's in your blood."

"How do you know?"

Ruger rubbed his chin and eyed the green folder. "Because only a powerful Adept could access the Torrent just by accidentally touching some calligraphy in a simple spell. When you did that…we all felt it. That's why I came. You summoned me."

"I summoned you…right. But what if it was a fluke?"

"Then we'll bounce you and you can go back to Vanderbilt and live your sedate life, forever locked in the Vandy vaults."

"I told them I was sick." If her bosses knew her better, if she'd been at the job longer, they'd have known she was never sick enough to skip work.

"So you didn't quit the moment I presented my offer? I'm shocked."

My God, he was teasing her. She answered in all seriousness. "No. I didn't know if this would work out. Still don't."

"You should have more faith in yourself," Ruger said roughly.

"You don't even know me."

"I know more than you think. I'll get us some food, and we can try again."

He grabbed the folder and headed out of the door.

❧⊱〜 ✦ 〜⊰❧

Ruger walked into Amanda's temporary office. She looked up, her eyes a little wild. He supposed he appeared about as ruffled. "You still think we should let her bring up the Book of Leinster?" he asked.

"If she's the one to mention it, we'll know it truly is calling her. You have to train her anyway, so we might as well wait to see how strong the pull is and if this mission is truly worth the risk everyone will be taking. Including Jayne."

Nodding, Ruger rubbed his temples. "Any more chatter about her?"

"They assigned a tracker to follow her."

Ruger's heart snagged on a beat. "We haven't even decided where to place her."

"The Kingdom knows more about this woman than we do."

"It's easy enough to check out her studies in grad school."

Amanda tapped her stylus against her lip and studied her iPad. "I think it's more than that. Perhaps she has something in her possession that will speak to her tie to the necromantic grimoires."

"Should I ask?"

Amanda set down her stylus and met Ruger's gaze. He remembered the day she'd found out Aaró's mentor had killed her husband, how bloodshot her eyes were, the shake in her voice, the way she'd spilled her coffee. But she was still here, still holding them all together. "Do it. I'm not waiting on my superiors to miss this opportunity. Go ahead and question her about books she owns, old books preferably. Anything she's picked up at garage sales or during her time in college."

"She's incredibly powerful, Amanda. More so than we thought. The way she reaches into the Torrent. It's frightening, honestly."

"She isn't Deacon. Or Rosa."

"Please don't."

Amanda came around the desk and put a hand on Ruger's arm, her superior role falling away for a moment and his friend sliding into her place. "We know so much more now. And if we don't pursue this possibility, the Kingdom will, and they will use it to enslave every nonmagical person on the planet."

Ruger swallowed against a dry throat and touched Amanda's hand briefly, trying to think past the memories of his last two trainees' dead eyes. "Thanks."

"You're a rock, Ruger."

"No, I just have a poker face." He smiled sadly, then left to drag another innocent Adept into the depths of their war against the darkest kinds of magic.

CHAPTER TEN

Jayne practiced pulling up the Block while Ruger was gone, feeling less and less strange as she did. A quiet confidence was growing inside her, lifting her spirits, giving her a rather sassy vibe. She wondered briefly if it was the Torrent, flowing through her. Interesting.

A few minutes later, he returned with a tray boasting a sliced baguette, cheese, grapes, and a bottle of excellent Bordeaux.

Jayne almost laughed. "Do you have a Frenchman on retainer?"

Ruger poured her a glass of wine. "I sensed you wanted some wine. This will help you relax and get into the Torrent. We need you to gain some control. Today."

"Today?"

The hard planes of Ruger's face made her neck prickle with unease. "Time for more learning, Jayne. The biggest fear we have is that a Master will rise on the wrong side of humanity."

"A Master? You mentioned that word earlier. Explain, pretty

please."

"A Master is like an Adept, but with much more power. A Master can fully use all of the spells in the Torrent. A Master can bend the world to his or her will. Thing is, there hasn't been such a person in centuries, certainly not since magic became inaccessible. But recently, we've heard some disturbing chatter."

The wine slid down Jayne's throat, rich and familiar. She took a slice of the crusty bread. "I'm listening."

"A group called the Kingdom wants to bring the world back to a more primitive state. They don't accept that a spell ended the free flow of magic. They believe humans are separated from their true magic and full capabilities because of our reliance on modern technology."

Jayne cocked a brow. "As culty as that sounds, the premise isn't too crazy. During college I studied a tribe who claimed to have the ability to see events in their own near future. I don't think they were necessarily using magic or were Adepts, but being completely present in their environment without the distractions of phones or Netflix—may it live forever, amen—this tribe could read real-world signs of what was to come."

Ruger didn't smile. "That is a very Kingdom way of thinking. But they take it a step further. They believe everyone should have magic and that a Master they create should rule us for our own good."

Jayne rolled her eyes. "That usually works out. The whole *I'm being a tyrant for your own good* thing."

"Yes. Exactly. Hello, Hitler. They are terrorists, make no mistake. Terrorists under the guise of saving humanity. And they don't hesitate to eliminate people who get in their way or don't agree with them."

"They sound like fun. Invite them for cocktails. Or feed them to that class four dragon."

Ruger frowned. "They have been involved in two disasters recently. You know the Hong Kong–Zhuhai–Macao bridge explosion?"

Jayne's throat tightened. Nearly a hundred people had died. "That was the Kingdom?"

"Yes." Ruger's hand shook a bit as he downed his own glass of wine. "And the man who burned alive in Central Park?"

Terror buzzed inside Jayne's chest. "My sister and I just saw that on the news."

"He was attempting to access high-level spells in the Torrent. That kind of flame pattern is indicative of an Adept reaching a little too far. Maybe he thought he was a Master, maybe they pushed him, exploited his talent, but yeah, he belonged to the Kingdom. God only knows what he was trying to do in the middle of New York City. Some sort of attack. We have only been able to secure rumors so far, nothing concrete."

"I never thought I'd be glad someone was dead."

"This job is packed full of ethical dilemmas. Like any job involving security. We are here to protect humankind. And if we have to end some bad people in the process, well, I for one think that's just fine."

Jayne drained her glass. He wasn't wrong, but still. Murder was murder. Right?

Ruger set his glass on the table and spun the stem easily between his fingers. "We were going to wait on telling you this, but Amanda and I believe you need to know." He met her gaze, his eyes intense.

"I'm listening."

"An Adept may find magic in several ways. One is by joining a more advanced Adept in the Torrent like we do during training. An Adept may also call on the elements to search for hidden spells, but it is very difficult."

"I'm following so far."

"Good. Another way an Adept may find magic is through grimoires, which you seem to have done. But that was just a magical text, a regular grimoire. We believe there are five necromantic grimoires hidden within the world's ancient manuscripts."

"Hold up. Necro-what?"

"Necromantic. Having to do with raising the dead."

A chill gripped Jayne and shook her hard. "You're testing me again, right?"

"Unfortunately, I'm not. With one of these grimoires in hand, one can presumably raise a dead Master."

"To what end?"

"We're not sure. The legend, the story, it's all very vague. And those who study it tend to end up dead."

"I can't imagine messing with necromancy is good for your health."

"We don't know enough about it. It could be the spells are damning, it could be the action takes too much power."

"So what good is a Master magician who's a zombie?"

"You do catch on quickly, Jayne." He refilled his glass and took a healthy gulp of wine. "Like any Master, we think they can work magic the rest of us Adepts cannot. Each Master has some sort of key, for lack of a better word. If someone gets their magical hands on all the keys, they will unlock a metaphysical weapon that will end us all. If they are under the control of the wrong person…"

"Shit."

"Yes."

"And you think I might be able to help the Library and the TCO get their hands on the necromantic grimoires before the Kingdom has a chance to find and use said weapon."

"I do. Amanda does. Her superiors at the TCO and the CIA do as well."

"But why me?"

"Number one: you're incredibly strong with magic. And you have a talent for old books."

"Like the Book of Leinster?"

"That's certainly one we're interested in."

A pleasant shiver crossed Jayne's heart and the palms of her hands. It happened often when someone mentioned that particular book. Her mind argued against this madness. "But why me? A lot of folks study Irish mythology and manuscripts, and many more besides."

"You know it's different, though. Don't you?" He cocked his head and studied her face, and she sensed excitement and something else, something wary in his look.

She sighed. "Fine. Yes. Okay, I do feel oddly pleased when I talk about the book. When someone mentions the book. When I see an image of it. I always thought it was just my weird brain."

"Your brain isn't weird. It's special."

"I'm not sure I want to be the special zombie book witch."

"Too bad, child."

It was too much to take in. She leaned on the table, staring. "Right. So magic is real, there's a group of nasty terrorists trying to control humanity, and the Book of Leinster is a necromantic grimoire. What else ya got?"

"Let's drop the revelations for a bit. You ready to try some basic magic again?" Ruger was already getting up from the table. "In addition to the wine, I have something I think might help."

There was a tall black bookcase in the far corner, one she hadn't noticed until now. Ruger pulled a slim, leather-bound book off a high shelf, one he could reach without a ladder, curse him.

"This is a grimoire with spells not too different from the one that helped you into the Torrent earlier."

The book was heavier than it should have been. Jayne shook it, confused.

Ruger chuckled. "Waiting for some unicorns to fall out?"

Jayne laughed. "It's very hefty for its size."

"It's part of the spell. Open it up to any of the writings and let's give this a whirl."

The book suddenly felt even weightier, and a thought struck her. "What was the news you heard about the Kingdom? You mentioned something before…"

"Yes. They've gathered in Ireland."

Jayne's hands immediately began to sweat. "They're waiting for me. They know about the Book of Leinster."

"Most likely. A suspected member of the Kingdom was seen entering the Trinity College library last week," he said. "You'll have to work fast and smart to get access to it before they do."

She raised an eyebrow. "I doubt any of your little clandestine situations are easy. But listen, how am I the girl for the gig when I've only seen the Torrent once on my own?"

"When you did, we all felt it like a thunderclap."

"You mentioned you'd felt it."

He coughed a small laugh. "Because magic is…throttled, the first time a new Adept enters the Torrent, all casters feel the impact of the new power. If that person has significant abilities, the boom is resounding, to say the least. You boomed."

She shook her head, still unbelieving.

He cracked a smile and pointed to the spell book. "You still in? To fight for the good guys? Jayne, you have a power we haven't seen in ages. Truly. You can do this. I have trained hundreds of officers. None have had your natural talent."

If she succeeded here, she'd be in Ireland soon, and up against people willing to burn to death and who knew what else to achieve their goals. She swallowed the enormous lump in her throat. It was the same feeling she had before sparring at the martial arts gym but multiplied by a thousand. Her body's reaction was spot on. If she passed this test, she was headed into a fight of mind-blowing proportions.

"You also can't deny the adventure of it calls to you, Agnes Jayne."

"Please don't call me that."

"Only when I need to annoy you and get you moving. Let's do this." His gaze snapped to the book in her hands.

"Fine."

She turned the pages until she'd hit the middle. The writings were in English. It was talking about some sort of pathway through a forest in Wales. Closing her eyes, she set her fingers on the ink.

The Torrent welcomed her with a rush of floral scents and flowing lights.

"Visualize your Blocking spell." Ruger sounded both close and far away. It was very disorienting, but with that burgeoning confidence holding her steady, Jayne did as ordered. The lights gathered around her hands. She opened her eyes and felt the Torrent's cool touch still there, hanging off her fingers like rings. Ruger nodded encouragingly. She spread her hands and imagined the Block again, that case of invisible power surrounding her. The coolness enveloped her whole.

Ruger lifted a foot and kicked toward her. His boot stopped in midair and he laughed. "You did it."

Jayne let go of her concentration and felt the Block fade away. "I did!" Her face hurt from smiling. "I just did magic. Insane."

"Go in again. Now. Right away, while the feeling is fresh."

Jayne grabbed for the book, which had fallen from her hands to rest by her feet, but Ruger took her arm gently.

"No. Without the book."

"Okay." She closed her eyes and imagined the scent and feel of the Torrent.

And then she was there.

"Very good," Ruger whispered. "Now, look for the Tracking spell. Think of touching a book's pages and seeing faces and names and details. Concentrate on picking up the feel of the person who came before you…"

"I'm not sure what you mean."

"It's like a book's checkout history. When you work the spell, you'll see a magical text's history, anyone who's used the book. But instead of a list of names, you'll see their faces, smell their perfumes, hear a word or two maybe. If you're lucky—or good—you might even see their names."

The Torrent's bright stars flowed past Jayne's arms and legs, bringing goose bumps with their chill. She thought it would actually be very nice just to stay here instead of worrying about the outside world. A tune came into her head and she began to hum along. The sounds were mysterious and in a minor key. She felt relaxed, at peace, for the first time since she had touched the book in the vault. Maybe this wasn't so bad after all. She felt sleepy. Maybe she could just lie down, have a quick nap—

"Agnes Jayne! Get out now!" She opened her eyes, realized Ruger was shaking her.

"What? I was fine. Just sleepy. What happened?"

Ruger studied her eyes for a moment before releasing her. "You can get lost in the Torrent. It…welcomes you in. Unless you want to die, you have to make sure you don't let your guard down for too long."

"Do what?" Jayne's voice was shrill even to her own ears.

"It's okay. You're learning—"

"It is decidedly not okay! What just happened?"

"You felt peaceful, right? Well, if you give up your soul to the Torrent, you'll die here, but live there forever. You just won't be yourself."

"And you didn't think to warn me about imminent death?" Jayne got in his face. "Listen. If you expect me to go along with you and your beloved Agency, you'd better inform me more completely than that when my life is at stake."

"You can leave now," Ruger said coldly.

"What?"

Ruger pointed at the door. "Leave."

"What do you mean?"

"You aren't taking this seriously enough, and we can't take the risk," Ruger said.

"I am taking it seriously. I'm taking you seriously. Obviously, I'm taking the magic, seriously, too."

"Then understand this. My *beloved Agency* certainly will not always inform you when your life is in danger. You should assume you are always in danger. You will receive information as it becomes strategically relevant to your mission, and not before. What you must remember here is this: You are not the primary purpose. Neither am I. All of humankind is. To do this job, you must be willing to take some big risks. You say you believe in this? You're willing to take the risks? You're willing to die for us, Jayne?"

She hesitated. Was she? Was she willing to put her life on the line for these people? "I think so."

"You *think* so?" He ran a big hand over his face. "Well. I want you to go to your rooms. Have some more Chinese."

"How did you know—"

"And decide once and for all if you are in or not. If you decide to stay with us, to risk it all, in the morning, we will portal to the TCO training facility in Quantico, and you won't be back for at least two weeks. Perhaps much longer. Perhaps never."

His words stung, and Jayne did her best not to flinch. She wanted to do this. No way she was giving up this adventure, but to be away from her sister and keeping such seriously crazy secrets? That part wasn't her favorite. Maybe the possibility of dying wasn't exactly cool, either.

Ruger held the door open.

Amanda was there, arms crossed. Chick was a tad intense, to say the least.

"How did it go?" she barked.

"We'll talk later," Ruger said.

Amanda handed Jayne a slip of paper with a phone number on it. "Here is your office number. Your rooms are on the tenth floor. You'll find what you need there."

"Um, thanks?"

"Dismissed, Miss Thorne."

She followed the meager signs to the elevator, took it to the tenth floor. There was a row of doors, and she realized each had a name affixed. When she found hers, she opened the door and stepped into...

An exact replica of her apartment.

What?

"Portal," Ruger's ghostly voice said.

She rushed to the window. Sure enough, the familiar oak tree outside her window greeted her, the leaves green and lush. So she was back in Nashville.

Okay. That was a cool trick.

Jayne's phone buzzed. She had three texts from Sofia. She had no idea what to say to her sister. Maybe tomorrow she'd come up with something.

Jayne turned her phone off vibrate, pulled her hair into a ponytail, and headed to Jeni's for some well-deserved ice cream. If she was going to take a job that might include losing her very soul, there was going to be lavender and darkest chocolate before it all went down.

CHAPTER ELEVEN

The ice cream was perfection, an impeccable counterpoint to the sultry Nashville evening. She found a seat at a sidewalk table and luxuriated in the creamy goodness. It was so tasty she bought a second cup. Why not?

With every bite, she thought about it being her last. *The last time I'll eat this. The last time I'll see Nashville. The last time I'll see Sofia. The last time...* Was this what the prospect of working with the TCO was going to do to her? Rob her of being able to live in the moment the way she'd been doing for the past twenty-three years?

Ruger's voice echoed in her memory. "We need you, Jayne."

Damn you, Ruger.

Sofia's worried face blinked through Jayne's head. A heaviness enveloped Jayne's chest, and the sudden need to talk to her sister overwhelmed everything.

She picked up the phone and called. Sofia's voice whispered on the line. "Jayne?"

"Hey, sis. Sorry I've been avoiding you," Jayne said.

"And you're really sorry for being so standoffish?"

Jayne stood and began pacing. "Exactly."

Sofia breathed into the phone like she was smashing her face against it. "You had better tell me what you're up to, Jayne Thorne. Now."

"Don't be upset, okay? I was offered a new position at a library overseas."

Sofia's silence buzzed in Jayne's ears. She could easily imagine her sister's neck going red with hives.

"Sofia, it's a good thing. A great thing. The job is…with the government. In their national library system. They offered great benefits. I'll even be able to keep my apartment in Nashville and travel from here." Actually, she had no idea if this was true or not. Most likely not, but she could sense Sofia was fully freaking out, so this little lie was necessary.

"Jayne, no. You can't do this. We have to stay together. You don't even pay attention when people are following us. You need me to have your back."

Jayne shook her head. "There's no one after us. It's okay. If the government can't take care of me, who can? They have tanks," she said, trying to lighten things up. "I mean, come on."

"You don't understand."

"Then explain it to me."

Sofia breathed out, a world of fatigue in the sound. "I can't."

"Then give me a month with this amazing job. If something goes wrong in one month, I'll back out."

"They'll allow that?" A tentative hope turned Sofia's voice wistful.

Time for another lie. Jayne's stomach twisted. "Definitely. I asked already."

"No. It's not safe. You can't go away on your own, Jayne. I

forbid it."

"Sofia, I'm not just your little sister. I'm a grown-ass lady. I absolutely hate that you are upset about this, but I'm going. I've already accepted. Can you let it go and celebrate with me?"

"No. I can't. Reconsider. I'm begging you." Sofia's voice was thick with tears, and something else, panic. For the first time, Jayne wondered if maybe their attachment was for Sofia's sake, and not her own.

Jayne pinched the bridge of her nose. Her own tears burned her eyes, unshed. "Please. I need to do this. Just trust me, for once."

The phone went dead.

"Sofia?" Had she hung up on her? No way. Sofia didn't do crap like that. She dialed again, but it went straight to voicemail.

Exhaling all her frustration, Jayne pocketed the phone. She would call Sofia tomorrow once her sister had time to cool off. Jayne would promise to check in once a week, religiously.

But a voice in Jayne's head asked if she would be able to keep that promise. What if she was in Vatican City or Prague or lost forever in the Torrent? She suddenly realized how stupid she'd been, thinking Sofia would be okay with this. The way her sister had clung to her growing up, trying to protect her from everything and everyone…rushing off headlong into an adventure was the antithesis of Sofia's approach to life.

And Jayne herself knew practically zero about what her life with the CIA's TCO branch would be. Would she truly be able to reach Sofia whenever she wanted? Would she be able to quit if she wanted to? Would Ruger always be there to pull her from the abyss?

And with all these unknowns, all the questions, and doubts, and worries, bailing on her dream job, upsetting her sister, upending her life, maybe even ending it, why was she still even considering this?

You know why.

A flicker of green appeared in her peripheral vision. Power. So much power in that river of stars. Power, and excitement, and magic. Actual magic. What she'd always longed for, what she'd always wanted, waiting for her to master. For her to control.

Jayne looked around, taking in the normalcy around her. The park, the lights, the leaves on the trees, the happy cries of children on the slide. If she wasn't going to do it for herself, she sure as hell was going to for them.

She brushed off her skirt, tossed away the ice cream container, and headed back to the apartment.

Ruger had said it was time to save the world.

Jayne Thorne, CIA Librarian, was ready.

CHAPTER TWELVE

Back in her apartment, Jayne set about tidying, throwing out all the perishable food and washing down the fridge. She took the garbage to the chute, then vacuumed and dusted, folded her laundry, her thoughts consumed with Ireland, with Trinity College, the Book of Leinster, and all the other amazing tomes she could see there. The werewolf novel, although packed with twists and turns and pleasant sarcasm, couldn't hold a candle to the frightening and awesome idea of grimoires that held the spells that would allow her to master magic.

As she had the thought, she heard a gentle susurrus, and a note appeared under Jayne's door. Man, they were stealthy. It was surreal to think that on the other side of the door, someone had opened a portal from DC to slide her a note. She was tempted to throw it open and shout "Boo!" at whoever was standing there, but she contented herself with calling, "Would it kill you to just knock?"

The note was typed. *We have a bag for you with everything you could possibly need. Leave your belongings behind. Be ready to step through at 7:00 a.m.*

Jayne crumpled the note in her hand, wondering if she was required to eat it or if it would explode on its own in a second.

Despite her cleaning, the apartment still smelled like Chinese food. Normally, that would make Jayne happy and wistful for more nights spent perusing Goodreads for the next great epic fantasy and stuffing dumplings into her mouth. But tonight, surprisingly, she only felt bored. She suddenly felt ready for her real life to start.

Ancient texts. Spells. Magic.

After all she'd seen today, she wondered if she'd ever be content with reading on the couch again.

When all was as tidy and clean as a late-seventies-era apartment could be, Jayne set the half-finished werewolf book on the kitchen counter, patted its cover fondly, then went into her bedroom to lie down. Closing her eyes, she pictured the Torrent and her own version of the Tracking spell Ruger had told her about. If she was going to start working for the TOC tomorrow, she couldn't rely on Ruger being there every step of the way.

Wait. Her eyes flew open. Ruger hadn't said he was going along on the mission. What if she had to go on her own? He was like a magical father figure—the Gandalf to her Frodo. She needed him. Didn't she?

She took a breath. Well, all the more reason to see if she could do this without help.

The memory of Ruger's panicked voice rang through her ears. He'd sounded so worried when she had been tempted to give up this dimension for the Torrent, to give in to that beautiful feeling. But now she knew what to watch out for. She'd be fine.

Breathing deep, she imagined the emerald stars flowing around her. The chill and scent of the Torrent bloomed around her legs and torso. Attempting to call up the Tracking spell, she envisioned old books with cracked spines and sheets of ancient vellum. Faces spun through the air, and the mutterings of names echoed through her mind. The Tracking spell gathered like blue light in her palms.

She opened her eyes.

The light in her hands wasn't quite there anymore, but she could feel the power in her flesh and bones, tickling and pushing against her fingers like a creature crawling and jumping between her palms. The sensation drove her out of bed and back into her minute living room. She pulled a book off her bottom shelf—her father's journal. Sofia had given it to her as a child, and it was the only gift Sofia had ever given that seemed...weighty. Even as a little kid, Jayne had noticed Sofia's reluctance in handing it over, like she'd been admitting their parents truly were gone for good.

"It was Dad's," she'd said long ago. "He told me you should have it if something happened to him."

Jayne swallowed the familiar grief and squeezed the edges of the book.

The title read *Entreaties and Proverbs*. It was a dull book, full of paragraphs that didn't make any sense, penned in Dad's scrawling hand. When the words did come together to mean anything, they only spouted advice like one's crotchety old aunt would. *Be wise about who you talk to, for they may talk back. Keep your treasure away from your heart, for your heart will be swayed. Save your pennies and know that someday you will use them well.*

Yeah. Not exactly groundbreaking literature up in here.

Jayne barely remembered her parents, but Sofia had consistently spoken highly of their dad, mourning his disappearance and mysterious death as she'd moved Jayne from place to place, gaze cast over her shoulder like someone was after them.

The thought of Sofia's pain brought Jayne's own hollow ache to life. It twisted inside her and she clutched her chest, the sadness so familiar, like a sickness with no cure. Her father had been so kind, from what she could remember—his hand soft on her head and his voice rumbling and gentle.

She whispered a quiet prayer for him and for her mother, too, though she and Jayne had never been close. Memories of her mother included scoldings and cold looks. Sofia had been the favorite, no doubt about it. But hopefully, both Mom and Dad were at peace, and someday, Jayne would find out what exactly had happened. They had been expert hikers who would never stray into an area when there was a chance of fire, so the entire tragedy made no sense. But failing to accept the explanation the authorities had given Jayne wouldn't bring her parents back.

With her grief back under control, Jayne resumed wondering about this book, this battered little journal. Jayne opened the book to a page on the intricacies of beginning a friendship. She pressed her hand against the paper, and for a moment, nothing happened.

But then a face materialized, and it knocked the breath out of her.

It wasn't her father.

It was her mother. Forbidding. Frosty and fierce.

Jayne forced herself to keep a hold on the book even though her arms shook and her heart pounded. Ruth Thorne was saying something in the vision, doing something. Why did her mom care about her dad's journal?

Ruth's thin lips uttered one phrase. *To begin again, the world reborn.*

Before Jayne could hear or see more, the image disappeared

and the magic in Jayne's hands faded.

A world reborn. Death by fire. Was it possible Ruth Thorne had magical abilities, too?

Don't be ridiculous, Jayne. You're imagining things. You want to feel a connection with her. It's normal, after all this time.

She sat down hard on her bed, the book in her lap. A headache attacked and, finally exhausted, Jayne submitted, crawling into bed with her memories.

CHAPTER THIRTEEN

The next morning, after trying and failing to reach Sofia five times, Jayne buttoned up her jacket, opened her door, and stepped through as instructed...finding herself in the same long hallway she'd exited from the night before. She made her way to the elevator, took it to the lobby, where Ruger was waiting for her, glancing at his watch and frowning. He looked torn between fussing at her for some imagined fault and giving her a cup of chicken noodle soup before sending her back to bed.

"What? I feel okay. And I'm early, right?"

"Never early enough, Jayne. Let's go."

"No portal?"

"Not today. Where we're going is top secret, totally classified, and too vulnerable to risk anyone finding it from the Torrent. The Kingdom could destroy us from within if they discovered the locations of our training facilities worldwide."

"Lovely. Lead on."

A black sedan waited for them at the glass doors. The trees

of McLean, Virginia, were similar to Tennessee's greenery, but she could spot a few differences between their complementary foliage as the car drove them farther into the country. Redbuds and pines lined the winding road, and Ruger kept quiet the entire time, fiddling with his phone. Maybe he was loading her briefing, maybe he was playing spider solitaire, she had no idea. Though she wanted to pepper him with questions, she contented herself with reading, always a safe choice. She'd grabbed the werewolf book off the counter at the last second. The werewolf in question had just revealed the reason why he'd first approached the main character. He'd been working with the vampires. Shocking.

"Of course you were," she mumbled.

Ruger's gaze flitted over Jayne's book, then to the window. A muscle near his ear twitched. "Excuse me? Did you say something?"

"I was talking to myself. Sorry." She held up the book and wiggled it. "There be foul finagling afoot."

"There always is." Ruger looked out at the blur of leaves in jade, chocolate, and the start of pumpkin orange.

"It wouldn't be a good story without some major problems. Speaking of troubles, can you give me a clue on what my days are going to look like for the next couple weeks?"

Ruger's gaze snapped to the driver. "Read your book."

Okay. That answered that. Obediently, Jayne pushed her glasses up her nose and went back to the werewolf and his complicated explanation of why he'd originally sided with the vamps but was now firmly against them.

Two hours later, the driver passed through a series of gates, and dropped Ruger and Jayne at a large, rectangular building. Green-painted walls stretched into the highest pines, above a gravel parking lot. Trucks, cars, and three black vans filled three-fourths of the spaces.

The double doors opened into a cavernous space complete with exposed venting shafts and hanging fluorescent lights. Three box-like rooms sat at the edges of the warehouse, the one on the left resembling the inside of an airplane's coach seating. On the right, someone had built a mini grocery store and what appeared to be half of a house.

Amanda approached them, her Apple Watch lighting her face, then she shook Jayne's hand. "Welcome to the Farm. I'm glad you're here."

"You are? I mean, thank you."

"I should hear something about you shortly," Amanda said.

Jayne tugged at the collar of her shirt. "About me?"

Ruger, eyeing Amanda, switched his black bag to his other hand. "Anything I should know?"

"Not yet." Amanda checked her watch again. "I'll keep you in the loop."

On Amanda's right, two men fought hand-to-hand in the tiny kitchen beside a round, wooden table similar to the one Sofia had bought for their last house together, before they'd moved to Nashville. A black-haired man raised his arms, and his opponent, a man with absolutely huge biceps, fell to the tiled floor, his legs apparently not functioning. The black-haired man must have performed some quick move that Jayne didn't catch.

A thrill buzzed through Jayne. Someday she might be able to do that. "Where do I start?"

Ruger made a grumbling noise. "Slow down, cowgirl. You need to watch for a while before you begin that level of training."

Amanda had been nodding, but when she glanced at her watch again, she cursed quietly and pulled Ruger closer. Her eyes were sharp. "Ruger. She may not have that kind of time."

"What?" He scowled at her watch to see the message, then swore himself.

Amanda's gaze flicked to Jayne. "The director says we need to move on the Dublin situation ASAP."

Ruger began walking again. The bicep guy on the kitchen floor found his feet and clapped a hand on his opponent's back. Jayne couldn't hear what he said.

"No," Ruger said. "She doesn't even know how to use her massive magical strength yet."

"I'm a fast learner." Jayne couldn't help but love that he'd said *massive magical strength.*

Sighing, Ruger rubbed his chin. "I'm sure you are, Jayne, but this shouldn't be rushed. There are dangers. Remember the man in Central Park?"

How could she forget? The flames behind the reporter. Sofia's horrified look. The burned outline of a human body in the early autumn grass. Jayne's stomach turned.

Amanda gripped Jayne's arm. "You'll have to learn fast. This has to be done. You agreed to work for your country and the human race, and this is what we ask of you." She glared at Ruger. "The director's orders are not something we can negotiate."

Ruger nodded, looking as green in the face as Jayne probably did. "Fine. But I'm taking her to Dublin myself and overseeing the entire operation. I brought her into this, and I will bring her back out with her flesh still on her bones."

"Jayne?" Amanda's face stared into hers. "Hello?"

Jayne blinked, trying not to freak out. This couldn't end well, sending her into battle without training. But she nodded and squared her shoulders. "I'm fine. Let's do it. I wasn't born with this insane ability for nothing."

Amanda's smile finally seemed genuine. "Well said. I'll make the arrangements. I'll check on you both at five. Crash course, Ruger. Get as much into her head as possible, starting with defensive spells." She walked off, her kitten heels clicking across the concrete floor.

Half of Jayne wanted to run after her and beg for a way out of this, but the other half hummed with excitement at the possibility of saving the world, or at least a part of it.

"Let's head into the conference area at the back."

He led her around the corner of the fake grocery store to a spot where someone had shoved a long table and twenty chairs into a corner. It was a bit dark, but Jayne found herself glad they had some privacy. She didn't want the other recruits seeing her mess up on her first day.

"We're not going to worry about physical combat for now. You don't have the time, and you're already a decent fighter, from what I've seen of your training videos online."

"You've seen the videos from the dojo?"

"Yes. We'll cut straight to your spells. But first, let me brief you on your mission."

"Yes, it might be helpful to know what I'm supposed to be doing. Thanks."

Ruger bent and unzipped his carry-on suitcase. "You'll need to befriend a woman named Deirdre Green. She is not an Adept, but she works in the Early Books Department at Trinity College library, and we believe she might have ties to the Kingdom. You'll have to keep a close eye on her as you work to access the Book of Leinster."

"So I can trip her as she walks through the library? That would be effective."

"Jayne," Ruger growled.

"Sorry. Yes, I figured as much."

Ruger's look cut her. "Just listen."

Jayne nodded.

Ruger rubbed his lips like he had an itch. "Get her to like you. You'll need to find her weakness. Or a need she has. A cousin who is tangled in a gang. A mother with breast cancer and no way to pay for treatment. A friend who's fallen on hard times."

"What?"

Ruger acted like he hadn't heard the question. "Use the feelings you have about your sister to bond with her. Everyone has a tragedy. Remember, we are the good guys, saving the world. Besides, we will help the woman with whatever her need is, if she looks away as you work. It will be a trade. Good for all."

A bitter taste touched the back of Jayne's tongue. It was too bad that doing good didn't always feel good. Talk about a morally gray area... "And if she doesn't have a tragedy for me to exploit?"

"She will. Everyone does. You need to be prepared for situations that arise when you get close to Deirdre. If she introduces you to any Kingdom members, you will be in immediate danger. But you'll have to put that aside, Jayne. You must find out what they're up to by feigning interest in their cause and joining their organization."

"You're going to send me right into the line of fire on my first time out? Undercover? Are you mad?"

He laughed a little. "Mad, desperate, what's the difference? It's a big risk, I agree. But you're the best shot we have, Jayne. You're stronger than us all, and the Book is calling to you. You'll need to be very, very good with more-advanced spells. Go into the Torrent, please. Now. We don't have a minute to waste."

This is insane this is insane this is insane. But she didn't doubt the sincerity of his words for a moment, so she forced a grin. She'd agreed to this. Time to show them what she was worth.

Oh. Salary. She'd need to ask about that at some point. Surely the pay would be awesome, if she was defying death regularly. Not that it mattered. The library would have any book she could possibly want to buy. Plus, there was no way to put a price on saving the freaking world from enslavement.

She cracked her knuckles. "Ruger, you better be planning to teach me some kick-ass magic."

His dark grin was all she needed to see. Ignoring the twist of her stomach, pushing away the environs of the Farm around her, the shouts and calls, Jayne envisioned the Torrent.

CHAPTER FOURTEEN

Ruger entered the Torrent alongside Jayne. She couldn't see him, but she could feel his presence, solid and sure.

"Try to guess what spell I'm calling up," Ruger said.

A shape appeared beside her. It looked like a tiny doorway. Pale sage-hued lines cut across the opening.

"A trap of some sort?"

"Good. How might it work?"

"Maybe you could set it behind you, and then, when someone passed through it, trying to hurt you, they'd be cut to ribbons?"

"I hadn't thought of placing it behind me, as a moving spell. Interesting. It's not aggressive enough to cut anyone. But your thought process is promising. How else might I use this spell?"

"I don't know." Her brain felt like sludge.

"Come on. You have more ideas. I can practically feel your gears turning."

"My lightning brain." Sofia called Jayne's mind a storm, and they'd joked about her lightning brain crashing through perfectly normal conversations and leading them down wild paths.

Ruger frowned. "Your what?"

"Nothing. Never mind. Okay. Um. I think you could set it up across a real-world doorway and maybe the spell would alert you when someone passed through it?"

"Yes!" Ruger's shout made Jayne jump and the Torrent dissolved, leaving them back at the Farm.

Ruger smiled. "Sorry. I am very pleased with you, Jayne. You really do have a natural talent with magic. It's impressive."

"Thanks."

"Now, back in we go. This time, you bring that spell into being."

After five tries, she managed it and a second one, too, quite accidentally. The extra spell looked like the doorway with its slashes, but instead of being a rectangle, the spell formed the shape of an egg. Ruger immediately cut across it with a word and a rush of magic from his presence beside her in the Torrent.

"What was that?" she asked, curious at his haste.

"A Birth spell."

"You're going to have to give me a little more than that."

"It's actually more of a transformation. If you cast that spell along with another one to guide the change, you can make a bird into a dog. Or turn me into you. Not actually, but it would look like that creature or person in the flesh. Not in thought patterns or soul. Just the flesh. It uses the energy of the living creature that passes through to re-create the physical being and strength of whatever spell you layer on top of it."

Whoa. That would be crazy. "What do these layering spells use to define the form? A name? An image from my mind?"

"It can be either, or both. Magic is intuitive and oftentimes uses metaphor. Castings can vary from Adept to Adept. If your will is strong enough and your symbology makes sense to you and the Torrent inside you, the spell will work."

"That's pretty froufrou."

Ruger barked a laugh. "It won't look whimsical if you use the Birth spell to age yourself."

"Holy crap. That sounds horrifying."

"I've done it. It is."

She couldn't help herself. "How does that work?"

"Let me show you."

They reentered the Torrent, and the egg-shaped Birth casting appeared beside Ruger's invisible presence. Then another symbol settled over the first spell like a blanket. The spell looked like a fist and a heart. Maybe not a heart. It was tough to tell. But then letters shimmered over the symbol to spell out Ruger's full name. Ruger Fitzwilliam Stern.

"Return," Ruger said.

Jayne let go of the Torrent, then watched as Ruger climbed through what looked like an oval of pale light in the middle of the floor. He turned to face her.

She gasped. His hair was gray, nearly white at the temples. Wrinkles crowded his eyes and tugged his lips into thin lines. His back was bent at the shoulders, and he looked like he'd lost at least fifty pounds.

"Hot stuff, eh?" He shook his behind at her, then passed the opposite way through the spell. When he came out on the other side, he was normal again. Middle-aged Ruger. Not ancient as the mountains Ruger.

"That was pure bananas."

"Want to guess another spell? Come on." Ruger closed his eyes.

Jayne followed him into the Torrent again. The cool air brushed over her cheeks as Ruger called up a spinning ball of dark emerald green. The sight of it made her slightly nauseated.

"It's so fast."

"Exactly. If you call this up, you can move more quickly than any regular human. But it'll suck the energy right out of you, so be careful with it." The spell dissipated.

"Here's another."

The Torrent seemed to hold its breath for a second.

"Ruger?"

"It's okay. Hold on."

Light gathered, weaving and crisscrossing, layering edge upon edge, until it built what looked like a basket.

"Is this for all that berry-picking I'm going to be doing in the middle of Dublin?"

"Ha. You can use this to keep things hidden on your person or to carry heavy items a short distance. Once again, it sucks you dry, so watch it. Let's take a break."

They returned to the training facility. Ruger's face had paled, so Jayne brought him a glass of water, which he guzzled down.

"I want you to master all of these spells before we leave for Dublin."

"But I'm halfway to exhausted already!"

"And you think you'll be nicely rested and prepped if an emergency occurs?"

He made a good point. "Fine."

She worked all day and into the night, casting and thinking and willing things to happen right there on an unadorned concrete floor beside an eighties-era conference table until she dropped to her knees back in the real world.

"I have to take a break."

Ruger looked at his watch. "We're done for the day. I'm surprised we haven't heard from Amanda yet."

"I got the sense the world was about to end."

"The world is not going to end while we teach you, Jayne. Be patient. Let's get some chow and rest while we can. The 'hotel' is this way."

Legs feeling distinctly wobbly, she followed him across the garage ground of the Farm to a small building that looked like a roadside motel.

At the door, he clapped her on the shoulder. "You did well today. You're going to do well in Dublin, too. Don't worry too much. Get a shower. I'll have food delivered."

She forced a smile of thanks, but worry chewed at her nerves. No matter what, she had to get in touch with Sofia tonight.

CHAPTER FIFTEEN

The Farm's hotel was not exactly James Bond worthy. Built to house exhausted recruits who couldn't care less about their environs, it was about as no-frills as she'd ever seen.

She mentioned that to Ruger, who laughed.

"What did you expect from the middle of nowhere, Jayne. The Ritz? Eat."

Jayne had been too tired to eat much, despite the lovely freshly made carbonara Ruger had placed in front of her. After she'd pushed the plate away and only picked at her blueberry pie, yawning about fifty times in a row, Ruger had suggested she get some rest and crawled away to his own room, making noises about finding out when they'd leave.

With her new phone, she tried Sofia again. Still straight to voicemail.

"Listen," she said into the phone, imagining the perpetual worry lines between Sofia's eyebrows. "I'm sorry you don't approve. But it is what it is. We're still sisters. I love you, and you love me even if you're too angry to admit it right now. I'll call you again when I can."

Clicking off, she pressed the phone to her chest. "Please stop hating me, sis." Her whisper sounded loud in the small room.

And now she was too geared up to sleep. Wet hair wrapped in a towel, PJs on, Jayne stretched out on the faded sheets and stared at the ceiling. Her hands tingled from doing magic, and with every heartbeat, she heard the word *Kingdom*. What would it be like to go up against them? Hopefully, she would only have to skulk around behind the scenes and find information. After working with Ruger, she knew very well she'd lose a supernatural fight if it came to that. Yes, she had raw talent, raw power, but that was nothing if she couldn't keep a clear head during a high-stress situation. There was no way she'd be ready in two weeks. Not even a full year of training would do it. Even with her martial arts experience, she would be toast if she came up against an experienced and passionately driven Adept terrorist.

Frustrated with this knowledge, Jayne crossed the room to the coffeepot and used it to heat some water for tea. She had three packages of tea in her purse, her emergency stash for when she found herself in uncivilized locations. Earl Grey, green tea with mint, and an herbal one—chamomile. Perfect. She dipped the chamomile bag into the mug she'd prepped, and the scent of flowers filled the hotel room. Inhaling, she pretended the room was filled with the ancient texts she'd see in Dublin. She imagined a page from the Book of Leinster, the age-dulled red and green ink, the way the letters—even on a laptop screen—had shimmered in front of her eyes and lured her in like a would-be lover. She'd spent every minute of her off hours studying Middle Irish to better understand the metaphors used in the ancient tales.

A short knock on her door had her scrambling to her feet.

"Come in," she called.

Ruger opened the door.

"Good news. Well, sort of. There's been no more suspicious activity at the library, and nothing's blown up, so the director feels it's better for us to stay here and train you a bit more thoroughly. We're on call, though, so the moment we get the word, we're on a plane. Get some rest tonight, because tomorrow, I'm going to kick your ass all over the Farm."

He grinned, looking like a pirate's middle-aged dad, and shut the door before she could retort.

"We'll see about that, *sir.*"

She got lucky with the reprieve. The next few days were filled with more information than she thought her brain would ever be able to soak in. Not only was she practicing spells, defensive, offensive, and everything in between, she was learning the ins and outs of being a TCO officer. How to lose a tail when walking/riding/driving. Which code phrases meant what. How to reach the TCO when things went awry.

Ruger had Jayne give Sofia an "office" number for her new job. When Sofia called the number, the TCO phone service would put the call through to Jayne's new phone. Her calls would be monitored, but she was encouraged to text and phone Sofia fairly regularly to keep suspicions from rising. The whole communication system was "spoofed," as Ruger called it, and used two minor spells in the process.

Too bad Sofia still hadn't returned a single one of Jayne's texts, calls, or voicemails.

During one of her training sessions, Ruger had ordered Jayne to drive a car alone into a wooded area near the training facility. A group of people speaking some language she couldn't identify surrounded the vehicle. Over the phone, Ruger demanded that she escape the situation, no matter the cost, without magic.

A man in the crowd pounded a fist on the windshield and shouted through the glass. Two more people swung bats at the rear lights, making Jayne shriek despite knowing this crowd had to be other TCO officers like herself. Their angry expressions just seemed so real. She put the car in reverse and the people in the back jumped out of her way, but as she turned the wheel, readying to switch to drive to speed out of there, a woman wearing a balaclava leapt onto the hood. Heart pounding her brain to bits, Jayne slung the car to the right, threw the woman off, then slammed the gas.

Only then did she realize the car had morphed into a dragon, and she was literally flying.

The ground dropped away to show starlit clouds and the forest, dark and speckled with the angry crowd's flashlights below. The dragon roared and moved its sinuous neck, its black scales tough but smooth under Jayne's shaking hands. Wings the size of a ship's sails caught the wind. The base of the dragon's wings shifted under Jayne's thighs, and still she hadn't accepted the fact that this was happening. An exhale of charcoal-scented breath came from the creature's mouth and ghosted over Jayne's wind-strewn hair.

Sucking a shocked breath, Jayne let the unintended spell go, and she was on the ground again in the car, the steering wheel cold and soft, completely unlike the dragon's scales.

A dragon, for God's sake. What was this life she was living?

Trying very hard to drive and not pass out, her mind whirred. She couldn't have been as high up as it had looked from the dragon's back. She hadn't felt the fall. It had been an illusion then, like the spells Ruger had used on that other trainee, Mark, during the morning's sparring session.

But by the look of admiration on Ruger's face, and the shock of the other trainees, that wasn't the case.

She stumbled from the car. "What just happened?"

"You needed to get away. So you created an escape. It was a little flashy, and maybe too informed by your Harry Potter obsession, but it worked. Well done."

"*I* made the car into a dragon? Get out of here."

"I keep telling you, Jayne, your power is endless. You have more innate talent than any Adept I've seen in years. This is a good thing. Remember this moment if you get yourself in trouble. Imagining your way out will always work."

That night, Ruger had taken Jayne to a dive bar on the Farm's grounds for a much-needed shot of tequila.

The next evening, exhausted from twelve full hours of working spells and answering questions about her new identity, Jayne stepped from the shower to see Amanda waiting in her room to inform her it was time to head into the fray.

"I know it's quick, but you've got this," Amanda said, checking her watch. "Ruger will continue your training in the field. Have you memorized your legend?"

"I'm Jayne Thomas, adopted sister to Lane Thomas, my troublemaking brother who is constantly running from the authorities. Jayne Thomas shares a very similar background to the real Jayne, a past job at Vandy, degrees out the wazoo, and a talent for magic."

"Jayne Thomas is the only Jayne who exists now. It is vital that you don't forget that."

"Yes, ma'am."

"I know we've pushed you hard these past few days. But I believe you can handle this."

Jayne glowed a bit under the praise, but she couldn't help herself.

"How do you know I won't screw this up? I spent my life training to be a librarian, not a spy."

"The two disciplines are not terribly different, actually."

"I'm not sure that's a compliment. One could argue that subversion isn't attractive when the world is at stake."

"We aren't subversives, Jayne. We're trying to keep the world safe. We're trying to keep our knowledge, our history, our good works, intact. The Kingdom wants to unravel everything we stand for—democracy, freedom, equal rights, broad education—and will do it in such a way to hurt and enslave countless millions of people in the process. They pander and flatter, and they don't care who they hurt in their quest for ultimate power. Remember that, should you find yourself in their presence. Now, you'll leave for your flight in one hour. Just enough time for us to fix your eyes. Take off your glasses, please. And look at me. No blinking."

"What?"

Amanda shined a horribly bright light into Jayne's left eye, making her curse. "That hurts!"

"Once more. And stand still this time."

One more massive flash in the left, then another. Amanda turned Jayne's head slightly and did the same to her right. Three flashes, the first super painful, the last two not as bad.

"Now blink."

Jayne did. Her eyes felt gritty, but the world around her was crystal clear.

"Oh my God. I can see! Without my glasses! What did you do to me? Some sort of magical LASIK?"

"Essentially."

"You could make millions, Amanda."

"It only works on Adepts. You'll find a pair of glasses in your bag that look just like yours, but with clear lenses. We can't have you getting your frames knocked off during a fight and you not being able to see."

"It's very cool. But next time you want to alter my body, Amanda, you could ask first."

"Your body, your mind, and your soul belong to the TCO now, Jayne. Remember that. Good luck in Ireland."

The air shimmered, and Amanda was gone.

A bit ill from Amanda's declaration, Jayne rummaged in her bag until she found the promised clear glasses, set them on her nose. As awesome as it was to be able to see without corrective lenses, she liked the way she looked in glasses. They gave her a studious air.

A heavy knock told her Ruger was outside. At least he had the decency not to apparate into her room. She flung open the door to see him holding two carry-ons.

"Ready?"

"As I'll ever be."

"Then move aside and shut the door. The portal is through the bathroom."

"Hopefully not through the toilet." He cast her a brief, dirty look. "What?"

"You have a very smart mouth, Jayne."

"That's me. Jayne Thorne, CIA Librarian. Cracking wise and saving the world, one lame joke at a time."

He rolled his eyes. "My point exactly. After you."

CHAPTER SIXTEEN

Her foot landed in Langley; she recognized the long, nonde-script hallway. Ruger stepped through behind her and gestured for her to follow.

"Oh. I thought..."

"We can't portal into Dulles, Jayne. A car is waiting."

"Dulles?"

"That's the international airport here in DC."

"Why aren't we just portaling straight to Dublin?"

"Long story, but ultimately, there needs to be a record for customs. We've arranged a work visa for Jayne Thomas, so you need to be seen entering the UK officially. Plus, we don't want to alarm any Adepts in the area that two of us have arrived without notice. A long flight ahead for us both, I'm afraid."

"At least tell me we're in first class."

He laughed out loud at that. "You'll be more comfortable than me, trust me."

As it turned out, they were in the bulkhead by the mid-cabin door, so Ruger at least had room for his very long legs. He gave her a wink, put on a set of Bose noise-cancelling headphones, and was asleep before they took off.

Not. Fair.

Jayne fretted. She worried. She drank too much tea. She ate Ruger's cookies off the plate the flight attendant left for him. She pulled off her fake glasses and marveled at being able to see perfectly, both distance and close up. She resisted tunneling into the Torrent for an escape, unsure what might happen at forty thousand feet, instead using her remarkable memory to go over her legend again and again, revisiting her training, the copious instructions.

Then she pulled up the screen in her seat's arm and watched movies, delighted to find the first two Harry Potter films. The books were better, obviously, but this was a welcome escape. Because she could finally understand exactly what Harry was going through.

When they landed, Ruger sent her through customs alone. He joined her on the other side from the opposite direction, and she wondered if he'd portaled through so he wasn't on the radar.

They grabbed a taxi, and she tried to enjoy the quick trip from the airport into the gorgeous city of Dublin as much as she could, despite the worry lingering around her like a shroud.

The taxi dropped them at an time-worn gray building, and Ruger escorted her to the flat she'd be living in.

Flat was about the right word for it. It was on the fifth floor of the ancient building, accessible from a two-person lift that had a metal cage door. Furnished in faded teak woods and gray curtains, it was utterly devoid of personality. Nothing like her charming old apartment back in Nashville. They probably dated from the same era, the mid-seventies, but this was a gray box, and not because the walls had been painted that way.

"Wow. Impressive."

"It wouldn't do for you to have something splashy. This is anonymous, and close to work. Look out the window."

She pulled back the curtain, and her heart sparked. The spires of Trinity loomed over the undulating lines of Dublin's many pubs, busy traffic, and buildings in all shapes and sizes.

"Not a bad view, huh?" Ruger said. "Though I suggest you keep your curtains closed at all times."

"Yeah, that won't look suspicious at all. Where are your digs?"

"Two floors down."

"Is there a portal in the toaster?"

He looked pained and she laughed. "Okay. I'll take the stairs if I need anything."

He dumped the contents of a manila folder on the table.

"Here is everything you'll need. Memorize the dossier on Deirdre Green, then burn it. I suggest you get some rest. They'll be expecting you bright and early tomorrow morning. And remember, your primary goal is to befriend Deirdre and get her to lead us to the Kingdom."

"You're a hundred percent sure she's tied to them?"

"No, but it's a strong possibility. The nature of her previous tenures suggests she's looking for something. She's high profile, granted access to special manuscripts, and very smart. So be careful with her."

"Cross my heart and hope to die."

"Jayne…"

"Too soon for death jokes?"

Ruger just shook his head and turned to leave.

Jayne reached for his sleeve, suddenly feeling lightheaded with nerves. She closed her hand before making the grab, not wanting to appear desperate. "Wait," she said, schooling her voice. "Aren't we going to eat? And train? I'm not ready for all of this, Ruger. We both know it."

Ruger rubbed his eyes with the back of his hand. "Jayne, trust me. I have your back. Okay? You're not in this alone. We'll keep training, keep learning. But right now, I'm going to sleep. Your fridge is stocked. I believe there's even a pie. And makings for lunch tomorrow—the librarians bring their own."

At least there was pie. "My hero. But…" Jayne turned in circles, looking at the dingy walls. "There are no books."

With a deep sigh, Ruger closed his eyes. Moments later, the walls were covered in bookshelves and a rainbow array of titles. Her books. From Nashville. Wow.

Jayne couldn't stifle her surprised cry of delight. "Wicked. You *have* to teach me that trick."

"Good night, Jayne. Do well tomorrow. You know your assignment. Fit in. Make friends. Get Deirdre to trust you, and—if she tries—recruit you for her cause. If she's not the Kingdom member herself, it's possible someone close to her is the conduit. Do whatever you must to become her friend. Get invited to her home and make nice with her husband. Act normal, and fit in. Oh, and in the meantime, if you come across any nasty books, let us know. Now, go forth, and make us proud."

He let himself out.

It took her all of five minutes to unpack. Ruger had somehow managed to bring all her favorites in that tiny suitcase. *Magic, Jayne. It's magic.*

Happily, the refrigerator did hold the promised pie. Blueberry, from the looks of it. She grabbed a slice, poured a glass of wine, found a battered copy of Sharon Penman's *Here Be Dragons*, something she hadn't read in at least a decade, and lost herself in the world of Joanna and Llywelyn.

Something was trying to strangle her.

Jayne shot to her feet, her Farm training kicking in. Block. Shield. Attack.

The pressure on her neck released, and she crumpled to her knees, eyes searching the darkness for her assailant.

All she saw were the long, deep shadows of the Dublin night, and a crocheted afghan laying on the floor next to her. She laughed shakily, blowing out her breath. What the hell had just happened? Had the afghan attacked her?

Her door flew open and her lights flashed on, momentarily blinding her. Ruger bolted into the room, hands up, ready to do battle. When he saw her sitting on the floor, he grabbed her by the shoulders and pulled her to her feet.

"What happened? I felt a surge of energy, heard you yelling."

"You heard me two floors away?"

He gestured to the lamp. "You're miked, obviously."

She flushed. "I don't want to be miked."

"Too bad."

With a glare she told him exactly what she thought about that.

"It's for your safety, Jayne. And mine. And the mission. You can yell at me about it later. Tell me what happened."

"Something was trying to strangle me. The afghan was knotted up around my neck. I must have fallen asleep and it twisted around me. I think I was dreaming about our lessons."

Ruger shook his head. "I'm not so sure. Go look in the mirror."

She flipped the switch, heard the light hum to life before it actually lit the space.

There were bruises on her neck, like someone's thumbs had

pressed hard against her carotids.

"Holy shit."

Ruger was there now, too, taking up all the available space.

"It didn't take them long to come looking for you."

"They? You think this was the Kingdom?"

"In a way."

"Is my cover blown?" She was shocked to find herself thinking operationally instead of like Jayne the innocent but oh-so-worldly Vandy librarian.

Ruger led her back to the living room, muttering some spells that made the air around her constrict. She felt like she was wearing a very tight shirt and her goal-weight jeans, though she was definitely not there. It wasn't exactly pleasant.

"Ow."

"Sorry. You need extra protection right now."

"Again, I ask. Is my cover blown?"

"Just…give me a minute to examine you." His hands ran lightly over her arms, her neck, her shoulders. He looked around the room, and his eyes fell on her *Here Be Dragons* book.

"Were you reading this when you fell asleep?"

"Yes." She flipped open the front cover, showing him the Ex Libris stamp, one of her prized possessions, now with the tiny alteration that would help seal her identity. *From the Library of Jayne Thomas*. "It's one you packed from my shelf in Nashville."

He retrieved a dish towel and picked up the book gently, examining it from all angles.

"What is it?" Jayne asked.

"A nasty attack spell. They must have broken into your apartment and left this behind."

"Who?"

"The bartender who gave you the spiked drink, I presume. He was working with Aaró. They were trailing you in Nashville."

"Aaró?"

"He was the redhead from the bar. I took care of him." His face was grim, and Jayne understood *took care of* meant *killed*, and shivered. She'd suspected as much, but still.

Focus, Jayne.

"There are spells that can be attached to inanimate objects to attack people? That can happen?"

Ruger ran a hand across his broad face, looking extremely worried. "It can. It's only a variation of the Tracking spell you learned." At the look on her face, he added hastily, "Though I haven't heard of it happening for a very long time. I'll need to let Amanda know immediately. I'm not sure how this was missed."

He started toward the door, but Jayne put out a hand. "Wait, you're just going to leave me here, with no real explanation and no way to defend myself against phantoms in the night?"

"You're totally equipped. You chased that spell away. That was your doing, not mine. And I've added a few extra layers of protection. No one will be messing with you here again. I swear it. This was a leftover from Nashville, that I'm certain. The spell smells like Aaró, and he is no longer with us. No one knows we're here. Your cover isn't blown."

"I don't have a lot of choice in this, do I?"

"Try to sleep. You're safe."

It was not lost on her that he hadn't actually answered her question. "Sure I am, buddy. I'm living in a world where a book can somehow attack me in my sleep. What else might be out there that you've never seen before?"

He blew out a breath. "I guess we'll find out."

"Get rid of the mike."

"Jayne—"

"If you want me to do all this crazy crap, I have to at least know I have my privacy."

Ruger's jaw worked, and he looked at the ceiling.

"I'm not giving up on this. Tell or don't tell the rest of them. But I want it gone."

He shook his head and, moving fast, ripped tiny devices from her lamp, a spot behind the bedroom door, and one somewhere in the living room. He leaned his head back in. "Sleep well."

She didn't.

CHAPTER SEVENTEEN

Despite the lack of sleep and terrible jet lag, Jayne's first Dublin morning sparkled with hope. The bruises were faded enough that she simply wound a scarf around her neck, the ends trailing happily down her back.

Just a five-minute walk from her flat, Trinity College's front arch welcomed her into a majestic quiet—such a dramatic shift from the busy streets of Dublin. The morning sunlight glowed along old columns and spilled over the cobbled square. She took a minute to leave yet another voicemail for Sofia, this time her message more positive, only asking for one single text to let her know she wouldn't hate her for eternity.

She got it.

Fine, the text said.

Love you, she typed, smiling. Shoving her concern about Sofia away, Jayne soldiered on.

A giddy mix of excitement and fear rushed through her, battling her attempts to look chill as she walked past art students and headed for the old library. Her first day on the job. Another university library, a stunningly beautiful campus. She would see the Book of Kells, and stand inside the Long Room at Trinity, the ultimate library porn. She was magical, and a newly minted CIA officer. And she would eventually find her way to the Book of Leinster.

Today was going to rock.

Could the people she saw glancing her way tell she was different somehow? Did the aura of magic shimmer around her at all? If the TCO's info was right, she was currently the only Adept in the immediate vicinity, though surely there were plenty in the Dublin area. The Kingdom had to recruit from somewhere. Or maybe she just looked über American. She was wearing a deep green skirt and a sleeveless gray shell under a matching cardigan, the scarf, and black flats. Conservative librarian clothes. She didn't think she stood out, but...

Just act normal. Be cool and confident in your role as the newest staff member in the Early Printed Books and Special Collections Department.

A breeze stirred the air in front of the open door of the Old Library, and the scent of ancient books made Jayne swoon. She couldn't help herself, she craned her neck to peek past a Trinity student talking over the heads of a small group of tourists, just to see if she could catch a glimpse of the Long Room from the doors.

"You should probably head toward the Berkeley Library." A tall, blonde woman smiled, pointing at Jayne's staff tag. "You'll get to your department through the basement. That way."

Heat rose to Jayne's cheeks. Now she remembered what the orientation email had said. The woman was correct. "Oops. Thanks."

"You'll get a chance to see the Book of Kells. It's not going

anywhere." The blonde smirked, looking down at her phone.
"Right. Of course." Embarrassed that she'd acted like every
other tourist to wander onto the campus, Jayne took five steps
backward, thanking her again before turning away.

A woman on a bike zipped past Jayne's elbow and nearly
knocked her down in front of the Old Library's entrance.

"Sorry," the woman on the bike called, already half a block
away.

Jayne brushed off her skirt and started walking again but
slammed directly into a man running toward her carrying a
massive black duffel bag, yelling at the woman on the bike,
"Stop, you gowl!"

Jayne, the man, and the duffel bag went down in a tangle.

"Sorry!" she yelped.

Blushing furiously at her double dose of clumsiness, Jayne
scrambled to her feet and tried to help him get his massive bag
back onto his shoulder. The man—he looked like a movie star
with his sculpted shoulders and arms—grabbed the duffel as if it
weighed nothing, adjusted the strap, then grinned at her, dimples showing. His light blue eyes sparkled in the morning light,
and Jayne took a step back, thrown off by how good looking
the guy was.

He raised a thick eyebrow and jerked his chin toward the first
person who'd run into Jayne. "So much for my bike."

"That woman stole your bike?"

"*Stole* is a strong word. I prefer to think it's simply been
borrowed and will be returned in some other life. So sorry I
knocked you down."

"Thank you. And I think that was my fault, not yours." She
knelt to pick up something that had fallen from his duffel. It was
a Thai kickboxing mitt similar to the ones Jayne used back at
her gym in Nashville. She handed it to him.

"My name's Cillian," he said, his full lips pouting in a deliciously Irish way as he pronounced the hard K. "Cillian Pine."

She shook his hand, trying not to stare at the small scar that ran across his nose. What had happened to give him that? "I'm Jayne Thomas." Her throat tightened around the small lie. She'd have to get used to the deceit of using her false last name. It was all for a good cause. "Are you into kickboxing? Or perhaps just into carrying the oddest things ever onto collegiate campuses?"

He laughed, the Adam's apple in his throat moving. The yellow of an old bruise colored the skin beside his nose. He must've had a black eye about a week back.

"I teach Muay Thai kickboxing," he said. "Just up the way. Northside. But how did you know this pad was for kickboxing?"

"I work out at home. In Nashville."

"That explains your accent. It's deadly."

She frowned. "Um, I'm not sure how my accent would kill anyone."

Covering his mouth, he chuckled. "Ah, no. *Deadly* just means awesome or great. Do you not use the term in America?"

"Not where I live."

"Why are you here, hanging with the Trinnies? Let me guess, you're a Rhodie."

"Roadie? I'm not with a band."

He laughed again. He had a nice laugh. "Rhodes scholar."

Good grief, Jayne. A band? "No, I've taken a job with the Early Printed Books and Special Collections Department. This is my first day."

Oh, wait. Should she be telling him this? Her wild training course had obviously not been strong enough to imprint the most basic of rules into her mind. One handsome guy and suddenly she was spouting like a broken hose. No, it was fine. *Make friends. Fit in.* This qualified, right?

He whistled. "Wow. That is something. I wouldn't have the first clue what to do with an old book. I haven't read in donkey's years."

Had she heard him right? No reading? She would have to reassess his cuteness forthwith. And what did a donkey have to do with it?

He grinned, showing white teeth. One of his incisors was a little crooked. "It means *in a long time.* What do you do with the books?"

"We help students, faculty, and other scholars with their research. And we make sure no one damages the manuscripts, books, and photographs so they'll be legible when you and I are long gone."

"I like that. Keeping things safe for the children."

"Exactly."

"Since you train, would you like to try one of my classes? I always offer a free session to newcomers. Tonight, maybe?"

"Tonight? Well..." Play it cool, don't look too anxious. How else was she going to fit in if she didn't meet new people and try new things? "I wouldn't be able to get there until 7:30. Oh, I mean, 19:30."

Adjusting to living overseas was going to be more complicated than she'd thought. At least she wasn't trying to conquer an entirely new language. Not that this sounded like her version of English, with all the Irish idioms and the accent.

"Perfect. That's when we start anyway." His accent made the word sound like *par-fect,* and the R even had a subtle trip to it. It was decidedly...cute. Even if he didn't read. She could fix that. She firmly believed a nonreader was simply someone who hadn't found their jam yet. She'd bet he would like fantasy. Robin Hobb, to start. And then they could have a few lazy weekends, chatting about the stories. *Stow your ovaries, Jayne.*

Lifting a muscled arm, Cillian shielded his eyes against a stray sunbeam, stared past the reading room building. "Gotta scram, I'm off to meet some mates in the Global Room. Do you happen to know where the Watts Building is?"

"You're asking an American who was lost the moment she walked through the arch?" He laughed once more, and Jayne decided it was one of the best laughs she'd ever heard.

"Excellent point, Miss Librarian."

"Go ask that blonde over there by the Old Library entrance," Jayne said. "She's the one who told me where to go."

"I'll do that!" He started off, the mop of dark blond hair on top of his head lifting slightly in the breeze. He turned, grinning. "Lovely to meet you, Jayne from Nashville."

Giving him a shy wave back, she resumed her journey to the reading room and tried to clear her mind for the task at hand. Kickboxing and hot guys would have to wait.

She had to snort at that. It's not like she had a serious boyfriend, ever. She'd dated a couple of guys a couple of times with no real relationship resulting. They were never as exciting as her work.

"You're lame, Jayne," she said as she finally found the proper entrance.

CHAPTER EIGHTEEN

Cillian made a show of asking the blonde where the Global Room was even though he already knew. As the blonde explained which way to go, he glanced back at the target, Jayne Thorne. She was far more beautiful than his Kingdom contact had led him to believe. Hair the color of whisky, eyes that flamed with something—maybe curiosity—and a body that had its share of curves and the lean muscle gained from time working on their shared interest. She had smelled like berries and something else, maybe books? Or ink? His nostrils flared, trying to pick up the scent, but the breeze had mostly carried it off. He'd recognize it again, though, no doubt.

When his contact had informed him about Jayne's kickboxing background, he'd known immediately how to approach her and get close to her. It had been a solid guess that, new to the country, she'd be on the lookout for a gym.

It was all falling into place nicely.

"Did that woman steal your bike?" the blonde asked. "You

should report it."

Of course, that hadn't been his bike. It'd been a ruse to run into Jayne and earn him some automatic sympathy from her.

"Thanks," he said absently to the blonde before heading back toward Early and Special, where Jayne would be.

He needed to get his information to Jayne. It wouldn't take but a minute or so—surely they'd deliver a note to an employee—and doing it belatedly would make giving her his number seem like an afterthought and less suspicious. He did need to hurry, because he actually did have a gig in the Global Room, just as he'd told Jayne.

He'd found throwing truth into his somewhat deceitful work made the whole thing more tolerable for his own peace of mind and also helped the mission go more smoothly. As he walked across campus, he recalled the quick conversation with Jayne, her ignorance of the location, her overly open demeanor. The Trinity staff would likely eat the newbie alive. Poor gal. She didn't stand a chance if the Kingdom was interested in her.

With the help of signs and three kind strangers, Jayne wove through a labyrinth of glass walls, numerous banks of computers, and myriad students dressed in everything from striped ties to basic trousers that looked needful of a wash to her department. A lean man at the door asked Jayne some questions—his accent was as London posh as it could possibly be—then he took her bag and handed it off to a stocky boy with jet-black hair and thick glasses.

"Take this to the break room, please," the man said to the boy. "Locker 225."

"Whatever you say, Gerard." The boy hurried away.

Gerard turned to Jayne. "Your key." He dropped said object in her hand. "Don't lose this."

"I'll do my best not to."

At long tables, a dozen or so folks read books that had been carefully tucked into foam cradles and were held open by weighted white ropes fondly called book snakes. Most had a staff badge, but a few proudly showed the hollowed eyes of grad students, researching their hearts out.

A smile tugged Jayne's mouth despite the danger. It was amazing that she was actually here. In one of the world's most hallowed libraries. Well, the back room of one, anyway. At one point in her life, post-school, pre-Vandy job, she'd thought she was destined to flip burgers despite her level of education. But now she was here, in Dublin, at a college many chose over Harvard. The very air smelled like philosophy and literature.

Rolling her eyes at her own misty academic snobbery, she pocketed the key, then trailed the tall doorman to a bloodred desk, where a gray-haired woman wearing glasses on a chain around her neck looked her up and down. This woman didn't match Deirdre's description. Jayne wondered when she might run into Deirdre, the employee she was assigned to befriend, if one could call it that. Spy and deceive, that's what she was really going to do. Truly the basis for a lifelong friendship if there ever was one.

"What is this, Gerard?" the gray-haired woman asked.

"*This* is your new Early and Special. Although"—he looked at his gold watch—"she is more late and common, if you ask me." He quite literally looked down his nose at her.

Stung, Jayne glared. "You don't know a single thing about me."

"I know you're American," Gerard said. "And Southern."

"So I'm automatically not good enough for you?"

"I didn't say that. I am often ten minutes late. And I am completely common. Not at all special."

Fabulous. An expert in passive-aggressive behavior was going to be her greeter every morning. Jayne's middle finger twitched, but she forced her hand to still. Flipping off the first staff member she'd met probably wouldn't be great for her mission. Or her career.

"Gerard." The woman with the glasses put her hands on her hips. "Go away."

"Scurrying away, Your Highness." He bowed sarcastically. Jayne hadn't realized such a move was even possible. "See you at lunch."

The woman sighed heavily and stuck out her hand. "I'm Rosalind. Keeper of Public Services."

"Thomas. Jayne Thomas." She inwardly cringed, realizing she said that just like the old James Bond movies Sofia had binged the summer she broke up with her first boyfriend.

Jayne laughed to herself. Jayne Bond, CIA Librarian, at your service. Would she be 007? No, according to Dewey, that was Computer Science, unassigned. Maybe something in the 130s, Parapsychology and Occultism. Or 141—Idealism and related systems and doctrines.

You're making Dewey Decimal jokes in your head, lame-o. Stop thinking and focus.

"So you're to be our new Public Services assistant. The same role you played at Vanderbilt University, yes?" Rosalind, thankfully not noticing Jayne's amusement at her internal monologue, brought Jayne behind the red help desk and into a back room.

"Yes," Jayne answered dutifully, hating the small talk. Chatting with her new boss was making her palms sweat. Jayne longed to demand immediate access to the Book of Leinster, but Ruger had urged her to feel out the situation before plunging in, so Jayne held her tongue.

The woman's glasses swung over her ample bosom as she leaned close. "Excellent. Then we won't need to do much training, just acquaint you with the logistics. This is the key to the restricted areas." Rosalind handed over a tiny skeleton key. "Visitors must first sign in at the desk and fill out the appropriate forms before putting in a call slip for our materials. We don't expect anyone this morning, so it will be nice and quiet to get you oriented."

There was a far-off crash, which sounded for all the world like a bundle of very old books hitting the floor, then a small voice called, "Rosalind? A little help here."

Rosalind shook her head. "I spoke too soon. Keep an eye on the desk, will you, dear?" She hurried away, calling over her shoulder, "I'll be back shortly, and we'll get you set up."

Jayne gripped the key firmly in her palm as Rosalind walked away, leaving her alone in a room of books that had once belonged to ancient noble families and kings long forgotten in the world of technology and caramel macchiatos. And magical texts. And a possible terrorist or two.

Was she really prepared for this?

Man the desk. At least that was simple enough.

A few seconds later she realized she had her first real opportunity to start the covert part of her job. Okay. Okay. What had Ruger told her to do?

"Any opportunity you have to access the Book of Leinster or information regarding the manuscript, take it," he'd said. "There will likely be more magical tomes hidden there. You might learn from them as well. Touch the spines of the books in the Early Printed Books and Special Collections Department. Feel for magical traces. If you feel a buzz, a strange heat, or anything out of the ordinary, take the book from the shelf. Access the Torrent and attach the Tracking spell."

She rubbed her neck, remembering the attack from last night. Tracking spells, attack spells. She'd known books were powerful, but never imagined they were capable of true physical malice. Outside of having one tossed at your head, of course.

I can do this. No problem. She wanted to practice accessing the Torrent just one more time before she got started. Closing her eyes, she held her hands open, palms up.

"What are you doing?" Gerard's voice broke over Jayne like a bucket of ice water.

"I...I'm concentrating."

"Yes. Of course you are. Very special, indeed." He held out a slip of paper. "This was delivered for you. From a young man who looks like he has been in quite a few nasty rows of late."

She took the note, and Gerard sped off.

The paper read:

Nice to meet you this morning. Text me and we'll set up a class if you want.

—Cillian

The note had his phone number and, she supposed, what must be the address of his kickboxing school. He must have circled back when he realized they'd have trouble finding one another without any contact information. Well, well, well. She smiled, tucked the note into her pocket, and went back to work.

With Gerard gone and Rosalind still conveniently absent, Jayne breathed deeply and imagined the Torrent's emerald light and smoky rose scent. And then she was there.

A river of stars rushed past her knees and over her shoulders, chilly and clean. Ignoring the uneasy fact that there was no earth beneath her feet, she envisioned a book with tattered pages and hands—long and bony, short and fleshy, young, old, in between—turning and pointing to the book's words and illustrations. A shimmering, pale white glow eased its way over her eyes and around the back of her head. She'd summoned a perfect Tracking spell. Keeping all her focus on the spell, she left the Torrent and found her feet back in the library.

Excellent. She had the spell in her hands, nice and strong. No time like the present to start checking books.

The shelves nearest the desk held literature from ages long gone. Running her fingers lightly along the spines and feeling every inch a criminal for potentially damaging these texts with magic, Jayne watched the world through the Tracking spell's shimmering, white light. Most of the images that passed over her vision when she touched the spines were too faint to make out. A veil. Two dark eyes that might have actually been stones. A hand gripping a sword, knuckles brushing the book's cover.

But then, on the fourth shelf, a bright, clear image surfaced.

Jayne's fingers paused on a thick, black leather spine.

The image showed a man wearing a cowled robe—a monk? He gripped the manuscript in his big, meaty hands, very unlike the way Jayne would've guessed a scribe would handle such a costly item.

What was this, then?

Removing the handwritten book the way she'd been taught—with two hands and careful not to pull at the spine—Jayne took a deep breath of rose and campfire, of magic. She carried the book to the staff tables behind the desk and set it on a foam cradle. She checked over her shoulder to make sure no one Gerard-ed her again, then began smoothing the edges of the pages gently with her palms.

The manuscript resembled MS 492, a twelfth-century Bede from Bury that detailed geography after the Norman conquest, with its bright sapphire, jade, and ruby capital B for Britain at the beginning of the Latin text.

In her vision, the monk's hands clenched, then one ran along a line three-fourths of the way down the page. Jayne took a moment puzzling her way through the elaborate lettering.

"...*ambagesque tenebris*...tangle the dark," she whispered to herself. "...*uti anima*...use the soul."

Then the monk's hands blackened to the blue-dark of rot, and a name shrieked into Jayne's head. "Bekkr!"

Jayne gasped as the spell fell away from her, chased away by fear. She felt all wrong. Scared, breathless, heart pounding against her ribs, like an ax murderer had jumped out of the stacks and chased her. Damn. What the heck was that? She shook her head. She knew so little. How was she supposed to do this job?

By doing the job, Jayne.

She gathered herself, attached the Tracking spell. Keeping an eye out for Rosalind, she quickly put the book back on the shelves. She would definitely report her experience to Ruger. Anything that dark and soul-sucking had to be pretty foul, right?

A strange tingling bloomed in Jayne's chest, and her thoughts of the dark book sifted away. She looked around. What was the source of the feeling? It had to be magic. The sensation was familiar, but she couldn't quite put her finger on it.

Ignoring the feeling, pushing it away mentally, she went back to work, searching for more magically touched manuscripts at this wild new job of hers.

The rest of the morning went smoothly. Rosalind returned and showed Jayne how to set up her email account. Within an hour, she was online and working on a request for research help from a faculty member. Jayne gathered the manuscripts the professor had listed and put them on a shelf behind the desk for the woman to pick up later. Once she finished, she pretended to have another research request so Rosalind wouldn't question why she was perusing the stacks again.

Secretly taking notes on her phone, Jayne worked her way through several more rows. She'd only sensed two more fully formed images on two other texts. Nothing as frightening as that first glimpse of the monk and the rather evil-sounding bits of his manuscript, thank heavens.

Finally, Rosalind set down the library phone and looked up, smiling. "Jayne, are you excited to get a look at MS H 2.18?" She eyed a table beyond the shelves where Jayne had been working.

Jayne's heart stopped. MS H 2.18 was the assigned label for the book that had drawn her interest for years.

The Book of Leinster.

CHAPTER NINETEEN

"Now?" Jayne's voice held a tremor of excitement, but worry crowded in, too. She had known she would be granted access to the book, but she hadn't wanted to push it and ruin her cover by seeming too eager. Now that the moment had come when she would finally see and possibly touch the tome she'd pored over online, her nerves sent her body into a tailspin. After what had just happened with the monk's text, how could she control her reactions if the book really was a necromantic text? Maybe she shouldn't be accessing it in front of strangers. If it shouted at her, she might react strangely. She needed to be more prepared and was wildly relieved when Rosalind shook her head.

"Not *right* now, we need Deirdre, and she won't be back until after lunch. But when she does, yes. We're most anxious to get your take on the translations and condition, to help us preserve it." Rosalind's glasses slipped down her nose.

Gerard's head appeared over Rosalind's shoulder. "You Americans are always in such a hurry. I'm telling you. Our future is lost."

"It's the past I'm worried about," Rosalind said, then frowned. "Are you well, Jayne?"

Jayne's nerves were settling. She patted her stomach. "Oh yes. Just hungry. I think my body is still on Nashville time."

"Let's break early, then," Rosalind said. "I'll show you the staff break room." She waved a frizzy-haired intern over to the desk and barked orders to keep a good watch on the room.

Rosalind and Gerard walked down the hall with Jayne, heading toward a door Jayne hadn't noticed on her way in. The break room consisted of a long marble countertop with stools, five tables surrounded by gray chairs, a microwave, and a large fridge. The lockers Gerard had mentioned at the start of the day covered the back wall.

They retrieved their belongings and sat down at a table near a long window. The light was gray and showed the corners of another building. Jayne stared at the lunch she'd packed, unable to even consider eating.

Rosalind's phone dinged, and she looked at the screen over what looked like a ham sandwich. "Ah, brilliant. Deirdre says she'll be back after lunch. Jayne, I think she might be a help to you with the interpretation. Though she hasn't studied Irish mythology to the degree you have, she has made a concentrated effort of late. When she returns, she'll bring the book up for you, and you can test her knowledge."

Jayne's heart took off at a gallop. *Play it cool.* "Great. Um, who is Deirdre?"

Gerard spread jam on a piece of toast. "The woman is a pillar of decorum and you should follow her about like a puppy, if you ask me. Not that you're asking me. But you should. That's just my opinion."

Rosalind smacked his arm. "Don't listen to his snobbery,

Jayne. Deirdre is quiet and a bit...odd, but kind, nonetheless. She comes from money, I think, though she hides it well."

"Tacky, Rosalind."

"Stuff it, Gerard."

Jayne ignored their banter and picked at her own sandwich. After lunch, she was going to meet her target, and her book.

Jayne and Rosalind worked for almost an hour before the door opened to show a lovely woman with wide-set cheekbones and dark eyes. With a quick wave, she scurried to a second table.

"Deirdre," Rosalind called for her, smiling. "Come here, dear. This is Jayne Thomas. She's our newest, I know you're going to enjoy working with her."

Jayne studied the woman's face so she could report back to Ruger like she learned in training. Calm, clear-eyed. Nothing shifty, nothing defensive. Just a shy smile and brief eye contact.

Jayne left Rosalind and extended a hand to Deirdre. "Nice to meet you. I hail from Nashville. Vanderbilt University Library. I'm so glad to meet you. If you have any tips on where to eat or how to get Gerard to not hate me, I'm all ears."

Rosalind snorted a laugh over her seventeenth-century text. "Good luck to you on that."

Deirdre's grin was there and gone in a blink. "Pleasure to meet you, Jayne. I do hope your time here at Trinity is very pleasant."

She shook Jayne's hand with warm fingers, then grabbed a stack of papers and scooted off before Jayne could request she bring up the book. Jayne's mission to befriend this woman wasn't going to be a cakewalk.

"Don't be offended," Rosalind whispered. "She was a bit shy with all of us at the beginning. She'll thaw."

"Where did she work last?" Jayne's cheeks heated. *Slow your roll, Jayne. Don't make Rosalind suspicious about your interest in Deirdre.*

"The Bodleian, in Oxford. She was at the Library of the National Academy of Science in Rome prior to that. She's young, but she has a decade of experience in ancient texts. We're lucky to have her, she's very sought after."

Jayne knew all of this from Ruger's briefings, but she imbued her voice with awe. "Wow."

"Indeed."

"Think she'll be back soon? I'd love to see the book."

"I think so."

But Deirdre didn't return for an hour. Then two more hours. Giving the excuse of going to the restroom, Jayne set out to find her.

But she never succeeded. Deirdre had gone home sick.

Great job, Jayne. You let your mark slip right through your fingers.

At five o'clock, Jayne gathered her purse to head out.

Gerard tipped his head to her as she walked past. "Didn't make any paper airplanes today or accidentally set any priceless tomes ablaze, did you?"

Jayne wished she could think of a fantastic retort, but her mind whirled with what she'd seen today and what Ruger would say about it. "I'm not nearly that exciting, Gerard, but thank you for thinking I am."

"We don't care for excitement around here. I'd tell you to remember that, but I know exactly how well Americans listen to advice."

"You know what they say. The best advice is this: don't take advice and don't give advice."

"Ah. Of course you would quote an unknown."

Jayne stopped the door with her foot. "Maybe you like this one better. 'Good advice is something a man gives when he is too old to set a bad example.' François La Rochefoucauld."

Gerard's eyebrow lifted toward his receding hairline, and something close to a grin crossed his mouth. "Touché, my dear. Touché."

Jayne laughed aloud at that, then strolled across the sun-warmed cobblestones and toward her flat. She needed to update Ruger, and then... then she was going to go enjoy her first Irish kickboxing lesson.

CHAPTER TWENTY

In the midmorning sun, Ruger sketched the arches and walk-ways of Trinity for two hours. Though he'd worked a disguising spell to make him look like a white man with a fittingly artistic, wild beard instead of his own dark skin and closely trimmed goatee, he still worried the man he was waiting for would somehow recognize him. The run-in with Aaró and his crew had thrown Ruger more than he liked to admit. No doubt Aaró's branch of the Kingdom would be searching everywhere for him, pining to avenge their iconic leader. Ruger certainly hadn't shared that with Jayne.

Ruger lowered his pencil and scanned the crowd for any sign of the man with the duffel bag. A cluster of elderly tourists passed by, followed closely by a knot of Trinity students. Perhaps this man's run-in with Jayne had been nothing. Amanda hadn't been able to dig anything up with the scant description he'd given her, but Ruger's gut told him to stay on this. Chatter about Jayne had gone quiet, and the silence was more worrisome than anything.

As Ruger tipped his sketching pencil to shade a trail of poorly drawn cobblestones, a flash of movement caught his eye. He looked up to see the man with the duffel bag leaving the building. Moving slowly, casually, Ruger packed up his sketchbook and pencils and began the work of tailing this man who'd dared launch himself into Ruger's newest trainee.

Keeping watch on the man's head moving within a crowd of Trinity staff wearing badges and looks of disdain, Ruger maintained a good distance. It wasn't easy. Off campus, the Dublin crowds grew more dense as folks headed to the pubs for lunch and bustled into shops and onto buses. The man slipped away from the crowd and into an alley between buildings. Ruger hung back and pretended to seriously consider the paintings of the Irish countryside in the shop window at the corner. When he'd counted to twenty, he rounded the edge of the building and trailed the man down the alley. The man reached a doorway and disappeared inside.

Ruger walked past the doorway, glancing at the sign above with a practiced air of ease and confidence.

The man had disappeared into a tattoo parlor. The Tinker's Tats. Ruger turned the corner and made his way back to the main thoroughfare as he sent a message to Amanda through his encrypted phone. Hopefully, they'd get more info on this fellow based on this location.

At the end of the day, Ruger portaled into Jayne's apartment.

She jumped and dropped her bag. "Ruger! Ugh! I'm never going to get used to that." The pink in her cheeks had faded, and she was chewing her lip.

"What happened?" He picked up her bag and set it on the

table as she took a seat.

"Freaky monk in a nasty book. Met Deirdre. Almost saw the Book of Leinster."

As Jayne, eyes dark with worry and face paler than usual, explained the details of her day and answered all of his questions, Ruger adjusted their plan.

"You'll see Deirdre tomorrow. Assert your position as an expert with regard to anything involving Irish mythology. Don't downplay what you know, Jayne. Don't be self-deprecating. Show them you know this stuff and you are the one they can rely on. They'll soon give you full access to the Book of Leinster without a minder, and you'll be able to find out if it is indeed one of the necromantic texts. And if Deirdre is tied to the Kingdom, she will definitely attempt to bring you in. Remember what we practiced. How you are ignorant of the organization and love the outdoors, how you used to sit in your yard and stare up at the stars and imagine a different world."

"And you really think they'll swallow that?"

"I do. I've seen it happen. Sometimes zealotry can be blind to the obvious, and that works in our favor."

Jayne nodded like her report was finished, but Ruger could tell she was holding something back. And he knew what that something was. The man with the duffel.

"Anything else?" he prodded, testing the depth to which she valued fully informing him and the Library Division of every development in her life.

"Uh, no." She shrugged, not making eye contact.

Damn. Now he'd have to play this out and see if she would tell him soon or if he would have to report her lack of disclosure to Amanda. "All right. Get some rest. You need to be on your toes for tomorrow."

Ruger left Jayne nibbling on a slice of pie. He immediately

called Amanda. "Our girl met her new friend today. She will proceed with the plan tomorrow. Most likely, she'll have access to the book as well."

"Good. Now, about the man and tattoo parlor. The place was owned by one Aaron Offlinger."

Ruger swore. It was one of Aaró's pseudonyms. "So the most unpredictable branch of the organization has their eye on our girl."

"It would seem so."

"How do you want us to play this?"

"Have Jayne stay the course. He didn't attack her. She's safely in her apartment with the wards up."

"She is."

"Then they don't want to take her out. Not yet, at least. They want to lure her in, and that's what we want as well. It's good. Between Deirdre and this new operative, Jayne has an even higher chance of infiltrating the Kingdom. How did Jayne respond to this man?"

"She didn't bring him up."

"You didn't ask? Oh, never mind. You wanted to see if she would mention him. The guy must be a looker, hmm? Afraid of a repeat of the Meredith case, are you?"

"I am," he said, thinking of his third trainee, Derek, the one who'd fallen for the Kingdom operative, Meredith, and ended up dead. "But Jayne isn't Derek, Amanda. She isn't. She has a really good head on her shoulders."

"So did Derek," Amanda snapped. "Until he didn't."

Ruger ran a hand over his beard. "I'm on it, boss."

"You'd better be. And I need to hear how things progress on a very regular basis."

"Understood."

"Is it? Because when Derek took off—"

"It's understood, Amanda."

Her labored sigh carried through the phone. "Fine. And you can handle trailing the male operative as well as keeping a good handle on Jayne?"

"You know I can," he said quietly, feeling very tired of the world in general.

"I just wanted to hear you say it."

He switched off and turned his mind to strategy, wondering who this Aaró follower was exactly and what his plans were with Jayne. How much did that branch of the Kingdom know? He wanted to find the guy right now and demand answers, but that wouldn't be the smart play. Patience was what this plan needed, and Ruger fell back on his training in that area, a professional calm enveloping him as he portaled into his own flat and sat down to eat some leftover lasagna that he was too preoccupied to enjoy.

CHAPTER TWENTY-ONE

Once Ruger was gone, Jayne threw some workout clothes in her purse, and headed out to get the lay of the land around her flat. She noted the restaurants, coffee shops, and shops with increasing approval. Anything she could possibly want or need was only a few moments' walk from the flat. Convenience was paramount on an operation like this, when she had to live in plain sight, this she knew from her training. The TCO didn't want her to make herself a target any more than necessary, wanted her to focus on her goals and not be bothered by hopping a bus to a shopping mall to buy fresh underwear. She had to laugh. She was actually thinking like a real CIA officer.

Her stomach growled. She needed some food. Maybe that cute Irish guy was free. It wouldn't hurt to get the lay of the land from a local, right? Surely not. Phew. Who was she right now? The flirty side of Sofia would've been proud. Sweating a good bit, Jayne texted him a hello.

Cillian answered almost immediately.

Hello, Jayne from Nashville. Any chance you're hungry?

Swallowing and thinking of his deep, kind voice, she typed back *Famished. And I just finished up. Want to grab something to eat?* Oh lord. Had she really just asked him out? Juggling her phone, she wiped her palms on her skirt.

He didn't answer right away, and she tucked her phone back into her purse. Oh well. It was probably better anyway. She needed to—

She walked into a wall. A very tall, male wall.

"Sure thing." Cillian smiled down at her.

Her heart did a tiny flip. "What are you doing here?"

"You're the one who suggested we get something to eat."

"But..."

"I like the seafood chowder they make over there." He nodded toward a pub that looked like a small castle called The Auld Hall. "I eat there fairly often, and when I saw your text, I thought I'd just pop over and see if you were around. So you want to kick back some food, then some targets?"

"Can you work out right after eating?"

"No problem."

"Well then, lead on."

Let the world know, Agnes Jayne Thorne had a date. A real date.

The chowder was, as promised, excellent. The conversation, too. They'd chatted about kickboxing (his passion), Nashville (bucket list), and books (Jayne was right, after being force-fed a diet of schoolbooks and history tomes, he was simply bored, not anti-book). It wasn't a bad start to a friendship.

Oh, who was she kidding? Cillian was almost perfect.

His dojo was a little bit less than perfect.

They'd hopped a bus over after dinner, and sure, he had a nice line of heavy bags to kick, a clean workout floor that was properly padded, and a tidy restroom, but the walls of the gym were bare concrete blocks, and the sad fluorescent lights fluttered in a way that made the place look like the set of a horror movie.

Cillian waved a hand toward the expanse of it and smiled. "Welcome to my home!"

She didn't have the heart to suggest improvements. Gerard might think she had no manners, but she knew what not to say here and now.

Ignoring the peeling paint and the potential mold problem on the back wall, she said, "It's great! Can I change in there?" She pointed to the restroom.

"Of course."

When she came out of the surprisingly not-too-terrible restroom, Cillian had one leg stretched up a wall in a standing split.

The gym suddenly felt too small for two people. The whole world was too small. Tugging at her shirt collar and forcing her naughty brain to stop imagining other scenarios in which flexibility could be a true asset, Jayne forced herself to stop staring. She rolled her eyes. "That's not intimidating at all."

Cillian chuckled and walked across the floor. "How about we do some parries and counters to warm up?"

"Sounds good."

Cillian put on a pair of flat mitts. He punched one lightly toward her nose and she pushed it away with a parry, slipping slightly to his dead side. "How's the new job?" he asked.

"It's amazing," she said. "I get to hang out with the most rock-star books in history."

"You make it sound exciting."

"Ha. Well, I think it is."

"And that's what's important. You have nice coworkers, then?"

Was he getting too much into her business? Or was she being neurotic? "Yes. They're pretty great. Except for Gerard."

"What's his story?"

"He's a snob. Like of *Downton Abbey* proportions."

Cillian's eyebrow twitched and humor sparked in his light blue eyes. "But without the kind heart that will learn from snobbish mistakes?"

Oh, man. He knew *Downton Abbey*. Her heart was in danger. "Exactly. But it is kind of fun to snark right back at him."

Cillian nodded. "Yep. You are a fighter. In every sense of the word."

"I suppose I am." Jayne parried another jab, then countered, punching the other mitt with a quick overhand left.

"How did you get into martial arts?"

Jayne recalled that day so long ago when Sofia had dragged her into the dojo. Hiding behind her older sister, Jayne had watched the kids kicking Wavemasters and running back and forth. Their confidence had seemed like magic. But this wasn't part of Jayne Thomas's backstory. And now she had to flat out lie to this cute guy.

"My brother insisted I start taking it."

"Smart guy."

"Yes."

"Maybe he had a premonition that you'd end up traveling all over the world, following your sexy books."

Jayne laughed and it came out a bit strangled. The way he said *sexy*... "Maybe. We had a rough childhood, so I guess that's why." Jayne looked up to realize she'd said some pretty heavy stuff for a first evening out. "Sorry. I don't want to be a downer."

"We're getting to know one another. Don't hold back. Unless

you want to."

Stomach churning, Jayne hit the mitts with a quick jab/cross combo. The thunk of her fists on the solid targets allowed her voice to work. "My parents died in an accident. My brother was old enough to take custody. He's very protective."

"I can't say that I blame him," Cillian said. "I'm sorry about your parents, Jayne."

The sadness that never truly left touched her heart with cold fingers. "Thanks. It was a while back." Not that the pain had gone anywhere. At least now she could distract herself from it most days.

"I wish I had a brother like that. It's only my dad and me in our family now. My mum died, and I have no siblings. Dad's all right, I guess." That lost look in his eyes plucked a string inside her. She seriously wanted to hug that sadness right out of him. "Hey," he said, face clearing, "would you like to meet my mates tomorrow night at that pub? There's a game on."

A lightness filled Jayne at the thought. Sure, he made her nervous. Guys did that to her. But he was kind, and hot, and she could see herself feeling comfortable with him eventually, unlike her previous dates. Except for the lying. "I could do that."

Smiling, Cillian put the mitts away and pushed his hair out of his eyes, his strong jaw angled as he grinned. "Let's kick the bags, hmm?"

Jayne got into her guard stance, stepped forward, then pivoted, kicking the heavy bag with her shin.

"Nice one." Cillian whipped around in a blur and whacked the bag with a fantastic tornado round kick.

"Showoff." Determined not to be cowed by his obvious talent, Jayne spun and launched the bottom of her foot into the target.

Cillian clapped twice, laughing. "That's a deadly turning back kick you have, woman. I don't think there's much I can teach you on the basic moves. How about we do some real sparring next time?" He wiggled his eyebrows, and his bright blue eyes sparkled with mischief.

Next time.

Well, dating a local was one way to fit in.

"Definitely."

CHAPTER TWENTY-TWO

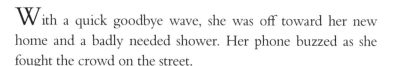

With a quick goodbye wave, she was off toward her new home and a badly needed shower. Her phone buzzed as she fought the crowd on the street.

It was a text from Ruger. *Where are you?*

I went for dinner and a workout.

Get back here. Now.

If Jayne hadn't already been sweating, she would've started then. Ruger sounded majorly pissed off. Ugh. Something had happened, no doubt. She never would've gone off with Cillian if Ruger had asked her to stay home after work. She needed a shower and a glass of wine, not an angry magical TCO officer. The crazy pressure of this position was already bothering her, and she hadn't even gotten to the dark stuff yet. *Get it together, Jayne.*

Two blocks later, she walked up the narrow stairs to her apartment and unlocked the door. Ruger sat on her plain gray couch, flipping TV channels, anger plain on his face.

"Sorry. I didn't realize you were waiting."

"I was." He set the remote down.

An old Taylor Swift interview roared through the apartment.

Jayne threw her stuff onto the kitchen counter and glared at Ruger through the window that looked into the living room. With a dish towel—the tag still on—she wiped cool water down her face and neck.

Ruger joined her in the kitchen. "Where have you been? Exactly."

"What, you don't have some kind of magical GPS tracker attached to me?"

"Stop joking around. I'm serious." He *was* serious, he was practically growling at her.

"What's wrong?"

He blew out a breath. "More Kingdom activity. We caught a small group trying to set off a bomb at a power plant on the Scottish coast. I had to go deal with the disposal."

"Are they a danger to our mission?"

"That's just it, Jayne. We're blind right now. That's why it's so important for you to get into Deirdre's good graces. You have to work fast. They are up to something big. I can tell. The Torrent seems…disturbed since you accessed it the first time."

"Well, that's just lovely. Pissy magical dimensions. Hey, so I met a local guy."

Ruger's eyebrows rose.

Jayne filled him on Cillian and how they'd met.

"What did you two talk about at his gym?" Ruger asked, his voice neutral. Jayne was glad he didn't seem worked up about Cillian.

"Just getting-to-know-you stuff," Jayne answered before taking a swig of tap water from her glass. "I stuck with Jayne Thomas's background." She told Ruger what Cillian had asked, and Ruger listened, nodding every once in a while.

"Thank you for being honest with me. Now it's my turn. I was watching this morning when he bumped into you, and I followed him. Jayne. He isn't what he seems."

Jayne's hand shook around the water glass. She didn't know if she was furious or scared by this news. Damn. Had she already screwed everything up? "Don't hold back, man. What's up?"

"This afternoon, he visited a tattoo parlor that was once owned by a member of the Kingdom."

Her heart sank. "No."

"Yes."

"But that doesn't mean he is with them. Right?" She set her glass on the countertop a little too hard, sloshing the water over the edge. "I bet a lot of people go there. Dublin is a big place."

"Maybe. Maybe not. The odds are not in his favor, not with everything going on. I'm just saying you need to be very careful. We've decided you should continue this friendship, just in case he is Kingdom. See what you can find out. Perhaps you'll learn what we can't."

"Are you checking him out further?"

"We are. Remember, even if he is an innocent, he can't learn anything about what you're doing. If he's not involved with them already, the Kingdom could get their hands on him at some point. He could be killed for what he knows."

Jayne swallowed around the lump in her throat. "Of course. I thought perhaps going on a date might make me stand out less. Loners are the ones up to stuff. Regular gals go to pubs."

"That's true." He gave her a speculative look. "Nice guy?"

She narrowed her eyes. Was this professional interest, or was Ruger being a bit older brother-ish? "Ahem," she said tartly. "Very nice."

She wanted to get away from the topic of Cillian. It was honestly embarrassing that she'd developed a crush so soon after arriving in Dublin. And of course it would be on someone her superiors found suspicious.

"So, about Deirdre," she said. "I can't just ask her about the Kingdom, can I?" It would be so much easier.

Ruger raised a very judgy eyebrow. "No, you cannot, and you know that from your training. Remember, this must be handled with subtlety and caution. If you are too eager, our mark will disappear. I've seen it happen a thousand times. You must take your time and reel her in. But you have to do it quickly."

"Might be hard to do both, Ruger. And you make me seem like the bad guy. Or a fisherman. Neither of which I relate to."

Ruger wasn't amused. "You are the good guy who must participate in ethically gray activities to achieve the good for all. Make no mistake, Jayne, you are already a hero."

Her chest ached. She suddenly missed Sofia and her dad more than ever. They would've been proud to see her now, risking her life for others. They would've called her *lightning brain* like they always did. *Let's see some electricity!* Dad used to say when she was stuck on a problem. She'd always been two grades ahead in school, doing fifth grade work in third. Her dad's belief in her never waned, and his genuine faith pushed her further than she ever thought she'd go. Though he died while she was still little, it was the memory of him that got Jayne through grad school.

Ruger lectured on for a while, and they did some cool moves in the Torrent, working on her defensive spells. By the time he left, she was so tired she didn't even want to read. She collapsed into bed.

And her old, familiar nightmare came for an unwelcome visit.

The heat was always the first thing she noticed. It bled into her cheeks and burned her hair. The smell...

Then came the screaming. Not hers. Dad's hoarse shrieking.

Mom's shrill peals of agony.

Jayne, silent, standing over them as they burned, her hands raised. Flames gnawed their skin from their skulls, white bone showed through cracked flesh. Fire blanketed their clothing, blackening their lips as they shouted for help. And all Jayne could do was burn with them.

The fire never finished her. It seared her flesh, but never ate it away. She was doomed to live on and on while they turned to ash at her feet.

The last part of the nightmare was the only thing she'd actually experienced in her waking life. The tears. When she'd first lost them, she hadn't realized how many tears a person could create. It was shocking, the amount of fluid, the ferocity of the sobbing. Her own grief was a calamity.

And as always, she woke with a start from this recurring horror, soaked through with sweat, a ghost of those tears sticky on her skin.

CHAPTER TWENTY-THREE

Cillian pushed through the door to The Tinker's Tats and strode past the two guys getting ink, all the way to the back, where a door hid behind a ratty curtain. He knocked twice, then once again lower down below the doorknob.

The door swung open and he slid into a room lit by large black candles. Posters of seventies bands covered the walls, and Mac sat on a stool near the exit, smoking one of those foul cigars of his. Thick smoke curled around his buzzed salt-and-pepper hair, then fell to gather around his ample gut like he was floating on a cloud of cancerous mist.

"Ah, Cillian." He set the cigar in the glass tray on the side table and rose to clap a hand on Cillian's shoulder.

Cillian stiffened. "Mac. What's the craic?" Aaron's desk in the corner was dark and clean of its usual stacks of old laptops and mobile phones. "Where's Aaron? He's been gone forever."

Mac swore, vehemently.

"Shit, Mac, what is it?" Mac normally said two words in a

month. Cillian had never seen such passion from him.

The big man ran a hand over his head and sighed. "Aaron's dead."

Cillian stepped back. The walls closed in. "What? No. What do you mean?" The man had been the only steady thing in Cillian's recent life. He couldn't be dead.

Mac wiped his nose with the back of a hammy fist. "The bastard feds got him. Didn't like our work."

This was mad. "They can't just kill people. They're the government. There has to be like a trial or something, right?"

"I don't think this particular branch of the American government cares for following anyone's rules."

"But Aaron's work, our work, is just to help the Earth. How... why would that be...I don't understand."

Sighing, Mac shuffled to Aaron's desk and picked up a tiny notebook, and a small silver flask. He handed them to Cillian, who took it with shaking hands. "He said to give these to you if he ever failed to return after a visit to the States."

But Cillian couldn't even look at it. Tears were welling behind his closed eyes, and he had to get out. Now, before he made an idiot of himself. "Fine. All right. Thanks, Mac." He spun and headed for the back exit to the far street.

"You going to be all right, mate?" Mac's voice followed Cillian out the door and into the chilly afternoon air.

Aaron was dead. Dead. He'd never ask Cillian about his crap intramural rugby team again. There'd be no more trips to the countryside to plant trees and camp under the stars with the rest of the Kingdom members. Cillian didn't know how to get there. Aaron had always made him wear a blindfold to those larger meetings, to protect Cillian in case he landed in the wrong hands during a job. Cillian could almost feel Aaron cuffing the back of his head like an older brother would, could almost hear the chuckle in his words, could almost see the fire in the man's intelligent eyes.

The crowd on the main road bumped into Cillian, but he hardly noticed.

"I never asked how he died," he whispered to himself. "I should've asked." What would Aaron do in this situation? Cillian had always asked himself this question. Aaron made the right moves, knew what to say when. "He'd have done the job. The journal. He would've nabbed that journal for the cause."

Fighting the ache rising in his chest and the tears burning his eyes, Cillian looked up and began to run.

CHAPTER TWENTY-FOUR

Gerard rolled his eyes at Jayne when she walked into the reading room the next day.

"You really should cut back on partying while you're employed at Trinity. Such"—he waved a hand at the dark circles under her eyes—"unwise life choices do indeed show themselves in your work and on your face."

"My face is none of your business, Gerard." She knew very well she looked like she felt. After the late-night training and the nightmare and the jet lag, she had slept through her alarm and had to rush to get to work on time.

"Everything at Trinity is my business. My entire family attended this college, and four of my dearest relatives work in various departments around the campus."

"That's actually really cool."

"I'm so glad it passes your *cool* test. I may go to my grave a happy man now."

"Here's your eye roll back in case you were missing it." Jayne nearly sprained a newly LASIKed cornea giving him a good one. She could have sworn she heard the ghost of a chuckle follow her down the hall.

In the back room, Rosalind worked at a table opposite Deirdre. Rosalind winked as Jayne shut the door quietly. Deirdre glanced up, then pushed a curl of black hair behind her ear, not smiling or saying hello or anything at all to indicate a new person had entered the room. And if Jayne had been a betting woman, she'd have put money on Deirdre's face looking even more tired than her own.

Jayne set her purse on the smaller table by the door and cleared her dry throat. "I don't know about you all, but today feels too much like a Monday for my taste. Are we allowed coffee in here?"

Both women's mouths dropped open in horror. Their hands hovered over the manuscripts like mother hens over chicks.

Jayne held up her hands. "Kidding. I was kidding."

Rosalind laughed. "Did you go on the lash last night, Jayne?"

Jayne was fairly sure Rosalind meant *go out drinking.* "No. I just...I couldn't sleep. New town, new bed, jet lag." She hated lying even a little to the kind woman, even if it was for a good cause. But it couldn't be helped. There were a million reasons Jayne couldn't say *Well, I stayed up 'til two o'clock doing a load of magic so I could learn to fight radical baddies who want to make us all cavemen and then enslave everyone who isn't magically fabulous, and then I had a horrible nightmare about my dead parents.*

It was wild to think that the Kingdom wanted the world to go backward. Sure, humans needed to stop trashing the ocean and belching crap into the sky, but to knock everyone into history? Even if there wasn't the whole slavery horror, she'd still be wowed by the Kingdom's insane goals. Jayne shook her head, realizing Rosalind was speaking to her.

"…since we finished with the Italian manuscript yesterday, I was hoping we could get to a far older one sometime this morning." Rosalind took her glasses off and let them hang on her beaded necklace. She pointed toward a rolling cart that held a dark metal box.

A buzz traveled through Jayne's bones. Older. Yes. She rubbed her hands together and headed toward the box. As curious as she was about this old book, her interest in this text was a flicker compared to the flame of passion she had, thinking of gaining access to the Book of Leinster. "And then maybe can we bring out the Book of Leinster? Assuming Deirdre's good with it?"

Deirdre kept her eyes down. "I am."

"I can get the book myself if you like."

Rosalind clicked her tongue. "Later, Jayne. A top-priority request came in this morning. The British Library is requesting our thoughts on whether or not this manuscript might have once been a part of the Lansdowne collection, specifically the Shaftesbury Psalter."

"Twelfth century?" Jayne took the box from the cart to the second table, making sure she was in easy conversation distance from Deirdre. She could chat her up while she worked on the codex. Two birds, one stone.

"That's what they're hoping. Do you have much knowledge of the psalter?" Rosalind studied the way Jayne handled herself, and Jayne was confident that her treatment and procedural behavior was up to speed.

"I studied portions of the Lansdowne manuscripts in grad school. It was written for a female reader specifically, yes? So perhaps there will be illustrations featuring the women of the church."

Rosalind's smile stretched wide. "Indeed." She hummed a little as she bent her head to her own work.

Jayne glanced at Deirdre, so silent and mousy. "So what do you do when you're not skulking around old words with Rosalind?"

Rosalind snickered. "At least she said 'old words' and not 'old Rosalind.'" Jayne decided she liked Rosalind very much.

Deirdre shrugged. "I stay home, mostly. I do like to watch movies. Alone." Her voice was quiet, but it held a strength to it.

"What kind of movies?" Jayne shifted the wooden-backed stack of vellum from its shelter and eased it onto the table. It smelled like olive oil and dust.

"Horror."

Jayne turned, surprise jerking her attention from the manuscript. "Whoa. Really? That's intense."

Deirdre's smile was genuine, and it was the first time she'd actually made eye contact with Jayne. "Yeah. I like to see ridiculously scary things. I'm not sure why."

"The thrill of it?" Rosalind glanced at the clock on the wall.

Deirdre shook her head. "No. I guess I like the idea that the things in the movies aren't real."

"You can turn the movie off," Jayne said, "unlike the horror stuff that happens in real life, hmm?"

Deirdre's stare bored into the side of Jayne's face, and she froze, realizing this might sound like she suspected Deirdre was up to some bad stuff. Jayne had been caught up in the task of opening the codex without damaging the pages and hadn't been paying attention to where the conversation was headed or how it would relate to the TCO mission at hand. She had to say something, anything, to break this tension and bring the conversation back to safe waters. It was too soon to press, even beginner Jayne knew that.

"The scariest thing I can stand to watch is *Frozen*." Jayne shuddered dramatically. "Anna almost married that prick! Kristen Bell isn't allowed to be so stupid."

The women paused, then the silence cracked, and their laughter filled the room.

"And here I thought American women were so tough," Deirdre said.

"Oh, I'm super tough. Unless I'm in front of a screen. Then I'm a marshmallow," she said, a nod to Kristen Bell's Veronica Mars.

"Well, get to work, Miss Marshmallow."

She looked over her shoulder to see Rosalind's raised eyebrow and smirk. "Yes, ma'am," Jayne said, grinning.

She had to figure out how to get Deirdre out of the library, away from her house and television, and into the real world. Jayne would never get to know Deirdre in the small amount of time she had if they were constantly being shushed and put back to work. She appreciated Rosalind's dedication, and honestly would have completely been in line with her regimen, but it didn't work toward Jayne's most important goal: to discover the Kingdom's secrets.

"Before we get down to business," Jayne said, "Deirdre, can I ask you to dinner? I'd love to hang out sometime."

"Yes. You girls should go out. That would be grand." Rosalind's voice was light and happy.

"You're welcome to join us, Rosalind."

"Oh, no. You and Deirdre need to bond without your boss looking over your shoulders."

Jayne wished Sofia could find a friend like Rosalind, younger of course, but just as positive. Maybe a person like Rosalind could rub some of the tarnish off Sofia's rough exterior. But that would never happen. This was a secret mission, and Sofia didn't even know what Jayne was up to. She didn't even know she was here. A heaviness sat on Jayne's chest, and she breathed through it.

"You all right?" Deirdre's shy eyes blinked, and Jayne nodded.

"I suppose I'm a little homesick."

"Starting over in a new place is always hard. I would love to have dinner with you."

Jayne hadn't meant to evoke pity, but if it got the job done, then she supposed it wasn't poorly done. She pressed her case.

"That's great. How about tonight? I met a kickboxing instructor yesterday and he invited me to The Auld Hall pub to watch some game on TV. I'm about as interested in cricket or soccer—sorry, football or whatever it is—as I am walking on the moon. If you're there, it will be a ton more fun. What do you think?"

Deirdre bit her lip. "I don't know. My husband—"

"He's welcome to come. And if he doesn't want to, he'd be cool with you joining us yourself, right?" He'd better. Jayne sure as hell knew she wouldn't put up with a husband so controlling that he wouldn't be fine with her going out without him.

"I'll call him at lunch and see what he had in mind for tonight. He might have a meeting anyway."

"Perfect. He can do his meeting and you can have fun with us."

"Maybe."

Jayne nodded, a stone settling in her stomach. Deirdre might be a member of the Kingdom, and Jayne was about to introduce Cillian to her. If Cillian was as innocent as Jayne hoped he was, this little hangout might put Cillian in danger down the road.

Then again, if they knew each other, which would be not great, at least she'd have something important to report.

Breathing through her nose, trying to calm down, she made a decision. She'd just have to act like Cillian wasn't a big deal, that he was no one she cared about. He wasn't anyway. She'd just met him. Jayne would simply sit two seats down from him and flirt with his friends. It would mess up any chances she might've have with Cillian romantically, but the mission had to come first. She set her jaw and forced herself to breathe easy. She was a CIA officer. She would not let hormones ruin her chances at saving the world.

After lunch, Deirdre shot Jayne an email that said she'd love to join in. Score one for the team! And then Cillian texted to remind her of the time and place.

Is it cool if I bring a friend from work? she texted back.

Of course.

Okay. It was all going to work out. "Can we bring up the Book of Leinster now?" Jayne asked Rosalind.

"Tomorrow, dear. I promise."

Jayne forced herself to smile and get back to the work in front of her. They were feeling her out, testing her bookish skills. But if they kept putting her off, she'd have to figure out a way to examine the book without them.

She didn't relish the idea of breaking and entering one of the most prestigious libraries in the world.

CHAPTER TWENTY-FIVE

At the close of the day, Jayne said goodbye to Rosalind and popped into the restroom to brush her tangled hair. When she was a kid, she hated her slightly wavy brown locks. They were the color of mud. Of tree bark. But when she began studying old books, she realized her hair was the hue of leather-bound classics. Funny how being a complete nerd sometimes made Jayne feel very sexy indeed. Who cared if she was the only one who thought it? Giving herself a smile in the mirror, she left to find Deirdre, who had been hiding away like a shy mouse the entire afternoon.

At the exit, Gerard stood straight and perfectly still. He was looking out the windows.

"Gerard?"

He opened the outside door for her. "That is my given name."

"Have you seen Deirdre? We're supposed to go to dinner."

"She left ten minutes ago."

Jayne's stomach dropped. "What?" She'd bailed on their

plans.

"She headed to the right. Toward the rugby fields."

There was a chance Jayne could catch her and see what was up. "Thanks!" She hurried into the square, dodging students with smug grins and tourists taking selfies.

She should have nabbed Deirdre's phone number. Then she wouldn't have had to stalk her like this. Why was Deirdre going to the rugby fields when she said she'd eat with Jayne? Did she play the sport? She didn't seem big enough, but then again, Jayne had read a book about rugby once and learned the scrum half didn't have to be giant.

Blinking against the bright late-afternoon sun, Jayne slipped into the shadow of the museum building and ran right into her prey. Her friend, she meant. Of course.

Deirdre blinked and pulled away, staring as they righted themselves. "Jayne!"

"Hi! Sorry. Went a little sunblind there for a minute. Are you still coming with me to eat?"

"Oh yeah. I am. I just had to give my husband something."

Jayne sighed. Okay, no big deal. The evening was still a go.

Deirdre looked toward a compact fellow leaving the area, winding his way through the crowd and past College Park. A beanie obscured most of his head, and a tidy button-down shirt covered his lean frame—the kind of shirt men wore under nice suits. The shirt was too formal for jeans, but Jayne wasn't the mistress of being en vogue or anything, so what did she know. Under his arm, a manila folder pressed against his side. It appeared thick, even from this distance. A book?

"You two read the same stuff? Like a little husband-wife book club? That would be amazing."

Deirdre glanced at her ankle boots. "No. It's just work stuff." She looked up and smiled and it was super fake. "So where are we going? I can't remember which pub you mentioned." Without waiting for Jayne, she headed back the way they'd come.

Every alarm in Jayne's head was going off. Work stuff? Like her work stuff for Trinity? As far as Jayne knew, Deirdre's husband didn't work at Trinity. Maybe he held a position in another department and Deirdre was actually required to hand deliver a book to him. But that just didn't seem right.

"The Auld Hall," Jayne answered, her mind whirring as their feet matched in step. "It's not a long walk."

"Oh, I know the place. Good live music."

Jayne swallowed her questions and attempted to focus on Deirdre. "Excellent. My time in Nashville spoiled me on live music. Bluegrass is my favorite. Well, second to indie rock. Or maybe classical. Ah. I can't decide."

As they slipped around a family of six arguing about a bus route, Jayne realized Deirdre was staring into space.

Was she thinking about her husband and whatever she'd handed off to him? "What music do you like?" Jayne asked, keeping her voice light.

"What? Oh. I don't know. Whatever is playing on the radio, I suppose."

"Come on." She elbowed Deirdre gently. "You must have a song you love. Or hate."

Deirdre laughed. "Not really. I don't listen to a lot of music."

Jayne decided that maybe a quick, unexpected question might garner some good intel. "Where does your husband work?"

Pausing for a moment, Deirdre stuttered. "Erm. He's an engineer. He builds things."

So what sort of book was she handing off to an engineer? If she'd given her husband something from the collections…

"I figured he worked here. Since he was here…"

"No. No, he just came to meet me."

"Rosalind said you've moved around a lot. Does he follow you from place to place? Or are you following him?"

"He follows me," she said lightly, clearly ending the conversation.

Fail. Oh well. There would be time later on to press more about whatever Deirdre had given to her husband and why, once they had a few drinks in them. That would loosen the woman's tongue a bit, right?

As they crossed the street beside a man selling Irish flag pins, Jayne took stock of what she'd gathered thus far on Deirdre.

nervous

good at her job at Trinity

into horror movies

husband who's an engineer

shy

checks with husband before making plans

husband is sometimes close enough to Trinity to receive mysterious packages

probably doesn't play half scrum

interested in Irish mythology

Yep. That was about it.

Jayne cleared her throat and tried a new topic of conversation as they neared the pub. "I can't wait to see the Book of Leinster with my own eyes. I studied that thing obsessively in grad school."

In the crowd, a man with large arms and even larger sunglasses perched against the neighboring gift shop and glanced their way. Jayne's mind whispered a warning. She flexed her hands, palms sweating. He was familiar. Before she could get a good look at him through a pack of uni students, he turned and began gesturing wildly to a woman in a pink dress.

Frowning over her shoulder, Deirdre looked at Jayne as if to ask if she were coming or not.

"Sorry. Thought I saw someone from my flat." Jayne followed Deirdre under the arch in the front of The Auld Hall. Kegs of Jameson lined the stone walls.

Deirdre pushed a strand of hair behind her ear. "What specifically interested you? In the book, I mean."

"How much do you know of its history?" Jayne asked.

The corridor of sorts led into an open courtyard. Jayne stretched up onto her tiptoes, looking for Cillian's bright blue eyes. She was more excited to see him than was probably wise, considering she was supposed to act like she didn't care much about him in front of a possible magical terrorist.

"Well, I've gleaned a bit from Rosalind, of course."

Jayne laughed. "Of course. I just wouldn't want to accidentally talk down to another expert."

"You're the only expert between us on this particular book. No worries on that." Deirdre's eyes were wide, but Jayne couldn't help but look for the lie. It sucked not knowing for sure what to say and what to keep hidden from this woman.

"Jayne!" Cillian broke through a group of old men, his cornflower-blue Irish eyes a-smiling. It was ridiculous how handsome he was. He pulled her into a hug and she tried really, really, really hard not to swoon at the scent of his soap. For God's sake, she was pathetic. She should have gone on like ninety dates to improve her tolerance to his charms before coming here with Deirdre on a freaking mission.

"And who is this you've brought with you?" He stuck out a hand to Deirdre, and Jayne introduced her. She watched them both carefully for any signs they knew one another but sensed nothing. *Please don't be a terrorist,* she thought, sending Cillian a relieved smile.

"Deirdre's in Early and Special with me."

"Another book expert then." Cillian raised an eyebrow.

Deirdre waved his compliment away. "Not really. Jayne here is the expert. In Irish mythology, no less, so watch your metaphors. She'll call you out if you reference the wrong goddess or some such."

"I definitely will."

"You are the biggest nerd." Cillian smirked.

"We both are." Deirdre's voice was hardly audible amidst the laughing patrons and the shouts from the televisions.

CHAPTER TWENTY-SIX

Jayne and Deirdre followed Cillian through one of the three doors off the courtyard. In a room covered in what looked like soccer—no, *football*—stickers, Cillian gestured to a wooden table that had once had a finish on it, long, long ago. The sign out front had stated that the pub opened in 1201 AD, so yeah.

A very skinny guy with a haircut like a Marine waved and called himself Ned.

A red-cheeked fellow beside him raised his drink and whistled a little tune before saying his name was Aldie. "Eh, Cillian. You feeling all right now, mate?"

Jayne glanced between them as Cillian smiled, showing those dimples of his, and shrugged. "Fine, man. Thanks."

Aldie puffed a breath, his red cheeks swelling. "You sure? You seemed full—"

"Leave it, Aldie." Cillian smiled again ruefully, like he wished he hadn't snapped at his friend.

"Were you sick or something?" Jayne asked. "Because we can

reschedule. It's not a big deal."

"She's going to reschedule the football match?" Ned grinned and clapped, lifting his hands toward Jayne. "That'd be a good trick."

She snorted and gave him a flat look.

Cillian ran a hand over the back of his neck, took a breath, then chuckled quietly. "I'm all right, everyone. Aldie's just a mother hen."

That urge to hold Cillian close washed over Jayne again. She wondered what it would feel like to lace her fingers at the nape of his neck and pull him to her, how a press of those lips would taste, what the heat of his hands on her lower back would do to her.

Goodness, Jayne. Focus. Something about the way he's reassuring them is off, and you know it.

Aldie and Ned laughed and the tension fizzled away, and Deirdre started to scoot in but seemed to realize she would be sitting between Cillian and Jayne. She gently pushed Jayne in front of her. "Go on. Sorry, there."

What a sweet gal. "No, you go ahead," Jayne said, gesturing to the seat. If Jayne had to sit right next to Cillian's hot self all night, there was no way she'd be able to pretend there wasn't a little spark between them.

"No, no," Deirdre insisted.

Jayne gave in and sat next to Cillian as he ordered another beer from the hassled-looking waitress.

"What do you want?" he asked Jayne. "I'll get it, if you don't mind."

Deirdre took a menu from Ned and asked, "How long have you and Cillian been dating?"

"Oh no. We're not. We just met."

"Come on!" Cillian put a hand over his heart like Jayne

had stabbed him in the chest. "We kicked bags together. We bonded!" He raised a fist.

Happiness bubbled inside Jayne and she fought a ridiculous grin. He was incorrigible. "We had one kickboxing session. We aren't dating." She faced the waitress. "Could I get a Guinness? Is that too touristy?"

"If there's one thing we true Irish can agree with tourists on," he said, "it's showing love for Guinness."

The waitress nodded sagely. She took everyone's drink order, then shoved her way toward the back of the pub.

Cillian touched Jayne's arm, sending lovely sparks across her skin. "We could be. Dating, you know."

A wave of heat rushed over her, a longing for more of his touch. The sparks from his hand rode all the way to her neck as he focused those blue eyes on her. An array of small freckles below his left eyebrow created a pattern like a fanged tooth. They weren't like any of Jayne's freckles. In fact, she hadn't noticed these on him until now. It was like they'd just shown up.

Cillian crossed his arms on the table and fiddled with a beverage napkin. The tendons and muscles of his arms moved under his skin, his veins standing out as they did on most athletes. Her fingers itched to run along the lines of him, to map his body.

Crushing, girl. You're crushing hard. That's all. He might not be a good person.

"Aldie, Ned," he said, "you should know that Jayne here is not only a very valuable nerd at Trinity, but she also can deliver a delightfully nasty turning back kick."

Ned and Aldie howled encouragingly, and Jayne felt her cheeks heat. "Thank you. Deirdre, tell us about your background. You come from the Bodleian, right?"

Deirdre was checking her phone. She looked up, distracted.

"What?"

"Your background? You've studied Irish mythology too, yes?"

"Oh. Yes. But you all don't want to hear about that stuff while we're having a pint, do you?"

"I do!" Cillian sat up straight. "I'm a proud Irishman. You should educate your countrymen on such matters." He edged toward Jayne and whispered, "Although if I'm honest, I'd much rather hear the tales from you."

Jayne leaned into him and breathed in the scent of soap and clean cotton. His muscles tensed under his T-shirt. She was melting, but she needed to put on the brakes. No matter what kind of tattoo shop he'd been to, Cillian just didn't seem at all the type to be involved in the enslavement of the world's non-magical folk. Ruger and the TCO were just being overcautious. It made sense, and she was glad they were on it, but she really hoped they were off about Cillian.

Regardless, she needed to keep her distance. Especially when she needed to draw out Deirdre.

"Hey," she whispered into Cillian's ear, "can you go get me a napkin? And maybe one of those little cherries they keep at the bar?" Her voice cracked slightly with nerves. She hoped he didn't notice.

He frowned at her odd request, but shoved Aldie and Ned from the booth to fetch the items. When he returned—napkin in his pocket and cherry stem pinched between two fingers—Jayne forced herself to ignore how adorable he looked.

"Ned and Aldie don't need to move again. Just sit there at the end. It's fine. Really." She forced an overbright smile. *Boy, you do know how to make things awkward.*

Poor Cillian looked like Jayne had punched him in the balls. "Yeah. Of course," he mumbled as he took a seat.

This was awful. Jayne focused on her mission. She had to. Ruger and the TCO were depending on her. Who knew if what she discovered might save the world from a bunch of lunatic magicians? And she couldn't feel too bad about Cillian. Not if he might have a tie to the Kingdom. *Focus on your objective, Jayne.*

"Deirdre, how long have you worked at Trinity?"

"Not long. I like to spread out my research when it's possible."

"Why is that?" Jayne gave Deirdre a little smile, hoping she didn't look suspicious.

The waitress arrived and handed out drinks. She tossed a basket of fries—no, *chips*, Jayne reminded herself—toward the center of the sticky table.

"My interests aren't restricted to Trinity." Deirdre took a chip and twirled it absentmindedly. She was blinking at twice the normal rate. "There are texts I need...that I want to see in the Louvre, the British Museum...all over the world. From the great libraries to the ones few have ever heard about."

"Makes sense." Jayne dumped ketchup beside the pile of chips. "So what are you looking for in the Book of Leinster?"

Deirdre set the fry down without taking a bite, but Ned clicked his tongue. "It must be stories about Queen Mab, hmm? That lass was a ball-breaker." He rubbed his buzzed hair and swigged from his pint.

"You know about her?" Deirdre asked, clearly surprised.

"Naturally. We Irish love our stories."

Deirdre froze, her lager in hand and her eyes trained on Jayne. If she wasn't mistaken, Deirdre looked downright terrified all of a sudden. Was there more to the tales of the ancient warrior queen than what Jayne knew? Something that tied to the world of magic? She was going to have to tell Ruger this, and fast.

Working to break the tension, Jayne patted Deirdre's back.

"You're not choking on that weak beer, are you?" Jayne asked. "Need a real brew to fix you up?"

Deirdre shook her head and let out a small laugh. "I'm fine. It was a long day."

"I love her," Aldie whispered to Cillian.

"Aye," Cillian said, staring at his glass.

Jayne pretended not to hear them. "Are you surprised Ned has heard about Queen Mab? She is in all the regular fairy stories. Shakespeare and so forth."

"She is." Deirdre gulped her drink. "But not many people are like us, Jayne." Jayne thrilled at Deirdre's friendly smile. "I would have expected us to be the only two in this place who would rather be reading a dusty book in bed than watching the football match."

Jayne bumped Deirdre's shoulder. "You're probably right."

"You're definitely right," Cillian and Aldie said in unison.

On cue, the TVs in the pub grew louder and the match began with a shout.

The crowd's *oohs* and *aahs* destroyed any chance Jayne had to gain further information about what Deirdre thought of Queen Mab—known to academics as Medb. Frustrated, Jayne was forced to watch the match, sipping her Guinness and eating the chips as they came.

When the guys' team lost, the group wound their way to the street to bemoan clumsy moves and slow service.

"Thanks for inviting us, Cillian." Jayne squeezed his shoulder and kept back a step, her officer training battling the rest of her.

He gave her a puzzled look, but then he smiled, tucking his hands into his pockets sheepishly. "Any time. See you around, Jayne."

Her heart squeezed. He looked so deflated. She felt like a complete jerk.

The men walked off, into the moonlit street. A red four-door buzzed too close to Cillian, and Aldie pulled him away. Cillian just lifted his chin and laughed. The moon poured silver over his cheeks and hair. She knew she was being crazy, but it almost looked like his skin drank the moonlight and reflected it back again, and he was taller than she'd realized earlier.

Deirdre bumped her shoulder. "He is a looker. Do you want to go after him? I can get back to my car just fine without you, if you do."

Jayne cleared her throat. "No. I barely know him." But that didn't feel true. She felt like she'd known him for far longer than she had.

"If I wasn't married, I'd want to." Deirdre's neck flushed. "Oh, I shouldn't have had that second lager."

Jayne linked her arm in Deirdre's. "Yes, you needed that drink. As did I. We work hard, us nerds."

Deirdre's shy laugh rained guilt on Jayne. She wished she was simply making a friend instead of securing a possible asset. She inhaled the sharp air. But she had a mission. A job. A duty that she'd promised to perform. And Jayne never shirked her duties. Not when she was a child unloading the dishwasher, a college student with an essay due, or a librarian with a stack of work a mile high, and she wasn't about to start now.

"What first interested you in Queen Mab? Or do you call her Medb?" Deirdre asked.

"I usually say Medb or the anglicized form, Maeve. I see that quite a bit in essays. But you know that, don't you? It's fun to talk to someone like me for once. Medb was amazingly tough. No one pushed her around."

Deirdre studied Jayne's face. "No, no one did. Have you always been a librarian? A historian?"

Make her feel comfortable. Draw her out.

"Well, once upon a time I was a pretty fabulous grocery bagger."

"Fabulous?"

"Very. My apron was far whiter than anyone else's. And my sorting skills were unparalleled, let me tell you."

"I'm sure." Deirdre gave Jayne one last look. The beers the other librarian had imbibed made her eyes shine a little too much. "It was actually my husband, Alarik, who sparked my interest in the legends."

A buzz reverberated between Jayne's eyes. Magic? Intuition? "But I thought he was an engineer? Does he peruse ancient lore just for funzies on the weekends? I mean, we do, but as you said..."

"Not everyone is like us, to be sure. It is related to a hobby of sorts. He has some friends that have gotten him interested in history. Like Ned said, the Irish love their stories."

A hobby? With friends and legends and old books? Jayne could barely contain herself, but she managed.

"It's great you have that in common."

Deirdre glanced at the pavement. "I suppose."

"Is it not?" A streetlamp flickered overhead, and a car horn blared.

"It is. It's lovely. I'm just tired. I don't know what I was saying. Jesus, Mary, look at the time. I'm parked just there." She pointed at a compact two-seater in the third space beside the parking lot's curb. "I'll see you tomorrow."

And with a wave, Jayne's asset was into her car and gone.

But Jayne had certainly gained intel tonight.

Deirdre's husband, Alarik, and his friends were very interested in history, were they? Hmm. Yeah. Jayne knew what they were interested in. The magic hiding in old books. Alarik had to be the Kingdom member that Ruger and the TCO had heard about.

Jayne couldn't wait to tell Ruger. She pulled out her phone and texted him.

If you can, meet me now.

CHAPTER TWENTY-SEVEN

With the back of a hand, Cillian wiped the clinging sweat from his face. Trying not to let on about how terrible he felt, he waved good night to Aldie and Ned. Was it just the grief of losing Aaron? He didn't think so. Maybe something about how alluring Jayne was, and how much of a gobshite he felt like, betraying her? Maybe he was just coming down with something.

He looked at the moon and the nausea inside him faded. Something about its light eased the sick feeling churning in his gut. He turned to see if Jayne was out of view. He needed to be following her, getting into her place to find that journal for the Kingdom, for the contact who messaged him, the anonymous contact that Aaron had always told him to trust completely. But his head was swimming and he had to get home. He couldn't work on Jayne tonight. He'd be worthless.

He slid into his car and tore down the street, the streetlights strangely crystalline and bright. A tiny part of him wondered if he should message the Kingdom contact, something he'd never done, something Aaron had instructed him not to do. Though the messages had self-destructed, he knew the number they came from. It was against all the rules, but he needed to know how pressing it was that he find the journal. And how necessary he really was. Did they truly need him, or had it all just been Aaron's good graces getting him into the organization? It was pathetic, but he needed reassurance. A new mentor who would take him under his wing.

Frustration bubbled under Cillian's skin, and he slammed a hand on the steering wheel. No, he missed Aaron, the only person who had ever treated him like family. The view out the windscreen blurred, then cleared. Passing a row of shops, Cillian realized he could discern individual cracks in the plaster between the stone walls of the buildings, tiny cracks that he shouldn't have been able to see. He'd only had three pints of the black stuff, over three hours. He shouldn't be fluthered. This had to be some odd fever.

He found himself turning the car toward the tattoo parlor, and before he could sort out what he could possibly accomplish at a place that would be closed by now, he was parking and getting out, heading for the back door. Of course, it was locked. He leaned against the building as his fever sent chills over him.

His phone buzzed. It was from his contact with the Kingdom, the one Aaron had taught him to trust. As if they knew he needed them.

We mourn his loss. He would have wanted you to find that journal. Cillian's heart raced. *Who are you? I need to meet face-to-face.*

Not yet. Soon. Get the journal. Text this number when you have it. You honor him with your dedication to the cause.

The heat began to fade from Cillian's neck and face, his fever abating. He couldn't maneuver his way into Jayne's place tonight. She was long gone and had been a little standoffish all night anyway. It was bad enough he had to steal from the girl. He wasn't about to force his company on her like a creep. Tomorrow he'd text her and get where he needed to be.

Any info on journal's appearance? What am I looking for? Cillian pressed Send.

Perhaps twenty years old. Leather bound. Don't forget the flask. Drink from it before you enter the flat.

I'm on it.

Weird instructions, but whatever. Cillian spun and put a hand against the tattoo parlor's door. Aaron's face flashed through his memory, the steady way he'd always been there for Cillian, the absolute confidence the makeshift elder brother had shown in his words, his actions, his advice.

"I'll do this for you, my friend. Brother." His voice caught, and he swallowed, using the promise to steel himself like a dram of whisky. He still had the Kingdom, and they still had him. Though Aaron was gone, Cillian wasn't alone in his dedication to the way life should be: simple, clean, less screwed by the modern world. And though he hated the idea of stealing from this lovely Jayne girl, it wouldn't hurt her, surely. It was just a book he was going to take. The Kingdom was worth the small crime.

On his way back to the car, he picked up a white paper bag on the ground, from one of a hundred tourist shops. He smashed it into a ball, anger seething through him at how little those who visited cared for his country. The world deserved better than what the humans were giving it, and the Kingdom knew how to save the beauty that had been lost.

Cillian looked up at the moon, soaking in its comforting light. "For you, brother. But please don't make me do worse than this, all right? I'm not keen on finding out how prison life would suit me."

He could imagine Aaron's sideways grin, the shake of his head as he put up with Cillian's irreverence toward the Kingdom's orders.

Shit, he was going to miss him.

CHAPTER TWENTY-EIGHT

In a welcome turn of events, Jayne walked into her apartment to find Ruger making a plate of cheesy scrambled eggs.

"If that didn't smell so heavenly, I'd make mention of you getting comfy in my place."

"Hey, I'm making these for you, so don't—" Ruger whipped around, skillet in hand, spilling eggs all over the kitchen. "You were touched by a Rogue."

Jayne dropped her bag and purse to the floor and wiped her clothes off like she was covered in ants. "A what? What do you mean? What are you talking about?"

The terrible odor of burning eggs wafted through the air, but Ruger didn't let her past him to get a wet towel. He grabbed her and stared into her eyes.

"Jayne. What is your third-level code word?"

Ah. That had been part of the training before they'd left for Dublin. First level was "Rabbit." Second was "Blueberry Bookend." Stupidest code words ever. It's like the organization had zero imagination. Third. What was third? Her mind didn't want to find it. "I know it, Ruger. I do. I just had a couple of beers and I'm really tired and—"

He had a very large, very sharp knife at her throat in a second. "Tell me the third-level code word or you are dead right now, Rogue."

Sweat beaded on her upper lip as his fingers dug into her arm. "I'm not a Rogue. I don't even know what a Rogue is." Her brain finally clicked its gears and became worth a peanut again. "It's 'Jumping River Owl.' Which makes zero sense! And you should change it if you're going to perhaps slice people open for not remembering it!"

She pushed him away, hands trembling, trying hard not to think about what he might have done if her brain had refused to function.

Ruger slid the knife into a sheath under the back of his sweater, then met her gaze. "Are you okay?"

"I'm fine." But her knees wobbled, and she let him help her into a chair at the dining room table. "That sucked. I want pie. And for my apartment not to smell like torched breakfast foods."

"And I want a million dollars and two months off, but neither one of us is getting any of that."

Jayne crossed her arms in an attempt to stop shaking. "Tell me what a Rogue is." She suddenly felt like she had a stranger in her apartment and every decision she'd made felt wrong, wrong, wrong.

Ruger pinched his nose and exhaled in a rush. "Did you see anyone that appeared...off?"

"Off?" Jayne shook her head, anger itching beneath her skin. "What does that even mean?"

"Like, not a normal human."

"Okay. Hold up. Magic is real. Fine. But *not a human*? The heck?"

Ruger held his hands out. "Take a breath."

Smoke spooled from the skillet that was still half on the stove's burner. "I will if you stop the Eggpocalypse in there."

Ruger hurried to wipe up his mess, and Jayne took the time to breathe deeply and slowly.

Not human. Not human. Not human.

When he sat on the corner of the table, she didn't wait for him to begin questioning her again. "Tell me what you are talking about or get me some pie. Preferably both."

"There are creatures in this world that most don't know exist. But they, like magic, haven't been seen outside of the Torrent for decades. We call them Rogues. Generally loyal to one magician at a time, and the bond is lifelong. When their magic rises, around full adulthood, maybe later due to chemical variations, they can take on an animal form written into their DNA. After they bond with a magician, the magician can help them extend that shifting ability into other creatures. Magicians use them in battle, to attack, to spy, to defend."

"Do you have a Rogue?"

He shook his head, eyes growing sad. "They're the stuff of legend, really. No one's seen one for a very long time."

"Then how do you know what they smell like? How did you know I'd been around one?"

"Learning the scent of various types of magic and creatures, including Rogues, used to be part of TCO training, but the higher-ups left it off the last few years in an attempt to streamline."

She just couldn't absorb this. There were nonhumans on Earth and had been forever. This was somehow even more insane than magic simply existing. She clasped her shaking hands. Imagine looking into a person's eyes only to realize that yes, they were just as clever as a human, but shock of all shocks, they weren't anything of the sort. A set of shimmering eyes dazzled Jayne's imagination and she took another shuddering breath.

"Are Rogues evil?"

"Rogues are no more evil than their magician," Ruger said. "There are good Rogues and bad Rogues, just like there are good people and bad people. But they are unpredictable, incredibly strong, and can be controlled by a high-level Adept if they've bonded."

"Right. Of course. So you're saying someone sent their Rogue after me, a weapon that hasn't been seen in a century? You've got to be shitting me." What else was out there that she knew nothing about?

"I'm really not shitting you. Though I suppose, all things being equal, it's possible the Rogue was looking for you to bond with. They only give off their particular scent when their magic is high." He scratched his beard, his gaze distant. "Or when their bodies are preparing to shift for the first time..."

Head whirling, Jayne marched into her bedroom and retrieved the werewolf book Sofia had given her. She held it in front of Ruger. "Are you going to tell me every fiction I've read isn't really fiction? That this kind of stuff might hold a painfully big element of truth?"

Ruger gently pushed her book aside. "No, this isn't a world of vampires and werewolves, Jayne. Not like in your books."

"But you're telling me there are beings in this world who appear human but can transform into whatever they want. That is a werewolf, dude! Spin it how you like, but they might very well have abs like that"—she poked the book cover—"and turn into furry forest legends during the full moon!" She tossed the book on the dining table and shut her eyes, fully freaking the freak out. Why was there no pie?

When she opened her eyes, Ruger was studying her like a puzzle.

"First off, shifting has nothing to do with the full moon. And I don't know anything about their abdominal situation, but yes, Rogues can take the form of a wolf. They could just as easily be an asp or a coyote or a crow. Their forms are limited only by their magician's power, imagination, and need. But they are very, very dangerous. And we'd thought them either extinct or very nearly so."

Jayne closed her eyes slowly and sat. "So you think that a real-live-not-extinct-or-dead Rogue put its hands on me at some point this evening?"

"I do."

Her eyes flashed open. "Do you not think I might notice that happening? I did only have three beers. Not three dozen."

"Rogues look like humans. Like us. Especially if one's lain dormant all these years due to chemical variations and hormone levels. Who touched you tonight?"

"I was in a crowded pub, Ruger. It was very close quarters, I was bumped and touched all night. It could have been anyone. Are there any more dormant magical monsters out there?" She was proud that she sounded only slightly hysterical.

Ruger finally looked amused. "Oh, Jayne. We haven't had time to train you thoroughly, but yes, of course there are. There's no way of knowing what you unleashed back in the Vandy vault. Yes, it seems some ancient magic has returned to the world. Does that mean everything we'd ever heard of has as well? There's no way of knowing. We have to muddle through it together."

At least he'd said *together*. She had to admit, she always felt safe when Ruger was around.

Jayne chewed her lip, picturing Deirdre nervously twisting her hair around a finger and Aldie tapping the bar table. "You asked if I saw someone who looked...'off' was the word you used, I believe. I don't know anyone here well enough to judge whether their behavior was unusual for them or not."

Ruger stood, striding to the window. Pulling the curtains apart and back together again, he sighed. "It's hard to explain if you've never noticed it. Rogues have a different look to them when they're in certain light. Their size can be tricky. They can appear smaller or larger, depending on how the magnetic field is acting in their specific location."

Jayne's throat went dry. She flexed her hands, a buzzing rising inside her, curling around her ribs and sparking against her heart. *Different look in certain light. Size can be tricky.* No, it couldn't be. She was attaching meaning to what she'd noticed in the stupor of alcohol.

Jayne realized Ruger was staring. "Who was it, Jayne? Who did you see that fits that description?"

"I don't know," she lied, pushing her memories of the night out of her mind. She knew nothing concrete and refused to endanger or accuse an innocent based on her knee-jerk response to this new information. She hadn't seen anything that meant anything. "I really do need pie." On her phone, she googled *pie Dublin.* "There should be a pie delivery service. That should be a thing. If Dublin doesn't have one, I think I'll start a side business."

Ruger pried the phone gently from her hands. "Jayne. We can talk more about the Rogue tomorrow. I'll set greater wards on your apartment. But right now, you need to tell me everything you discovered about Deirdre and her husband."

CHAPTER TWENTY-NINE

An alarming shift of focus. *Deep breaths, Jayne.*

"Deirdre's husband is called Alarik. I'm sure you already knew that. She said he works as an engineer, but didn't say where. I saw him today from afar. He met Deirdre at Trinity and she gave him a manila folder. A thick one. Could've been a book, but I'm not sure. He was wearing a hat and I couldn't see his face. Wiry build. Questionable fashion sense. Not that I'm judging."

"Did you talk to him?"

"No. He'd already walked off when I got there. Deirdre didn't seem to want me to meet him, honestly. At least, that's how it felt to me. I was just running after her because I thought she was blowing me off for our drinks date."

"You invited her along to meet you and Cillian and some of his friends at a pub? And she said yes right away? No strange behavior?"

"She texted her husband about it first to ask permission,

which seems totally bizarro, but what do I know? No one I marry will get to tell me what to do." She glanced at Ruger's left hand, then his right. No rings. "Are you married?"

"Moving on," he said.

"Touchy, touchy."

"Jayne," Ruger warned, and she flipped him an angelic smile. It felt good to throw him off, considering she was the one on unstable ground.

"Deirdre seemed happy to have the invite. She's really shy, though. I could tell it wasn't easy for her to socialize. Rosalind, our supervisor, calls her a mouse. She's not wrong."

"Did you get the number she dialed?"

"Number?"

"Deirdre's husband. When she texted him. Or did his name just appear at the top of her screen?"

"Oh, I don't know. She didn't do it right next to me."

"Next time, you get close and see if you can grab any more info. Even a nickname she uses for him might end up being useful. You never know what will move a mission forward. The smallest pieces of intel can be the keystone. We can have a trace on her phone, via spells. I'll see if someone higher up can put a push on that, level up the magic some. See if we can't track down Alarik. Maybe he's the key to all of this. We've seen nothing alarming, but we could have missed something."

"Gotcha. There's more."

Ruger nodded and gestured for her to go on.

"Deirdre wanted to know why I was interested in the Book of Leinster. She asked what drew me to the book, which reminded me of what you'd said, how it possibly is calling me and I'm meant to unlock its secrets."

"Could be coincidence."

Jayne nodded. "Deirdre later asked me about Queen Medb,

the warrior queen in the Book of Leinster. She asked what first interested me in her, and I hadn't even said anything about her. Deirdre seemed very interested in that bit of the mythology, though we didn't end up getting into details. She left like she was suddenly nervous. Could she be the Rogue?"

Ruger shrugged. "It's possible."

"She said her husband has friends who got him interested in history and he is the one who would be interested in Queen Medb. Sounds fishy to me."

Two lines formed between Ruger's eyebrows. "What do you know about these stories?"

"I could bore you for years."

"Go for it."

"Medb was married off to a couple of guys. Her last marriage was all going well until they began comparing cattle."

"Like…cows?"

"Bulls, actually. One of her cows bore a bull that was supposedly the greatest thing since hot mead, and her husband took it for his own. She was not okay with this and went to war. It goes on and on. Even the bulls fought. Suffice to say, the historical Queen Medb was a mighty woman who knew what she wanted and went after it. She was a warrior and a strategist and lived to be over one hundred years old, if those accounts are accurate."

"That doesn't sound at all like the Queen Mab in poetry and Shakespeare."

"Not really, no. The creatives through history turned Medb into a beautiful and powerful fairy queen. Statuesque and full of fantastical magic. The original—the mythological one—was just a badass."

"A powerful queen. And animals. Perhaps the bull she went to war over was no mere animal, but a Rogue. Her Rogue."

Whoa. That was a take on the mythology she'd never heard. But it made sense. If the legend was just a line or two off, then the bull could've been one of these magical creatures that bonded with a magician.

Ruger typed something into his phone, then looked up. "What did Alarik say specifically about the topic to Deirdre? Did she mention anything more about his interests?"

"No. Like I said, she got all squirrelly and left."

Fatigue rode over Jayne's body. She put a hand on Ruger's shoulder. "I think I need to rest. Seriously. I feel like my head is about to roll off my shoulders." She went to the fridge and pulled out a bottle of water, nearly dropping it. Her nerves were rebelling against all these wild revelations, not to mention the fear that whispered about the Rogue she'd encountered. Drinking down the cold beverage, she hid her face from Ruger. She didn't want to seem incapable of handling this information, this world, her job. To say she was shocked by the thought that there were not only magicians but also people who weren't people— well, that was an understatement on a level with discovering ancient Alexandria's library hadn't been destroyed and calling the find *cool*.

Ruger gathered his jacket and bag and headed for the door. "All right. One night off training. But we have to talk about this Rogue again tomorrow. Write up everything you did tonight, every person you were near, even if you didn't notice them touch you. We'll figure out who it is."

Jayne faced the open fridge, pretending to look for something to munch on. Really, she just needed a minute to get a handle on the idea of Rogues. It actually bugged her more than learning magic was real and that she was a practitioner. Why? Why did the idea of nonhuman creatures in human form freak her out this much?

Continuing his very father-style lecturing, Ruger said, "And you must avoid everyone, except Deirdre and Rosalind, of course, until we do."

"Are we sure Deirdre isn't the Rogue?"

"No, we're not. But since she's your target, we'll have to risk it. And Jayne, you need to understand the risks. No more messing around with the locals. I'll handle surveillance on Cillian going forward."

She went back to the fridge, rustled around inside, hiding her face. Damn.

"Jayne."

"What?"

"That is an order from your superior. Not a request."

"Aye aye, Captain." She met his gaze, which was stony at best. As a CIA officer, she just had to buck up and face this. "I understand. I will follow your orders."

"If you don't, and you somehow run into whoever that Rogue may be, we may have to take you in."

"What does that mean?"

"It means you'll be off the mission and detained."

"Detained? Like, you'd throw me in prison?"

"Possibly."

She slammed the refrigerator door. "I understand."

Ruger left, and she locked the door, took four very deep breaths, forced the night from her mind, and plopped onto the couch with an airport copy of Brandon Sanderson's *Mistborn*. She turned the book over and over in her hands, looking for any traces of magic, but it was simply paper and cardboard. Its magic was within the pages and wasn't out to hurt her.

Why did this magic feel more real than her own? A strange alchemy, books.

Shutting out the real world, Jayne dove into the epic fantasy.

It took a bit for her mind to settle, but soon enough she was reading about clandestine meetings between folk who wore rippling cloaks and used coins to fly. It thankfully allowed her mind to rest, to escape the dangerous truths Ruger had laid on her today. She didn't resurface until she was halfway finished with the doorstopper of a book and the clock said something gross like 2:15 a.m.

The ice machine in the fridge knocked around while she turned off lights and moved closer to going to bed. With just five hours before she had to get ready for work, she really needed some shuteye.

But she knew very well sleep wasn't going to come floating into her room on a magical mist. Especially since there were...

She couldn't even think the word.

Instead, she thought about the paranormal romance Sofia had loaned her. Clearly, some Adepts were authors. Had to be. It was just too close to the truth. And here she'd thought writers were just wildly imaginative. Nope. They had accessed magic, or at least some of them had, and then they'd passed the ideas onward via fiction.

Jayne's mind turned from one crazy thought to another like her brain was a grad student who'd downed a triple espresso.

Why hadn't Ruger just told her about the danger of Rogues to start with? What about the risk? When she first got back to the flat, he'd acted like the Rogue was about to smash through the apartment window and gnaw on their livers. Then he got all philosophical on her. She was confused.

And this whole thing about how when she had accessed the Torrent, she had somehow unlocked all the magic in the world? Or juiced it up? Why her?

Jayne shook her head, her pillow wrinkled softly against her cheeks. She rolled and shoved her face right into the cottony surface and prayed for sleep to use some *Mistborn* magic, burn some brass, and soothe her brain into submission.

Ruger had ordered her to avoid everyone but the specific individuals she worked with at the library, so she had to give up Cillian.

Cillian.

That fear in the back of her mind whispered what she'd seen. The moonlight on his skin. The way he'd seemed taller. But no. It couldn't be. Her imagination was going wild. Poor Cillian didn't know a thing about magic. He was no Rogue or anything like that. He was far too innocent.

She plugged in her phone to charge and noticed a text from earlier in the evening.

It was Cillian. *I feel as if I did something to upset you.*

"Ugh." She set the phone back down, her limbs like lead weights against the comforter. She longed to assure him, to joke with him, to make him feel better. But it was best if she just cut him off now before she imagined something else and got him into trouble. Besides, Ruger's order meant they couldn't see one another anyway.

Lacking the energy to properly break it off with him, she ignored the text and set the alarm. Shutting her eyes, she pushed Cillian out of her head. She had a job to do here in Dublin, and it might help the TCO save lives. And it was the job of her dreams. She was fully committed and would just have to shake off the rest of the distractions.

CHAPTER THIRTY

Jayne woke after only a few hours of restless sleep, thinking about her sister.

Two hundred forty-five. That's how many messages Jayne's sister Sofia had ignored. Jayne pressed the freckle on her arm, the match to the one on Sofia's, the freckles they'd pretended were communication devices as kids.

"Hello?" Jayne whispered into her arm, tears springing up around her eyelashes. Thankfully, she hadn't put her mascara on yet. She pressed the spot again, knowing she was being insane, but not caring at all. "Sofia, please answer. I'm sorry I went out on my own. But it can't be helped. I'm saving the world. Or trying to. Please answer. Please just talk to me."

Maybe she would break her vow of secrecy and tell Sofia everything. Sofia was great at keeping secrets. And they couldn't go on like this. Jayne had been tucking all her worries about Sofia into a far, dark corner of her mind, but now that she'd opened that corner to the light, she couldn't think about anything else.

A knock shook her out of a continuous stream of guilt and worry.

It was seven in the morning, not even time to leave for work yet. Who would be knocking? Ruger didn't knock.

Jayne peered through the peephole. Cillian. Her heart did a small samba, and her mind started to race. But wait. How did he know where she lived? Would Ruger be pissed if she let him in? Was that coffee she smelled?

She slid the bolt free and opened the door, hoping she didn't look as awful as she felt. "You'd better have coffee. It's the only thing that will turn this," she said, pointing at her frown, "to this." She smiled.

Wearing a baggy hoodie with the insignia from his football team on the chest, a grin, and rumpled bed hair, Cillian looked gorgeous. He raised one thick, dark blond eyebrow and presented a steaming paper cup he'd had hidden behind his back. "I thought this might make up for whatever I did."

Despite Ruger's warning, Jayne didn't have it in her to be curt with him. She couldn't forget the sadness in his eyes when he'd spoken of his mother. And he'd been so kind… "You didn't do anything wrong. Come on in."

The scent of hazelnut trailed him inside. He handed over a cup, then turned a kitchen chair around backward and sat in it, hanging his arms over the back. "When do you have to report to book duty, smarty pants?"

Jayne laughed, drank deeply from her cup, wishing she could take him to work. The coffee burned its way down her throat and she was just fine with that. A tiny part of her worried about him showing up at her place like this, but at the pub they'd discussed good places to live in Dublin and she'd told him what building she was in. But she hadn't said what flat was hers, so how he knew where she was… In retrospect, it wasn't a very spy-like move on her part. Still, if she'd been too cagey, it would have sounded weird. Oh, well. She had skills to fight him off if need be, and the TCO at her back too.

"I have to clean up this mess and head out right after," she said. "Not much time to chat, unfortunately." She fought the urge to smooth her hair and lick her lips. If he didn't like how she looked au naturel, all the better. He'd leave her be and she wouldn't have to break off this thing-that-hadn't-yet-become-a-thing.

Cillian sipped from his cup, then eyed her, his gaze sliding across her cheekbones and down her neck like a caress. "You are lovely in the morning."

Damn. That. Irish. Accent. "Oh, sure. I bet I'm winning all the awards at the moment."

The way his thumb moved over the rim of his cup warmed her as much as the coffee.

"Just say thank you, woman."

"Don't boss me."

Cillian chuckled. "What will you be working on at Trinity today? In layman's terms, if you don't mind."

"I'm hoping to see the Book of Leinster."

"Is that the one you and Deirdre were talking about? With Queen Mab?"

"Queen Medb, but yes. You know, it is the mythology of your homeland. I'd think you'd know more than me."

"I never was much for school." His dimples appeared as he smiled and glanced around her place, his gaze going to her bookshelves.

"You got by on shiny apples for your teachers and notes from all the girls, didn't you? I know your kind."

"My kind." He laughed and finished his coffee.

Jayne clicked her tongue before drinking more of her own. "I'd say 'shame on you,' but the words would be wasted." She set her coffee down and started toward her bathroom to do her makeup. "I'm going to work on my face in here, but you can keep talking."

"What else do you know about my kind?" A teasing note danced through his question.

"That you get away with everything."

"Correct."

"Incorrigible."

"Highest marks for you, library vixen."

Jayne's cheeks warmed. She leaned around the bathroom doorway to glare. "Simmer down. We haven't even been on a formal just-you-and-me date yet."

"Yet? You mean I do have a chance?"

She needed to shut this down. Her body and her heart didn't want to, though. "We'll see. Honestly," she said while applying eyeliner and leaning over the sink, "I really have to focus on work. This is the job I've always wanted. I can't be staying up late and coming in tired or hungover."

Quiet bumps and shuffles came through the wall. He was perusing her bookshelf. "I get that. But you get off work at a decent time. I can meet you for a meal right after. We don't need to stay out late."

"Text me." Jayne applied a nice red lip, noticed it was crooked, and wiped it off, going instead to her usual cherry ChapStick. She zipped up her makeup bag and walked into the living room to find him perched on the chair's arm, reading a dictionary. "We'll see."

"I'll do that," he said, glancing up, his smile wide.

"Interesting read?"

He stood and shut the dictionary. "Expanding my vocabulary

so we can communicate, slacker to nerd."

She laughed as he shelved the giant tome before strolling to the door behind her. The lights outside her doorway made his rumpled hair shine.

"Well, I'll be off. Have a good day, Jayne Thomas."

She cringed inside at the use of her fake name. "You, too. And thanks for the coffee."

He looked good walking away, and she refused to feel guilty about seeing him. After all, she hadn't initiated it and gone against Ruger's order. Cillian had come to her. What was she going to do? Refuse to talk? That would've been strange behavior and suspicious, certainly. No, she'd done the right thing. She hoped, if the TCO's Library Division was watching, they would agree. Just in case, she wrote it up and slipped the note under Ruger's door, then headed to work. She'd better get her hands on that book today. If Ruger came in yelling, she needed some good info to keep him on her side against Amanda and the rest of the TCO.

CHAPTER THIRTY-ONE

The book Jayne had studied, dreamed of, and fantasized about was sliding in a cart toward her. Deirdre gave her a timid smile as she wheeled the box that held the manuscript into the workspace beyond Rosalind's red desk.

Rosalind's eyes shone, the wrinkles at the edges expanding as she glanced between the Book of Leinster and Jayne. "Are you ready for this? You did just wash and dry your hands?"

It was a question for a new librarian, not a woman with her level of expertise, but Jayne had no room in herself for irritation now. She simply nodded to Rosalind like a good schoolgirl. Jayne's heart hammered in her chest, and she felt a sensation like a hand pressing against her forehead, warm palm over the space between her eyebrows. "I am."

Deirdre slowly removed the text from the protective box and set the Book of Leinster in a foam cradle that would keep it from opening too widely and damaging the ancient pages. It was a voluminous vellum manuscript.

"Magnificent, isn't it? I know we see old books all the time, but this one is special. Can you imagine what the pages must have looked like in 1160 AD? So beautiful."

Jayne's nostrils flared as she took in the book's scent. Dust and mold. And something else. A smell that reminded her of magic. Gently, Jayne touched the edges, and the spring-green stars of the Torrent sparkled atop her view of the monk's elaborate calligraphy.

Careful, she chided herself, and not just because the pages could be damaged by the wrong touch. She couldn't allow herself to be thrown into the Torrent in front of them. She couldn't let on that magic was here, that she was a magician. Rosalind would most likely freak out and possibly Deirdre, too, unless the woman was truly tied to the Kingdom. Perhaps Deirdre was a magician as well, but now, in front of the lady who ran their department and oversaw this manuscript, wasn't the time to find out. At the very least, exposing her ability to manipulate the world magically would jeopardize Jayne's place at Trinity. Worst case, Rosalind would deem Jayne had gone bonkers and report her, making her unemployable anywhere.

So she fell back on her schooling, and talked. Rosalind grinned like a proud mother as Jayne spoke about the various works inside, details about the monk who'd written it, and the culture that had thrived during its creation.

"What about Medb?" Deirdre asked.

Jayne carefully found the Táin Bó Cúailnge—the Irish Iliad—and smiled. This was happening, and it was magic in its own right.

"Tell us the story." Rosalind's voice held a unique blend of childlike wonder and academic reverence.

Jayne, the smoke-and-floral scent of the Torrent in her nose and the steady warmth of some new kind of magic between her eyebrows, gazed over the Old Irish text, the faded ink, the crisp shape of the monk's lettering. She didn't translate directly. Instead, she told the tale like a bard, tweaking the pacing for her audience.

"Queen Medb's new husband, Ailill, claimed he had more than she did and that she was lucky to have married him. The queen wasn't the type to let that go. She called up all the servants and workers, and the royal couple compared their riches. Medb was sure she would come out on top. After all, she was the best of her siblings, the daughter of a great man. She was the strongest warrior, most powerful in mind and body. It turned out that Medb and Ailill had equal wealth except for one bull. Ailill owned a massive, swaggering bull the people called White-horned, and even Medb had to agree the possession of this creature put her second to her husband. To right this wrong in her world, she decided to do a trade for a neighboring, lesser king's brown bull, a creature that was said to rival White-horned in every way. Sadly, a drunk at the celebratory feast said something nasty about the neighboring king, and the trade turned into a war. Medb lost many warriors, but she did claim the brown bull. The beast tore White-horned to pieces."

Rosalind shook her head. "All of that bloodshed for a bull."

Deirdre stared at the page, brow furrowed.

Jayne's mind whirred as the magic around her drifted in and out of view, obviously invisible to the other women. Perhaps Ruger was right, and that brown bull had been a Rogue, a powerful being capable of changing shape and increasing a Master magician's abilities. Power like that would be worth spilling blood, especially to a warrior queen like Medb.

Words whisked through Jayne's ears. Startled, she looked up from the Book of Leinster. "What was that?"

Rosalind frowned at Deirdre. "I didn't hear anything, did

you?"

"No," Deirdre answered, eyeing Jayne.

The sonorous voice whispered, and Jayne strained to decipher the sounds. "Old Irish."

"It's lovely, isn't it?" Deirdre said as she and Rosalind looked again at the manuscript, Jayne's question forgotten. She must have thought Jayne was talking about the calligraphed words.

The page held the same story Jayne had studied for so many years, but seeing it with her own eyes, smelling the vellum, feeling the texture of the calfskin under her fingertips...

"I wonder what she was really like." Jayne smiled to herself, as paintings and drawings in reds, golds, and blacks swirled through her mind's eye.

"Who, dear?" Rosalind's voice sounded far away to Jayne.

"Medb. The warrior queen of Connacht."

Deirdre moved beside Jayne, though Jayne couldn't tear her eyes away from the text to see what she was doing. Her voice was filled with grudging respect. "She had several husbands and lovers. Unusual for her society."

"Yes," Jayne said. "Women had standing in her time and place, but the degree to which she held influence, to which she married and divorced and possessed her own vast holdings, that was unique. She had a singular ability to rouse those around her to battle. People either loved her or trembled before her."

"Or both, I'd wager," Rosalind said.

Deirdre chuckled. "Let's look at the illuminated pages, shall we?"

The whispering voice threaded through Jayne's thoughts again, the words twisting around themselves until vowels and consonants rounded, flattened, and took on the cadence of...

"English?"

Jayne's face heated as she realized she'd spoken aloud. "Sorry.

My mind is spinning."

Rosalind put a hand on her shoulder. "I understand that. Don't you, Deirdre?"

Jayne tore her gaze from the book to watch Deirdre's reaction. The woman smiled kindly. "I do. When I had the opportunity to study one of the original copies of the Magna Carta, I couldn't focus my thoughts properly for days. My mind kept wandering to what it must have been like, that day they cornered the king."

Heart warming toward her fellow book nerds, Jayne turned the page carefully as she'd been trained, both hands moving confidently to shift the sheet of vellum. She found a page painted with shades of red, gold, and green. All three women leaned closer to look.

The page wanted to lift up in the middle. Without thinking, Jayne gently set her freshly washed and dried palm on the center, and the world fell away.

Jayne's stomach dropped, and she gasped internally as the Torrent sprang to life around her. But she knew how to handle this now. She quickly focused on the real world, and Deirdre, Rosalind, and the book came rushing back to view.

"Are you all right?" Deirdre studied Jayne's face like she might find answers.

Jayne cleared her throat, still seeing green stars, and nodded. "Yes. I just had a moment. You know." She gave Deirdre a smile.

Deirdre grinned. "I do."

As Rosalind and Deirdre peppered Jayne with questions, the voice returned.

And it spoke to Jayne in terrifying clarity.

We are bound, Master to Master, for you have found my grimoire. You feel my essence now, know it as surely as you know your own. And you will come for me. It has been foretold.

Jayne's heart snagged on a beat, and her hands grew clammy. She pulled her fingers away from the text. What in the world did that mean? And whose voice was it? This was some sort of magic, but Ruger hadn't trained her in anything like this. She had to see him. Now.

"Ladies, I hate to end our fun, but I'm not feeling well. I think I need to go lie down for a bit. Would that be all right, Rosalind?"

"You do look green around the gills, dear. Of course. All the excitement, completely understandable."

They tucked her things together for her and sent her home. Jayne didn't even acknowledge Gerard's absence at the front door as she rushed away.

CHAPTER THIRTY-TWO

Standing in the hallway in front of Jayne's door, Cillian pulled the flask Aaron had left for him from his pocket and drank, wincing slightly at the bitter taste. It tasted like Jameson's, but with a mossy, grassy tinge that momentarily made him want to vomit. The feeling passed quickly, though, and the whisky warmed its way down his throat into his stomach, then worked into his limbs. He could almost envision it traveling through his body, his bloodstream, not the clean amber of regular whisky, but something verdant and old. Hopefully he hadn't just poisoned himself with something nasty. Why in the world Aaron would want him to wait until late afternoon and drink old whisky before breaking and entering, he had no idea, but he'd learned not to ask too many questions.

Stashing the flask in his jacket pocket, he slid his credit card into Jayne's lock, then bumped the doorknob, his rough youth coming back in flashes of memory. His friend Hugh following him into a dark package store and grabbing a bottle of vodka, shouting a delightfully inappropriate version of their school's song.

Cillian had always been the lockpick in their group—gaining Hugh and his brother, Mikey, access to cars with owners daft enough to leave phone chargers, stashes of small bills, and spare credit cards in glove boxes or under seats. Cillian felt like an arse for stealing when he was a kid, and he hadn't used his nefarious skills in years. Not since Aaron had bailed him out of jail.

He sighed as he pushed into Jayne's flat. "At least it's for a good cause," he whispered to himself.

Repeating the phrase like a mantra, he ran a finger along the spines of the books in Jayne's impressive set of shelves. *Celtic Lore and Secrets, Gaulish Art, Tuatha Dé Danaan Encyclopedia*. The history and art books went on and on. How could she read this stuff? He chuckled, thinking of her wrinkling her little nose as she pondered something he'd said at the pub. Damn, that girl was cute.

His finger stopped on a leather-bound spine. He slid the small book out and opened the front cover. A messy line in blue ink said *Entreaties and Proverbs, Property of Henry Thorne*.

Cillian froze. *Thorne*. This was it. The journal. But it belonged to her father? Had to be. How many journals would be hiding in one woman's flat? Well, well. Jayne had lied to his face when she said her last name was Thomas, he knew that, but this confirmed it. He might be lying to Jayne, but Jayne was lying to him, too.

He had to admit, he was interested in what skeletons resided in cute Jayne's closet. But if the Kingdom was interested in her father's journal, he had to look at her as an enemy to his cause. And that hurt.

He looked around her flat, debating. Technically, his job with her was finished. He could walk away now, never see her again.

Or you could stick around...just to make sure she doesn't harbor any more dark secrets.

A breath of relief coursed through him. Maybe he didn't have to give her up just yet. He had his secrets, too. He'd be careful. The Kingdom might want more information about her, so he needed to stay close. It would be fine. He could handle this. Aaron would have, so now Cillian would do it for him.

Curiosity begged Cillian to read the journal and figure out why the Kingdom wanted it. But Jayne could be on her way back from work unexpectedly, or she could have hired someone to come in and clean. He had to leave. Now.

Tucking the journal into his jacket pocket, he slipped out of the flat, feeling justified but also really damn guilty.

Cillian walked through the gates of Glasnevin Cemetery, the spot his new Kingdom contact had chosen for the journal handoff. Gravestones lorded over deeply green grass and walled rectangular burial sites, lined up somewhat evenly row after row after row. The sidewalk, cracked and sporting sprigs of defiant growth, led Cillian to a lean man with eyes he had to call sharp. The look he gave Cillian was nothing like Aaron's brotherly concern or fiery passion for the cause. This man looked like he was either going to hire you for a high-paying job or slit your throat. Or one right after the other.

The man spoke before Cillian had a chance. "You're Aaron's old friend, hmm?"

"I am." The journal was heavy in Cillian's jacket pocket.

"Call me Lars." He touched a hand to his heart, the Kingdom's version of shaking hands. "Sorry for your loss."

"Thanks. Can you tell me anything more about his death?"

"There isn't much to tell. The branch of the US government

that is tasked with tearing our organization apart found him and killed him. He died quickly, from what I was told. A small mercy, but a mercy nonetheless."

Bitterness pricked Cillian's tongue, and he forced himself to breathe. "Did you know him?"

"Aaron? I met him once. Impressive man."

Cillian pulled the journal out of his pocket and handed it to Lars, who accepted it without a glance and slid it into a large shoulder bag. "What is so important about that journal? Looked like nonsense to me, to be honest."

Lars's smile was thin, his eyes cold. "There are things experts can see that many cannot."

Nodding, Cillian let the tension flow out of him. At least that ugly chore was over and done with. He hadn't enjoyed nicking the book from Jayne.

"We need you to gain more information from this woman."

Cillian's stomach turned. "Why? Who is she other than a librarian? Why is she important to the cause?"

The autumn breeze skirted across the cemetery, carrying the scent of rot and old bones.

"If Aaron had asked you to inform on someone, would you have questioned it?"

His words were loaded weapons. "Aaron wouldn't have demanded it of me."

Lars tipped his head back and looked at the night sky. "Ah. I see now." He leaned toward Cillian, whispered something, and a pale, red light washed over Cillian's eyes.

"What was that?"

Lars tilted his head. "What do you mean?" He glanced at the street that lay beyond the cemetery. "Oh, you mean the siren. I think that was an ambulance."

"What? No, the light. I couldn't..." Whatever Cillian was

about to say dissipated in his mind. He shut his eyes to think, his thoughts scattering like startled gulls.

When he opened them, he was alone, standing in a cemetery.

What was he doing here?

He whipped around. "Hello?" A chill speared his chest, and he felt...foggy. He tried to recall his evening and failed.

Why the hell was he in a cemetery?

Had he experienced some kind of stroke? Surely not. He was too young and healthy for that. But he had absolutely no memory of coming to this place or why he would've done such a thing.

Heart hammering away inside his chest, he hurried from the cemetery and began to look for his car. A light rain started up as he crossed the street. He needed a nice, familiar beer right now, and possibly, a good think. He texted Aldie and Ned. They'd meet him at the pub and he'd do his level best to forget about this. It was all too strange.

At the car, he shivered, fumbling with his keys. Maybe instead of the pub he should have called for medical help.

Nah. He was fine. Right? Besides, if he admitted to anyone he'd come to alone, in a cemetery, they'd haul him off to be examined.

Racing down the wet streets, he sped toward Dublin city and the pub, determined to shake off the whole night.

CHAPTER THIRTY-THREE

Ruger met a frantic Jayne in his flat, which was decidedly less personal than her own. Ruger didn't need much. He was too focused on the job at hand to be bothered by settling in and comfort.

He'd been worried about her all day after her casual note—*Cillian stopped by. I had a coffee with him then gave him the brushoff. Leinster today!* And a damn smiley face. A smiley face. It wasn't dignified.

But now she was upset. The skin around her mouth had gone pale, and she was breathing too quickly. He sat on the lumpy brown couch and waved her over to take a spot beside him.

"I'm listening. Take three deep breaths. Then talk."

Setting her bag and purse down on the dining table, she did as he asked, her eyes open, her gaze accepting of his order. He was glad to see her subtle gratitude, pleased that she wasn't taking offense to his direction. He needed to continue building the trust between them. She didn't seem to be holding a grudge that he had put a knife to her throat, but he was already aware Jayne contained multitudes. She wasn't telling him the whole truth about everything, not yet. Her attachment to Cillian was more than casual, he feared. And considering Cillian was most likely working for the Kingdom? Ruger didn't want her getting hurt. Not on his watch.

Jayne's color mostly had returned as she sat on the couch beside him. Her eyes locked onto his. "Today I opened the Book of Leinster."

A buzz seemed to fill the room, Ruger's pulse ratcheting up. "And?"

Rubbing her hands on her suit pants, Jayne took another slow breath. "I saw the Torrent."

"So it *is* a grimoire," he said with satisfaction.

"Without a doubt. And I heard a voice."

Ruger scooted closer. "What kind of voice?"

"A woman's voice. First in a language I couldn't hear well enough to identify, then in Old Irish, and finally in English."

Ruger's hands had gone cold.

"The voice said, 'We are bound, Master to Master, for you have found my grimoire. You feel my essence now, know it as surely as you know your own. And you will come for me. It has been foretold.'" Jayne looked up, staring at him again like she needed him to explain this, to give her a hand.

He stared back at her. It wasn't possible.

Wasn't it? Amanda's voice rang in his mind. How else could magic have returned to them, if not for a Master moving among them?

Chills rippled through his body, and he forced down the excitement. This was everything they'd dreamed of. Everything they feared.

Ruger had, at last, found a Master. And she belonged to the

CIA.

"Why do you look like you want to dance a jig?"

"Because, my dear Jayne, this is it. A necromantic text. It has to be. And you have opened it. It wouldn't have opened for me. For Amanda. For the Kingdom. It opened for you, Jayne."

"I'm not following."

"Do you know what it means that the spirit bound to the book called you a Master?"

A small dawning registered on her lovely young face. "No."

"Yes. It explains everything. Why magic came back to the world. It's you, Jayne. You're a Master. The first in centuries."

She was shaking her head as if clearing buzzing bees from her mind. "Impossible, Ruger. I can't be. Masters can do higher-level magic than Adepts. I can barely tie my shoes in the Torrent."

"We don't know what you can do yet, girl. But we do know this. Based on what you heard, the trapped spirit of the book is also a Master, and somehow bound to you." He put a hand on her shoulder as if he could give to her some of his experience and strength and help her down what would be a dark and uncharted road. "Jayne. At this moment, you are possibly the most powerful magician in the world."

She sat very still and her voice quavered when she spoke. "I don't know any more than I did when I woke up this morning."

"But this bond, if it is what I think it is, will give you access to that spirit's abilities. Master to Master. I've heard of such things, but I never imagined I'd live to see the day."

She put a hand to her stomach, like the idea of being caught in a manuscript for eternity made her sick.

"Whose spirit is in the book?"

"I don't know. But we need to find out."

Jayne sat with Ruger in silence. His mind had to be whirling around this insanity just as hers was.

Finally, he spoke. "Do you have a guess who might be speaking to you?"

She did, but Jayne didn't dare voice it. Could it really be true? Could the voice in her head be Queen Medb herself?

Correct, the voice echoed in Jayne's mind, the cold sound slithering down her spine.

Ruger's hand was on Jayne's arm, starkly warm compared to the chill running through her.

"It's the warrior queen," Jayne whispered. "Queen Medb. The most powerful woman in Irish history."

His gaze roamed over her face, awe glinting in the eyes' dark depths. The awe scared Jayne. She didn't know what to do with this development.

"And now," Ruger said, "you are her voice in the realm of the living."

The truth of his statement burned through Jayne's blood.

Then Ruger's face broke into a smile so wide it nearly blinded her, and he whooped for joy.

"Wait until Amanda hears this."

PART TWO

But I who have written this story, or rather this fable, give no credence to the various incidents related in it. For some things in it are the deceptions of demons, other poetic figments; some are probable, others improbable; while still others are intended for the delectation of foolish men.

—O'Rahilly 2014, page 272, lines 4901–20
The Book of Leinster

CHAPTER THIRTY-FOUR

After a full week by Deirdre's side at the library, bringing up her own struggles with her odd childhood and the way they'd moved from place to place, Jayne felt fairly comfortable the other woman's barriers were finally dropping. She'd learned about Deirdre's deceased brother, who died from the flu when he was just ten years old. Deirdre had understood the grief Jayne talked about over their notes on the day's collection work, the way Jayne kept looking for her parents around every corner despite their being gone for so long. Jayne felt dirty about the whole thing, but it was necessary. Deirdre seemed like a good person, and Jayne truly hoped she wasn't tied to the Kingdom, that Ruger and Amanda were mistaken.

On Friday, Rosalind stayed late to finish a report, waving off offers of help from Deirdre and Jayne. Together, they walked toward the exit and Gerard.

"I'm glad to see you two ladies have made friends," Gerard said, a book he'd been reading tucked under his arm.

Jayne raised an eyebrow and leaned toward Deirdre. "Why does that sound like a veiled insult?"

Deirdre smiled. "Because everything he says is a veiled insult."

Gerard huffed. "That's not true. I praised your biscuits at lunch today, didn't I?" he said, looking at Deirdre.

"You did. I'm glad you liked the treat."

"Oh, please," Jayne interjected. "If you had an insult for baked goods of that caliber, you'd belong in the nuthouse, Gerard."

Laughing, Deirdre left with Jayne, walking into the twilight that cast Trinity College in watery shadows that reminded Jayne of smeared mascara.

"Jayne, would you like to come to dinner tonight?"

Jayne's heart skipped across three beats. Ruger would be thrilled. "Of course!" She coughed to cover her overloud response. "Of course. Thanks. When is good for you?"

"How about now? I already spoke to my husband and he—"

"Jayne!" The familiar voice hit Jayne like a smack to the back of the head.

Sofia.

Jayne turned to see her older sister's flyaway hair and big, gorgeous eyes. Sofia pulled her into a hug, and Jayne squeezed her back even though her head was spinning.

This was bad. Very, very bad.

Sofia couldn't find out that Jayne was here for the CIA's magic branch. Or that magic existed. Or that Jayne was using a fake last name. And with Deirdre here...

"What are you doing in Ireland?"

"I should ask you the same thing, young lady."

"Deirdre, this is my...this is Sofia."

"It's good to meet you. Looks like you need to catch up. Take your time. I need to text my husband."

Deirdre stepped back, giving them some space. Jayne waited

until she was out of earshot.

"Sofia." Jayne exhaled. "Give me the address of where you're staying and I'll meet up with you after dinner tonight."

Hurt spread across her sister's face. "What? I come all the way across the pond and you're putting me off?"

Ugh. This timing couldn't have been worse. Jayne leaned in and whispered in Sofia's ear.

"Please understand. I have a work thing that I can't miss. It's really important. Just a few hours and then I'm yours. And I'll explain everything."

Deirdre was still texting and politely giving them space. Sofia studied Deirdre, caution in her gaze and her body tense beside Jayne's.

"Please, Sofia. I'm so glad to see you. You have no idea how happy I am right now. I just…have to do this."

Sofia nodded, then planted a kiss on Jayne's cheek. She smelled like she always did, that musky perfume of hers from Victoria's Secret. She lifted Jayne's hand and wrote an address on the back. "No later than ten, please. I'm super jet lagged. And I'd better get points for being so calm about all of this."

Jayne forced a jaunty grin. "It's because you're proud of your sister, aren't you? Didn't realize I could get a gig at Trinity, did you?"

Sofia smiled half-heartedly. "I always believed in you, sis. I just… We'll talk later. I'm sorry for cutting you off like that. I was worried. I'm trying to change, Jayne. I really am."

Jayne squeezed Sofia's arm gently. "Thanks. Ten it is."

They hugged once more, then Sofia waved to Deirdre and hurried off the way she'd come.

Jayne expected Deirdre to say something along the lines of "you could have invited your friend to join us," but she didn't. She seemed glad to see the back of Sofia, and honestly, at this moment, Jayne was, too.

"Ready to go?" Deirdre started toward the car park. "Alarik is waiting."

"I'm ready. Starving, in fact!" She forced a laugh and caught up to Deirdre, who was walking quickly toward the lot.

Deirdre offered to drive and Jayne agreed, not really knowing quite how to proceed. She wished she had time to meet with Ruger first. This invitation had come out of nowhere. Jayne had to at least let Ruger know that Sofia was here. He might already know, but...

"Hey, that was an awkward goodbye. She caught me off guard. We've been...estranged. Do you mind?"

"Not at all." Deirdre backed out of the parking space and started down a road leading out of the city.

Jayne dialed Ruger. When he answered, she said, "Ah, got her voicemail."

"I'm here. I'm listening," Ruger said. His voice was comforting.

"Hey, Sofia," Jayne said into the phone, knowing Ruger would get what was up. "Sorry about having to run off. You surprised me there on campus just as I was leaving. Like I said, I'm going to dinner at Deirdre's house, but I'll see you right after, as promised. Thanks for understanding."

"Sofia is in Dublin?" Ruger's voice was pinched. "And you're headed to your asset's home?"

"Oh yeah, and I hope the"—Jayne flipped her hand over to read the hotel Sofia was staying at—"Baymel Hotel isn't as terrible as it sounds. Ha. See you soon."

"We will be on the hotel and send someone to watch over Deirdre's house. Don't worry, Jayne. Just listen and act interested in their cause."

Jayne ended the call and tucked her phone into her purse.

Okay. That was better. At least the TCO would be aware of her location, and they'd know what to do with Sofia.

Deirdre's voice broke through Jayne's worried thoughts. "Alarik, thought it would be nice to go to our house on the coast tonight."

Jayne gripped her seat belt. "You have two houses? Wow. Sounds great." *Except for the fact that you are most likely going to murder me and chuck my body into the sea and the TCO won't know where I am until they find my floating corpse in the surf.*

Could she call Ruger again and pretend it's someone else? Cillian maybe? She lifted her phone to do just that.

Deirdre frowned at the phone. "I hope you like steak. My husband makes a fantastic meal of it."

"Definitely. Who doesn't like steak?" Jayne dialed Ruger and held the phone to her ear. But the ringing stopped abruptly. The screen said Powering Off. Her battery had died.

Damn it.

Of all the days to forget to charge her phone.

"Do you have a charger with you?"

Deirdre glanced at Jayne's phone. "Yes, but not for that kind of phone. Sorry."

"No worries. I'll live without the outside world for a few hours. So, it's a vacation home?" Jayne asked, lamely.

"Yes." Deirdre steered them through a hairpin turn. The scent of saltwater blew through the car vents. "It's not actually ours. It's a friend's, but she's letting us use it."

"Very generous."

Deirdre nodded, but she shifted in her seat as she spoke, and Jayne sensed this friend of theirs made her nervous.

Jayne looked in the side mirror, praying the TCO had someone following her. But no cars trailed them. The road was completely empty. Maybe they had a magical GPS tracker on her somewhere. She rubbed sweating palms on her pants. "It's really sweet of you both to invite me."

"Alarik thought it would be fun to chat about your shared interests."

"I'm sure it will be."

Still no tail on them. She was on her own. Jayne took a slow breath to calm her racing heart.

The ocean-side cabin was lit up when they pulled into the gravel drive. Yellow light poured from two front windows, and they'd put an interesting pale green bulb in a large lantern that hung near the door, spilling a watery, sea-tinged light onto the steps.

Deirdre opened the door and they walked into a room decorated in shades of blue and green. A long, wooden table boasted two flickering pillar candles and a steak dinner all laid out. But there were only two places. A note sat beside one of the salads. Deirdre picked it up, touched her mouth while she read silently, face paling.

"Are you okay?" Jayne asked.

"Alarik couldn't stay. Something came up at work. He said he wants us to enjoy the dinner and he'll meet you next time we all have a free night."

Jayne didn't know whether to be pleased that the strange man wasn't going to be here or more worried. "It's super nice that he went ahead and made us dinner."

Setting her purse down and taking Jayne's, too, Deirdre glanced toward the back bedroom. "I suppose we should sit then."

The dinner was awkward, to say the least. Deirdre kept looking out the bay windows at the far end of the room like she hoped her husband would pull up in a boat or something. The water was gorgeous, limned in moonlight and shifting with easy waves. The steak was hella good, so at least there was that. Deirdre visited the restroom far more times than was normal. Perhaps she was sick. But the whole time, tension simmered in the cabin. Jayne startled at every noise, thinking the place was about to blow up or that terrorists were about to blast their way inside. She was relieved when Dierdre asked about work as they put away the last of the dishes.

"When did you first come across the Book of Leinster?"

Jayne leaned on the kitchen counter and sipped at the red wine Deirdre had opened at the start of this weird evening. "I was in high school, I think." If Deirdre truly did have connections to the Kingdom, Jayne needed to become even more interesting, a possible convert to their cause and an asset for the organization. "I dreamed about the book, and when I saw pictures of it, I felt this…sensation of it being familiar to me even though I'd never seen it outside of a computer screen."

Deirdre's eyebrows lifted. "Really? That sounds…almost supernatural."

She sounded skeptical.

Jayne met Deirdre's gaze. "I have seen things that defy explanation. I know it sounds nuts, but I can't deny it. I think there is more out there than most think."

"More?"

Turning, Jayne set her elbows on the counter and took another sip of wine, the liquid puckering her tongue. "I don't know. Maybe the physicists' theories about alternate dimensions are more accurate than we'd like to believe." She downed the last of her wine.

"Does the Book of Leinster tie into your thoughts on these theories?"

"It does. I believe it has something hidden in it. Something otherworldly, for lack of a better term."

"Fascinating." Deirdre sighed and dumped the rest of her wine down the drain. "I suppose we should head back to Dublin now. Your friend will be waiting."

After quietly turning off the lights and blowing out the candles, Deirdre led Jayne out of the cabin and back to the car. "Alarik will definitely want to try this dinner again."

"I hope so. Especially if he wants to chat more about the possibility of the supernatural existing."

Deirdre exhaled, almost laughing and shaking her head as they drove down the moonlit road. "You two would most certainly get along."

"You don't believe in anything like that?"

"I have yet to experience it, so…"

"But your husband has?"

"Alarik? Oh yes. But I'd rather let him tell you, if you don't mind. I don't want to put words in his mouth, as they say."

Alarik had to be the tie to the Kingdom. A man who believed in magic. One who wanted to know about Jayne's interest in a book that turned out to be a necromantic text? All the puzzle pieces fit. So why had he bailed on them?

Deirdre dropped Jayne on the street, a block down from the flat. She didn't want Deirdre knowing exactly where she lived, even if it was protected by Ruger's fatherly and highly skilled eye.

What a strange evening.

Inside the flat, Jayne dialed Ruger first, debriefed him on the evening. "I didn't introduce her as my sister, only as Sofia. I said we'd been estranged. But Deirdre didn't seem to care. She was totally preoccupied."

"I understand. We'll take care of it. You convince Sofia that you are just fine and to get back on a plane. She's in too much danger if she stays here."

"I will."

"Good. No training tonight. I have things to attend to. I'll see you tomorrow."

Jayne, exhausted, dialed Sofia's number, but her sister didn't pick up. "Hey," Jayne said, leaving a voicemail, "I'm back from dinner. Want to come over for movies and wine? I'm really sorry about everything." She knew Sofia couldn't be allowed to stick around, but hopefully with one night of sister time, she'd agree to go back to the States. "Call me."

The phone never rang.

After an hour of flipping through shows, a shower, and another two glasses of red, Jayne began to worry. Sofia had been in such a rush to see her, and now she was going AWOL? It made no sense.

Unless Sofia was in trouble.

She called Ruger, but he didn't answer. She called the Baymel Hotel, but they didn't have anyone by the name Sofia Thorne. Jayne figured she must have gotten the name wrong, but without Sofia returning her calls...

A Tracking spell? Could she do that, with a person? She'd only ever tried with inanimate objects.

Jayne accessed the Torrent and threw out a Tracking spell. Nothing. It was as if Sofia had vanished off the Earth.

Great. Just great.

CHAPTER THIRTY-FIVE

Ruger portaled into a gray room where Amanda sat at a long table stacked with books, old and new. "Tell me your people added Sofia to Jayne's false background in case Deirdre or whoever is tied to her and the Kingdom does their homework?"

"Hello to you, too. Yes, it's done. Jayne has an estranged friend named Sofia who she spent a great deal of time with growing up." Amanda stood and pulled out a chair for him. "You look tired. How is Jayne doing?"

He had to look exactly how he felt if she was being more friend than boss again so soon. "She's incredibly worried about Sofia. There's been no word from her since she left Trinity."

"No clues on where she ended up?"

Sitting back in the chair, he linked his hands behind his stiff neck. He'd been up all night trying contact after contact, looking for Sofia and taking in any and all Kingdom chatter. "Nope. I have two officers looking, but they've come up empty-handed. I have a bad feeling about this."

"Tell me why, exactly. I have my ideas, but I want to hear yours." Amanda tapped a pen against one of the older-looking books. He realized they were all reproductions of the Book of Leinster.

"The chatter is strange. It mentioned the Head wanting two. That in and of itself is tough to decode, but you and I both know when the Head of the Kingdom gets involved, shit gets messy." The TCO knew next to nothing about the mysterious leader of the organization except that his or her presence in the chatter almost always preceded great violence.

"Do you have any idea what *two* they're speaking of?"

"No. Maybe they've identified another necromantic text?"

Amanda sighed, opened up the cover of a reproduction, then shut it again. "You were in Jayne's flat while she was at work, weren't you? Any more signs of the Rogue?"

"I was. There was a scent, but it was faint, just a leftover vestige from the night she met the Rogue. Thankfully. That's one good thing. Whoever it was seems to have moved on."

"As far as we know. There is so little research on Rogues and how their bodies and minds operate."

Ruger ran a hand over his beard. He needed a trim. He opened his mouth to ask about the texts, but another officer burst through the door.

"Officer Thorne's sister was just spotted at Logan Airport, coming through Customs. It seems she came back to the US after all."

Amanda smiled grimly as the other officer left the room. "Well, that's a relief. And now Jayne can focus. Ruger, go home. Take a nap." Her hand clamped onto his arm, her fingers hot. "I mean it. You can't help Jayne when you're operating on emotions and exhaustion."

He patted her hand and nodded. "Fine. But they want her.

I'm firmly convinced Deirdre's husband, Alarik, is the tie to the Kingdom. You read the brief on their conversation, right?"

"I did. And I agree. They're trying to lure her in. They have no idea what they're dealing with. Our Jayne has been well trained, and she has sound instincts. She's managed all of this beautifully. Let her do her job."

Ruger turned to leave, his skin feeling itchy and his steps uneven, but Amanda stopped him.

"Is the dead Master still speaking to Jayne?" she asked.

"Not that I know of. Not since that first day. She was rattled enough I think she'd tell me."

"I agree. She will. I'm not a gambler, but I'd bet on that. She's strong, and she's capable. You don't need to worry."

Squeezing his eyes shut for a moment, Ruger steeled himself against losing another mentee. No way this was going to work out with Jayne alive and well.

And he was the reason she was here, tangled in this mess.

"Did you ever think, in a million years, she would be a Master?"

Amanda leaned back in her chair, a small smile on her face.

"Honestly? I didn't dare hope...but I suspected. When that thunderclap resounded the first time she touched the grimoire in the Vanderbilt vault, I felt it all the way to my bones, and I knew she was something very special. It was clear she had powerful magic, but the way she's grasped your training, growing stronger by the moment...yes, the thought crossed my mind."

The smile fled, and she leaned forward, elbows on the table. "Which is why it's even more vital now than ever that you protect her. She's capable of things we can't even imagine. But she's young, she's impulsive, and she's much too stubborn for her own good. Her sister is a loose end we can't afford. This Cillian boy, too. Keep her focused on her mission and keep her safe.

Jayne's power will take care of the rest. I'm sure of it."

"You're the boss," Ruger said, stepping back through the portal.

CHAPTER THIRTY-SIX

In the faculty break room, Jayne polished off the last of her egg salad sandwich and tossed her lunch bag into her locker, errant thoughts of Cillian's laugh and the way he kicked a bag sparking through her mind. What would it feel like to have his arms around her, to feel his whisper brush across her ear? Her pulse ratcheted up a notch, and she rolled her eyes at herself. She'd seen or heard nothing from him since their coffee escapade, and she somehow doubted she would. She was surprised by how sad that made her.

Across from the long countertop, Deirdre put a bag of popcorn in the microwave.

"Hey, thanks again for dinner."

"It was fun." Deirdre's fingers paused over the microwave buttons. "How is your friend? Sofia?"

"Good. We had a nice catch-up, and she's gone back to the States." This was at least partly true. Ruger had told her that Sofia had returned home. She wished Sofia had left a goodbye message, but at least she would be safely away from the mess Jayne was getting into here in Ireland. She could fix things with her sister when this mission was finished. She hoped.

Change the subject.

"You sure you'll have time to eat that?" Jayne asked, pointing to the microwave. Their break was almost over.

"I think so. I can do some damage to a bag of popcorn. I'll see you up there."

Deirdre's hair was knotted at the top of her head, and the strands drifting down onto her neck stuck to her skin. Why was she sweating? The temperature in the library was pleasantly cool and kept consistently so to protect the materials. Maybe Deirdre had simply been up and down the hallways more than Jayne had realized. Those grad students could really run the staff ragged with their research requests.

Or maybe Rogues were a sweaty bunch.

Jayne shook her head. If she was truly a Master, wouldn't she be able to tell if a Rogue was standing right in front of her? Maybe the extra magic would give her X-ray vision? As far as being conferred special powers, being a Master was somewhat underwhelming.

Still, she couldn't help but wonder. What would Deirdre try to do to Jayne if she were a Rogue?

The hallway's dim light beyond the break room shone down on the last of the lockers and the door to the stairs.

Jayne popped into the restroom to wash her hands, as Rosalind and common courtesy demanded every other second, then she headed up to the reading room and research area.

At the red registration desk, a dark-eyed, middle-aged man wearing a starched, striped button-down was filling out a call slip. He had a full head of silver hair, much more than normal for a man his age, and Jayne couldn't help but notice he was quite attractive.

Rosalind took the slip from the man and walked into the staff area where Jayne met her.

"Is Deirdre still downstairs?"

"Scarfing popcorn, the lucky duck. I can help, if you like."

"Brilliant. This gentleman is a professor from the Beinecke at Yale," Rosalind whispered as the man began strolling around the reading room, "and he's requested to see the Book of Leinster. You'd be the perfect one to answer his questions. I'm supposed to be at the dentist in a half hour. I completely forgot about my appointment and I must leave now." She turned, smiling. "Ah. Speak of the devil."

Deirdre, still looking flushed, entered the staff area behind the desk and set her purse on a shelf. "Did you need me?"

"As a matter of fact, yes," Rosalind said. "I have to leave for an appointment. That man there, Dr. Albon of the Beinecke, has requested the Book of Leinster for his research into prose patterns in medieval Irish literature. Can you and Jayne help him?"

Deirdre took the call slip from Rosalind. "Of course. Jayne, I'll get the book ready, if you want to grab your notes?"

The gal was sweating up a storm.

"You're sure you're feeling okay, Deirdre?" Jayne asked. "I can handle this myself if you need a break."

"I'm fine. Thanks." Deirdre gave Jayne and Rosalind a quick smile, then hurried toward the elevator that led to the vault, presumably to get the book.

Two wrinkles formed between Rosalind's light eyes, but she shrugged, shaking off Deirdre's strange behavior. "See you before closing," she said to Jayne before scurrying toward the front door with her bright pink purse over her shoulder.

As she was leaving, Gerard said something to make her laugh.

The visiting Professor Albon glanced their way, but quickly

went back to perusing the shelves at the far end of the room. A grin slid over his thin lips, and Jayne's stomach turned, her creep meter going off. Not attractive at all, she amended.

With Rosalind and Deirdre suddenly gone, Jayne took the spot at the red desk. She didn't need notes to talk about the Book of Leinster, as Deirdre had suggested. Every fact about the manuscript was burned into Jayne's brain after so many years of study. She sat at Rosalind's computer, feeling jumpy. It wouldn't hurt to double-check this Professor Albon's registration, would it? She couldn't help him until they had the book in hand anyway. And no one was waiting on anything at the moment.

She pulled up the screen on the computer. All the blanks were completed correctly. Yale. Research project started in July of last year. He even had four references. Most people didn't bother to fill in that section so thoroughly.

Hmm.

The first reference was to a professor at UCLA. Why not another Yale pal?

Jayne opened a tab for the internet and searched the reference's name, a Barbara Tillington. Nothing about UCLA appeared in the search results. She searched again, this time including the university's name and the word *faculty*. UCLA's staff page came up, and she clicked on it. No Barbara in Literature. None in Humanities at all. She ran through the graduate studies program list as well as their library staff. Nothing.

Deirdre emerged from the elevator with a rolling cart, the Book of Leinster in a gray box, and a foam cradle. She didn't look at Jayne as she passed by.

"Hey, Deirdre."

She stopped, turned, a sheen of perspiration over her wide-set cheeks. "Yes?"

"Can I ask you something?"

Deirdre's face pinched. "I'm sure it can wait, Jayne." She jerked her head toward Albon.

"I'm not sure it can, actually." Jayne waved her over. "See this?" She pointed to the man's references on the registration page. "There is no Barbara Tillington at UCLA. I just checked."

Deirdre wiped her forehead with her sleeve and laughed weakly. "Really? Did you check his second reference? Maybe Tillington recently transferred."

"I will check the second one. Hold on."

"I'll go ahead and get him set up with the book. You check and wave at me when you have an answer, all right?"

"Maybe you should wait." Jayne began her search for the second reference, but Deirdre was already rolling the cart across the room. Jayne listened to them as she typed.

"Dr. Albon, I'm Deirdre. Nice to meet you…"

They began to chat about the book as Deirdre set the foam cradle on the table. As the search results loaded at a sloth's pace, Jayne watched Deirdre carefully. With smooth and slow movement, the woman extricated the ancient tome from its box and arranged it properly in the cradle, adding a book snake to carefully weigh down the page the professor wanted to view. Everything she was supposed to do.

An odd scent reached Jayne's nose. Her hands hovered over the keyboard. It almost smelled like something was on—

The fire alarm wailed.

Jayne jumped, heart climbing her throat.

Gerard—face pale and tidy hair askew—ran toward Jayne as the sound blared through the room. "You know the Health and Safety protocol for a fire?"

Jayne stood. "I do."

"Then get to it!" He sped past her toward the stacks beside the desk.

Sirens began to scream outside the building.

Deirdre was gone.

Jayne leaned over the desk, looking side to side, her pulse thrumming against her wrists. Where was she?

Professor Albon lifted the Book of Leinster, shut it, and held it against his chest.

"No! Put it down and go!" Jayne shouted at him. He was trying to save the precious book, but that was definitely not allowed. "Out that exit. Leave the book. I'll deal with it. We have protocol for this. Take that door behind you. Now!"

Either he couldn't hear her over the alarm, or he didn't want to listen. Book in hand, he turned and shoved his way out the emergency exit and into the bright sunlight.

Behind her, Jayne realized Deirdre was shouting down the hallway, toward the stairs.

A hazy smoke filled the room. Burned popcorn. That was the smell. Jayne knew what she was supposed to do in the event of a fire. She'd read her manual. But she wasn't about to let that shady Albon leave her library with that book in his hands.

Yes, a voice said in her mind. *Follow my grimoire. It is ours. Not his.*

Jayne didn't have time to freak out about hearing Queen Medb again. Instead, she sprinted toward the emergency exit.

Gerard flew out of the staff area, two black boxes in his arms. "Jayne! What are you doing?"

Ignoring him, she pushed the door's bar and fell out of the door into the grass walkway behind the library.

Albon was there, eyes closed, hands outstretched, the book at his feet.

The scent of woodsmoke and rose petals and the sea swirled around Jayne's head, and she gripped the grass, feeling like the world might suddenly disappear.

He was an Adept.

Albon took no notice of Jayne just behind him. He drew a triangle shape in the air with both hands. The scent of magic overcame even the smell of Deirdre's burning popcorn.

Emergency vehicles zipped past to the front of the building. The noise was deafening.

Before she could fully process what was happening, a green-blue light filled Albon's triangle. He grabbed the book and leaped inside, disappearing completely.

Travel through the portal, Medb whispered into Jayne's mind. *He must not have our grimoire.*

Her mind spinning, Jayne dove through the portal after him.

Jayne felt as though she'd been strapped into the seat of a rocket and launched with no countdown. The world ripped past in a blur. Long strips of gray city streets. Swaths of green that might have been forests and fields. A stretch of smeared lights like a thousand highways at night.

Her lungs struggled to suck in oxygen, but they couldn't inflate against the incredible pressure of the speed. The scent of magic oozed from her pores, and instinctively she knew her inborn affinity for the Torrent's power was the only thing keeping her alive.

What was this place?

What was happening? This was nothing like the simple zip of Ruger's portal. This was something far larger, more powerful, a dose of magic unlike anything Jayne had experienced. Her body was pressed hard from all sides, and she couldn't see Albon anywhere. He'd gone through, so he had to be experiencing this same horror. Why on earth would he cast a spell that did this?

Then, as suddenly as the experience had started, it stopped.

Jayne's body rolled onto a firm surface, and she opened her eyes to see Albon standing above her.

His smile made her shudder. He almost looked as though he had expected her to follow him. "What a lovely surprise. You are an Adept, a powerful one, too." Lifting his hands and shutting his eyes, he drew a spell from the Torrent and cast it toward her.

Stomach roiling from the vicious portal experience, Jayne reached for the magic of the Torrent, blindly waved around for a Blocking spell, then cast it.

The last thing she saw was a wave of misty white before she fell into a deep sleep.

CHAPTER THIRTY-SEVEN

Ruger pinched the bridge of his nose. "Play them again, Gerard."

The TCO's undercover officer had been placed at Trinity years ago, when Ruger first began watching the Early Printed Books and Special Collections Department. He'd successfully placed a new, spelled bug on Jayne's assigned phone after the smart, rebellious woman had found and removed the earlier version. At first, Ruger had been secretly proud of Jayne's defiance. It was that sort of spark that could keep an officer alive. But when Sofia had shown up out of the blue, then taken off again, making her motivations even more murky, Ruger knew he had to keep a very close watch on Jayne's interactions. The device sent all messages to Gerard, and Ruger decided what to return to Jayne's phone. The bug served as a holding cell, so to speak, for Jayne's voicemail.

"Of course, sir," the older man said with his crisp British accent as he pressed the button on the recording device.

Sofia's voice echoed off the gray walls of the interrogation room that Ruger had decided to use for this particular branch off his main mission. He didn't want Amanda knowing anything until he'd had time to digest it and decide what to do. Gerard was Ruger's officer, and not even Amanda knew the work the older man had accomplished for Ruger over the years.

"...sorry for scaring you, Jayne, but you don't understand. I hate to say this over the phone." The woman stammered. "You, I..." She blew out a breath. "Our parents weren't who you think they were. The world isn't what you think it is. Just call me. I can't tell you over a damn voicemail."

And then Gerard started the second message.

"Jayne. I had to leave just in case they saw me and recognized me. The woman you went to dinner with, she wore a pin. Did you notice it?"

Gerard and Ruger exchanged glances. Ruger had long suspected the Kingdom had a visual clue for those involved. Never anything brazen, but something subtle. A colored scarf or tie. Buttons in certain shapes. Earrings or rings that echoed some similar design. Something subtle to identify them to other Kingdom members. But they'd never found a consistent trend in the few Kingdom operatives they'd encountered. Many of the bodies were destroyed before he could get a good look.

"It showed the shape of a hand, the mark of a fingerprint most likely, to echo the powers they hope to gain. This isn't making sense. I need to see you. Now. Listen, I'm not crazy. There is an underground organization, Jayne. And they are killers. Murderers. I...I want to tell you everything. You need to know. You need to get away from that woman. I shouldn't have left you with her, but I wasn't sure. I've been wrong so many times over the years. I began to think you were right about me being paranoid. But Jayne, our parents weren't who you think they were. They got into something, something terrible. They were killed, Jayne. Murdered." Her voice hitched. "This sounds insane, but I'm telling you. Magic is real."

The woman was spewing everything she knew of the Kingdom and her parents' involvement and subsequent murder. Her information made little sense, tangled as it was, but one thing was clear.

Ruger crossed his arms. "Jayne and Sofia's parents were members of the Kingdom."

Eyes serious, Gerard stood and tucked the device in his coat pocket. "And were killed by them as well. Do you think the organization found Sofia?"

"After she left Boston, she disappeared entirely. We haven't found a single clue. Not many can pull that off. So yes, I do." Ruger winced, thinking of telling Jayne this news. Sure, Sofia might still be alive, but it was doubtful. "Thanks, Gerard."

Gerard gave him a nod and slipped out the door, leaving Ruger to his thoughts.

If Jayne heard Sofia's messages now, she'd take off to find her sister immediately. There wasn't a chance Jayne would be able to move forward with her mission to infiltrate the Kingdom and discover their steps with regard to terrorism and the necromantic texts if she knew this information. He didn't blame her, either. He was shocked by the news. Jayne would be rocked to the core.

No, he had to keep these messages away from her for the time being. The TCO already had some of their best officers searching for Sofia. That had to be enough for now.

CHAPTER THIRTY-EIGHT

Jayne woke up in shackles. Pain swamped her. Her heart slammed into her ribs, and her mind felt scrambled. Was she a hostage? What was happening? *Think!* She'd been through capture training with her fellow recruits. *What do you do, Jayne?* Finally, she locked onto step one.

Breathe.

And so she did.

In and out.

It wasn't easy for three reasons. First, her lungs felt very, very sleepy. Like they'd rather take a sick day on the whole processing oxygen thing. Also, she was scared more than she'd ever been. So frightened, in fact, that her body locked up for a few seconds and she couldn't make herself move at all. Which was fine with her lungs, but not so much for the rest of her that did seem to want to live. Lastly, red splotches on her pulse points burned like she'd fought with a curling iron and lost. She knew exactly why her skin had been scorched.

Portaling.

And not just your average portal, the stable, preprogrammed type that remained active in one place for a particular person or persons, like the one Ruger used to enter her flat and so forth. No, she had jumped into Albon's triangle and ended up as an unwitting stowaway in his incredibly powerful, frighteningly dangerous portal to…wherever this was.

Most Adepts who tried portaling too early, before they'd learned the subtleties of the Torrent and focusing the mind— well, they ended up like the man Jayne and Sofia had seen on the TV in Central Park.

Burned to cinders.

During training, they had only touched on Jayne creating her own portals because of the dangers, the instability, the possibility of setting oneself ablaze. She quite literally knew one emergency portal protocol. Essentially a 911 call to the Torrent universe. It was designed to get her out of a tight spot if she was about to die. That was it. It wouldn't work any other time.

Ruger drilled the dangers into her before they'd traveled via magic the last time. If a portal wasn't prepared properly, or if it was altered in some way, things could go awry. If an Adept wasn't thoroughly prepped, and they attempted the feat unsuccessfully, they either burned or they ended up far from the spot they wanted to be. Instead of a nice hotel in Hong Kong, they'd land in Siberia and freeze to death before they had time to cast another spell.

And those were the two best-case scenarios.

Don't think about that, she told herself.

And then she remembered Medb speaking into her mind, persuading her to go after the professor who most likely wasn't really a professor. Another breath. Okay. Maybe Medb would be of some help here. Wherever here was.

Are you there? she asked tentatively. Nothing.

Crap.

A magical mystery voice to help her out of a bind was a bit much to ask, yes, but still. What was the point of all this power if it wasn't useful?

Jayne turned back to her training. She needed to take stock of her environment, look for possible exits, and note threats, items that could be used as weapons, and supplies if she could indeed escape. Because if not, it was time to enact Emergency Protocol No. 856. Even if it burned her alive.

But until she caught her breath, her very own version of dis-apparating would have to wait.

She felt something tugging on her arm and looked down at the inside of her elbow. A cotton ball, held down with tape. Either they'd taken her blood, or they'd drugged her. Or both. The bastards. Being drugged would explain her lungs' apathetic attitude.

Looking around, she realized the room she was in was actually nice. Someone had set her up in a simple bed with soft, cool sheets. Two plain oil lamps glowed on top of minimal-ist side tables that looked like sanded tree trunks. The cleanly swept floor showed reclaimed wood's dents and uneven texture. Shelves, neatly stacked with books of all types, lined the walls.

The shackles weren't so great, though. The metal was heavy on her wrists and ankles and made it impossible to change her position much. Her neck was stiff, probably from all that portal blurry weirdness.

Other than the books and the lamps, the room was empty. She didn't even see her shoes anywhere. Wiggling her toes, she felt her own socks on her feet, soft and familiar. Tightness filled her sleepy chest, and she forced herself to breathe again. Slowly. In. Out. In. Out. Panic was the enemy at this moment.

It would have been great if she could ascertain how much time had passed. Something about not knowing made her dizzy. The real question was, should she lie here and wait to see what opportunities popped up, or shout in hopes it would start a chain of events that might spark some chance of escape? If she had only been out an hour or two, waiting would be best. If she called out, struggled, or tried to be clever, Albon might just decide to kill her. An hour or two wouldn't make or break the mission, she hoped. But what if she'd been unconscious for days on end? It was unlikely. Her body would've insisted on peeing, right? And her pants felt dry. It was gross to think about, but this was an emergency. Was she suffering brain damage from the knockout and the drug they must have given her? Were these dumb questions to ask? Yeah, her mind was definitely a little foggy.

Use your magic, and your training, Jayne. She certainly wasn't the same person she'd been in Nashville. She was an officer now, trained in mind, body, and spirit. The old Jayne would've freaked out beyond all reason already.

Breathing slowly, she envisioned the Torrent—grass-green stars and power flowing like a cool river around her fingers. But heat suddenly seared her wrists under the shackles, and the scent of hot flesh touched the air. She shoved herself out of the Torrent and hastily brought herself back to her prison, and just in time, too.

The door opened and Albon walked in. He looked nothing like the distinguished professor who'd come calling at the old library. He wore a chunky wool sweater that looked like it had been knitted by some medieval auntie. No dye. No modern style. His trousers were nubbly-textured, hemp maybe, she thought, and a natural pale gray. His sharp eyes flicked to her, and he ran a hand over his freshly shaved face.

"And how are we this morning?" He came close, and with every step, Jayne had to work harder and harder to keep her body from locking up in fear. It really didn't help that he held a syringe in one hand. His fingers rested on the bed, right beside her arm.

Then she knew. He had a wiry build like the man she'd seen walking away from Deirdre at Trinity. And Deirdre helped him with the book. This wasn't Professor Albon. It was Alarik, Deirdre's husband. But she didn't think she should say a thing about that quite yet.

Well, Ruger, you were right. Deirdre was the conduit to the Kingdom.

"I need to know some things about you, Adept," Albon/Alarik said. "Before we can decide where we go from here."

Pretending not to know what an Adept was wouldn't get her into the Kingdom any faster. If he believed she knew the basics of magic, he might move more quickly into recruiting her.

"What things?" she asked, her voice scratchy. "Like deciding whether or not to kill me?" *I'd like to see you try. Get me out of these shackles and let's go a few rounds.* She took brief pleasure in imagining the ass kicking Cillian, Sofia, and she could give him, if one took magic out of the mix.

The ghost of a smile crossed his lips. "We do not want to kill you. We want to…talk."

Ruger's pleased face floated through her mind. He would be thrilled to know she was inside one of the Kingdom's hidey holes. This was the opportunity the TCO had been looking for and exactly why they'd sent her to Dublin.

Now she had to convince this man that she was worthy of his cause, but she must do it in a way that didn't seem suspicious. If she immediately fangirled all over him and his secret organization, her mission would be dead in the water. Maybe she could just stick with vague and let him fill in the blanks and show her where to go with the convo.

"Well, that's good to hear. Want to let me loose, then? These hurt."

His eyebrow lifted a fraction. "Soon. You, my dear, are very powerful. Do you know much about your abilities?"

"I know that I can sometimes…accomplish tasks in ways others can't."

He nodded. "I suppose you are angry with me. For taking the book. The book that has always interested you."

She blinked at his quick change of direction. This was so much more difficult than training. He was right here. The bad guy. A man who could kill her right now if he chose to do so. Whom she could kill herself, were she not chained and shackled. The thought made her stomach turn.

"Not angry. Just…confused." She forced herself to breathe and let him talk. And like every villain in every book she'd ever read, he did.

"Do you know why I stole the Book of Leinster?"

"No."

His sweater made a soft noise as he crossed his arms, and she saw the syringe clasped in his fingers. "So you simply followed me into a portal because you wanted to protect a valuable piece of history?"

"Partly. I felt the magic in it when Deirdre brought it out. I couldn't just let it walk away." She wouldn't tell him she had already guessed he planned the fire and that Deirdre was in on this with him.

"Why do you think I stole it?"

"You already asked me that."

"Answer the question truthfully this time." He adjusted his hold on the syringe.

"Because you can also feel its magic, and you want the power you think the book can give you."

He smiled, that creepy, thin-lipped smile, and she shuddered inside. How could Deirdre have married this guy?

As if he'd read her mind, the smile widened. "Deirdre mentioned your interest in the book, the draw it has on you. Why do I want its power, do you think?"

"How should I know? You have a nice place here, hidden away with your eco-smart self. Such spots cost money. Maybe you need more, and the book will get it for you?"

"Perhaps. Why are you, an American, working at Trinity College? Why would they hire you?"

"Because that's what I do. Books. Manuscripts. And the Book of Leinster is my specialty. It is a dream job, being able to work there. Well, it was until you kidnapped me."

"I did no such thing. You jumped into my portal without permission."

If she appeared too eager to listen to him, to be agreeable, he would notice. Jayne had to keep this realistic, believable. And so she brought the salt. Nothing was more natural to humans than a nice blend of sarcasm and attitude. "Do people usually ask before they speed across the Earth with you? My bad. I forgot to pick up my *Miss Manners Covers Magical Thieves* manual."

His eyes flashed. She was annoying him. Good.

"I did not kidnap you." His voice was too quiet.

"No, but you aren't exactly calling up an Uber to get me back home." Jayne clanked her shackles.

His eyes grew dreamy, like he enjoyed the sound of her imprisonment. "If the world could be exactly how you wish it to be, what would that look like?"

Jayne's pulse picked up the pace. The drug they used on her was waning in power, at last.

"The heck kind of question is that?"

"As an Adept, don't you wish you could use your magic openly and embrace the real you?"

A snarky comment rose to Jayne's lips, but she held it back. She'd shown enough resistance for the time being.

"I don't even know what being an Adept truly means, but as for power? Of course I do." She stared at the ceiling, wishing this room smelled like anything. It didn't have a smell at all and therefore brought to mind a clinical kind of clean, which made Jayne focus too much on that horrible syringe.

Alarik breathed out slowly, like he was trying to remain patient with her. "That is what I want from the book."

"How can a book help us do that? Regular humans would go bananas if we showed them what we can do. We'd be locked up in labs our whole lives. ET comes to mind."

Alarik's glance flicked to the door and back.

Jayne continued. "Not that this path I'm currently on is turning out any different." She wiggled her shackles for the second time.

"You've said it just right. The path you're currently on is a prison of its own. And I'm not just talking about being restrained here and now. I'm talking about your entire life. You can't use spells that might help you preserve and learn from history at the library. You must always look over your shoulder when you access the magic."

"You mean the Torrent."

"I do. Who taught you what you are and how to use magic?"

Ruger had prepped her with a backstory. She'd been sure to casually mention the fake brother, Lane, who was really Ruger, to Deirdre, saying she hadn't spoken to him in a long while.

"My brother. He's like me. He can do things, too."

"Your brother, Lane Thomas?"

Deirdre, dutiful as ever, had told him everything. But did

Alarik know the rest of the fake story? The part about Ruger aka Lane being on the lam after a breaking and entering?

"I did some digging," Alarik continued. "Lane is quite the troublemaker, isn't he?"

Bless you, TCO, for your impeccably backstopped identities. She nodded. "Yep. That's him. Look, if you just let me go, I'll forget about your precious book and all the really illegal drugging and chaining up you did to me here. It'll be our little secret, hmm?"

"What if you and your brother could live in a world where you aren't the ones looking over your shoulder? You could be benevolent leaders in this world. Lane could stop running and live."

Jayne did her best to act super guilty and worried about her fake brother. It wasn't tough. This whole situation had her sweating already. "You could do that?"

"With your help."

"What would I have to do? I have a good job. I don't want to lose all that I've worked for."

"Even for Lane?"

She pretended to think about this. "I would give it all up if you could promise he'll be safe, and not forced into illegal work anymore. But I'll believe that when I see it."

"I can take care of everything if you agree to hear us out, to listen to our arguments."

"Our arguments?"

"With the power of magicians like you and the plan we have developed here, we could change the world. Jayne, have you ever heard of a group called the Kingdom?"

She forced herself not to grin like a fool. *Bingo.*

CHAPTER THIRTY-NINE

If Jayne could throw her hands in the air and cheer, she would have. Creepy Alarik was truly trying to get her to join the Kool-Aid-drinking group of maniacs. Success!

Instead, she just raised a brow. "Sounds dramatic," she murmured.

Alarik began pacing, tapping that awful syringe against his pant leg. "The Kingdom's goal is to heal the Earth and humankind. To rid us all of the corruption that technology has bred into our peoples and lands."

A dangerous, arrogant laugh echoed through Jayne's mind—Medb. *And to enslave the world through telepathy,* the ancient queen said. Jayne sucked a breath, the sound of Medb in her mind jarring.

Where have you been? Get me out of this!

Nothing.

Alarik didn't notice Jayne's reaction. He was obviously too caught up in his cause. "We want to go back to a time when magic-workers lived openly, lived free. When we helped our fellow creatures and lived in sync with the seasons and the Earth. The Earth hums with magic. Surely as an Adept you can feel it. The core of our planet and the magnetic fields pour energy into the Torrent. Long, long ago, our ancestors were in constant contact with that energy, with the Torrent."

"They didn't have to concentrate to see it, to be there?" Jayne's mind was in two places. Would Medb always be popping in to comment? *How would they use telepathy?* she tried to ask Medb silently. But there was no answer. Only Alarik's ongoing evil seminar.

"No, they didn't have to focus as we do, because the Torrent lived all around them." Alarik sounded wistful. "It flowed through the tree limbs and in the rivers. It lit up sky and sea. Then, it wasn't unusual for an Adept to become a Master, and they lived far, far longer than our kind do today, because the Earth was as it should be. Pure. Simple. Clean. Their synergy with nature was perfection."

"How does technology disrupt something so powerful as the Earth's energy?"

"Wonderful question, Jayne. Everything throws waves through the air. Radio. TV. Phones. Wi-Fi. The list goes on and on. These frequencies jar the Torrent's flow and cause it to separate itself into its own dimension."

Remember, Master, not to trust this magician. Remember. Remember.

Jayne shook her head to clear it of Medb's warning. Clearly their connection was one-way, only allowing Jayne to answer when Medb was open to it. She had to listen to Alarik and respond appropriately.

"That actually makes a lot of sense." Her statement wasn't a lie. It did make sense.

Alarik turned toward the door. "Teresa. Maximus."

A woman with narrow eyes and a man who looked like he'd just stepped out of an episode of *Vikings* walked into the room. Teresa was a tidy brunette, and Maximus had a red beard like a pillager of old. They both wore the same simple clothing as Alarik.

Smiling shyly, Teresa began unlocking Jayne's shackles. She tucked a piece of dark hair behind her ear as she worked. Her fingers were calloused and scarred, as if she'd been doing a great deal of hard labor.

Maximus crossed the room and pushed the bookshelves, and to Jayne's surprise, they slid back to reveal a tub and a sink. Both were made of stone, with what looked like copper and polished wood pipe and handles. Maximus raised a lever above the tub, and steaming water poured into the black-and-white stone basin.

"My friends will give you whatever you require to clean up and be comfortable until our next conversation," Alarik said.

Jayne sat up and rubbed her wrists, watching Alarik closely. She was too nervous that this was a trick to be excited about a nice bath. "Do you promise to refrain from drugging me anymore? I can already guess I'm not allowed to leave."

"No, you're right. We can't allow you to go yet, but we won't need to use the medications if you can behave in a reasonable manner."

"I don't think I have behaved otherwise. If you'll recall, you spelled me before I had a chance to do much of anything."

"You tried to cast a spell."

"I was defending myself."

Alarik lowered his gaze on her while Maximus checked the bath's temperature with a finger and turned off the water.

"Fine," Jayne said, standing. "I promise I won't do any more magic. But you can't keep me here forever."

"We won't," Teresa said. "Just give us one week."

"Um, people might notice if I don't show up for work tomorrow."

Teresa smiled. "No one will notice. Believe me."

Jayne studied the woman's body language. She was angled toward Alarik, with her arms loose. She wasn't afraid of him. She trusted him.

"We can explain ourselves to you, and hopefully, gain another—" Maximus was interrupted by Alarik.

"That's enough information for now, friends." Alarik waved the two helpers out of the room, then followed them. Before he shut the door, he said, "Just soak and think. I will be back in an hour."

"Seriously, I can't be here for a week. My employers *will* notice. My co-workers, too. You'll have trouble on your hands for sure. Trouble for you and your group."

"They won't know you've been gone a week. We are surrounded by a Time Catch spell. Time moves for us here, but it is in another dimension."

So that was the reason the portal had been such a nightmare.

"A branch off the Torrent, if you will," he said. "When you return, it will be as if you were only gone for about ten minutes. Maybe a minute or two more. It's not exact, this magic. Not yet."

Jayne felt her mouth hanging open but couldn't seem to get it to close even though she knew she looked like an idiot. They could pause time?

"You have a lot to learn about the magic inside you, Jayne Thomas. And we are more than willing to help you along your journey." And with that cryptic message, Alarik shut and locked the door.

Jayne rubbed her wrists, relieved to be rid of the shackles. Did Ruger and Amanda know about Time Catches? If not, she'd be earning her keep informing them about this amazing magical setup.

The bath was nice, though Jayne did her best not to enjoy it. She wished she were the kind of person who could say *I'd rather have my enemy hit me in the face than coddle me like this because I know it's just part of your game!* but she just wasn't. The hot water, scented with some kind of floral salts, relaxed her muscles and soothed her mind. She knew this was their first step at brainwashing her into being all in for the Kingdom, but she couldn't get herself to care at the moment. She should have asked if there was pie involved in this psychological warfare.

A funny question shadowed her thoughts. What happened if they killed her here, inside a Time Catch? What happened to her body? Would she just be gone in the other timeline? Would her corpse appear at some point? Ruger had said you could get lost in the Torrent. Could you be kidnapped and kept inside it, too?

She held up her wrinkled fingers and shuddered.

Well, that ended the nice bath.

The towel Maximus had left beside the sink was a simple length of linen. It wasn't very cozy, but serviceable. She dried off and donned the little cult outfit her captors had left folded by the bed. There was a wide-toothed wooden comb on the night table, and Jayne paced while she untangled her wet hair.

What to do now...

In the original plan, Jayne was to infiltrate the Kingdom and/or get Deirdre on the TCO's side. By jumping through that portal, Jayne had set herself firmly on the path to infiltration.

She rubbed her wrists, remembering the sharp burning sensation. For now, she would keep her word and not try to escape using magic. She would pretend Alarik had won her over, little by little. She would become a Kingdom member. She had no access to Deirdre here, no access to anyone outside of those already in this weird pocket of the Torrent. No allies or people who might be coerced into becoming allies.

She was on her own.

Eventually, they had to let her out, right? If she played the good Kingdom girl, they would release her to play a part in their plan. Hopefully. Or would they expect her to live here for some bizarre reason? Did Maximus and Teresa live here in this Matrix-ish otherworld? Should Jayne try to wake them up, so to speak? Oh.

A seriously creepy idea crossed her mind.

What if Teresa and Maximus weren't even real people? What if they were constructs of this place, made of magic?

Another shudder broke over Jayne's body. She grabbed a wool blanket from the bed and wrapped herself up tightly. Leaving now would be good. She was done with this shit show.

She could practically hear Ruger growling in her ear. *Work it out, Officer Thorne.*

Her mind shuffled through all the research she'd done on Medb and the Book of Leinster. There must be something… She had a connection to a powerful Master who called *her* a Master. If she couldn't talk with her directly in her thoughts, maybe Jayne could access Medb through the Torrent.

Jayne tried to conjure up the river of stars, but it felt wrong, somehow, warped. The flow of the Torrent wouldn't open itself to her. It was as if Alarik had placed some sort of shield on her magic.

Great. Another thing to figure out.

CHAPTER FORTY

It could have been a few minutes, or a few hours, before the door opened again and Teresa and Maximus came back in.

They didn't seem surprised to see Jayne curled on the bed, shivering. They helped her sit up and pushed a cup of hot tea into her hands. She'd never felt so cold.

"Poor thing. It'll be okay," Teresa murmured over and over while Maximus draped Jayne in a magically heated blanket. "Going through a Time Catch portal without preparation is hard on the body. Makes you feel like you have a fever."

Jayne was glad that's all they thought was wrong.

Finally, the chill slid away from her body and she began to feel like herself again. Mentally shaking herself off, she sat at a table they'd brought in and ate a plate of roasted chicken and some sautéed greens.

"I'm going to let Alarik know Jayne is fine," Maximus whispered to Teresa, closing the door behind them.

Good. Time for a little girl talk. Jayne set down her fork.

"Teresa, I don't want to sound rude, but…"

"Go ahead." Teresa's smile looked real enough. Then again, humoring the condemned was a smart move.

"What is your position here? How did you end up in this… place?"

"It's a long story, but I can sum it up. I never felt like I belonged. I was an orphan at ten, then I had a foster family that was kind but clueless on what to do with me when I began showing odd behavior. They didn't have magic. Knew nothing about it, of course. I actually ended up homeless after losing a string of jobs. Albon found me at an intersection, begging for money. He showed me what I could do and how special I was. And I don't stay here. No one can stay here for long. It begins to wear on you, being in this dimension. I go back to my family in Wisconsin."

She was using Alarik's false name. Interesting.

"Do they know what you do on your *business* trips?" Jayne did her best to grin conspiratorially even though the whole thing was super weird.

"No. I will share everything with them when the time is right. Today, they need to remain ignorant so our plan can go forward."

"What is the Kingdom's plan?"

"I can't tell you that yet." She smiled as Maximus returned and took her spot as Jayne's babysitter.

"Teresa, Albon wants you."

"Of course." She waved goodbye and scurried out of the room. Maximus took her seat.

"I really am fine now. You don't have to stay with me if you have work to do," Jayne said. To demonstrate she had her sea legs back under her, she stood and pulled off the wool blanket. "That's a cool trick, heating it up like that. Thanks."

"It's no bother, Jayne." Maximus's voice was slightly accented. He might've been from Scotland, but she had no idea what region. "This is our job when we're here. And hopefully, you'll come to believe in our vision for the future and you'll have the chance to pay back the kindness."

Yeah, well it wasn't kindness to hold someone prisoner. But Jayne knew it would be counterproductive to mention that.

"Maybe. Can I ask you something?"

"I wish, but Albon said we shouldn't tell you much just yet." He ran a hand through his bronze hair. "If you're all right, I'll go now and let you have a short sleep before the meeting with our leaders."

"I didn't know there was going to be a meeting."

"Aye. With Albon and the other elders. They're the strongest Adepts I've ever met. I hope they show you some of their skills. I remember my first day with them. I was shocked, let me tell you." His eyes danced as he let out a laugh.

The corner of Jayne's mouth lifted. It was going to be tough to remain stoic and TCO officer-like with Maximus. He was the kind of person who was easy to love. She already felt like they could be friends if the situation were different.

When Maximus left, Jayne tucked herself into the bed so it looked like she was resting in case they were watching her, and tried again and again to access the Torrent, to no avail. She finally stopped, worried that Alarik would be back without a smile and holding his nasty syringe. Maybe something in the sedative they'd given her messed with her magic.

It had to be at least an hour before Teresa entered and extended a hand, pulling her upright. Maximus waited by the door.

"Where are we going?" Jayne asked.

"You'll see soon enough," Maximus replied. He pursed his lips and gestured for the two women to go on ahead.

Teresa led Jayne out of the room and down a tunnel of rock, with Maximus walking quietly behind them. The passageway, lit by actual torches, led into a one-room cabin with a high ceiling full of rough-hewn timber and fat candles that made Alarik and his cronies glow like angels in their soft, white sweaters.

Twelve men and women, including Alarik, sat in simple, wooden chairs at a round table reminiscent of the tales of Arthur.

Alarik stood and opened his arms.

"Welcome, Jayne. I must open with the fact that my name is not actually Albon. I will reveal my true name as well as everyone else's once we get to know one another better."

Jayne was just dying to say *Yeah, I know exactly who you are, and you aren't the only one with tricks up your sleeve. Thomas isn't my last name. Bwahahaha!* but of course she could do no such thing.

She forced a polite smile. It was tough indeed to project *I am captured and unhappy about that but willing to listen to your ravings* in one look. Once again, Jayne was reminded why Ruger had been so upset about the TCO assigning her, a complete newbie, to this mission. Amanda and the higher-ups had decided Jayne's innate ability with magic was worth the risk to all involved. But without being able to access the Torrent, what magic could help her here? Worse, there was no way they'd just let her go after a week if she didn't pull off her fake conversion to the Kingdom's beliefs and goals. *Get them to believe your heart is with them. That is the only way to survive this.*

Jayne stood straight, trying to look interested. "What would you like to know about me?"

"We'd like to know what you thought of our talk."

"About what the Kingdom is and what you long for?"

"Exactly. What do you think of a world where Adepts like

you are honored instead of hidden away?"

"Why should I be honored? It's not like I could be some great benevolent queen if the nonmagical folks decided we should rule over all of Narnia."

Most of the crowd looked confused.

"I mean," Jayne added, "just because we have magic doesn't mean we should be in charge of the world. Having magic doesn't automatically make one good. Does it?"

"What a fabulous question." Alarik's upper lip curled, but he smoothed the sneer away and pasted on a smile. "Sit, Jayne. Join us."

"Thank you. So, what is your exact purpose?" Jayne took a seat at the table. "Like, nuts and bolts it for me."

Maximus and Teresa sat on either side of her, giving encouraging smiles.

"I think Maximus should answer this one. Would you?"

Maximus cleared his throat. A red flush crawled up his neck. "I don't think the Kingdom argues that everyone with magic is good."

"Of course not," Alarik said.

Maximus continued. "But we believe Adepts should oversee Earth's government organizations and law enforcement, but only those who show the ability to do such a job."

Jayne wanted to argue. Why couldn't a regular human be allowed to do such a job?

"Further," Maximus said, "Adepts have the ability to rule with a force that most of the population can't fight. With the right intent and the proper spells, we can control the population. If we behave as fits our purpose, we can do it without hurting anyone."

Ah, a veiled reference to the telepathy power, the ability they hoped to gain from the necromantic texts.

A silver-bearded man to Alarik's right frowned, but Alarik waved away the concern.

"Jayne, can you tell us, in your own words, what you think the Kingdom believes in?"

She frowned, wondering if she'd heard him correctly. "You want me to repeat what you've told me?"

"Exactly."

Jayne smoothed the wrinkles in her pants. This request of his was probably another step in brainwashing, so she had to keep playing along. "The Kingdom wants a world where Adepts are heads of government, and magic is honored and respected."

His grin was luminous, and it filled Jayne with relief.

"Very good," Alarik said. "And how would life be for you and Lane in such a world?"

"Better."

"In what ways?"

"Lane wouldn't have to run from his past. He'd be forgiven. And I could live openly. I wouldn't have to restrain myself when accessing the Torrent. We would be free."

Maximus looked at his lap and grinned, and there were murmurs from the assembled Kingdom members around the table. She tried to make eye contact with each of them, assign them mnemonic names so she could report back to Ruger, but Alarik waved a hand.

"Well said, Jayne. Because you survived an unexpected first trip through a Time Catch portal, I believe your power is significant. You could be an immense help in rescuing our Earth and every Adept in it from the evils of today's civilization. Using the magic of the Torrent, we plan to…" He paused and glanced around the room. The other Kingdom members almost tittered with excitement as they grinned, luminous with joy. "…eradicate some of the more disruptive elements of the modern world."

She was starting to see exactly why this fellow had been chosen to lead this cult. He was the type of person one wanted to please. In the outside world, he'd set off her creep-meter, but here, it was different. In this shadowy half-world, he belonged. It was something in the bearing and the way he had with words.

Deirdre's words trickled through Jayne's memory. *He's an engineer. He builds things.*

A shudder rocked Jayne, and she masked the movement with a cough.

"I think that's enough for today. Maximus, Teresa, please take Jayne to her work area and show her the magic she can do while she's with us." Alarik lifted a hand in farewell as the two Adepts escorted Jayne out of the room.

Crap. Had she said the wrong thing? Everyone was still smiling at her, so maybe not. But she hadn't been able to imprint all the faces, either. Maybe Alarik had sensed her trying to. Crap, again. He was smarter than he let on.

And a work area? Jayne was suddenly having visions of Morlocks from H. G. Wells's *The Time Machine.*

They led her away from the meeting room until the hallway forked, and they went left.

"Um, what, exactly, are we doing?"

Teresa turned as they walked on. "Each of us trains when we're here helping, to get stronger, to improve our magical skills. Today, we'll show you how to access the Torrent to move objects without touching them."

"Cool." The TCO hadn't gotten to this level of magic with her yet. Might as well learn some new tricks.

"The leaders must trust you are a good person," Maximus said. "By the way, why don't you call me Max?"

"All right," Jayne said.

The firelit corridor opened into what looked like the out-doors. Huge trees stood in yellowed grass, and a cliff face loomed, gray and formidable.

"Wait." Jayne stopped dead, her breath coming short. "Are we in Yosemite?"

CHAPTER FORTY-ONE

Jayne reared back, heart pounding. What the heck?

"It's amazing, right? This is a magical construct of the Yosemite National Park," Teresa said. "The Head of the Kingdom thought it would be a nice place to train. Jayne, are you well? Is something wrong?"

"I...I have some really bad history with this place." Her parents had died in a wildfire just past the boundaries of Yosemite. In her mind's eye, the whole place was engulfed in the flames that had destroyed her childhood.

"I'm sorry. Albon suggested it because it's so beautiful and peaceful. But we can change it. Hang on." Max gripped a circular necklace he'd had hidden under his shirt—it looked almost like a fingerprint—and whispered some words, closing his eyes. Teresa closed her eyes, too, setting a palm on his arm. They were doing magic, but it didn't smell the same as when Ruger did. It was earthier, like fresh mulch. She tucked away that knowledge; it might be important later.

Yosemite's half-dome morphed into a sloping mountain covered in greenery. A waterfall splashed through the growth, and a grove of wide-leaved trees appeared. A bright bird fluttered overhead, and the sound of ocean waves echoed.

Her heart stopped racing, the panic receding. "Um, did you two just turn Yosemite into Hawaii?" It was impressive, to say the least.

Max's laugh boomed while Teresa just smiled. "It's a twist on the creation. A simple illusion. Nothing compared to what the Head developed underneath. But is this setting better for you?" Max asked. He was looking a little pale. Probably from working what had to be a tough spell.

Note to self: scenic illusions are higher magic. Got it. Jayne breathed more easily. "Yes. Thank you very much."

They walked under the trees for a while, and Jayne had the notion that they were waiting for her nerves to chill. It was nice that they weren't asking why she had freaked out. "So Albon created this entire other dimension?"

"Oh, no. Albon is very talented, very powerful, but even he can't create a full-blown Time Catch. There is another, a sacred one that Albon follows. She wasn't at the meeting," Max said as he spread his arms. He closed his eyes. "Let's not waste any more time. I have to leave soon to return to the real world. Jayne, join me in the Torrent."

So a woman Jayne hadn't met ran this branch of the Kingdom. Or maybe the whole organization, who knew? And they called her a sacred one? She wondered if the TCO had any information on this sacred leader.

"Will I get to meet the sacred one if I join you all?"

Max's eyes opened, and Teresa stepped toward Jayne. "Are you truly considering it?" Max asked, his face full of hope.

Jayne had to play this very carefully. "What you all say sounds sensible, and I'd do anything to help my brother."

"He's in a lot of trouble, hmm?" Teresa frowned in sympathy.

"Yeah. If he is tracked down, he'll spend the rest of his life in prison." Jayne closed her eyes. She couldn't summon tears at the moment but hoped the gesture would convey a certain gravity.

Max, chin tilted, gazed at Jayne when she opened her eyes. He spoke quietly. "Honestly, you shouldn't be too excited about meeting the sacred one. She is really, really scary."

"Maximus!" Teresa gripped his sleeve.

"I'm sorry, but come on. You know it's true. If I'd met her before Albon, I'm not sure I would've joined up," he whispered, looking over his shoulder.

Teresa was positively incensed. "Because I care about you, Max, I will keep this to myself. But let me remind you, our leaders must be fierce to go up against our enemies. This revolution requires complete devotion and will demand the utmost from each of us."

Jayne hadn't been freaked by Max's mention of the sacred one, but Teresa's little speech did make her sweat. Complete devotion? Demand the utmost? They were sounding more and more culty all the time.

But Jayne had to stop and think.

Those phrases were also quite reminiscent of the promises she made to the TCO. Of course, they were set up to keep the world safe from magic-wielding maniacs.

But here was a group that also believed they were protecting the world. Well, protecting the Adepts of the world, anyway. Both Teresa and Max seemed like decent people. They were just doing what they thought was best, too. Jayne wished this was all more black and white. Good versus evil. But it was all shades of *sort of* right if she looked at it from a certain angle. Nothing about this mission was clear-cut or simple in its ethics.

Uh-oh. She was becoming compassionate toward her captors.

With that thought, a snippet of Ruger's training whispered through Jayne's head, and she realized Max had just showed himself a good candidate for recruitment as an asset. He'd shown doubt about the Kingdom's leaders, fear, and a willingness to confide in a relative stranger.

If Jayne could get further into his circle of trust, she could possibly use his fear to weaken his devotion to the group. If she could get Max alone, get him to talk more openly about his doubts and desires, hopefully she could find something to promise him in return for helping her bust open the Kingdom and stop them from committing whatever evil they had planned. Maybe she could even get him on the side of the TCO.

Now she needed to know what he wanted, aside from a world run by Adepts and swimming with magic. Something that, if he wouldn't do it willingly, she could use as leverage. It felt squicky to think about, but this was the whole world they were supposed to be saving.

But she had a gut feeling that Teresa would get in the way.

"Teresa, I'm feeling a little…" Jayne sat on a large rock and pretended to be woozy. "I'd have better luck with the Torrent if I had a little something to eat. Do you think you could…I don't know…"

"Oh." Teresa squeezed her hands together. "Of course, I can get you some food. I'll be right back. Will you stay with her, Max?"

He nodded, and Teresa disappeared out of the fake Hawaiian forest, presumably into the corridor that had led them here.

"Do you want to wait for your food before we get started?" Max squatted beside Jayne, his dark eyes sincere.

"Yeah. Let's just talk, okay?"

"Sure. What about?" Max crossed his legs and got comfortable in the grass.

"I need to just hear some normal stuff. I'm kind of freaking out. Tell me about yourself."

Max chuckled. "I understand. All right." He rubbed his hands on his knees. "My first job as an adult was teaching middle school. That was far more difficult than doing any kind of magic."

"Ha. I bet. Worse than herding cats. More like rounding up lions who would prefer to eat you alive and share the video with friends."

Max's laugh echoed through the space. "I met my wife there, though, so it was worth the trouble."

"Teresa?"

He blushed. "Oh, no. We just work together."

"Does your wife teach?"

"School psychologist."

"Is she an Adept? Does she know about the Kingdom?"

Max picked some grass and slowly released it into the breeze. "She can't do magic, but she supports our cause."

"That makes me feel better."

"Why?"

She heard Ruger's voice. *Careful, Jayne. You aren't much of an actress, but he's starting to bite. Go slowly.*

Talk about brainwashed. In a few short weeks, Ruger had become her conscience.

She played with her ponytail. "Because I have a lot of non-magic people I like, and I want this new world the Kingdom talks about to take care of them, too. If your wife is cool with the Kingdom's plan, it must not be too terrible."

Max chewed his lip and stared up at the false version of a large hibiscus bush. "She doesn't know the details."

"Which details?" *Controlling every nonmagical person in the world with telepathy? Yeah, I can see how you'd want to leave that out.* It would be very good if Jayne could get the actual telepathic control statement from him right now.

"Jayne, you have to get those from Albon and the rest."

She nodded and gave him what she hoped was a shy smile.

"My wife, well, she knows I believe it's the right move."

Something about his expression made Jayne shiver. "How did you convince her it's the right move to trust the Kingdom?"

"We worked five summers in the Peace Corps. Saw some terrible, terrible things. I can't…"

"Hey. If you don't want to talk about it, it's okay."

"No." He sniffed and blinked. "I need to. To be honest about this. The world today is full of wrongness. You know what I mean?"

"I definitely do."

"I think we need an overhaul. To start over and find the elements that make us who we are again. To bring down the fat cats, the abusers of power, the witch-hunting humans."

The more he spoke, the more impassioned he became, the more Jayne had to fight to stay where she was. Every cell in her body shouted for her to run away from this seemingly kind man. His words were the words of terrorists, anarchists, extremists. The killers of today's world. Butchers of innocents. Shooters and bombers and hijackers. The worst kind of villains. Those who truly believe they are in the right and will stop at nothing to see themselves in power.

She tried to speak, but her throat had closed up. Lowering her face, she pretended to be deep in thought. She took a deep breath. Another.

Then Teresa was jogging over with a brown paper bag. "I brought you a sandwich. I hope you like hummus."

"I do," Jayne squeaked.

Nothing like delicious Middle Eastern foods to fix an awkward stall in the conversation. The sandwich was wonderful, but it churned in Jayne's stomach like a ball of snakes.

Max finished a bottle of juice Teresa had brought him, then stood. "We should get back to work. Ready to give the faster access work a try?"

Finally. She gave them a tremulous smile, hoping she looked like an anxious, excited recruit. "Definitely."

CHAPTER FORTY-TWO

Max handed Jayne three bracelets. They were made of leather, with adjustable ties for size. Three stones hung from twisted metal. The first was clear crystal, the second was the color of moss, and the third was lined in purple, a teal green, and some transparent material.

"Clear quartz to regulate energy and increase your power. Green jasper to keep you grounded and focused. Fluorite for spells. It enhances your intuition as an Adept and can make finding spells much easier."

"They're really beautiful."

"And powerful." Teresa wiggled her own bracelets as Max held out his necklace of stones.

"You didn't have those on earlier." Jayne would've noticed them.

Max adjusted Jayne's second bracelet for her. "We keep them in a pocket or whatever until we need them. Kind of bulky, you know."

Jayne moved her arm around. They were heavy even though the stones weren't very big. Max and Teresa were already closing their eyes. Taking a deep breath, Jayne joined them.

The second she thought of the Torrent, she was there. The stones were amplifiers. Groovy.

"Do you need these inside the Time Catch? Do they work in the regular world, too?"

Teresa spoke into the starry place. "Stay focused, Jayne. Find the spell for Movement."

Jayne imagined a person running, and before she had time to think whether or not that was the right train of thought, the spell was there, floating and ready to go. "Wow." She focused on it and was back in Hawaii with a speed she'd never experienced.

Max stood before her. "Try to move that boulder you were sitting on."

She spun to face it, and Teresa chuckled a little behind her back.

"Maximus, give her something that makes sense," Teresa whispered.

"A little hazing is all right. It'll help us bond with her," he answered.

Jayne knew she could do this, though. She felt it in her core. Hopefully, her core wasn't jerking her around. Ruger and Amanda both had crowed about her power, and this felt as simple as some of her first tasks during training with the TCO.

She threw the spinning cloud of almost invisible white at the boulder. She felt the magic lock on with a jolt, then she lifted her arms. The great stone heaved past the canopy, into the blue sky, and then kept on going.

Max whooped, and Teresa shouted something.

Jayne's body trembled as she slowed the rock's descent and

lowered it gently, allowing the boulder to hover over Max's head. She inhaled the scent of the magic pouring out of her.

"Hazing, hmm?"

He laughed and held up his hands. "Sorry, Jayne. Sorry!"

She set the rock in its place.

"What power you have!" Teresa ran a hand through her hair. "I can't believe what I just saw. That was more than even Albon could do."

"Now who is being disrespectful toward the Kingdom leaders?" Max elbowed Teresa teasingly.

They set her several more tasks, each harder than the next. Jayne accomplished them with ease. Just as she was starting to feel powerful, the ground started to shake.

"Oops. I overdid it, I guess."

Max and Teresa were staring at her, fear slinking across their faces. They both looked shaken, and Jayne realized whatever had just happened, it wasn't part of her training.

She had the horrible sense they were afraid of her now, and that was going to make her recruitment all the harder.

"Um, someone want to clue me in on what just happened? What was that?"

Teresa looked around frantically. "The construct is unstable. Max, we should go."

Jayne put a hand out to Teresa, who'd been knocked to the ground. Teresa just shook her head, obviously shocked at Jayne's ability. Max grabbed Teresa by the shoulders and reached out for Jayne's hand.

The earth shook under their feet, and all three fell. One of the massive, wide-leafed trees crashed to the ground.

Teresa shrieked and pointed.

Beyond the tree, a swirling mass of emerald stars exploded from the ground. A sound like a roar and a thunderstorm combined pummeled the air, and a cloud of sickeningly sweet magic poured over them, blowing back their hair. Jayne jerked herself to her feet.

A shape loomed from the starry mass.

Human in form but over twenty feet tall, the thing stalked toward them, flattening flowers and bushes, sending up waves of rocky dirt, and snapping trees with its blurry hands like the ten-foot trunks were no more than toothpicks.

Max got to his feet, shouting something at Teresa, who seemed incapable of movement. He ran to stand in front of Jayne, then faced her, spittle at the corners of his mouth and the glint of fear bright in his eyes. "Jayne. Go. I'll hold it off."

"What is it?"

"A Rogue. A trapped Rogue rebelling inside the Torrent. Now go, before it's too late!" He shoved her toward Teresa, who stood a few feet away, hand outstretched toward Jayne.

This was her doing. Her power had loosed this...Rogue. Max said *trapped*. Was this the same kind of Rogue Ruger had been worried about?

There was no time to think. If she had started this, she would end this. Or Max and Teresa both would die.

"You go, Max. This is my fault." He shook his head violently as the Rogue stomped toward them, its magic's light pulsing with every step closer. Jayne pulled on Max's sweater and jerked him backward. "Go!"

And then there was no more time to argue. The Rogue spread its arms and opened its maw.

Control the Shifter, Medb said into Jayne's mind. Did she mean Rogue? *Your blood holds the power. Listen to your own blood, Master.*

Chills raked down Jayne's back as she took a deep breath, the burning air choking, and accessed the Torrent. The cool river of power immediately poured over her limbs and twisted around her fingers. She had no moment to think of which spell to use. Instinct drew a spell into her hands, and she threw it at the Rogue, with no idea what was about to happen.

The spell held Jayne in invisible hands, shaking her as hard as the ground trembled underfoot. She felt as though she was being sucked dry as the spell pulled energy from her heart and palms, funneling it into three wavering, glowing arcs toward the Rogue. The grass around her and Max blackened and smoked as the Rogue shouted, the sound like disjointed screaming and a high-pitched, inconsistent scratching. Fallen trees erupted into flames.

Jayne's hands and arms began to warm, to sizzle.

Shaking, she screamed, fear lording over her completely. She was going to die like the man in Central Park. Like her parents had died, consumed by flames that, magical and nonmagical, destroyed with a shocking speed.

Magic shunted from her body and flowed from the Torrent. She tried to drop her arms, to curl her outstretched fingers. The spell was too strong. It fought back, jerking her forward into a stumbling walk toward the shrieking Rogue. The creature whipped into the shape of a flaming sword, and a high, scratching sound tore at the air. Jayne's spell wrapped blue-green light around the sword and pitched it backward. As the creature fell, it transformed again, this time into a house-sized raven, its wings expanding and its talons slashing toward Jayne. She leapt aside, and the talons dragged against the brittle and blackened grass under her feet.

Max and Teresa shouted her name behind her, but their voices drowned in the noise of the Rogue's cacophony.

The Rogue morphed from raven into an owl with empty eyes. It lunged for Jayne, razor-sharp beak coming at her with a dizzying speed. Her spell blazed white. The creature exploded into a cloud of black smoke and floating ash.

All went quiet.

Jayne dropped to her knees, her back slicked with sweat and her hair plastered against her forehead. Max and Teresa ran to her, shouting questions that she had no energy or information to satisfy.

CHAPTER FORTY-THREE

Teresa's face was flushed, her eyes burning with excitement. "Wait until Albon hears. Though he must already have a sense of your abilities. No wonder they're willing to accept you so quickly."

Jayne drank from the bottle of water Teresa had brought along with the sandwich.

Max just kept shaking his head, red beard shuffling over his shirt. "I can't believe it. Teresa, have you ever seen a Rogue? And a tortured and trapped one at that?"

"No, and I'm rather glad Jayne was here."

"That was brilliant, Jayne. Wild. We will need to report this immediately." Max led them out of the Hawaiian island scene and back down the corridor. "I wonder what Albon will say about the Rogue."

Play dumb, Jayne...

"Um...what is a Rogue, exactly?" Jayne asked, fingers brushing the bracelets. The stones caught the light of the torches.

Teresa and Max eyed her, then one another. Teresa nodded, then Max shrugged.

"They are creatures who look like humans but can morph into animals."

"Into mountain-sized birds?"

Max snorted. "Apparently."

"What did you mean, that it was tortured and trapped?"

Teresa was practically whispering, as if imparting the sagest of secrets. "Rogues look for Adepts who might become Masters. They bond with them, and the magician makes the Rogue stronger and sometimes expands their choice of form."

Jayne knew this from what Ruger had told her, but she had to act as though this was all a shock. "But that...thing, it was going to hurt us."

Teresa glanced over her shoulder. "Maybe. Maybe it was just trying to escape the Time Catch. They're really rare, and some think they've been trapped in the Torrent for a very long time."

"But I think we have some working with us," Max said.

"Let's wait on that, Max." Teresa's tone cut the conversation.

Jayne knew her next question would be pushing it, but considering what she'd just accomplished perhaps Teresa would answer. "Who would torture a Rogue, and why?"

"I'm sure it's nothing anyone would do on purpose. From what I've read on the subject, Rogues can become trapped in the Torrent when they stretch their magic too far, and are forced to blast their way out like our large friend did."

Max shuddered. "Not too different from us Adepts burning to death when we aim higher than our skill level."

Jayne rubbed her arms. The heat of the magic she'd done had faded, but she would recall the feeling of flames licking the inside of her skin with perfect clarity for a long, long time. Then she remembered the time she'd been training with Ruger and he'd had to rescue her. "I was nearly stuck in the Torrent once."

"Really?" Max said.

Teresa brought them past Jayne's room. Three more corridors branched off the one they'd taken to the meeting hall or whatever it was called. They took the last of the three, and Jayne committed the path to memory.

"Yeah. I heard this voice. It was really lovely, and I just wanted to stay in the Torrent."

"You were lured," Teresa said quietly as she pushed a swinging wooden door. "Someone must have noticed you in the Torrent, someone in the same magnetic field. I bet they realized how powerful you were and tried to tempt you closer, metaphysically, to see your face or hear your voice."

Well, that was comforting. Perhaps Ruger had explained that, but Jayne couldn't remember exactly. Everything had been so new. She might have simply skirted over that info, as overwhelmed as she was.

The room housed two long tables and a bevy of stools. Scratches marred the pinewood floor, gouges nearly five feet in length. What happened here?

Max answered Jayne's unasked question. "Magical experiments. It can get a little mad."

"Yikes."

"All subjects are willing participants." Teresa stopped them at the end of the room, where a brass bell hung from a hook beside a set of double doors that were barred with iron.

An uncomfortable sensation traveled across Jayne's skin, like someone had just run nails down a chalkboard and her body was made of sensitive ears.

Max was looking from the double doors back to the way they'd come in. He didn't seem any happier about this area than

Jayne felt. Even Teresa's hand shook as she raised it to knock. But perhaps that was leftover fear and adrenaline from battling the trapped Rogue. Completely understandable. Jayne wasn't likely to ever forget the terror the Rogue's enormous form wrought or the sound of its tortured shrieking.

Had she killed it? She blinked. Yes. She definitely had. She hadn't even thought of that, not really. Rogues were magical creatures, not humans, and it had attacked her. But still. She was a killer. A slayer of dragons perhaps, but a killer just the same. Her throat tightened. It wasn't as if she'd had a choice.

Teresa knocked again. One side of the double doors swung open, and they had to stumble backward, out of the way.

As Jayne tried not to step all over Max's feet, she glimpsed something odd in the next room. Inside a shimmering barrier, a man hung suspended and shaking, covered in a sheen of sweat. And his arms—

A harried-looking Alarik flew from the door, then shut it as Jayne processed what she'd seen and tried to focus on Alarik. His hair wasn't smoothed as usual, its silver strands wild and nearly on end. His eyes were bloodshot like he'd been up all night romancing a bottle of tequila.

"What are you doing here?" He was ticked. Really ticked.

"I am sorry," Teresa said, sounding like a recalcitrant schoolgirl. "But there has been a surprising development in regard to Jayne's training."

"It had better be an emergency."

Teresa nodded, wringing her hands. "A tortured Rogue, trapped in the Torrent, broke through the training illusion."

Max and Jayne moved to let Alarik by. "Then I must attend to this before—"

Max took his arm, then dropped his hold immediately when Alarik set an impressive glare on the man. "Jayne dissolved the

Rogue. On her own."

Alarik spun to face Jayne. His gaze drew a line from her face to her hands. "Are you injured?"

She rubbed her forearms. "I'm fine."

"How did you do it? What spell did you call and cast?"

"I don't know." No way she was going to tell him about Medb, not until she knew more and they trusted her. "I just...I just acted on instinct."

Alarik glanced at Teresa, then toward the double doors. "How bad was it, Teresa?"

"Bad."

Alarik's lips pressed into a thin line. But his expression quickly cleared, and a beatific smile crossed his face. "Well, of course. Now it all makes sense. We might have a future Master in our midst, friends."

Jayne's stomach dropped as if she'd jumped from a five-story building. Maybe she wasn't supposed to let on that she was quite that powerful. Now the bad guys knew her secret, too.

What would the TCO think about that?

Alarik took them back to the training room. During the walk, Teresa and Max detailed the fight for him. Jayne followed quietly, secretly longing for the vault at Vandy.

They spent the next hour working spells alongside Alarik, pushing Jayne to call up whatever spell she'd used to take down the Rogue. Though she felt it, lurking in her blood as if now imprinted there, she pretended she couldn't access it, only managed to use other spells, ones that brought rain, others that shook the ground, a few that sent branches and leaves flying into the air. They were powerful spells, but she wasn't going to unleash the hell she'd felt earlier, not in front of them. They couldn't know the extent of her control over her power. Not yet.

When Jayne was exhausted, her skin hot to the touch, Alarik called for a stop.

He took Jayne's hands in his. His fingers were slender and wiry, a bit wrinkled but strong. "We are very glad you're here. And indeed, you are fortunate to have found us, because in no other place would your talent be so explored and expanded." He smiled, showing white teeth. "Max and Teresa will take you back to your room. I will see you after tonight's rest."

He left, the Hawaiian trees they'd regrown waving in a magical breeze over his head.

Max was practically bouncing on his toes as they trailed Albon, giving their boss man a good head start. "Sleep well tonight," he said to Jayne when they arrived at her door. "Train with us again tomorrow. Then, maybe Albon and the rest will decide to let you in on all of our amazing plans. It's very exciting to think about having an Adept like you on our side. We'll raise—"

Teresa smacked him on the arm. "Hey."

Max clammed up. "Right. Okay. See you tomorrow morning, then. We'll come and take you to breakfast." He let Jayne into her cushy prison and locked the door after Teresa had waved goodbye.

Henry Thorne's timeworn journal safely hidden in his pocket, Alarik coursed down the hallway, heart pumping excitedly. The Head had been entirely correct; Henry's journal was the key to everything. Most everything, that is.

According to Henry, the necromantic texts had the power to call a modern Master to life, one who would have the ability to raise a dead Master. The newly raised Master would then bestow a gift on the chosen Master. Henry believed the gifts represented the five elements: Earth, Air, Fire, Water, and Spirit.

But this was where Henry's journal was maddeningly incomplete.

His writing said once all five elemental gifts were bestowed upon a Master, somehow the Whispering Tree—the symbolic phrasing for the ability to communicate with, nay, control every nonmagical individual on Earth—would rise.

But only a Master with the elemental gifts would know how to make that happen.

If only Henry was alive to finish his research. But the Head had killed him, years ago.

Still, Alarik knew the time was at hand. Jayne was so much more than he'd ever imagined. She'd been drawn to Medb's book and was surely the one he'd been searching for. He'd known the text truly was a necromantic work but needed the right magician to connect with Medb directly. With Jayne starting down the road to full mastery and the new work Alarik and his team were doing on Rogues, the Kingdom was sure to see their plan to fruition.

They would not be thwarted.

Alarik would be there to start the world anew.

Now, he had to get back to the lab and see how the Rogue testing was going. They'd successfully put one Rogue under the control of Adept Blaine, a man whose magical talent seemed destined for greatness and whose dedication to the cause was complete.

He pushed the double doors open to the sounds of a Rogue shrieking. Alarik gritted his teeth against the unpleasant noise, wishing there was no need for pain.

The bars of light caging both Blaine and his mastered Rogue

glimmered as the Adept slashed a hand through the warm air. The Rogue dropped to his knees, twisted his torso, and screamed as his head turned backward, somewhat like an owl's.

Alarik tapped on the Torrent-made bars. "If you'd fully give in to the partnership, the pain would be far more manageable." He had found if he called "mastering" a "partnership," the Rogues tended to be more compliant.

The Rogue's eyes filled with hatred, and then he began to shimmer. His cries broke into a tinny sound like a metal ball thrust onto concrete as his body contorted and shrank, his skin going silver, smooth and uninterrupted by feature or limb.

Alarik fisted his hands. If this worked, it would change everything. Fifty-two trials and none of the Rogues had survived this particular extension of power, this drastic morphing.

The lab went silent. Only the bars hummed with power while Alarik and Blaine held their breath.

The Rogue hovered a foot above the floor, alive and yet not, his human shape transformed into a steel sword.

Blaine met Alarik's gaze, his eyes gleaming with the success. "We've done it!"

A small, cruel smile spread over Alarik's mouth. "Indeed we have. Well done. Well done!" He clapped the younger man on the back, full of fatherly pride. "Continue on and keep me informed of your discoveries."

There was still so much to explore with regard to this development. They needed more Rogues, to start.

When Alarik had first met with that fool Aaró's man, Cillian, Alarik had thought he smelled Rogue on him. He'd hoped he'd stumbled upon another Rogue to work with in this testing. But sadly, the scent had faded, and Alarik had apparently been mistaken. That Cillian fellow was only a human. If he'd been a Rogue, surely by his age he'd have shifted and smelled of the breed.

It had been a difficult decision, figuring out whether they should wipe the man's memories of the Kingdom. He was a fighter. He had potential. But in the end, Cillian hadn't possessed the fervor of his mentor. Aaró, with all his faults, had never once wavered in his dedication, his absolute sacrifice for the cause. Cillian just didn't have that strength of character necessary for getting one's hands dirty.

But this Rogue in the lab? The one who they could shape into an inanimate object? If he stayed alive, this one would do nicely for their long-term plan.

CHAPTER FORTY-FOUR

For a full week, Jayne played her role. She trained in fake Hawaii with Max and Teresa. It was rather similar to her work with Ruger and Amanda, but instead of suits and legal jargon, the Kingdom encouraged a kind of individualism that was exactly as false as the vine-covered, volcanic mountain lording over their magical sessions. Kingdom members were free to work in this dimension when they chose and to use magic only as they saw fit. But—and it was a huge *but*—this creepy, judgy feel hung on every word and action. Like they were free, but if they chose an option that varied from Alarik and the other bigwigs' opinion...well, it didn't seem like that was going to be a point in their favor. Jayne hadn't seen any consequences to such divergent behavior, but the pointed looks that Teresa gave Max when he dared to voice his doubts made it pretty clear that the supposed freedoms they enjoyed were nothing of the sort.

Standing beside the rainbow-hued trunk of a eucalyptus, Jayne followed Teresa's guidance and plunged into the Torrent to search for a spell that would help her use the power of the Earth's magnetic fields to improve her strength.

"Think of it like photosynthesis," Teresa said.

"Um…" Jayne spun, and the Torrent's lights curled around her arms like cats' tails, soft and gentle. She'd been encountering these moments regularly, felt so relaxed in the Torrent now. It was a good thing that Ruger had been there when she'd first been tempted to stay for too long.

Teresa's voice rose, and Jayne realized she'd been talking, but Jayne hadn't heard her last few words. "…and feel the power settling into your flesh."

"So I'm a big, magical sponge." Jayne could handle that.

She relaxed further and a spell came into being right in front of her nose. It looked like a meteor shower, lights streaming down in rays and spurts. She moved her hands like an orchestra's conductor to collect the top edge of the shower, then opened her eyes to see Max and Teresa.

Jayne grimaced. The spell wiggled between her fingers, harder to hold than any she'd tried yet. "Now what?"

Max pointed to a spot beside the river. "There is a strong magnetic field there. It won't feel like Stonehenge or anything, but you should get a pretty good jolt if you do it right."

"And a jolt is a good thing?" Jayne asked as she maneuvered the invisible shower of light toward the place he'd indicated.

When she reached the fabricated force, the spell shook Jayne's hands like it was about to explode. She took another step. She was going to lose it. Being the overachiever she was, Jayne gritted her teeth and took three more solid steps. The shaking grew, and she felt as though her bones were about to rattle right out of her skin. Then the spell took hold. The trembling stopped and power surged through Jayne's body.

"Oooh. Me likee."

Behind her, Max and Teresa laughed. "Try another spell while you have it reined in," Max said.

She entered the Torrent and it felt like going down the biggest hill on a roller coaster. She was just there. Too distracted to try for originality, she simply grabbed for the magic symbol she'd used to move the boulder on her first day here. Holding two spells and having magnetic force rolling through her body? Nope. Not easy. But it did feel pretty amazing to have that much power at her fingertips. She saw Teresa and Max watching her with wide eyes. The air around Jayne waved, with the magic swirling like she was in the middle of a mirage. She focused on Max and Teresa.

And lifted them into the air.

They both shouted and threw up Blocking spells. But Jayne's power dwarfed their efforts. Max's mouth seemed stuck in an O shape as he flew above the trees.

"Jayne!" Teresa waved her arms as her feet brushed the eucalyptus branches. "Are you focused enough for this?"

"I'm not going to hurt you," Jayne said, although she had to admit it was fun to control the one who had originally been in charge of her shackles. "Max! You okay up there?"

"Shocked, but fine, Jayne! Nice work! Very focused power you have there!"

She lowered them to the ground, then released both spells.

They ran to her.

"That was my strongest Block. I can't believe you worked right over it like it wasn't even there. But then again, that is nothing compared to what you did with the Rogue." The skin around Teresa's mouth was pale. She panted and shook her head.

"Wicked stuff, Jayne." Max clapped Jayne on the back.

They kept talking about Jayne's abilities through lunch, and afterward as they moved toward the exit for some rest time. With all the smiles and new trust she felt she was gaining, it was time to push these two a little in the name of the TCO's mission.

"Hey, if we take over," Jayne said, talking like she'd already been fully accepted into the Kingdom, "and the Kingdom rises to power, what will the world look like? We won't, like, shut down hospitals and stop air travel and stuff, right?"

Max swallowed and watched his feet as they walked.

Teresa sighed. "Every revolution has casualties."

"What do you mean? You'd close hospitals? That seems reckless."

Max's face lightened. "Oh, they will stay open. But we'll use natural sources of healing."

"So no ventilators for the babies in ICUs? What about people getting treatments, operations, comas? How do you treat a heart attack or stroke with magic? And how will people get from point A to point B? I mean, we can portal, but nonmagical folk have to be able to get places, right? What about the power grids? Food supplies? Basic sanitation?" She was pushing, but she really did need to know these things.

Teresa's smile grew a little plastic as they stopped at Jayne's room. "You should ask Albon these questions during your next discussion. He can explain all."

The tone of her voice didn't sound like her. It was canned. Robotic. Scary as hell.

Jayne nodded and waved as Teresa left her and Max in the hallway.

Max eyed the top of the wall. Jayne squinted and noticed something black, small, and circular. A camera? Not very primitive. The great villains of old would've been disappointed in these zealots. They weren't nearly consistent enough.

"Listen," Max whispered. "Your arguments have merit. If you bring up this topic during the discussion tonight—"

"There's one tonight?"

"Yes. And if you mention this, I promise to support you. The Kingdom's plan is amazing. I want it to happen. But there are certain elements that I'm not comfortable with. Sacrificing people for the greater good… I can't sleep, thinking about how my nephew will have to deal with no longer having the power of his nebulizer. I'm fine with dying when it's my time, but my nephew? Asthma isn't his only problem, and he is such a good kid. And only thirteen. Multiply that by millions of people? It seems…drastic."

Ya think? My God, they were going to create a mass extinction event. Unthinkable. She had to get out of here and warn the TCO.

Max was looking at her oddly. *Play along.*

"Thanks, Max. You're a good guy, too."

"Thanks for not tossing me onto the cliff top today."

"No problem."

Jayne made a valiant effort to sleep, knowing that her mission required good health. Images of the tortured Rogue she'd killed flashed through her mind, making her tense up. And she remembered the glimpse of the man she'd seen beyond the double doors in the place that made her skin crawl. The sweating man who hung in the air, his arms covered in a thick, brown fur. Like a bear's pelt.

Jayne gripped the sides of the bed, head pounding.

He was a Rogue.

Two Rogues spotted in one day, and both of them in severe

duress.

What did it mean? No one had said a thing about the Kingdom using Rogues in their work, so was this a secret? Why?

Jayne tried to shut off her brain. Her poor body needed sleep if she were to figure out any of this. She missed her books. She missed her dingy flat, and her pie, and Ruger, and Sofia, and the library, and damn it, she even missed Cillian though she barely knew him. It was strange to think that time wasn't passing with them, that no one knew she was here.

After lying awake for endless minutes, she finally imagined the last scene she'd read from Sofia's ridiculous werewolf book and managed about two and a half hours of shut-eye. And then Teresa was at her door telling her it was time for the meeting.

An idea had formed during Jayne's brief rest.

If she brought up what she and Max had discussed, maybe she could sway the whole group and stop their plans in their tracks. But if she asked about the ethics of their plans, how many people could be hurt, and then no one backed her up and none were moved into second thoughts on the Kingdom's goal of a new magical world order? They might just toss her out on her bum.

Or kill her on the spot.

If she didn't pose any serious questions, though, would her fake conversion to their side even be believable? Her head hadn't stopped pounding in twenty-four hours.

"Come on," Teresa said, handing Jayne a tiny apple. "They're waiting. I'm late because I thought you might need a snack."

Jayne couldn't eat. She thanked Teresa and slipped the fruit into her pocket, wondering if she'd just skipped out on her last meal.

CHAPTER FORTY-FIVE

Once everyone had taken a chair at the enormous King Arthur-esque round wooden table, Alarik/Albon set his palms on the rough wood and eyed Jayne.

"We should start with how you are feeling about all of this, Jayne Thomas."

Everyone stared, and Jayne found herself as shy as she'd been on her first day of college, out of Sofia's direct control. The same fears rose up. Would she sound like an uneducated hick? Was she experienced enough to even be here?

But just like that first day of school, Jayne shoved her fears down and raised her chin proudly. She was a TCO officer now and trained for this. She had power to boot. Neither these people nor her inner critic would cow her today.

"I find your mandate interesting," she said, not a trace of nerves showing. "I enjoyed training with Max and Teresa and learned there is so much more to the Torrent than I knew before coming here. I appreciate their efforts, and yours."

The two smiled from their seats on either side of Jayne.

"And considering the Kingdom is willing to help my brother…well, I'm in."

Alarik's smile spread across his weathered cheeks as he clapped his hands together. "Wonderful. We had hoped you had the mind and heart for this. And now," he said, gazing from person to person, "I have an announcement about our Jayne here. I've never seen such power from a young Adept before. I have reason to believe she is on the path to becoming a true Master. With Jayne dedicated to our cause, we cannot lose."

Conversation broke out, peppered with questions and gasps.

Alarik raised his hands, quieting the group.

Now was the moment she had to decide. Push the issue or not? Those seated at the table ranged from people about her age through those who had to be pushing eighty. Varied skin tones. Some serious. Others with kind smiles. Every set of eyes held the glint of intelligence. That, and magic, was what they had in common. This was no group of fools. They knew what they were getting into here. A debate had to be expected. They'd wonder about her commitment if she just went with it all too easily. And maybe, just maybe, she could move their hearts toward mercy and change enough minds to tangle Alarik and the head of the Kingdom's plan.

"I do have one issue, though," she said. "If I may ask…"

"Of course," Alarik said. "Ask anything." His smile kept its breadth but lost a touch of its sincerity.

"If our aim," she said, making certain to include herself in their ranks, as she'd been trained, "is to return the Earth to a simpler state, what will happen to those who rely on technology to survive?"

Alarik put his hands in his lap and his smile fell away. "Please expand."

"Hospitals, for example. If the electrical grids are shut down, what happens to everyone? And the global supply chain? Medications, food, transportation? The military? If you remove access to basic services, people will die, won't they? Especially the most vulnerable. That doesn't seem...fair."

Alarik pushed away from the table, and Jayne had to fight panic. Was he going to spell her into oblivion right here and now for her question? He left the table and paced slowly behind his chair, his gaze on the ceiling.

"With your education, I'm sure you studied the various revolutions throughout history."

"Yes."

"So you know well that change oftentimes requires great sacrifice."

"But we have magic. Why would there have to be sacrifices? Can't we take care of the weak among the nonmagical somehow?"

His smile returned and he stopped. "Your compassion makes you strong, Jayne. I admire that. You see, there are limits to what we can do as a group, but we will certainly have members in place to provide strength to those who can live through it with a good push of power. We also will end this place"—he held up his hands to indicate this Time Catch place they were all hanging out in—"and open up a new facility in the Torrent to care for those who need more than just a quick surge of supernatural power to live."

"You'll fit everyone in every hospital in the world in this new facility?"

Max frowned at the table. Teresa traded a look with a woman across from her.

Alarik sat again. "No. We won't be able to fix the whole world's ills from the start. Even I can admit it would be too much. Worry not, Jayne. All is under control. We won't take on more than we can handle to start. We'll focus on the United Kingdom first. Magicians will flock to our cause. I am sure of it. And then we will move."

Jayne wanted to force him to share more information. What specific areas would be affected? What was this terrible plan that could do so much? How bad was the next stage if this first one was this terrible? But she bit her tongue and nodded. Silence oftentimes brought answers out of people.

Alarik's jaw tensed. "We're prepared to invite you to the meetings that will lead to the first stage of our plan, but first, you must show your loyalty."

"How?" She fought a shiver.

"When we return to the moment just after you and I went through the portal, you'll begin your own mission. To steal the dark grimoire you found on your first day at Trinity College. The monk's ledger."

"How do you even know about that?"

"The touch of the book lingers on you. That's how dark magic works. As for how we know where the book is, there are spells that allow us to peer into our forebears' past if we know exactly what we're looking for. That book belonged to one of our enemies. It is full of foul magic, and it should be destroyed."

Jayne wanted to say *But aren't evil spells the Kingdom's favorite thing?* but she kept quiet.

"Such manuals into the darker areas of our ability should be dealt with. It is the Kingdom's responsibility. We don't want dark magic unleashed on the world accidentally."

Jayne's mind whirred. It was possible that she could steal it. She had the access, and as far as she knew, the TCO hadn't sent anyone in to recover it yet. Ruger had told Jayne to leave it alone, that it was too dangerous for her, but all of this was deadly.

"I'll try, but I can't promise you I'll get away with it. After losing the Book of Leinster, they will put new protocols in place. And if I'm caught, there will be major consequences that might keep me from helping the Kingdom."

"If you're caught, we'll rescue you. Have no fear about that. We won't let an Adept of your power slip through our fingers."

Well, that wasn't creepy. "What about my coworkers? If they know about it, they'll talk, and you'll have a big mess on your hands. Trinity won't let it go, and you know this. Can you wipe their memories or something?"

"There is a spell for such a task. We don't like to use it, because it's tricky, and done improperly, it can cause permanent damage. We don't seek to cause people pain, Jayne. You must understand this. Our goal is to liberate them."

Oh yeah, liberation through magical enslavement. Rock on, Alarik.

She must have looked worried, because Alarik said, "Don't worry. If you are caught, you won't be punished. You will disappear. We will make a place for you."

"Like a magical witness protection program?"

"Exactly like that."

Jayne swallowed the acid rising in the back of her throat. She'd be trapped with them. And it would be far more difficult to contact the TCO and manage any type of escape. If she tried to steal the grimoire, she had to be sure she'd succeed. Failure was not an option. Ruger would help her manage this, naturally. *Don't push back too hard, Jayne. You don't want to risk losing them.*

"Okay."

"Don't look so nervous," Teresa said. "You are very powerful. You can slip that book into your bag with your mind like *that.*"

She snapped her fingers, smiling. "What kind of exit precautions do they have in place for staff?"

"I'll have to see what they'll do once they realize the Book of Leinster has been stolen. For now, each book has a hidden identity card, and the detection device at the door goes off if the book leaves. But there isn't a manual check for staff members."

"It won't be a problem for you, Jayne." Alarik tapped his fingers on the table. "You can cast a Blocking spell around the book, and the electronics won't detect the hidden card. When you have the grimoire in hand, leave the library immediately. You'll deliver the book to a man wearing a yellow scarf near the rugby field."

"My coworkers will notice if I'm drumming up spells in the middle of the staff work area and leaving during work hours."

Alarik glanced at the old man next to him. "I was going to wait on telling you this, but if everyone is agreed…" He looked around the room. The other Kingdom members nodded, murmuring. "All right then. Jayne, we have a loyal assistant inside Trinity. Deirdre is my wife. She'll assist you in your endeavor, alert us when you've taken the grimoire."

Jayne tried to appear appropriately surprised.

Alarik continued. "You can do this, Jayne. You have been invited to become one of us because of your power and your mind. You pay attention to details and make strong decisions."

She fought to keep from rolling her eyes. He was talking to her like she was a child. "Like leaping into a flaming triangle to nowhere?" she asked, playing along.

The Kingdom members chuckled.

"Deirdre will distract Rosalind while you protect the world from that dark book," Alarik said.

"Why didn't she just do that when you took the Book of Leinster?"

"Because I'm not a staff member. I couldn't take the book out via spells. I would have had to deal with the man at the door's manual search."

"Why couldn't Deirdre just take it?"

"I bet you know the answer to that."

Jayne had some guesses. "She's not magical. And maybe you want Deirdre to retain her position in the library so you have access to another book or something else stored there? But it's possible they will fire her because of the incident."

"They won't. It was an accident, and no damage was done to any books. It's a stain on her record, but just a stain. Now, let's prepare for your return. I will not be there, of course, but there will be authorities swarming, so be ready to answer questions."

"I'm not bringing the Book of Leinster back with me, am I?"

"Of course not. We will introduce you to the book's potential after you prove yourself. Now, about the questions the library and the authorities will ask…"

Medb's hissing whispers flowed through Jayne's mind. She didn't have to speak that language to know the ancient Master wasn't a fan of Alarik. *Agreed,* Jayne thought to Medb.

CHAPTER FORTY-SIX

Alarik walked her to her room, going on with a script Jayne was to follow when questioned back at Trinity, post-fire. It went a little like this.

She thought she'd seen someone go out the door, but no one was there when she left the building.

No, she had never seen the man before today.

No, she didn't know him at all.

Deirdre hadn't acted strangely that day, nor did she seem to know the man who took the book.

The script was all very thorough, pretty much expected.

Until Alarik started talking about Rogues and their dangers.

"Not that I have to tell you after what you experienced. But some dangers are more subtle. Jayne, another Rogue has been near enough to touch you. Before you interacted with the trapped one. A different Rogue, in Dublin."

It was all Jayne could do to not mention Ruger. She'd been so close to a slip. "Really?"

"Yes. The trace of the other Rogue is faint, but it is there. We don't know of any in that city."

"Why can't you just track them down?"

"For one thing, it is rare to find one. And in a large city such as Dublin, it would be nigh on impossible to find the creature. They only give off the Rogue scent when they are close to changing. Most have this under control and do not change near humans. I warn you because we noticed it, and if you are to be one of us, we want you to be on your guard."

"What can a Rogue do to me? I mean, aside from turning into a berserk thing and bashing me to bits like the one in the training area."

"To be truly powerful, a Rogue needs a Master. Their shared power is difficult to challenge. They feed off one another. It's said Rogues can even share thoughts with their Masters, if they are truly matched, that is. But no one has seen a true match before. It is legend only."

"Whoa." Ruger hadn't told her that. Seemed like a pretty damn important thing to mention.

"Rogues live in loose packs, and when the moon is full, they head off into the more rural areas to hunt, grouping up based on their shifted form. Their human selves, their clothing, their human personalities, their human knowledge—it's all still there, hiding under the magic woven into their DNA."

"Do they pass on the gene?" she asked, her brain in two places.

Why was this bozo telling her all the things she needed to know? Ruger should've forced her to sit down and hear him out about the Rogue she'd crossed paths with. She gritted her teeth. She was a TCO officer. She shouldn't have been so poorly informed. In Ruger's defense, her mind argued, her training had been cut short so she could take this insane mission and use this supposedly amazingly strong magical ability of hers. Still. It seemed rather important. Unless the TCO didn't know as much as Alarik about their magical world... But that was impossible. Wasn't it? *Focus, Jayne. He's still talking...*

"Yes," Alarik was saying, "genetics play a role in the propagation of all magical creatures. It's similar to being an Adept. Just because one parent has the gene, or even both, it doesn't mean the child will have the ability. Rogue and Adept traits are nondominant, which is why we are just as rare as they. But still, one has found you, attracted to your power, I'm certain. We wouldn't want a creature like that to learn of our plans. We don't have any reason to believe the creatures are aware of the Kingdom at all. My mentioning it is purely me being overprotective of my potential Initiate."

"Initiate. I like the sound of that." Jayne made herself sick saying the words. This guy was as creepy as history's worst baddies. Worse, maybe, if he was able to do everything in that scheming, horrible head of his. Jayne couldn't imagine the Head of the Kingdom. She wrapped her arms around herself.

"Nervous?" Alarik asked as he opened the portal with the fastest spell casting Jayne had seen yet.

"Yes."

"Understandable. Just remember. Deirdre will receive a message about you approximately one minute after your arrival back in regular time. She'll help you. Just don't...don't overshare with her, please. Because she isn't an Adept, she is frightened by what we can do. We'll keep her a bit in the dark for her own safety, yes?"

"Agreed," Jayne said.

"One last thing." Alarik held out his hand. "Your amplifiers."

She untied the bracelets from her wrist and handed them over. Then she jumped through the whirling triangle.

Alarik waved his hand in a circle, and his voice followed Jayne into the portal. *"To begin again, the world reborn."*

That phrase. She'd heard it before. When? And why did it make her feel so strange?

She tried to stop her body from hurtling into the portal, but of course, that was impossible. The portal swallowed her up and washed awat her thoughts for the time being.

The trip back did not feel like a million bucks.

Feeling like she had sat on a beach without sunscreen for a day, she landed on her rump in the grass outside the library, sirens wailing in her ears. She held up her arms. Her skin didn't look burned, but it felt sensitive to the touch.

"Where was the kind warning about the portal burns, Alarik?" she muttered, wishing she'd remembered the burns she'd received on her way in. She could've asked about preventing that at the stupid meeting.

A fireman came around the corner and rushed to help her up. "You hurt?"

"No, thank you. I thought I saw a man go out this door, but..." She looked into the distance, playing it up quite nicely, in her humble opinion.

"Come this way, please." He led her around to the front of the building.

Despite herself, Jayne was blown away. The Kingdom's Time Catch worked. She hadn't been away from the real world more than ten minutes, tops.

A crowd had gathered, and police held them back with outstretched arms. Smoke drifted out the front door, forming a gray haze over the cobblestones. Gerard was rubbing his hair back compulsively and talking a mile a minute to a policeman.

"Ah! Thank God!" Gerard ran toward her. A rush of kinship

flooded her. "I thought you'd been lost to the great popcorn debacle, Jayne."

She touched his arm. "No, I'm fine. Is everyone else all right? No one hurt? The books…"

"The books are fine, Jayne. Maybe a little smoky, but we can work with that." He sounded almost gentle.

"We've had no injuries reported," the fireman said.

"So it was a popcorn fire?" she asked Gerard.

"Yes," the fireman answered for him. "Someone had a bag going in the downstairs break room."

Gerard shook his head. "It was our lovely Deirdre. She is normally so responsible. Surely she was distracted by an insightful musing on her important work."

"Yeah," Jayne agreed, looking at the policeman who'd followed Gerard over. "This was an accident. Deirdre shouldn't be punished. She is such a great person."

The policeman glanced at his phone. "These things happen. Not usually here, but they happen all the same. I'm sure the college won't press charges."

Rosalind and Deirdre emerged from the group of authorities beyond the trees and the front entrance. Jayne made deliberate eye contact with a harried-looking Deirdre, who nodded slightly and chewed on her lower lip. Her eyes were bloodshot, and tears had dragged her makeup down her face. Rosalind had an arm over Deirdre's shoulder, and the older woman clucked what sounded like reassurances into Deirdre's ear.

When Jayne approached, Rosalind drew Jayne into the circle, hugging both of her coworkers. Gerard even gave the group a quick squeeze, which made Jayne realize she was making friends on all sides of this thing. And with the dangers involved in this mission, there could be a day she would lose some or all of them.

She hugged them harder, then found a quiet spot to call Sofia. Sadly, the call went straight to voicemail. "Stop being mad," Jayne said into the phone. "I'm fine. And we'll catch up as soon as term is over. Okay? Christmas will be great. I promise."

CHAPTER FORTY-SEVEN

Trinity sent everyone in Jayne's department home to recover and to allow the janitorial staff and the library's specialized archival unit to clean up Deirdre's mess. Jayne sat in her apartment bedroom, staring at the wall. Recovering, indeed.

There was so much to take in.

Her power. Rogues. Stealing books. She held her phone loosely, knowing she should've already called Ruger and made a full report. He was watching her flat. They all were. But thankfully after a simple *I'll make a report in an hour* text, they'd left her to herself.

But where to start on this report? There was just so much.

Setting the phone on the bed, Jayne decided a glass of wine and a slice of pie were in order. She didn't bother with the table. She just drank from the bottle and enjoyed the last bit of rhubarb from the pie she'd bought at the market down the street. Rhubarb was a good fit for her mood, as was the red blend. Sweet but also bitingly tart. She was excited about her ability to do magic, about her potential for protecting those who needed it, and helping the TCO in big ways. But she was thoroughly freaked out by her experience in the Kingdom's weird Time Catch hangout. She'd been outside of time. Time. And that tortured Rogue…

What was the Kingdom doing with that Rogue she'd seen beyond the double doors?

Shaking her head, she finished her wine and tossed the bottle in the recycling bin under the sink. The moon shone through the kitchen window and across the countertop. She couldn't put off facing what she'd been through for long. She had to contact Ruger soon.

Just then, her phone rang from the bedroom.

With one last look at the crumbs from her demolished slice of pie, she hurried to answer.

"Hey, Jayne!" Cillian's voice was bright, and it literally turned Jayne's frown upside down. "How are you?"

She exhaled for what felt like the first time in over a week. God, his voice was the most gorgeous thing. Even better than the pie. "I'm doing okay. A little tired. We had some excitement at the library today. Popcorn fire."

"Am I supposed to know what that means?" A laugh danced through his words, and she had a sudden urge to climb through the phone, rouse some of her newfound confidence, and kiss him senseless. *Goodness.*

"Deirdre put a bag of popcorn in the microwave and forgot about it. Nothing major was damaged, but it was kind of awful. All those sirens. She feels terrible about it." And Jayne wondered if any small part of Deirdre set blame on her husband, Alarik. How long had Deirdre been doing his dirty work without full knowledge of why? That had to wear on a person.

"Wow. I'm glad you're all right. What are you up to tonight?"

Giving my boss a full rundown of everything I've just seen in a magical realm you can't possibly imagine.

"Um…"

His voice dropped a bit. Deeper. Sexier. Gah.

"I thought we could try again, without the crowd. Say yes, Jayne. It will be fun. Promise."

Damn it, all she wanted to do was say yes. She would get permission from Ruger. She wanted to see Cillian. She wanted it badly.

"Why don't I just meet you at The Auld Hall again? Seven?" she asked.

"Great! See you then."

Already imagining Cillian's easy way of taking her mind off the horrors at hand and the way his jeans fit him just right, Jayne hung up and called Ruger. She wanted all of this information off her chest so she could feel normal again for a night.

"You're alive. Thank God." Ruger's voice was strained. She could imagine him rubbing that perfectly trimmed goatee and pinching his lips together. "One of our lesser officers heard there was a fire."

"Just a small one, but it played a big role in my recent adventures."

"But I just talked to you. You haven't had time for an adventure, Jayne."

"I'm an expert on Time Catches now, Ruger, and boy, do I have a story to tell you."

"A Time Catch?"

"Yep. A certain Professor Albon came to the library. He was really Alarik, Deirdre's husband, come to steal the Book of Leinster. With freaking Queen Medb urging me along inside my brain, I jumped through a nasty little portal he called up to escape with the book."

He kept quiet as she detailed her trip through the portal to the Kingdom's other mini dimension, the training she did there with Max and Teresa, the Rogue she fought, and the mission Alarik had set on her shoulders.

When she finished, Ruger actually laughed. "I am very proud of you, Jayne. You've succeeded beyond our wildest imaginations. Amanda will dance when she hears."

The thought made Jayne smile. He really did sound proud of her.

"Thank you. Now, how do you suggest I go about stealing the grimoire? Do you like Alarik's plan on that?"

Ruger was getting more and more excited. "You could use the spell I taught you in training. Remember the basket? It's a Capture spell that holds an item in a sort of…pocket of the Torrent. But it will drain you quickly. It's one of those spells that doesn't filter the energy from the Torrent as efficiently, depends on your own energy to do the work. Maybe you should stick with how Alarik told you to do it. If you complete his mission in a wildly different way, he might get suspicious."

"Agreed. But this is breaking and entering. Smash and grab. I could get arrested, and that wouldn't be fabulous for our mission, would it? Can I risk it?"

"I think you have to. And it will be better if we just stay out of your way. If you really get in deep and need extraction, try to send your code word to my number."

"What if I don't have my phone?"

"If you can access the Torrent from wherever Alarik might take you, use the Flare spell I showed you on your second day in Virginia."

The Flare was a complicated piece of magic that involved focusing on the person whose attention you needed, then finding and casting a flash of red light. Done correctly, the spell's target would see the blaze and an image of the caster's face and know to send help immediately. But it was tricky. She hadn't mastered it at the Farm.

"I can't believe you dissolved a trapped Rogue." Ruger's voice was distant. "Your power must have the Kingdom salivating."

"They gave me bracelets with stones that amplified my power, too. Quartz, green jasper, and fluorite. I wouldn't mind having them back. They made accessing the Torrent easier than blinking."

"Amplifiers are old magic. Earth magic. It's not something we normally use these days. Fascinating. They really are harkening back to the beginnings, aren't they?"

"I suppose. They helped a lot. Find me some."

"All right. Can you tell me anything else about the Rogue you saw with Alarik?"

"He was in pain. And they had him restrained. Is that unusual?"

Ruger sighed heavily. "It's been so long since we dealt with Rogues…"

"The Kingdom members claimed everyone there was a willing volunteer."

"Sure. But do they consider Rogues 'everyone,' or are they tools to them? Unfortunately, they have been mistreated in the past."

"Disgusting."

"Yes. From all we know, and what you've just confirmed, the Kingdom sees Adepts as a higher form of being than ordinary humans. I doubt they think Rogues are on par with magicians."

"But they have power. Real power. You'd think they'd want to harness it. Ooohhhh…how could I be so stupid? That's what they're doing. Alarik is trying to harness the power of the Rogues. He could use them to take over."

"Makes sense. It's a feral sort of magic. I can see the Kingdom using them like beasts of burden. But you need a Master to truly control a Rogue. The relationship is symbiotic—one depends on the other."

"Maybe they were trying new magic on the Rogue they had there. What if the one that I had to kill had been experimented on?"

Ruger sucked in a breath, the sound whistling over the phone. "Now that is an interesting idea. And a horrifying one."

"They could be pushing Rogues, forcing them to shift into creatures that don't come naturally, for lack of a better way to put it. The one I saw was clearly in distress."

"I'll talk to HQ about it. You could be on to something."

Jayne agreed, then moved on to the topic of what Alarik had said about the Rogue ability to read minds. "You didn't tell me that." Her chest heated, anger rising.

"There's no need for you to worry about it. Unless you think you're being followed."

"I'm not." She'd kept a good eye out for signs. "But I'd like to know everything, Ruger. I don't like being in the dark when I'm risking my life here."

"Jayne. I know. I am sorry. There is just so much to tell you. Thousands of years of magical history. I have to make judgments on what's vital for you to achieve your mission goals, or when you need to move on to other, more pressing topics for discussion and learning. You'll learn it all, I promise. I'm not holding back from you." His voice softened. "Jayne, you must remember, magic has been on a kind of temporary hold for a very long time. We're all feeling our way through."

Jayne relaxed her grip on the phone and took a breath. "I get it. Now, what do I need to know about handling the dark grimoire?"

"You'll have to keep a clear head. Make sure you drink the bottles I put in your fridge today."

"You what?" She raced to the kitchen. Sure enough, ten bottles of that red juice she'd had during training sat side by side in the refrigerator door. "Okay. Got it." It was still weird to have a team going in and out of her life like helpful ghosts. And rather creepy, too.

"Give me a second." It sounded like Ruger covered the phone with a hand. He was talking to someone else. "Jayne?"

"I'm here."

"Deliver that grimoire to Alarik and his people as quickly as you can. I hate the idea of them having access to it, but it can't be helped at this stage. We'll worry about it later. Don't keep that evil book on your person for a second longer than you must. It will influence you in bad, bad ways."

"Like Frodo and the Ring?" This was wild.

"What?"

"Never mind." It definitely sounded Tolkien-ish. The idea of a cursed magic leaking into her bones turned her stomach. "I'm going out with a friend tonight, if that's good with you all. I assume you're not nearby, since you haven't already knocked on my door?"

He didn't disagree, so she assumed she was right.

"I need to spend some time with Amanda going over all you've told me. Meet me tomorrow before work. Five a.m. at the safe house outside the city. We'll need a sketch of every face you saw with Alarik and any names or places you can recall." He gave an address on the outskirts of the old town.

"Why can't you just come here?"

"Patterns, remember? We have to break our patterns to keep from being noticed. Now that Cillian is hanging around your place, bringing you coffee…"

"In my defense, it was very good coffee."

"I assume he's the 'friend' you're seeing tonight?"

"Yes. If I blow him off, it will look weird. You want me to fit in, right?"

"Right. But be careful. Though we haven't found any evidence of wrongdoing, I still don't trust him fully. Do not let your cover slip, not even for a moment."

"Gotcha, boss. Oh, before you go, have you heard anything about Sofia?"

A pause. "No. We have people on that."

"What do you mean? Is the TCO following Sofia now?"

"Jayne, we want to keep you and yours safe. We know how much Sofia means to you. She's gone off the grid, but from what you've told me, she has a particular talent for that. We'll find her. Be careful out there. And try to get some sleep tonight. It's no small thing you're going to try tomorrow with that foul book."

CHAPTER FORTY-EIGHT

The pub was wild and packed to bursting. Cillian's lopsided grin greeted Jayne on the pavement just outside the noisy entrance. He held out a hand, and her mind went right on to imagine what that hand would feel like on her hip.

"Don't be afraid to use an elbow or three," he said over his shoulder as he pulled her inside.

They bumped and laughed their way past a bunch of women in very, very short skirts and a mixed group of older men and women sharing what smelled like whisky. Hair flopping sexily, Cillian leaned over the bar top and shouted something Jayne didn't catch at the white-haired man running the cash register.

The man turned away from his stack of bills and shouted toward the back of the pub. "Jon!"

A curly-haired man emerged from behind a curtain wearing a white apron. He waved to Cillian and Jayne.

"Thanks," Cillian said as Jon popped open a door that Jayne hadn't even noticed at first.

"We have to take care of our own. When term's in, there's only half a dozen of us native Dubliners still in this city, seems like." Jon closed the door behind him.

The room was just as noisy as the main pub. Old men joked with a group of musicians as they tuned up. Trinity students stood and talked, faces flushed from alcohol and the room's warmth. A clutch of women in their fifties played cards at a big, round table.

"Is this like *Fight Club*?" Jayne asked as she sat on a barstool beside Cillian. God, his leg muscles under those jeans were destroying her train of thought. The barkeep handed her a Guinness without even asking what she wanted. "Am I allowed to talk about Dublin's secret pub inside a pub?"

"Definitely like *Fight Club*. Only with fewer fights and more dancing. And honestly, they'll let anyone in." He sipped his beer, the tip of his tongue touching his bottom lip.

She swallowed hard, her mind filling with ideas on how to employ said lip. She had little experience with men, but this was the new Jayne, and she was determined to learn. "Well, I would hope so."

"It's just nice to know there's a better chance at getting a seat for those of us who know this room is here."

The beer was almost cold, and Jayne drank three big gulps before worrying about anything else. This was exactly where she wanted to be right now. A little bit of normalcy in her crazy new world.

A man with an impressive mustache started a slow tune on an accordion while the woman next to him began playing a small instrument that looked like a tiny flute. Jayne had no idea what it was called. A younger guy's fingers danced over the strings of a fiddle with worn edges, and another old fellow strummed a mandolin.

"This is so cliché," Jayne said. She elbowed Cillian gently in the ribs and he acted like she'd mortally wounded him, going so far as to half fall off his stool before popping back up with a laugh.

"No, Jayne, someone murdering Christy Moore songs would be cliché. This is an Irish traditional music session in its full and simple glory. It's lovely, and I dare you not to agree to that."

"It is."

The music picked up its pace and Jayne found her feet wanting to tap along the barstool's metal base.

A couple got up to dance, another joined them. Jayne gave Cillian a cheesy grin. "Jigs! Pretty please?"

"I thought you'd never ask." He grabbed her hand and pulled her into the midst of the dancers.

They didn't follow any set steps. They just spun and jostled and clapped for a chubby fellow who had traditional Irish footwork on lock. By the time five songs were through and three whiskies downed each, Jayne's hair was sticking to her sweating forehead and Cillian's arms were wrapped firmly around her waist. She found she didn't mind that one bit.

Bursting with nerves, she touched her forehead to his and eyed his whisky-scented lips. "I'm going to kiss you now, if you're okay with that." Her words were a bit slippery, but not so bad that she sounded terrible. Good thing she'd tossed some water down in between the heavier spirits.

Cillian's eyes turned smoky. "I am definitely okay with that. What's your plan of attack?" His gaze flitted between her own mouth and the rest of her face, like he was learning the curves and slopes of her cheeks, brow, and chin. "I wouldn't want to make it too easy on you. Most kickboxers like a nice challenge."

Oh, my. How was this her life right now? She couldn't believe she was flirting like this. Jayne's skin grew even warmer, and she touched his neck with her lips. "I have a simple plan. Distraction." She brushed her body against his and felt chills rise on the back of his neck. "And then I'll come in at an angle." Pulling away, she stared him in the eye. Then she kissed him full on the mouth.

He laughed in surprise, but then focused on the task at hand. His tongue found hers for a moment and Jayne felt his fingers tangle in her hair. He pressed against her like she had earlier, and sparks ran down her belly and thighs.

"Can we head to my place maybe?" he whispered.

The old Jayne would never say yes to a bold proposition like this. But Jayne was tired of that woman. She wanted Cillian, and if she failed at her mission and the world came to a smoking, fiery end, she didn't want to regret a thing. She tried to answer, but the words caught in her throat, so she nodded.

In the back of an old taxi that smelled like pipe smoke, Cillian pulled Jayne into his lap. "Will the driver mind?" she asked, her nerves warring with her newfound confidence.

"Not if I give him this." Cillian dug some money from his back pocket, which provided movement Jayne enjoyed far too much, then pushed it through the plastic slot. The driver turned up the music.

Cillian's warm hands snaked under the hem of Jayne's shirt, and goose bumps ran down her body. He cupped her back, then moved the fabric at her neck with his teeth and kissed her collarbone. His strong body pressed wonderfully against her, and she had the urge to draw up a spell to remove all their clothing and possibly mask the driver for modesty's sake.

Cillian rasped something accented and unintelligible and kissed her again, deeply.

And then Jayne was in the Torrent.

CHAPTER FORTY-NINE

A spell flew at her, and she was back in reality with its nearly invisible wavering cocooning her and Cillian. The taxi fell away and they were in a four-poster bed in a stone-walled room. A sword lay on the bed beside them.

Jayne held her breath. Oh no. Oh no! She'd done magic in front of him. Magic! What would he do now? What would the TCO say? Would she be carted off to prison?

Cillian jerked away. "Jayne!"

She sat back but didn't release the spell. What good would it do? He'd already seen what he couldn't believe he'd seen. Besides, her head was spinning a bit too much to try and be clever.

"Just breathe, Cillian. Everything is okay. You're safe."

He shoved his hair back from his eyes. "Like hell I am. What is this? Did you drug me? Are you drugged? Are you all right?"

"I'm fine. You're fine." She let the spell go and they were in the taxi again.

The car stopped and let them out at what Jayne assumed was Cillian's flat. They stood staring at one another in the scant moonlight.

What was she going to do? If she tried to lie, it wouldn't fly. She didn't have it in her right now. Both fatigue and the painful crush she had on Cillian would trip her up 100 percent. But if she told him...

"Jayne. Tell me you saw that. Have I lost it?"

"Can we go inside and talk about this? I'll tell you everything. Everything I can, that is." She was going to do it, break the most important rule of the TCO, put herself into the TCO's line of fire. And Cillian would be in trouble too, just by knowing. But what else could she do? There was no explaining away what she'd done, and though Alarik had told her there were spells that could alter memories, she had no idea how to do it.

Pulling her phone out of her purse, she switched it off. She doubted it would stop the TCO from tracking her, but having it off made her feel slightly better about spilling secrets she was supposed to take to the grave.

They climbed three flights of stairs in total silence, her face on fire and her mind whirling in incoherent circles. Cillian's hands shook as he unlocked his door. The flat was a studio with a fold-out couch still in bed mode and a galley kitchen to the right. One big window showed the night sky.

Tossing the keys into a bowl on the table with an impressive accuracy, Cillian crossed his arms and faced her. "Please tell me I'm not losing my mind."

"You're not. But you might want to sit down when I tell you what's up."

"On the bed? No, I don't think we need to go there right now, or I might forget that I was shoved into the fifteenth century in the back of a car just now."

There was no embarrassment greater than what she felt at that moment. "Promise me you'll listen and not ask questions until I finish. And that you won't tell a single living soul anything."

"Done and done."

"Really? Without any argument?"

"You are obviously capable of things my little brain didn't even know existed, so yeah, I'm going to let you run this show."

A slightly hysterical laugh tripped out of her mouth. He was amazing. She'd have thought he'd call her "freak" and head for the hills.

She began to explain, choosing her words carefully. Telling him magic existed was one thing. Clearly a number of the Kingdom members had lovers or spouses who were aware; she assumed the TCO was similar, though she hadn't asked. Telling him she was a spy for a magical branch of the CIA here to work at the Trinity Old Library to thwart magical terrorists? That was something entirely different. She wasn't stupid. Nor did she want to lose her position.

So she told him, in the most bare-bones way possible, about the existence of magic in the world, and a few of the minor spells she was capable of, including the mysterious one she had just cast without even meaning to.

"Magic."

"Yeppers."

"It's not as if I can deny it. I saw it with my own eyes." He raked his hands through his hair and let out a big breath. Then his gaze lifted and locked on her. Man, the looks he could give. It was like she'd downed a triple shot of espresso.

"Do you think I'm a freak now?"

He took a tentative step toward her. "Now how thick do you think I am? I wouldn't tell a witch that I think she is *freaky*," he said, using air quotes and an American accent, "when she could turn my balls into pigeons."

A laugh bubbled out of Jayne. "Pigeons?"

"Imagine it. It would be horrible. They'd be upset about being down in my trousers, and they'd peck at all the important surroundings."

"Oh, wow." Jayne smothered another laugh with her arm. "Okay. So. Have you ever seen any magic in your life?" She secretly hoped he might be an Adept. That might explain why she was so drawn to him. Not that Ruger or anyone had mentioned such a thing. She certainly didn't feel that way toward any of the other Adepts she'd met. But maybe their magic was special and linked and…

"Are you spacing out on me, Jayne?"

"I definitely was. Sorry. I've had a lot to drink. That's why I lost control. I'm sort of…new at this."

"And here I thought I drove you delirious with my touch." He grinned. "Have I seen magic? I don't know. I have had my share of strange experiences. A possible ghost at some ruins once during uni. And sometimes, I think…ah. Never mind."

Her curiosity was piqued. "No, tell me. Please."

"I'm good at reading people. Like what they're about to do. It helps with fighting, that's one good thing."

Jayne tried not to feel disappointed. That didn't sound like magic. Just simple intuition. A people person. "That's a great skill for a guy who fights for a living. Your intuition probably helps in business, too."

He opened his mouth, frowning, like he was about to argue what she said, but then he dropped his hands to his sides. "Hey, how about we eat all the ice cream I have in my freezer, then watch a movie?"

"You are a total dreamboat."

"I've been told as much."

"And humble to boot."

Cillian flicked her butt with quick fingers on his way to the refrigerator. To think she had worried he was a Rogue at one time. No, he was just Cillian and pretty much perfect. He returned, not with a tub of pistachio gelato or Moose Tracks, but with a box of Magnum white chocolate ice cream bars.

"Interesting," she said, trailing him to the sofa bed.

He flipped on the TV, muttering, "I can't believe magic exists. I'm cracked, for sure," and found some weird British mystery show that Jayne wasn't about to pay attention to when she had ice cream she'd never tried and Cillian licking his lips beside her. If tomorrow was going to be a nightmare, she was determined to make tonight a dream.

She took one of the bars. "This is good, huh?"

His face went as serious as a religious zealot. "The very best."

They gobbled two each, and when Jayne had tidied up, against all Cillian's arguments against cleaning, she sat next to him. Would he kiss her again, or was that all over for the time being because of the magic discussion?

He set the TV remote down and faced her, his eyes a darker blue in the low light. His lips parted, and she found herself staring at them. "I would like to kiss you again, but you must promise not to beam me into a Tardis or something."

"Oh lord. You've obviously never watched *Star Trek* or *Doctor Who*."

"Is that a deal breaker?"

"I shall allow it. You are after all, being very cool about my freakiness."

He grinned and she thought he might say something else, but instead he leaned forward, his mouth hovering over hers.

Her body warmed and tightened, wanting to close the infinitesimal space between them. But she hesitated, longing fighting reason. What if she did do magic again and something far worse happened?

Sitting back, he cocked his head and set a hand on her leg. "Eh, let's call it a night, hmm? You seem distracted."

A weight settled on her chest. "I'm worried about what might happen."

"I understand." He stood and she wanted to pull him back to the couch. "I'll get you a taxi. I'd drive you myself, but I've had way too much to drink."

"Kind, and responsible. You may take me out again, sir."

"You better believe it."

When she got home, she remembered to turn her phone on. There were several missed calls from Ruger.

Oh, great.

CHAPTER FIFTY

Ruger put his head in his hands and leaned on his desk. He'd been called back to DC for a mandatory debrief to share what Jayne had learned about the Kingdom, the Rogues, and the Time Catch. And he needed to do some research. He hadn't lied when he told Jayne there was much he didn't know.

The Library Division's main office was quiet this time of day, and he was glad for the silence, because Gerard had just let him know that while Jayne was out with the kickboxer who'd had a connection to Aaró, something had happened toward the end of the evening that seemed very much like magic. Ruger tried to call immediately, but her phone was off.

He was starting to realize Jayne Thorne was a bona fide trouble magnet.

It was possible the man had no Kingdom affiliations, that he'd been at the tattoo parlor for the obvious goal of getting a tattoo. Nothing else had come up in their research. But Ruger didn't like it. Especially when he was seen hanging around Jayne's building when he had to know she'd be at work. They'd let this Cillian fellow go inside the building, but he never entered her flat, and had returned to the street with nothing in his hands. Another officer had trailed him to his dojo, and Cillian hadn't shown any signs of being up to anything untoward. Ruger didn't want to push it by breaking into the man's home. Missions could get messy quickly, and there was no true evidence to show he was a threat.

"Trust her," Amanda had told him when he complained yet again about the problem. "We need to see where she goes with this. I have faith that she won't betray us, won't side with the Kingdom. We are testing her as much as using her."

"You know I don't like that term, 'using.' We are a team."

"Whatever you want to call it, Ruger. The point is, I'm telling you to back down a little. Just keep an eye on her from a distance. She's doing everything right, and on such an accelerated schedule that we're gaining on them."

"Back down? Even when we know it's very possible that the Kingdom already kidnapped her sister?"

"Yes. Even then. And don't you dare tell her, or she'll lose all her focus. I need you in Paris this afternoon, so have your meeting, and relax. She's got this."

He straightened a few papers on his desk, moved some files to his phone for reading, and blew out a breath.

Amanda was right. This mission was going fine.

Ruger messaged his man to lay off the couple, that he would handle it, and he left the beautiful quiet of the office and portaled into the streets of Dublin. He only had a matter of hours to focus on Jayne before he had to leave to quell an incident on the Continent.

⅜»— + —«⅜

Jayne winced at the frown distorting Ruger's normally granite features when he met her at the door to the TCO's safe house.

"You're late. And where have you been? I was trying to reach you, and you didn't answer your phone."

Uh-oh. She was in trouble. "Um, I went out? Remember? I said I had a date."

Ruger was silent for a moment, brows furrowed. "Jayne. You didn't happen to do any magic in front of your new boyfriend, did you?"

"Ummmm..."

"Oh, Jayne. You must be more careful. I should have warned you, but I didn't think you'd find someone so quickly. It happens sometimes, especially to new Adepts, when you forget yourself in the moment. We'll have to wipe his memory—"

"You were the one who told me to fit in. Actually, he's totally cool with it. I didn't give him a lot of info, just that yes, magic is real, and yes, some of us can do it. He rolled with it, no problem. He is Irish, you know. They believe in all sorts of mythical things."

"You told him magic was real."

"I think he'd already figured out that part for himself. I was just confirming it."

Ruger rubbed a temple. "Don't put him at risk, Jayne. That's all I'll say."

"Fair enough. But if he sticks around...it's sort of inevitable that he'd find out, right?"

"You think he might be sticking around?"

Her mind showed her the memory of Cillian's eyes going dark and sexy at his flat. "I...hope so? He's a really good guy. And a great cover," she added quickly. "I don't stick out with a local by my side."

"I'll speak with Amanda."

"Thank you. I really am sorry, Ruger. Why were you trying to reach me?"

He moved deeper into the room, gestured for her to take a seat at a sturdy table. "I have to go to Paris. There's been an incident with another case I'm in charge of."

"What?" Jayne felt that familiar edge of panic slide through her. "You're leaving me on my own? Now? Ruger, not a good plan."

"I'm sorry, Jayne. I have no choice. The Kingdom aren't the only bad guys in the world."

"They aren't?"

"Of course not. Now, focus. We don't have much time, and I want to talk more about the Time Catch and the players you interacted with."

It wasn't cake on a plate, trying to sketch all the Kingdom people at five in the dang morning with a roaring whisky-induced headache. But Jayne managed it, thanks to Advanced Art, junior year.

When she finished, Ruger stacked the sketches. "Thanks, Jayne. You've done so well thus far. Especially for an Adept who received less than half the training of a normal recruit."

Jayne popped her knuckles and grinned too widely, covering her fear with bravado. "Let's hope I don't go to Irish prison today to top off a job well done."

"You won't. I believe in you. Now, Alarik might have plans for you to join him immediately. You need to be prepared for that, and you should be ready in case he wants you to enter the Time Catch again unexpectedly."

"I wouldn't be surprised if he magically kidnapped me. But how will I reach you if that happens? I don't think I'll be able to pop in and out of the Time Catch at will."

"Now that we know it exists, if there's an emergency, send a Flare. We can tune things on our end to your frequency. If you're half as strong with the amplifiers as you said, it will work. Probably."

"Probably."

He shrugged. "New magic, old magic. Your magic. You'll be fine, Jayne. I doubt it will happen."

Jayne nodded.

"Hey, any news on Sofia? It would be great if she'd stop being a maniac and pick up the damn phone."

"No. Nothing. Time for me to go. See you soon, Jayne."

Jayne felt an urge to hug Ruger like she used to hug her father. She started toward him and he grabbed her hand, shaking it, while he clutched her shoulder.

He smiled wide. "You'll be fine. Call me right after, too, all right? I'll be waiting."

"Right. Will do." She felt stupid for getting emotional for a moment. Ruger wasn't her friend; he was her boss. And he was ditching her for some Parisian baddies, so she was on her own.

Jayne forced the thought aside and hurried from the room toward her mission of the day.

Stealing a book heavy with dark magic.

"I really should have a Samwise Gamgee on my six," she muttered as she boarded a city bus. Exhaust fumes tickled her throat and she coughed. It was so much easier to portal places, but of course she couldn't draw that kind of attention to herself today.

For her ride into thievery, she'd chosen to finish the were-wolf novel Sofia had given her. She'd put it away for a while when she'd learned Rogues were real. But now, she was ready to laugh a bit at how wrong the fiction was on the facts. It made her feel less like a naive idiot and more like she had control of this situation. "This is a pleasant fiction," she said to herself, quoting *Gladiator.*

CHAPTER FIFTY-ONE

Gerard rolled his eyes when Jayne walked in yawning. "Why do Americans think arrival time is negotiable?"

"I'm on time, Gerard." Already, Jayne's pulse was kicking up. She tried to calm her voice. "Like I always am."

"Barely."

"There is no barely on time. I either am or I'm not."

"That is debatable. Are you expected to be in the staff area or here at the door? It takes several minutes to walk from one to the other."

Jayne glared, but honestly, she was glad for the distraction. This thorny repartee was helping her heart rate return to normal because she was less focused on the upcoming snatch and grab.

"I'd say my arrival time should be noted at the main door, especially considering I am forced to spar with the doorman upon entrance."

"Developing proper work relationships with your fellow

employees is a job requirement, my dear. So sorry if the college did not make that clear in your paperwork."

Fighting a grin, she said, "Oh, it was there. But they failed to tell me my first interaction each day would include a painfully crotchety Brit."

Gerard looked dramatically offended. "I think *disdainful* would be the better adjective. But you best hurry on, now. You'll be late." An evil smile crossed his mouth.

Jayne shook her head and left him, wondering if she should've teased him about the paperback he was reading. He kept hiding it, so it had to be less than literary in style.

But now it was time to get to work.

She greeted Rosalind and Deirdre in turn.

Deirdre gave no indication that she knew what Jayne was about to try, so Jayne had to simply trust that Alarik had filled her in.

An hour crawled by while Jayne gathered three versions of eighteenth-century poetry books for a grad student who smelled like a wet dog. Rosalind still hadn't left the staff area for even a potty break. Red glasses in place on her nose, she scrolled through emails on the computer at the registration desk. Deirdre was labeling boxes for a set of Arthur Rackham illustrations with annotations from varying fantasy authors someone anonymous had gifted to the library.

Jayne cleared her throat and made eye contact with Deirdre. Rosalind didn't seem to notice.

Looking flushed, Deirdre looked away from Jayne and toward the front desk. "Rosalind?"

Rosalind took her glasses from her nose and let them swing on their little chain. "Yes?"

"Can you come with me to the vault? I want to store these until we have word from the English professor."

Rosalind stood. "Good idea."

Deirdre had been informed that since the fire was accidental, she wouldn't be charged or let go, but she did have to take another staff member to the vault with her for the next quarter. A fire in an ancient library would be a catastrophe of such epic proportion, and even something little like burnt popcorn meant punishment. Deirdre seemed to think hers was just and hadn't complained a lick.

The women disappeared down the corridor.

The moment the clacks of their shoes died away, Jayne left the poetry on the table and made a beeline for the grimoire. She carefully took the book from the shelf. The faded gold lettering along the spine almost seemed to flash. A fierce curiosity rose inside her, and she fought the urge to open it up and peruse all that evil.

Afraid Rosalind and Deirdre would return soon, and keeping an eye out for Gerard, she quickly accessed the Torrent, gathered a Blocking spell, and shrouded the grimoire in magic. She'd emptied her purse this morning, so the book fit neatly.

With a careful zip, the deed was mostly done. Now she only had to get out of there and get to the yellow-scarf fellow Alarik had hopefully put into place.

Two worries bit at her heels as she walked toward Gerard and the main exit.

Would Gerard believe her excuse that she needed to make a private phone call outside? And was this truly a Kingdom test she could pass? What if Alarik was setting her up?

She wiggled her phone when Gerard looked up from his paperback. "Got to make a call."

He frowned, slipping the book off his lap so it hid between his leg and the gray alarm post. "Why don't you just go to the staff room?"

It was time to use the ammo she had. "What's that you're reading there, Gerard? Something philosophical? A fine work of great genius?" Playfully, she grabbed at the book.

He raised it up to avoid her reach and she saw the title. "It's nothing," he said. "Just entertainment."

It was *Arrows of the Queen* by Mercedes Lackey. "I love that book! You shouldn't be hiding that baby away."

Gerard's grin was genuine. "It isn't half bad. My niece asked me to do a companion read with her."

"A buddy read. Sure she did." Jayne gave him a smile and hurried out of the door, heart in her throat. She felt like a dog, pulling this over on old Gerard. He was a pain in the ass, but she liked him anyway. If she were caught, he'd be canned.

A nauseated feeling swarmed Jayne's middle, and she stopped walking. A light rain began to fall. She touched the outside of her purse and felt the hum of magic. A ringing sound filled her ears as a bicycle zipped past and clipped her elbow.

"How about you don't run me over, jerk!" she shouted, anger roaring through her veins.

She bent, feeling like she might vomit.

Ah. This was the book's doing. The anger. The nausea.

"Samwise. I need you," she whispered, rising up and walking quickly toward the rugby field. But there was no good friend to help Jayne. She was all on her own now, earning her way into a group of terrorists who thought they were the good guys.

The book was as heavy as nine elephants inside her purse. The field seemed miles away, and there wasn't a yellow scarf in sight.

What if she passed out right here in the middle of the campus?

She would go to jail for theft. The Kingdom wouldn't want her. Gerard would get fired. Probably Rosalind, too. And who knew if any other TCO officer would be able to infiltrate the

Kingdom before they did whatever awful thing they were going to do?

Jayne simply had to get this book to the Kingdom.

She forced her feet to move. Sweat dripped down her forehead.

Why was the grimoire affecting her like this? It hadn't bothered her much in the library. Was it because of the spell she had on it? Was her magic fighting with its magic? What would happen if she let go of the Blocking spell? The evil thing might explode out of her bag and kill everyone in sight. She had no idea. Anything could happen. She really knew so little about this world of magic.

Why hadn't Alarik or Ruger warned her about the toll this would take on her? Maybe they had and she had just missed it, or dismissed it, more likely. *You're in over your head, Jayne. Pay more attention.*

A group of younger students passed by, one stopping to ask if Jayne was all right. She waved them on, and they talked about her as they walked away, calling her *quare sick* and using other Irish slang Jayne didn't understand.

The path branched to the right, and Jayne finally spotted something yellow in the distant rain.

She raised her hand in greeting. The yellow moved closer. Yes, it was a woman. It was Teresa, wearing a yellow scarf. She nodded toward a clutch of shrubbery, and Jayne obediently followed her into the semiprivate area.

"Put it in here." Teresa held out a thick, brown paper bag and snapped it open, keeping an eye on the people walking by.

Rain fell over Jayne's shoulders and gave her a chill. She transferred the book quickly and released the Blocking spell.

It was like she'd let go of a rabid dog on a leash. The relief was immediate.

"You'll be okay with this awful thing? It made me really sick."

Teresa gave Jayne a sad smile. "Yes. It probably affected you so strongly because your magic is very pure of heart."

"Really?"

"We can't talk. I must go and so should you. We will be in touch."

"How is Max?"

Teresa's eyes narrowed. "Why do you ask?"

"He was a nice guy. No reason."

Teresa seemed to relax a fraction. "To be honest, I haven't seen him. I'm hoping he just went home unexpectedly. Alarik won't tell me anything."

"Oh, wow. Keep me posted. Wait. I guess you can't. Well, I hope he is okay."

"Me too."

"You don't think Alarik did something to him because of my questions during the meeting, do you?"

"What did that have to do with Max?"

"I discussed the questions with him first. He told me to ask."

Teresa's throat moved against the scarf's loose knot. "I don't know. I have to go now."

"Take care," Jayne said as Teresa turned away.

Jayne's mind whirled as she made her wet way back to the library. Teresa's nervous retreat did nothing to soothe Jayne's fears about her line of questioning throwing Max onto the Kingdom's bad side. But surely just a few questions about ethical dilemmas weren't cause for kicking him out.

When Jayne dialed Ruger's number, she prayed he'd pick up quickly. No answer. Of course. She hung up and dialed again. After three tries, he picked up.

"Done," she said, her voice shaky. "But one member is missing now," Jayne added, hoping he'd know she meant a Kingdom member. "The first one I drew this morning."

Rosalind was coming out of the front door, gaze right on Jayne.

"Gotta run," she whispered before hanging up.

Pasting a smile on her face, Jayne tucked her deflated purse under her arm.

Rosalind met her, and they started back together. "Gerard said you had to make a call, and I thought I'd check on you, love. Everything all right?" She patted Jayne's arm with wrinkled fingers. "The fire shook us all quite a bit. I don't mind a bit if you need some time off this afternoon."

"I'm fine, Rosalind, Promise. Just something at home."

Guilt weighed down Jayne almost as much as the dark grimoire's magic had. Well, at least it was over for today. The book was dangerous anyway. She was protecting Rosalind and everyone else at Trinity College by taking it away.

After work, Jayne pushed through a crowd of tourists outside the Tesco to grab some much-needed chocolate. Irish sweets were pretty different from stuff back home. Sure, Jayne had perused the shelves of World Market in Nashville and tried some candy from other countries, but she really couldn't remember what she'd liked. Nothing even looked familiar. She decided on some aerated chocolate situation called Wispa. Seemed like a better idea than fooling around with questionable nougat or foreign caramel. Chocolate was pretty much chocolate.

Three bars in hand, Jayne shoved her way toward the street.

A hand shot out and grabbed her arm.

Turning, she eyed the person with a stranglehold on her jacket. Middle-aged, he had a narrow face and the strength of what felt like ten people twice his size, but maybe that was just her nerves talking. He pulled her close within the crowd and put his mouth to her ear.

"Tomorrow, at dusk," he hissed, shoving a slip of paper into her pocket before disappearing into the crowd.

The red light of the Tesco sign blazed above as she unfolded the message. Tiny lines made up the roads around Dublin, and someone had drawn a simple set of waves to indicate the sea. A spot on the coast was circled twice.

This was the spot where she would meet with the Kingdom operatives in the real world for the first time, as Alarik had promised in return for her theft of the book.

This was her chance. Hopefully she could retrieve the book and show off her magic, make them accept her.

And then she could take them down.

PART THREE

Many a ship is lost within sight of the harbor.

—Irish proverb

CHAPTER FIFTY-TWO

The sounds of the city faded—engines giving way to water, and human voices losing to the gulls—as Jayne dropped from the street and clambered down the rocks. Waves lapped at a rocky coast, and a far-off barge was the only break in the ocean's churning darkness. Good thing she'd picked up some waterproof boots. This was supposed to be low tide and the only time the sea cave the Kingdom was using would be dry. But the ocean didn't seem to want to give up the spot completely. She climbed over a damp boulder and landed squarely in a pool filled with crabs and some kind of green growth. Where was this cave anyway?

Out of the puddle, Jayne leaned on another tall rock and pulled out the map the man outside the Tesco had shoved into her hands. She was in the right spot, or so it seemed. There was the road and the bend in the coastline. A warning sign, put into place for those foolish enough to have a meeting in a cave that filled with wild ocean water most of the day, marked the end of an outcropping. Yes, she was in the right place. But where was the cave? And where did the rest of these Kingdom members store their cars? Had they taken the bus, or a taxi, like her? She shouldn't have taken the taxi. That man had to be reporting her weird behavior to his superiors right now. Why would a woman insist on being dropped off here, where there was absolutely nothing? Ruger was going to ream her for this. And she wouldn't blame him. She should've taken the bus and walked the rest of the way. Now she was—

"Jayne?" Teresa's voice carried over another row of black rocks. Then her head peered over the top. "Over here." Her lips were pressed into a line, and a wrinkle appeared between her brown eyes.

Despite her obvious stress, Jayne was glad to see her. "Oh, thank God, a friendly face." She wiggled between the boulders and gave Teresa a nod. "Where's Max?"

"He has...moved on."

"What does that mean?"

Teresa led Jayne around a flat area of jagged sea rock, then the cave mouth yawned wide, dripping with saltwater. The scent of magic was thick in the air, but it wasn't comforting. The cave was dark inside, but the flicker of a few torches shone inside its depths.

"Come. You're late," Teresa said, very clearly avoiding Jayne's question.

What in the heck did *moved on* mean? Like, broke off to another Kingdom cell, maybe a splinter cell like the one those men who'd attacked Jayne in Nashville had been a part of? Jayne wasn't supposed to know there were other cells yet, so she decided to simply bite her tongue and see what panned out. If there was a way to find out if Max was okay, she would find it.

Inside the sea cave, Alarik sat cross-legged on a wide, striped mat beside five others, who were likewise seated. Another ten or maybe twelve—it was dark, hard to see, and they kept shuffling around and talking—were in attendance. German, heavily accented English, and Dutch words echoed though the space.

"Ah, welcome, welcome, everyone." Alarik wore his usual medieval auntie outfit, but this time it had been dyed a dark red. The color did nothing to soothe Jayne's whirling, crashing ideas on what might go on here. She couldn't stop thinking about blood and the burns she'd received when she'd gone through the portal. "Today is very special. We have a new Initiate with a great power we haven't seen in a long, long time."

"Hello," Jayne stammered, taking a green striped mat from Teresa. She made herself as comfortable as was possible inside a wet and salty rock. "Forgive me if I don't know exactly what to do here."

"Honesty is the first requirement, so your admission of ignorance is a wonderful first step."

He addressed the entire group as they filled into the available spots and adjusted themselves on their mats. It was like a bizarre magical yoga class, and Jayne fought back the urge to giggle.

"Tonight, we have two of our groups here from Vienna and Amsterdam. Welcome, all."

Murmurs of "thank you" and "glad to be here" filtered around the cave.

"The Kingdom has two objectives for this meeting. A, to begin final discussions on the three spells we will cast to accomplish our twofold goal here in Ireland. And B, to find out what our new Initiate is capable of."

Uh-oh. She was part of the show? Jayne's stomach twisted. She was pretty sure she didn't like what that would involve, not if the nervous and pitying glances from the groups were any hint.

"Great," she managed to say, almost making the word ring true.

"Teresa, would you please find the sketchbook and shine your light on what we've done thus far?" Alarik asked.

Teresa pulled a large book from an oilskin bag set against the side of the cave. The cover was new, plain, and made of simple brown leather. A man in suspenders set a mat out for the book, and Teresa opened to a page near the middle.

A shape had been drawn with black chalk. Jayne moved onto her knees to see it over two guys' shoulders. Four slashes ran across a triangle, and a note was written below.

"Our Head wrote this note for us," Alarik said. "She'll join us as soon as she is prepared. She has explained the markers to look for inside the Torrent so we can find the spell that will work with the Book of Leinster, the book that has called to our Initiate Jayne." He granted her a smile, which she unsteadily returned. "It won't be an easy task, my friends," he said, "but worth it, yes?"

This was obviously a rhetorical question, because the Kingdom members just smiled and patted one another on the back like they were about to go into the final quarter of a game against the school's most hated rival. They were ready to play their hearts out and Alarik knew it.

But what was this spell? She thought maybe she knew the answer already but didn't want to really think about it. Not yet.

She decided to go for it and just ask, but Alarik cut off her thought.

"Jayne. Would you mind very much if we do a bit of training right now? The rest of you, attempt to locate a spell like our Head has requested."

"Okay," she said, trying her best not to sound like she was freaking out even though she was definitely freaking out.

Conversations began in three languages as Alarik approached Jayne. "Let's go to the back of the cave."

If he offered her a puppy and a lollipop, she was out of there.

He took a torch from a woman with a mess of curly hair and started toward the cave's inner recesses. "We must use all the tools we have to achieve a world safe for Adepts."

"And to protect the weak." Jayne just couldn't help herself.

"Of course. Though you have proven to hold enormous power, this testing of yours will not be easy, Jayne."

"Nothing ever is."

"True. I'm so very glad you found your way to us." He set the torch in a metal bracket covered in rust and medieval as hell. Facing her, he clasped his hands together. The light behind him made it so that she could only see his silhouette. "First, I want you to enter the Torrent and attempt to find a spell that can help you communicate with me in a mere whisper from the opening of the cave. I will return as soon as you manage it."

Stomach twisting, Jayne eyed the torch. "You're leaving the torch, right?"

"I am. It will last about…twenty minutes." And without another word of guidance, Alarik took off.

"Fabulous," Jayne muttered.

The back of the cave was the blackest of all blacks. Anything could be hiding. And it wasn't just bats or honey badgers she worried about. This group had to possess magic she'd never heard about in training. They were unpredictable. For all she knew, Smaug the dragon was about to saunter on out and have her for dinner. Oh, and she'd forgotten completely to ask when the tide would come back in and drown the cave. Great. This was all really perfect. She was a stellar TCO officer. She could just hear Amanda. *Ruger, your new officer is now magical dragon feces. Congrats on the pick, guy.*

Swallowing her fear, Jayne closed her eyes and eased into the Torrent's green speckled light and inky sky. Her muscles relaxed a fraction, and she began her search.

"Communication. Hmm...speaking. Listening," she murmured, mind whirling. Spells appeared and shuffled past, but none seemed to hit her in the gut with *rightness*. "The transfer of knowledge and...space...distance...vibrations of the throat..."

A wisp, no larger than her hand, floated at her feet. It was shaped like a cirrus cloud and didn't look powerful. But looks could be deceiving, and this one felt like exactly what she needed.

She pulled it gently into her hands and left the Torrent. Holding her palms near her mouth, she whispered, "Alarik. Helloooooo?" Snorting, she felt like an idiot. She tried again, this time a little louder.

A shout echoed from the front of the cave, and Alarik came jogging up. "No need to shriek, dear." He rubbed at his ears. His eyes were watering. "Your energy is truly impressive."

"Really?"

"You're a rare gem. Now, we must give you more of a challenge." He tapped his linked fingers against his chin, thinking. "Ah. Call up a spell that can mend this." Something glinted in the torchlight.

Blood poured over Jayne's knuckles.

Alarik had sliced open her hand.

CHAPTER FIFTY-THREE

Jayne swore. The cut burned and ached. A scream built in her throat, but she held it down.

"I'm sorry, dear. But you'll be able to mend it. I'm almost positive." He smiled and walked away again.

"Almost? Lovely. Thanks. Hey, when does the tide come back in?"

Alarik didn't answer.

Jayne's hand throbbed with pain, and sticky blood oozed from the small cut. Ruger had told her no Adept could heal, and that he hadn't even read any legends about any Masters who could heal, but maybe he was wrong. Alarik didn't say he was giving Jayne an impossible task that no one had ever accomplished. He obviously expected her to be able to do this. Did that mean Alarik or another Adept could call up a healing spell? What else had Ruger been wrong about?

When she entered the Torrent this time, the air smelled even more strongly of roses and woodsmoke, the scents that seemed to be her signature magical perfume. The lime-hued stars flowing around her body and down into a sort of waterfall past her feet and into the continuing midnight sky shone brighter than ever. The beauty of the place took her breath.

Why was the Torrent all souped up right now? She hadn't done anything different when accessing it. Same visualization. Same level of stress. Well, that wasn't quite accurate. Alarik had cut her with a knife, for God's sake. Of course she was more stressed. She was bleeding. Not badly, but still.

The blood.

Maybe the presence of her blood had jacked the Torrent into this new level of brightness around her body? A more natural amplifier?

Indeed, it is your blood, Medb whispered into Jayne's mind.

Jayne inhaled sharply. *Can you help me heal myself?*

You do not need my help.

Fabulous. Just fabulous. Now she needed magical stitches. She focused on thoughts of weaving flesh together, and a spell shimmered into view. It was a thatch-like pattern of solid white stripes that she brought back in its invisible form to the real world. A slight heat filled her fingers as she placed the spell over her cut. Okay, so far, so good. The spell soaked into her skin—a cooling stream of magic that would have made her sigh with relief if it weren't for that persistent burn in the fingers that had held the spell. The cut didn't completely heal up, but the blood stopped flowing, and the affected skin looked like it had been injured a week past instead of just a minute or two ago.

But the burn of the magic centered around her fingers intensified.

"Alarik!" Jayne shook her hand, stupidly hoping the feeling would fall away.

Alarik strolled up like he was simply enjoying a walk in the park. "Problem?" He took her hand and examined the cut. "Ah. You did so well! I knew it."

"My fingers feel like they're on fire, so I don't think this is a big, successful party moment."

"It will pass." But when he studied her face, he seemed less sure. He put a hand to her throat and checked her pulse. "You'll be fine. You are so very strong."

"*When* will I be fine?" The pain equaled the agony of the time she'd accidentally grabbed the cookie tray right out of the oven when she was twelve, far worse than the burn she'd felt after fighting the trapped Rogue.

"Kingdom members must promise to suffer for the cause, for the magic. Are you not willing? Because if you can't take the heat, as they say..." He held up his hands and shrugged.

"Then get out of the sea cave? At the moment, that doesn't sound like a terrible idea."

He sighed and crossed his arms while Jayne tried blowing on her fingers. It wasn't helping.

"That's enough testing for day one. Go home, Jayne. The next meeting will take place tomorrow night. If you don't show up, we will mark your inaction as a signal that you no longer wish to be a part of the Kingdom."

"I'll be there." Jayne gave him an awkward nod and trudged out of the cave, stopping only to say *bye* to Teresa.

Her hand was pounding with pain.

She'd healed herself. Queen Medb had spoken to her again. Alarik had disappeared Max.

And though she didn't understand it, she'd seen the first spell involved in the Kingdom's plan, as well as members from cells in Germany and the Netherlands. Ruger needed to know all of this right away.

Her mind spun with ideas and theories, and she couldn't help but worry about Max, too. If they had hurt him or imprisoned him or killed him, she felt some responsibility. She had to find out if there was any chance to help him. Sure, he was a bad guy, a member of a terrorist cell, but he had been kind and seemed like a genuinely good person. He'd just been duped by Alarik and the rest. And he didn't seem as brainwashed as Teresa. He could probably be won over to the right side. She'd have to ask Ruger about it, see if they could find any information on him. Right after she broke the news that she'd managed to mend herself. Ruger was going to have kittens when he heard this one.

CHAPTER FIFTY-FOUR

Back on the beach ramp, she called a taxi, and while she waited, sent Ruger a text.

Hella crazy weird stuff happening. Need to talk. Let me get somewhere safe.

Her phone rang immediately, and she casually reached into the Torrent for a spell to mask her words. It struck her that she was doing more advanced magic now, that it wasn't nearly as hard as it had been in the beginning, and she was doing it almost without thinking. *Practice makes perfect, Jayne.*

"What happened?

Jayne relayed the info about the Head's spell, describing its appearance to Ruger.

"The slash marks were drawn diagonally, left to right, across the triangle?" Ruger's voice sounded strained through the phone.

"Yes."

"Was the triangle complete?"

"It had three sides." Jayne turned her mostly healed hand over and studied the pink line where Alarik had cut her.

Ruger mumbled something, then said, "I mean, were there any breaks in the sides or corners?"

"Hmm. I'm honestly sure. I think there was a small break in the top corner, at the peak."

"Interesting."

"What do you think it is?"

"A sign for telepathy."

Jayne shivered. "Like the Rogues' skill? Or like the skill they hope to gain through the necromantic texts?"

"I don't know. It may be the less pervasive type of telepathy but they believe they can increase its power somehow. The severed triangle is an opening into the mind. Through suggestion, maybe. Through a drug or some type of bond or agreement."

"What about the slash marks? The slashes are claws, aren't they? To stand for the animal side of Rogues?" Jayne pinched the bridge of her nose.

"Probably."

"This is ridiculous."

"This is real life."

"It doesn't feel like it."

"I remember being in your place," Ruger said. "You'll acclimate. Give it time and trust me."

An argument sprang to her lips, but she forced it away. Part of her wanted to say *but you didn't tell me about a few very key elements of this new world. Can I truly trust you and the TCO?*

"Alarik tested me at the meeting." Ruger was silent, so she continued. Her fingertips burned with the memory. "He had me find a Healing spell. He sliced my hand with a freaking knife and then made me heal myself."

Ruger sucked in a breath. "Oh, Jayne."

"What?"

"First, I'm sorry he hurt you. You are strong, though. You can handle it. Second, what happened when you couldn't call up the spell? Were you aware he was testing your knowledge of the Torrent?"

"No...you're not listening. I healed myself. I did the spell. Though my fingers still sting like I dunked them in hot water."

"No one can heal."

"I did."

She heard a noise that sounded like he'd covered the phone. He said something to someone else. "That is unprecedented. Truly. I...I don't know what to say. I..."

"So you told me what you thought was the truth, that no one has healed anyone with magic in any recorded history?"

"That isn't what I said. The TCO isn't aware of any Adept in history being able to heal. That doesn't mean it has never happened. Obviously, it happens. You did it. I knew you were very special."

"That sounded hella creepy, and a little too much like our buddy Alarik for my taste, boss."

"Well, let's just say, I am very glad you're on our side."

Jayne wasn't honestly sure what he meant by that. Healing was a good thing. How could the baddies use it against the TCO and the less insane people in the world?

"What about the whole 'I'm going to burn alive if I try Master-level magic' thing? What kind of danger are we talking here? There's another meeting tomorrow night, and I have no idea what he's going to try next."

Ruger's voice was strained, the tinniness of the phone making him seem so distant. "What does it matter? You are a TCO officer. You are going to follow through. Right?"

He didn't play with his food, did he? Got straight to the meat.

"Of course I am. It's the world's safety at stake. I understand what I signed up for." Sort of. Not really. Not really at all, if she was honest with herself. None of this "getting access to every book in the world" job had been like she imagined. But Agnes Jayne Thorne was a full-on good guy, and hell yes, she was going to save the damn world.

"Are we good here? Because I need to talk to my superiors about this development."

"Yeah. We're good, Rug."

"You can't call me Rug."

"Just did."

"Agnes."

"Oh-ho! He plays the trump card. Jerk."

"But seriously," he said, dropping their game of teasing one another. "Check in with me later. I need to know if the lingering pain from healing doesn't ease up."

"I will. Before you go, any word about Sofia?" Jayne touched the freckle on her arm. "She still isn't answering my calls."

"No. Sorry."

"Hey, I almost forgot to ask you. Max, who helped me at their interdimensional hideout? He backed me up in a meeting when I argued with Alarik, and now he is missing, and no one will tell me what's going on with him. Can we get anyone to check out his home and family and see if he's okay? He stuck his neck out for me, and it's my fault if he is in trouble."

"This is the man from the first sketch. The one you mentioned before?"

"Yes. I don't know his last name, but you know what he looks like. Maybe the TCO could get someone to look out for him?"

"I will do what I can."

"Thanks, Rug."

"Ruger," he corrected.

"Good night," she said in the most singsongy voice she could manage.

"Bye, Jayne." She could almost see him shaking his head.

She texted Cillian and stretched her neck.

This is weird, but do you know a church where I could light a candle for my parents?

I do. How about Christ Church? Have you seen it yet? Not as lovely as St Patrick's but maybe less crowded. I can meet you there and after, we'll walk a bit. Good?

I'd like that. Thank you.

Jayne's taxi pulled up, and she jumped inside.

"Christ Church, please."

She hugged her phone to her chest as the taxi zoomed back toward Dublin.

She was so lucky to have met Cillian. Honestly, she would've gone crazy if she didn't have his normalness to get her through all of this.

CHAPTER FIFTY-FIVE

The taxi dropped her at the corner, and there was Cillian, looking not at all normal. He was definitely above normalness with his hands in his pockets, his broad shoulders tilted, and those shockingly blue eyes of his catching her off guard. His smile hit her like a punch. A good punch.

"Hey," he said, shyly.

She whistled. "You are a sight for sore eyes, Mr. Pine."

He bumped her hip gently as they walked off the pavement and through a set of tall, iron gates. "You're not so bad yourself."

Christ Church Cathedral was a beautiful beast. Started in the mid-eleventh century, it boasted myriad architectural styles, but not much looked original. It was too tidy. Jayne was pretty sure the Victorians had rocked out some serious Gothic work of their own on the structure. She had to smile. Victorian Gothic held a special place in her heart. She never knew why, only that maybe, just maybe, memories were passed down and some ancestor of hers had led the building work on something during that time period. She'd always chided herself for thinking that, but now that she knew magic was real, why not passed-down memories? It was hardly less believable.

"Soo...I'm still struggling with everything I saw and what you told me." Cillian's head fell back as he stared into the cathedral's vaulted ceiling. The soft light from candelabras glowed across his throat, and Jayne imagined the feel of that skin under her lips.

"It would be strange if you weren't." She took two small candles from a wooden tray, dropping a few euros into the donation box.

Cillian found a matchbox next to a stack of brochures about the cathedral and followed Jayne to the rows of flickering candles under a statue of Mary. The only sounds were a few far-off voices and the whisper of fire in the air. Cillian took a deep breath, and his jacket scraped gently against his stubbled jaw. Jayne set a candle each for her mom and dad directly in the middle of the rows, took the matches from Cillian, and lit each wick with a silent prayer. Should she also light one for Max? Was he really in trouble with the Kingdom, or was she worrying over nothing?

"Hey, I'm going to grab one more." It wouldn't hurt to light one for him. It felt right.

She did so and stepped back, standing beside Cillian in the quiet peace of the place.

"Do you want to light one for your mother?" Jayne asked, feeling nervous about the question, worrying it might be too personal.

"I never have been much for this kind of thing, but yes. I think I will." He smiled with half his mouth, then retrieved a fourth candle to add to their group of lights.

When he stepped back, he took Jayne's unburnt fingers into

his much warmer, larger ones. He looked at the candles, but spoke to her, his voice just a whisper. "I'm glad I met you."

She squeezed his hand. "I'm glad I met you, too."

Hand in hand, they walked out of the cathedral and into the sunset. The chilly autumn air gusted over Jayne's face, and she took a minute just to appreciate being alive. She was starting to worry about whether she could even begin to crack this Kingdom case. If their first major group spell was telepathy, what else were they planning? How would speaking into someone's mind turn the world into some happy, bizarre Garden of Eden? Would they just creep everyone out until they threw their phones into the trash and started living like cavemen? Somehow Jayne didn't think the spell they had in their little sketchbook could help them control the entire human population's minds. And if they were already searching for a telepathy spell, why did they need the Book of Leinster and Medb? And why did the queen float in and out like some distant radio station? Why couldn't Jayne stay connected with her all the time?

Cillian turned them down a side street. "I'm not an idiot, Jayne."

"I never thought you were."

"I can tell you aren't allowed to talk about what you're really doing here. With your..." He eyed the nearly empty road, then whispered, "magic."

"You're correct."

"What can you talk about? What do you do when you're not poring over ancient manuscripts?"

She laughed. "Well, I honestly just move on to other books."

"Seriously?"

"Yeah. I'm a complete nerd. You are dating a nerd."

"Oooh, we're dating now, are we? Is this official?"

Cheeks hot, Jayne stepped on his foot. "Mind your manners."

"What?" He chuckled and stopped, putting a hand through his thick hair. "I only asked a simple question. Are you my girlfriend?"

"You sound like a fifth-grade boy."

He shrugged and smiled wide. "I haven't changed much since then, really."

The urge to kiss his grinning lips overwhelmed Jayne and she gave in. He swept her up and spun her around. A streetlight blinked on as they stumbled, laughing and kissing, into a small park full of tall trees, just off the road. His hand found its warm way up the back of her shirt, then his fingers slid beneath her bra. Her breath caught as goose bumps rose over her breast and down her stomach.

Then Cillian stepped back, his eyes closed.

She gripped his arm. "You okay?"

He looked at her, his grin sheepish. "Yeah. Sorry. I'm not feeling quite right."

"Maybe you need to get checked out? Didn't you say you felt bad after our first night at the pub, too?"

"Aye. Yeah."

Jayne felt his head. "You don't feel like you're running a fever or anything. But let's get you home."

He nuzzled her neck, teeth grazing her skin. "Nah. I feel great."

She gently pushed him away. "You might just need some rest, kickboxing man. Let's go to your place and eat more of that weird ice cream."

"Never insult the white chocolate, Jayne Thomas." His forehead creased like he was momentarily confused, but he shook it off and smiled.

"I consider weird good," she said. "It's not a slight against your dessert of choice. I must say, it is no pie, though."

"Americans."

"Irish."

Cillian grabbed Jayne suddenly and tossed her over his shoulder like she didn't weigh a thing. Play fighting, she maneuvered onto his back and let him carry her piggyback to his apartment. He certainly seemed fine now.

Between ice cream and making out, Jayne's mind tugged at her. The next Kingdom meeting was tomorrow night. How hard would Alarik push her magic? Would this be the last time she was well enough to spend a somewhat carefree evening with Cillian? Would Ruger appear tomorrow morning, stern-faced, with tons of bad news from Paris?

Finally, it was time to go. Cillian kissed Jayne good night. "Are you sure you don't want me to walk you home? You could stay here, you know."

"You're sweet. I have to be up early for work, though. And I can handle myself." She took a fighting stance for show.

"I know you can, but you don't have to. I'm here."

"And I appreciate it. Good night, Tarzan."

"Ha! I just now realized the joke. Tarzan and Jane. I wish I was as quick as you, my bookish girlfriend."

"You were just distracted by my feminine wiles." Like some fantastic femme fatale, she ran her fingers over his forehead and down the side of his face. Lord, who was she becoming? She silently laughed at herself.

He sighed. "They're deadly."

With a laugh, Jayne took off into the night to think about what she could do in preparation for the next Kingdom meeting. She'd blown off some steam, and now it was time to get down to business.

As she walked, she had the strange sense that someone was near, watching. TCO most likely. She stopped under a tree, ducking behind its branches, only to see two people in the shadows by the front of Cillian's flat. She pulled out her phone.

"You're home and missing me already, aye?" Cillian answered.

"No, just down the street. Someone is hanging around outside your place."

"Ah." She could hear him stepping through the flat. "Hmm. I don't see anyone."

"They're by the—"

But as she said it, the two shadows disappeared. She smelled the now familiar scent of magic, wafting from behind the trees.

Had to be her people. TCO. And here she was busting them. They were just keeping an eye on Cillian because she was spending time with him.

"Oh, my bad," she said to Cillian. "They went into another building. I'm just being paranoid."

"You're sure? I'll come down and—"

"No, no, really. They must have just stopped to chat about something. Ignore me. I'll talk to you tomorrow, okay?"

She hung up and walked back up the street, toward the spot where the two had been. They had the perfect vantage point for looking into Cillian's windows.

At least, she hoped it was the TCO, and not some of Alarik's Kingdom members.

Ruger's voice played in her mind. *Don't put him in danger, Jayne.*

Damn. She needed to figure things out with Cillian, quickly. He was a complication. A welcome complication, absolutely, but she needed to be careful.

She started off toward her own flat again. She had to keep her head on straight to act normal at work, leading up to the next Kingdom meeting.

Her thoughts redirected, she started worrying about Max

again. Maybe Deirdre would tell her something that would point to him being simply off the job rather than in a freakish magical prison Alarik and his mysterious Head person had cooked up.

CHAPTER FIFTY-SIX

The library was a breath of fresh air. Well, it was a breath of old books, and really, that was so much better. Jayne smiled sadly, mourning the job she had thought she'd taken with the TCO. Too bad it wasn't more focused on simply studying texts.

Rosalind sat at her red desk, typing furiously. "Good morning, Jayne," she said, not even looking up. "Some pompous professor from Harvard is trying to order me around."

"He's got another think coming."

Rosalind looked up and grinned wickedly. "He certainly does." She paused in typing out her email and lowered her glasses. "How are you this morning, dear? You look a little wan. Mourning the Book of Leinster, I suppose?"

Rosalind must have a little witch inside her. "Definitely. I'm just so shocked we've lost it. But I'll be okay. What's on the docket for today?"

The two bent their heads over a list of various editions of poetry works to collate and a cataloguing project that had come in on Celtic tribal rituals.

Finger running down the list, Rosalind spoke in her library voice, all hushed excitement. "Four books to catalogue as well as this companion atlas dating to research completed in 1850. And Judith can forget about getting her hands on these. I don't care if she thinks they belong in her department. I want them here. It just makes more sense for our researchers."

"Agreed." Jayne wouldn't dare to argue with Rosalind when she was in this kind of mood. It would be akin to blasphemy in Jayne's book. Book. Ha-ha. Good thing she could make herself laugh when she was probably going to die in a great, magical bonfire while trying to heal an ear Alarik decided to lop off as a test.

The morning was pleasantly uneventful, just Gerard at the door pretending not to read the paperback he thought he had to be ashamed of, and Rosalind typing away. Jayne's Celtic ritual cataloguing project was fascinating, and to be honest, she was glad Rosalind was too close by for Jayne to attempt a Tracking spell on the books included. She just wanted to enjoy her work for an hour or three. The book currently under her careful fingers was about the studies of an Oxford professor on Celtic burials. Written in 1910, the research was dated and riffed off the renowned George Petrie. Jayne read snippets out of curiosity as she set up labels and shelving spots. At least her fingers weren't burning anymore. That would be bad for the texts.

The section she was working on covered Iron Age burials. She surreptitiously read as she catalogued. The earliest burials involved cremating remains in pits called ring barrows.

A chill slithered down Jayne's back.

Later in the age, the people of Ireland began burying bodies intact, either supine or prone, lining the graves in stones and personal items. It was comforting to her, the care they placed in their dead.

Jayne closed the tome carefully, placed the numbered, acid-free bookmark within its pages so she could later shelve it correctly, and then moved on to the next piece of the collection.

This second book was all about burial mounds, heaps of land over passage tombs or barrows. Some of the illustrations in the dusty book showed hills made up of innumerable stones, and others were blanketed with grass. One image showed a gently sloping plain, leading to an absolutely enormous hill, topped in a mound of gray stones. She read the caption.

County Sligo. Ireland. Tomb of Queen Medb.

Jayne's fingers tightened on the book, and she forced herself to relax so as not to damage the old text. What were the odds she would stumble across this information now? Perhaps some-one was sending her a message.

Are you there?

Nothing. It was like she and Medb only hit the same frequency every once in a while.

She had the cataloguing finished by eleven, when Deirdre returned from a meeting with the events coordinator. Her hair had fallen out of her low ponytail and her cheeks were flushed. She went to the desk she preferred and began sifting through some boxes Rosalind had left for her.

Jayne wanted to ask her about Max. And Alarik. And the Kingdom's plans. She nibbled her lip, thinking. She must've been doing it too loudly because Deirdre seemed to hear her and looked up, locking eyes with Jayne.

Deirdre discreetly shook her head and mouthed, *Later. Out front.*

So she was willing to talk to Jayne alone, outside. Well, there was no time like the present. "Rosalind?" Jayne got up and tucked her work to the side. "I'm going out for a breath of air.

I'll be back in ten. Is that all right?"

"Definitely." Rosalind smiled. "Deirdre, why don't you take a look at how Jayne's cataloguing is coming along? Let's make certain we're keeping with the Trinity process."

Jayne did her best not to be offended. This was, after all, Rosalind's job, and Jayne was still the newbie. But rookie status aside, Jayne needed Deirdre to come with her on this little walk. "I was thinking Deirdre might come, too. We can talk about that and take a turn around the front square and photobomb a couple of well-meaning tourists."

Rosalind laughed. "Go on, then. Don't be gone longer than ten, please. We have a great deal of work to finish today."

Deirdre's eyes narrowed as she looked at Jayne, but Jayne ignored her pangs of guilt and worry. Yes, she was most likely riding the line of what Deirdre's husband would want her doing, but still. This was about a man's life. If Deirdre had any information that might ease Jayne's mind about Max, great, and if she knew something that might help him get out of a Kingdom-style jam, that would also be worth the danger.

Gerard crossed his arms as they walked toward the door. "Where are you two going, if I may inquire? Must be nice to gallivant about the campus as you please. Grunts, such as I, must stay at their post, you see."

"Aw, poor Gerard." Jayne pushed her bottom lip out. "How about we bring you back something to brighten your day?"

Deirdre frowned, obviously confused that Jayne could joke around when they both knew some serious shit was going down. But Jayne had learned long ago that life would give you bad and more bad, even if you grieved and took things seriously. She'd decided to laugh and play and smile in the midst of it, because if you had to deal with the crap, why not enjoy the happy?

Gerard almost smiled. "I wouldn't be opposed to a small token of appreciation."

"Consider it done." Jayne grinned and led Deirdre out the door.

The sun fought a roll of blue-gray clouds above the college. Jayne savored the feel of the heat on her cheeks while she could.

"What do you want?" Deirdre's voice was tight and clipped. She looked over her shoulder, then leaned to scan the crowds. "We shouldn't be talking like this."

"Why not? Alarik told me you could help."

"Not like this. Only if you have a…job for them."

"I just want to know if you've heard anything about a man named Max. Big guy. A Scot. Hangs out with a woman named Teresa. Was he reassigned?"

Deirdre swallowed and wrapped her sweater more tightly around her chest. "I can't talk about that. We should go back."

Mouth pinched, she turned, but Jayne caught her arm. "I'm all in with them, Deirdre. And I'll never tell Alarik you talked to me. But I need to know if my friend Max is in danger. Or if I can help him in any way."

Deirdre looked to the sky. Then she shut her eyes and lowered her chin. "The Kingdom does not reassign people, Jayne," she whispered.

Jayne fought a shiver. "So…what then?"

Raising her chin, Deirdre met Jayne's gaze. "What do you think? Does my husband seem to be the forgiving and under-standing type?"

A wave of nausea swamped Jayne. "He's dead."

"Yes. Now, let's go back to what we're supposed to be doing so we don't join him, all right?" Tears wet Deirdre's wide, bloodshot eyes. She tore from Jayne's grip and hurried away.

Jayne stood, the flow of tourists and students slipping around her like the Torrent's magic.

A good man was dead because of her.

She couldn't help the thought. Was Cillian next?

CHAPTER FIFTY-SEVEN

Numb, Jayne passed Gerard, not even responding to his question. At least, she thought it had been a question. She hadn't really heard.

Her ears thudded in time with her pulse, and she fought to keep her magic from shimmering all around the room. TCO officers didn't lose control when they had terrible news. They gritted their teeth and got on with the job. She was here to save people from the evils of the Kingdom, and if she didn't get her shit together a lot more than one kind man named Max would suffer. No, she didn't know all of the Kingdom's plans yet, but if Alarik's behavior thus far was any indicator of the severity of the situation, she could safely guess the group's actions would be vicious, unabashed, and fatal to any who stood in the way.

In other words, shit just got real.

The afternoon passed in a blur. Jayne caught herself staring at an illuminated manuscript a gap-toothed professor had requested. She'd set it out on a foam cradle, but when she'd set the weighted book snake along the appropriate page, her mind had stalled out. She shook her head to clear it and realized the professor had been asking if she was ill.

"I'm fine. Sorry." She left the woman with the book and went back to the staff area.

Finally, it was time for Jayne to leave.

Deirdre had kept her distance and Jayne didn't see her go. At the staff lockers downstairs, Rosalind and Gerard talked around Jayne, joking and ribbing one another as they gathered their bags and scarves. She trailed them outside.

"Are you quite all right, Jayne? No joking here. You seem shaken, and you forgot my bribe," Gerard said.

Rosalind leaned toward his ear. "She's not been well since the fire, poor thing."

"No, it's not that. I'm okay. Honestly, I'm a little homesick."

"That's understandable, dear. Moving all this way, all by yourself. Quite brave, if you ask me."

Gerard eyed her, but nodded. "Very brave."

They nodded again and waved goodbye, and she headed toward her flat, realizing the truth of what she'd said. Of course, the depth of Alarik's cruelty was the main reason she was acting funny, but she was also very, very homesick. Or maybe she simply missed the life she'd had before the TCO found her. The safety of it.

But there was no use in pining away over something that couldn't happen. She couldn't go back to that life any more than she could keep this rain from falling before she made it onto her stoop.

As if to prove her point, heavy drops began to fall, tapping the back of her head and painting the pavement at her feet.

In her flat, she showered, relishing the hot water. That cave near the sea was going to be chilly tonight. Indulging herself, she used some lavender body wash she'd picked up at the Tesco. The scent calmed her sparking nerves but did nothing to assuage the guilt she felt over Max. Not only had he been a nice guy, she'd lost her very first potential asset. Great job.

"I'm sorry, Max," she said aloud as she slid on her boots and wrapped a wool scarf around her neck. "I will not let your death be in vain."

Tears pushed against her eyes, and her throat tightened. It felt stupid to say things like "in vain," but it was true. She wouldn't let his death be for nothing. At the meeting, in front of Alarik and the rest, she would use her overwhelming feelings to act the opposite of how she truly felt. She would pretend to be overcome by excitement at what the Kingdom had in store for the world. She would weep with joy at finding this family of fellow Adepts.

Only she would know her heart was with Max and his family.

Max. Cillian. Max. Cillian.

Sorrow. Joy.

It was amazing how quickly her heart could swing in either direction.

She had failed Max. She couldn't fail Cillian, too. She needed to talk to Ruger, see if he could arrange for some sort of protective spell. At least until she foiled the Kingdom's plans.

The taxi driver had the radio up, and she was glad for the noise. It kept her fear from taking over.

She people-watched as the driver wound out of town. American tourists, with their loudly colored T-shirts and white sneakers and selfie sticks, queued happily all over the city. Their camaraderie made Jayne miss Sofia. She pulled out her phone and sent a short text.

I wish we were watching Elf *right now.*

They'd watched it ten times last year, acting out the scenes and adding in new lines over bowls of parmesan popcorn.

No answer. Jayne pocketed the phone and tucked her sister into the far corner of her mind so she could focus on her job.

The taxi pulled up to the beach ramp, and the long road that would lead to a climb down to the ocean spread out in front of her, appearing like an impossible distance.

A clutch of thick-leaved trees marked a curve in the road. Stars pierced the cloudy sky and twinkled down on Jayne's head. A sudden urge to access the Torrent flooded her bones, to be in the magic without a nefarious dude at her side. It was like Alarik had dirtied the Torrent. Jayne wanted to spend a moment there, free of his influence and her own necessary, but still unpleasant, lies.

She ducked into the trees, keeping one hand on the knife she'd stashed at her waistband, under her shirt, in case someone might be hiding in the dark. But she was alone.

With a deep breath, she closed her eyes and fell into the comfort and power of the Torrent. The bright-green stars spun around her limbs as she floated. If she concentrated, she could hear a few voices far off. They weren't speaking to her, but they must've been nearby if she was hearing them. She was reminded of the training she'd received. There was no way to know how close they were. She had to be careful.

Determined to use this time for refueling her tank, so to speak, she ignored the voices and began spinning up spells for the fun of it. She imagined a beachy kind of breeze, and the spell rose up like a fish out of water, rising to kiss her fingertips. She kept it in one hand while she brought another spell to mind. This second one would back up the first and give the illusion of the smell of coconut sunscreen and piña coladas. Illusion spells, like Max and Teresa had done in the Time Catch. She knew full well she was being ridiculous, but she couldn't deny the urge to simply play with the magic. It felt right. She had no guilt about taking her time in getting to the meeting. Maybe the Torrent was leading her, helping her. Who knew if these spells might come in handy?

She left the Torrent, the spells still dancing along her palms, their shapes spinning. They were invisible, but she felt them with a sense she never knew existed until she'd started training. It was like seeing without seeing, similar to when you know there's a person behind you in a supposedly empty room.

Releasing the spells, Jayne took one more breath of vacation, letting the breeze wash over her head like a blessing.

With her nerves eased, she started toward the sea cave again. She wondered idly how much access Medb had to her thoughts and what the ancient warrior queen might think about her little vacay.

Alarik waited at the mouth of the hill's opening, arms crossed. He smiled. It looked forced as hell, and he felt more dangerous than normal. Not good.

"Jayne."

"Alarik." She wanted to put her knife to his throat and demand an explanation for Max's death. She wanted him on his knees, begging to be forgiven. The urge for power over him startled her. Not cool. Stopping him, yes. Controlling him? That was Kingdom territory. Where were these emotions coming from?

"You're late."

"Am I? Sorry. Traffic." She walked past him and into the cave like she belonged there, a trick she'd learned long ago. If she pretended she owned a place, people tended to go along with it. There were many of the same people she'd seen last time, and a few new faces. More recruits, it looked like. Alarik's army was growing.

Alarik caught up. "The others are already working on the next steps of our actions here in Ireland. I want to work with you on your healing for now. Head on back to where we worked last time."

"Great." Sweat beaded on Jayne's upper lip. Brave she might be, but knowing a creeper was about to slice you up and watch you try to fix the wound didn't make for fun times.

He wasted no time. The moment she was out of the main group's line of sight, his hand flashed in the torchlight and his blade shot across her chest, just under her collarbone.

She thought she might be about to pass out, so she joked to keep herself upright. "What did my scarf ever do to you?" Holding the ripped end of her scarf, she tsked. "Can you fix this with magic? I know I can't."

"You can do that and so much more. Now, stop joking around. You're bleeding quite a bit and should get to work. I do have the items needed to stitch you up if need be, but I don't have any pain relievers."

Shaking, Jayne shut her eyes against the pain and fear. She rushed headlong into the Torrent, like it was a parent's arms. She nearly crumpled then, wanting to cry and beg for help. But the Torrent only helped those who helped themselves.

As Jayne envisioned her wound and her flesh mending itself, the spell drifted into view and bobbed against her outstretched hands. It looked the same, solid white lines in a crossing pattern. It was the only spell—that she could think of—that wasn't partially transparent. She wondered if the solidity of the spell was an indicator of the level of mastery it took to cast it.

Pulling the Healing spell into the real world, she moved her hands back and forth about an inch from her wound. The flesh puckered, and she looked down, watching the edges of the cut draw toward one another.

It hurt. A lot.

And it wasn't only the pain of the wound and the flesh coming together. Her fingertips and forearms blazed with the heat of magic.

She smelled something off.

Sniffing, as she sweated and gritted her teeth against the tumult of agony, she realized it was burning flesh. Even as she was healing her cut, the spell was burning her from the inside out. Smoke rose from her fingertips and along the outside of her arms. She yelped, unable to hold it all in, and the spell broke apart.

The torches went black.

Jayne's head hit the cave floor.

CHAPTER FIFTY-EIGHT

J ayne sat up to see Teresa and Alarik, both wearing looks of concern that almost seemed real.

Teresa offered Jayne a glass of water and an Advil.

"One Advil?" Jayne took the pill and swallowed it down. "I think I'm entitled to at least three."

Teresa pulled out a bottle and gave her more. "Your cut is healed." She grinned at Alarik, whose eyes sparkled in the torchlight. It was a dangerous sparkle, and it made Jayne shiver.

Her cut *was* healed, and she wasn't burning anymore. But she wasn't going to let Alarik play this game with her again. She was more powerful than he was, even if she was new.

They helped her to stand and brought her to a circle of Kingdom members who were sitting around the Book of Leinster.

Jayne gasped. "Why do you have that book out here in the damp?" Her librarian heart roared at the horror.

Every head turned to face her.

"I mean, please, just…remember it's precious and this sea air is not good for that vellum or the ink."

Medb whispered in ancient languages, her melodious voice so loud that Jayne could hardly believe no one else could hear it.

Yes. Very good.

A man with locs pointed at a page. "A spell is hidden here. Can the Initiate retrieve it?"

Alarik helped Jayne onto a bench. "Perhaps. I do believe Jayne is the one to find this hidden spell. Don't you think, Jayne?" He sat opposite her and kept his eyes locked on hers.

The group smiled like they hadn't just murdered someone and weren't planning more terrorism. Jayne wished they would all cackle and rub their hands together like proper villains. It would be far less chilling.

Locs man continued. "Can you reveal it to us, Jayne?"

Medb had gone quiet. Jayne set her palm on the book, the others' eyes wandering from the blood on her shirt, to the healed wound along her collarbone, to her shaking fingers on the calligraphy. The Torrent welled up around her, sending stars over the group and around her arms and hands. She felt like she was falling.

Well, this was what she'd come for, so...

She closed her eyes and let go of her control.

The Torrent greeted her with open arms, and a feeling like warm sunlight poured through her veins. She searched for a spell that would help her see into the magic hiding in the Book of Leinster. Tracking spells floated by, followed by shapes that might have led to decoding or something similar. None of them felt quite right.

Jayne slipped away from the Torrent like she was shedding a soft cloak. She opened her eyes to see Alarik and the rest of his cronies staring. "Sorry. It's just not there. It's not quite right."

A flash of irritation tweaked Alarik's lips and eyes. "Of course.

I'm sure it will come to you soon."

A funny little spark of courage opened Jayne's mouth. "What spells am I meant to find in the book?"

Alarik looked at his hands. "We were hoping you could tell us. The Master who ruled this book, who used it and gave a piece of himself or herself to it, had powers we can't dream of."

"Medb." Jayne was through tiptoeing around. "It was Queen Medb, the warrior queen."

Alarik lunged forward and clasped Jayne's face tightly. "Oh, Jayne. Yes. I do believe it is. So you are somehow in tune with this grimoire? Have you...seen anything? Heard anything out of the ordinary?"

Jayne pushed away his hand and he narrowed his eyes but backed down, his gaze rapt. Maybe if she told them she could hear Medb, they'd keep her alive a bit longer, give her some power here. "Medb spoke to me."

The group began to whisper excitedly.

"This is incredible." Alarik clasped his hands below his chin. His eyes shone as he began to pace around Jayne and the Book of Leinster. "What did she say? Did she speak to you in a way you could understand?"

Medb didn't speak, but Jayne felt a pressing *No* nonetheless, so she shook her head. "Unfortunately not."

The Kingdom members discussed the issue in a variety of languages as Jayne set her palm on the Book of Leinster again.

A spell flashed into her mind, bright green and clear as if she'd drawn it on paper. "Wait. I see it. The spell we need."

Alarik was back at her side, nudging Teresa out of the way. "Yes? What do you think the spell is? What is its shape?"

"It's for...electricity?" Ugh. Jayne didn't like where this was headed.

Matching grins spread over the mouths of Alarik and the guy

with locs.

"Tell us everything," Alarik whispered.

"This spell helps the caster harness electricity. Part of the shape looks like a sword."

Alarik took over. "Perhaps that portion of the spell is a layer. A second spell set over the first. It turns the electricity into a defensive weapon."

Jayne didn't fail to notice he glanced at her when he said *defensive*, as if he still had to be sure to win her over by pretending he was less violent than he truly was.

Wind from the ocean blew into the cave and the torches fluttered, threatening to go out. The scent of salt and fish mixed with the perfume of her magic. The rose-and-woodsmoke hints clung to her bloodied clothing. She tried to focus on the surroundings and the conversation. There was a fresh burning pain in her fingers and arms. She gripped her elbows and leaned forward to try and stop trembling. This was so messed up. How could these people not see that this was not okay?

"Who is going to cast this spell?" Jayne's question was out of her mouth before she'd really thought about whether or not she should ask it. Well, that's what the TCO got with a rush training job.

Alarik chewed the inside of his cheek, looking nervous for once. "It might be possible for you to do it. You might be... Well, don't try it now. Definitely not. Even with your skills... not yet anyway." He traded a glance with another man to his right, who mumbled something in German. "This is only for a Master," Alarik said.

"But there aren't any Masters." Except that Jayne knew she was. Medb had deemed her one, and Ruger had confirmed the possibility.

Locs pressed his lips together and half-grinned at Alarik.

"Not yet."

"Is someone leveling up? How does that work?"

"What do you think I'm trying to help you do?"

Jayne's mouth had suddenly gone bone dry. *Disinformation, Jayne. Don't let them know what you're thinking.* "I… I'm not ready for that."

"Well, not yet. And maybe never. But don't worry. We certainly won't be placing you in a position to function as a Master for our first move toward the Kingdom's goal. You won't be ready in time."

She breathed out, relieved. "Good. Because I feel ready for very little at the moment."

They all chuckled like this was a big, happy sing-along and they were about to light up some s'mores. Jayne swallowed bile. Sick bastards.

She was angriest at Teresa, who had been Max's friend. How could she laugh and chat like he wasn't dead because of this group? How did she sleep at night? Jayne knew Teresa had felt the pain of his loss, because she'd nearly cried the day Jayne had asked her about Max, but now, she seemed to have climbed right over that mountain of problematic questions concerning her loyalties. Jayne really, really wanted to punch something. Instead, she bit her tongue and played her role.

"You are a key, though, Jayne." Alarik turned the page. "Medb chose you to read this hidden grimoire. You are the strongest Adept I've worked with in my life. Stronger than our Head. She will agree when she meets you." A strange glint passed through his eyes. "You are fated for this, and she knows it."

Jayne tried really hard not to wince at the thought of someone even more messed up than Alarik.

"Please examine the remainder of the Táin Bó Cúailnge. We are searching for the final layered spell we will use. This will take all of our combined efforts. Jayne, you will be very important in this step. Without your efforts, the Kingdom members who try this spell work will see death."

"Because it is a Master-level spell? What are you thinking this spell does?"

He took her hand gently and set it back on the page. "You tell us."

Medb, now would be a good time for some guidance. Jayne directed her thoughts at the warrior queen, visions of the endgame rolling through her imagination. None of the outcomes looked rosy. *Do you want me to see? Or keep this from them? What's our plan here?*

But the queen refused to speak.

In her life as a librarian, Jayne had quickly learned that more knowledge, not less, was best for making decisions.

She splayed her fingers on the vellum and pressed her flesh into the calligraphy, feeling a heaviness around her forehead and wrists.

A spell shimmered into the air, right in front of her nose. But Alarik and the rest were only looking at her. They couldn't see it, she realized.

The glowing markings were similar to the Birth spell Ruger had shown her, with its oval—that spell transformed flesh to make it look like something else. A dog to a cat. Present-day Ruger into old Ruger. That sort of thing. But this layered casting also showed a peak like a hill, and several lines and dots that disturbingly resembled a face, no, a skull. Jayne's fingers burned so hotly she was surprised her flesh didn't explode into flame.

She cleared her throat, her stomach twisting. "This is a Master-level spell, yes. Worthy of its name. I think this casting will raise a Master. From the dead."

Alarik loomed over the Book of Leinster, his eyes shadowed

by the uneven light. He held out his arms and took a moment to make eye contact with every member, Jayne included.

"This will be our greatest achievement thus far," he started, "if we can accomplish it. This, my fellow Adepts, is the spell of Necromancy."

Jayne couldn't make her mouth work the rest of the meeting. It was one thing hearing it as a hypothesis from Ruger. It was quite another thing entirely to hear an extremist murderer proclaim his plan to raise someone from the dead. Well, not just someone. They planned to raise Medb.

But to do what, exactly?

Jayne exhaled in a rush. She knew the necromantic texts were set up to raise Masters from the dead. But was this really possible? And why wasn't Medb present in her head right now, giving her a clue as to what might happen if they raised her? Jayne couldn't tell whether Medb was malevolent or not. Only incredible power and otherness pulsed from Medb's presence. Maybe she wanted to be risen. Maybe she wanted the Kingdom to achieve their goals. Maybe she was using Jayne to her own ends.

Alarik ended the evening with a declaration that there would be no more meetings in the sea cave and that he would contact her about the Necromancy casting and where to be and when. He instructed her to be aware of her surroundings, because the messenger would have to be blunt in his approach. That sounded super comforting.

As Jayne traveled home, the night-wrapped roads twisting under the moon, she rolled the same question over and over in her head.

What would happen if they managed to raise Medb from the grave?

CHAPTER FIFTY-NINE

Upon returning to their house in Dublin, Alarik tossed his keys into the stone bowl on the entryway table, then took Deirdre's hand. "Thank you for your unwavering support, my dear."

Deirdre smiled, but she still looked frightened as she pulled away from his grasp to turn the lock. The woman was always frightened. He'd married a mouse. He needed someone more fitting, someone more like...Jayne.

With Jayne at his side, he would be unstoppable.

Deirdre, as sweet as she was, no longer truly fit the bill. He still needed her, though. She was his ticket to the necromantic texts stashed away in the great libraries of the world.

Then again, Jayne spoke the same language as Deirdre, the language of dusty tomes and ancient knowledge. She could fulfill more than one purpose for him.

Would the Head allow such a thing?

Would he need the Head's permission?

He took Deirdre's face in his hands, much as he had done to

Jayne. "Don't you know that what we're doing, what you and I and the rest are doing, will change the fate of the world?"

Her eyes darted left and right. "I…yes, of course. Of course."

He folded her into his arms and held her, inhaling the scent of her apple shampoo. It mingled nicely with the lingering salt of the ocean cave permeating his clothes. "We will save the world from itself, Deirdre."

She kissed his neck. "Yes, we will. You are an amazing man, husband."

He leaned back and eyed her. She'd been so lovely in her youth and was indeed still quite beautiful now. "Please don't disappoint me, Deirdre. I don't ever want to lose you." Her soft heart was the problem. Of course, Alarik disliked the violence required to save the world from itself, but it was sometimes necessary. This was war. And if she let that softness override her loyalty…he couldn't take the chance.

Deirdre untangled her limbs from his and walked toward the kitchen. "I'll make tea."

Alarik studied her as she went. He wished he knew for certain she was wholly his.

A knock sounded at the door. Alarik wasn't expecting anyone, pulled a strong defensive Shield spell from the Torrent before he opened the door.

A man he'd never seen before stood on his porch. He touched a hand to his heart, one Kingdom member to another, and Alarik relaxed, dropping the spell away.

"My name is Lars," the man said. "I used to work with Aaró. I'm the one who shepherded Henry Thorne's journal to you. I have some information you might want."

"Information? About what?"

"You have a spy in your midst."

Alarik didn't sleep, plotting and planning and meditating on the news his new ally had brought. Alarik and Aaró had the same goals, but hadn't agreed on how to achieve them, and had broken away many, many years earlier. But with Aaró dead, his faction needed a strong leader. If Alarik could raise Medb, Lars and the rest wouldn't hesitate to pledge their loyalty to him. More recruits, more soldiers in his magical war, could turn the tide for the Kingdom. The Head would want these factions merged, he knew it.

The next morning, he met Teresa and a few others in the Time Catch. The woman they'd taken from the American airport parking lot sat at the round meeting table, her back straight and hands bound in front of her. At his entrance, her large, beautiful eyes flashed with hatred.

"Remove her gag," he said to Teresa. "If you would but calm yourself, I assure you we can explain."

Teresa tugged the bandana from the woman's mouth, then checked her bound hands.

The woman spat toward Alarik, who wasn't near enough to be hit with her spittle. "Why don't you just kill me and get it over with?"

"I don't want to kill you at all, Sofia." Alarik sat three chairs down and crossed his legs. "I want your help."

"I know exactly who you are, and I will never help you."

"You do?"

"You murdered my parents. To hell with the Kingdom."

Distasteful. Alarik looked away, wishing he'd given this chore to someone else. "Your sister is helping us willingly."

"She knows nothing! You must have...you must have blocked my messages to her. I tried to tell her about you, about everything—"

"And whose fault is it that she is so ignorant?" Alarik sneered. "Sofia, you are the one who is ignorant now. Were you aware your precious sister is working undercover for a branch of the CIA?"

"No. That's…impossible."

"It's quite possible, and quite true. But her mind remains uncertain. We don't know which side she'll land on. Hopefully, on ours."

His words landed heavily, and he saw her eyes grow wary. She either didn't know, or hadn't believed, that her sister was working for their sworn enemy.

"She won't. Jayne would never willingly break the law."

"Perhaps not. But if she thought your life hung in the balance…"

Sofia choked on an angry sob, her eyebrows drawn tightly together. "Just kill me. I'm tired of running."

"As I have already stated, we don't want to kill you, or Jayne. We want to work together. The Head will be so thrilled to have both of the Thorne girls in our fold."

"And who is your Head these days? Another of your protégés? Why didn't they make you Head, Alarik? Because you're flipping insane and a shitty magician to boot?"

Heat raged through Alarik's bones and he stood, knocking the chair over. "Gag her again, please. And make sure you work on her thoroughly tonight. She needs to understand what's at stake."

"I'll never give in to your brainwashing, Alarik! I'll—"

Teresa's gag stopped Sofia's incessant shouting. Alarik righted the chair and headed for the door.

Sofia didn't know her sister at all. Alarik had seen the look in Jayne's eyes. Medb had chosen her to be her bonded Master, just as Henry's journal had described. And once Jayne had that level of power at her fingertips, there was no way she would give it over to the weak TCO and their fumbling officers. No, Jayne wanted more out of this magical life, and the Kingdom would give it to her.

If Alarik failed in that, well, there were ways to persuade a good heart like Jayne's. Having Sofia was going to be beneficial, no matter how things played out. Though he didn't care for shouting, he had no qualms about shedding blood.

CHAPTER SIXTY

Collapsed on her couch, phone in hand, Jayne repeated everything that had happened at the meeting for Ruger three times. "I don't know how long I can act like I'm into this for Alarik. I won't let him hurt me again."

"I know this is hard, Jayne. But it's important that you continue playing your role. Should Alarik think for a moment you aren't under his control, he won't hesitate to kill you, no matter that he thinks you're a Master. He's playing with fire, and that makes men desperate. Don't give him a reason to react."

"I need my sister. I need to tell her what's happening. I need her to know I understand now why she kept us on the move, on the run. She has to have figured this out and was trying to keep me safe. That's what her message was about. Isn't that true?"

Ruger hesitated. "Sofia is fine. At home."

"Why didn't you tell me?"

"I did."

"No, I mean like that's the first damn thing you should've

told me."

"Careful, Jayne."

She gritted her teeth and sat up. "So she's fine. Just mad and not talking to me and being strange like she usually is."

"Exactly."

Jayne narrowed her eyes at the phone. He wasn't telling her something. "That all?"

"That's all you need to know, Officer Thorne."

"Oh. Is that how it's going to be? All right. Understood." She could taste her irritation, her distrust. What the hell was he keeping from her? "Good night." Her finger nearly bent backward as she clicked the call off.

Every bone in her body was tired, but she knew if she tried to sleep, she'd end up tossing all night. She dialed Sofia's number. "Hey, I get why you're mad. We need to talk. Please call me."

Her mind was spinning. She needed to come down from this magical high. She tried some wine, and some pie, and neither worked.

So she called Cillian.

"Please answer. Please be there."

"Jayne? I hoped you'd call."

His voice was a balm. It was the sun on a rainy day. It was every cliché in the book, and she loved it.

"Will you come over, please?"

Not twenty minutes later, there was a wonderful knock at her door. Yes, it was wonderful. It was exactly the sort of knock she needed at that moment. Solid but gentle. Inquiring but not demanding. All Cillian. Wonderful.

She swung the door open. "Hello, Mr. Wonderful."

"You're bleeding!" The alarm on his face told Jayne she probably should have taken a moment to clean herself up.

She pulled him inside. "I'm totally okay. Just a...little issue at work. I promise. I'm fine."

"Do we need to go to the hospital? Do you need stitches? Wait. Is that all your blood? Jayne. Did you do something terrible? You can tell me."

She put a hand to his warm cheek. "I am whole and well. I promise. And no, I didn't hurt anyone. I had an accident, but I'm okay. You have to trust me. There are things about all of this I can't share with you."

He looked concerned and confused. "You're shaking like an addict. Let's get you into the bath."

"Oooh la la."

"No." He steered her gently toward the short hallway, looking around. "I'm guessing your tub is back here somewhere. And no, no. This is not about seduction. Plenty of time for that when you're not covered in blood. Seriously, is all of that yours? Do I need to take you to the A and E? You promise you're all right?"

"I am." She tugged her shirt down a bit to show him that the wound was completely healed. "I got cut, but I was able to fix it. With magic. It feels weird."

"This is bizarre."

"I know. I feel bizarre."

When he'd filled her tub and poured in some of the lavender wash for bubbles, Cillian helped her get her clothes off. To his credit, his eyes didn't stray from the job at hand. Once she was situated in the hot water, Cillian left and returned with a cup. He began pouring water down over Jayne's hair. He hummed as he worked. She closed her eyes and soaked, let him wash her hair. It was bliss.

"How are you doing?" Cillian's voice was gentle and not suggestive, and she was so glad for it. She had no desire for romance right now.

"Much better. Thank you. Thank you very, very much." She turned to face him, keeping the bubbles strategically arranged to keep his job here from being harder. Ha-ha. Harder. She forced the joke out of her mind and gave him a smile. "Seriously. This is huge. You helping me when you have no idea how or why I'm...well, it's amazing. You're amazing."

"I've never met someone like you. I think I'm beginning to like you a bit."

"Like me. A bit. Awesome." She felt a little laugh inside her and let it out. "This couldn't get better."

"Ice cream."

"Okaaay?"

"We need ice cream. Now. That's what will make it better."

"I don't have any."

"Oh, we're going out. Just to the store. To buy your favorite flavor for me to try."

"We are?"

"It's in the directions. On how to deal with bizarre women."

An hour and a nice set of clean clothes later, Jayne and Cillian were eating from three tubs of frozen goodness. Rocky road. Strawberry, straight up. And Ireland's weird version of Moose Tracks.

Jayne finished her ladleful of that last one. "Yeah, it's not the same. At home, there are these ripples of fudge. This is just chocolate."

She watched, rapt, as Cillian licked his spoon clean. He leaned close, his scent all marshmallow and man. It was not a bad combo. "I am sorry that Ireland is such a disappointment to you," he whispered, his accent fully glorious.

"Oh, it's not." She tried to concentrate on her words as Cillian's tongue danced over her earlobe. A lovely warmth threaded through her limbs and down her torso. "The weather is a lot nicer than many claim. And the beer is great."

"I would've left you here if you hadn't said that."

"I respect the Guinness."

Cillian pulled away from her, touching the skin over her heart gently. "Are you all right? I can stay here while you sleep. Keep an eye out."

"Like I said, Ireland is not a disappointment." Jayne took his face in her hands and kissed him hard as desire glowed through her body. "Thank you for being a great person and not a jerk."

"There might be days when I'm somewhere in between."

"Medium is totally fine. I'm medium a lot."

"I don't think so." He took her hand and blessed each knuckle with soft lips, his bright eyes unblinking.

Her heart jumped, then sighed. She didn't know hearts could sigh, but damn if hers didn't. If she wasn't careful, she'd fall for this fighter.

She took him up on his offer to stay the night. Like a gentleman, he slept on the couch. And she had to admit, she was disappointed he did.

The next morning, Cillian was in her kitchen, wearing only jeans and a bright purple apron. Gods of the ancient world but his back muscles were more than she could handle, and his trim waist... Her palms itched to smooth the planes of his body and—

He turned, tossed a pancake into the air, and gave her a wink. "Fancy a flip?"

Her stomach took its cue and did its own flip. "Yum."

She ran to the bathroom, brushed her teeth, and yanked a

brush through her messy hair. Good enough.

When she returned to the kitchen, he was chuckling and plating up a nice stack with syrup. With one finger, she edged the plate away from them and to the far end of the countertop.

"I think I am in need of an appetizer first." Who was she right now? She couldn't believe the words coming out of her prim librarian mouth.

He spun and put his hands on her hips. "I'm not sure I can promise it'll only be an appetizer." Ruffling her hair, he grinned with half his handsome mouth. "You sure you feel up to it?"

She thought maybe she'd answer that with action.

Tugging the apron to pull him into the living room, she smiled. He leaned against her and pressed a kiss into her lips. His tongue danced over hers, the kiss growing more fierce and less gentle. With his hands in her hair, he shifted his hips. Jayne's pulse pounded in several interesting places as she decided the living room wasn't going to cut it.

She bit his lip gently, then zipped away, crooking one finger over her shoulder. "Come and get me, chef."

"Naughty minx," he hissed before running after her and into the bedroom.

Bliss was quickly becoming the norm with this Irishman, who was gentle and rough in all the right ways.

She forgot all about the pancakes.

CHAPTER SIXTY-ONE

Still mussed and glowing, Jayne hoped Gerard wasn't paying attention when she arrived at the library. Sadly, she did not get her wish.

"Well, good morning." Gerard raised an eyebrow. "Did we have another late night?"

Cheeks blushing, she glared. "*Live fast. Die hard.* It's my new motto, G. Get used to it."

He barked a laugh, his snotty demeanor broken for a moment. She smiled at him as she hurried toward the staff area.

The day was actually very uneventful except for one worrying thing.

Deirdre never came in. Rosalind told her that she'd called in sick. Not for one second did Jayne believe that.

Alarik must have somehow found out that Jayne asked Deirdre about Max. It was too much of a coincidence that she went off the grid the day after Jayne questioned her. Deirdre had seemed even more nervous than usual yesterday anyway. It was likely Alarik had already warned her not to talk to Jayne about the topic.

She really hoped she hadn't put Deirdre in danger. Surely Alarik wasn't going to off his own wife just for taking a walk with an Initiate who asked the wrong questions. Surely.

Protocol demanded she inform Ruger, so she did. He took her report, clearly in a hurry, and promised the TCO would look into it before dashing off on some adventure he couldn't tell her about.

The TCO would look into it. Right. Neither Max nor Deirdre were the TCO's priority now that Jayne had infiltrated the Kingdom. Alarik was the only one who mattered.

She walked off her frustration, not entirely surprised to find herself in front of Cillian's gym.

Through the window, she could see him. He was shirtless and kicking the dog shit out of a bag. His torso twisted, showing every muscle as he drove his shin forward.

When she opened the door, he pushed his hair away from his face and lit her up with a smile. "Well, hello. This is a nice surprise."

"I wish it was under happy circumstances, but I need help. Dangerous help."

He pulled out a folding chair for her. "I can be dangerous."

"My friend from work...her husband isn't a great guy. She didn't come in, and she's not answering her phone. I'm worried."

"Could she be at their house? Like, he's keeping her there?" Cillian wiped his face on a towel and put on a fresh shirt.

"Maybe. I say we go and find out."

"Now?"

"Now."

"It's on." He grabbed his bag and set of keys.

Jayne waited outside under the moon as he locked up. "I can get her address. I just have to go back to Trinity. Security will let me in, and I can snag it from Rosalind's computer. I don't think it'll be a problem. Her folders aren't exactly labeled in a sneaky fashion."

Cillian took her hand, and she smiled at the sweet gesture. "Something like *Staff addresses are here?*"

"That's about right."

His head dropped back as he grinned. "My girlfriend, the secret agent."

She fought back the shock. He didn't know. He couldn't know. No. He was grinning, playing with her.

"That's Officer Secret Agent to you, buster."

"Officer. Apologies. Don't arrest me." He gave her a wicked wink.

"Behave. We have work to do."

"Right."

At the college, Cillian held back, walking the front square and taking pictures with his phone like any old tourist.

A pudgy guard stood outside the entrance to the library, and Jayne showed him her staff ID. Ever since the Book of Leinster was stolen, the library had upped its security measures, so even staff couldn't get in after hours without a good reason.

He looked it over. "What business do you have?"

"I forgot my wallet."

"I'll have to ring for another guard to escort you. It will take a bit."

"Oh, seriously, it's just sitting there on my desk, I'll be back before he even gets here. I'm supposed to be on a date, and I'm going to look like an idiot, and I'm going to be late. Do you have a partner? Don't you hate it when they're late? It's soooo annoying, and I don't want to be pegged as the ditzy American girl who can't show up on time." Pulling a Charm spell from the Torrent as unobtrusively as possible, she leaned on him and laughed into his face. The spell went pink around him like a demented valentine, and he smiled. She had him.

"Go on, and hurry, please."

That spell was a doozy—she could still hear him chuckling as she slipped inside. The TCO wouldn't approve of her using magic to manipulate a situation...or maybe they would. Grinning to herself, she used the key Rosalind had given her to get inside. Gerard's post was shadowed by the window frame that let in a little bit of moonlight and a sliver of streetlight illumination. Only the emergency lights shone over the shelves, tables, and desks.

Jayne took a deep breath of the bookish scent of the place, enjoying the calm her beloved books always provided, and booted up Rosalind's computer. She typed in the password she'd watched the woman set up yesterday, the day she always reset it. The screen came to life, and Jayne began searching for the folder that would hold Deirdre's address.

What would Ruger say about Jayne going off book?

Nothing good, she knew that. But Jayne was genuinely afraid her asset's life was at stake. That was worth the risk, and if the TCO disagreed...tough. She wasn't going to let Deirdre suffer. If she and Cillian could get Deirdre away from Alarik and keep her, maybe at Cillian's place, then Jayne could move forward with the plan. She could lie about Deirdre like she lied about everything else to Alarik. What was one more?

Finally, she found the correct folder and memorized the address.

She joined Cillian in the front square, leaving the smiling

guard behind.

"Won't he report your visit tomorrow?" Cillian had donned a hoodie with a goat's silhouette on the front.

"I'm sorry. I can't take your questions seriously when you're wearing a goat."

"Goats are the best."

"I mean, sure. But…"

"Listen. If they're hungry, they'll eat any fookin' thing. No problem. If you give them trouble, they'll head butt your ass. If that's not gangster, I don't know what is."

"All solid points. Okay. I am an official goat fan."

They joked around while Cillian drove them to Deirdre's side of town, but both grew quiet the closer they came to their destination.

Jayne touched Cillian's knee. "We shouldn't park in front of the house. Let's stop here and walk in."

"Okay." He pulled the car to the curb.

"You sure you're up for this? It could get messy."

"Crack on, love." He gestured to the sidewalk, and Jayne led him into the night.

They found Deirdre and Alarik's house within minutes, and Jayne's adrenaline zipped through her bloodstream.

She went into officer mode. "First, we need to assess the situation. If Alarik isn't home, this will be fairly easy. I'll just go up and knock and talk her into leaving."

"And if he is home or he has someone keeping watch on her?"

"Then we smash and grab."

"Ooh. I want to do that."

The house was dark. Shrubbery surrounded the two-story brick home, and one small luxury car sat in the drive.

"I don't see anyone out front," Jayne said, sneaking to hide behind three close-knit trees near two trash cans at the end of the driveway. "But they could be inside."

How could they get a peek?

As trained, Jayne searched her environment for tools and ideas. A pizza box stuck out of the neighbor's trash can. She sprinted to it, pulled it out, and returned to the shadows.

"Take this to the door and ring the bell."

"I'm a delivery boy who's going to be rather nosy about how many people are home, right?"

"Correct," she said.

"You mean 'affirmative.' They always say 'affirmative' on the shows."

"Shut up and go."

"Got it." He stepped out of the shadows and strode to the door with an impressive amount of swagger. "Pizza! Hurry, please! My boss is a real arse-hat. Come on. Up ya bowsey!"

Jayne smeared her hand over her face.

The door opened.

CHAPTER SIXTY-TWO

A dim interior light washed over Deirdre's face. There was a mass of green in the doorway—there were wards of some sort, keeping Deirdre inside. Jayne's instincts were right. She was in danger.

Summoning the Torrent, Jayne sought a Cutting spell, one that allowed her to slice through the green mist protecting Alarik's house. Jayne couldn't hear what Deirdre was saying, but as she manipulated the cut and the mist peeled away, the woman's voice grew louder.

"I didn't order a pizza, and you need to leave, now."

Cillian cleared his throat, holding the empty pizza box high. "Well, since you seem to be completely alone…"

"Subtle move, pal." Jayne came out of the trees. "Deirdre, it's me, Jayne. Come with us, please."

Cillian tossed the box and pulled Deirdre firmly but gently outside. Jayne shut the door before her new friend could escape back inside, then removed the Cutting spell. The mist re-formed, the wards intact again. With luck, Alarik wouldn't know what had happened.

She fought back her excitement—her magical abilities were growing exponentially. Smiling, she hooked her arm in Deirdre's and started a quick walk back down the street.

Deirdre's hair was all over the place, and she was shaking inside her fuzzy robe. "Jayne! What are you doing? They'll kill us all. You can't do this. And how in the world did you get me out of there?"

"No, they won't. I won't let them hurt you, or me. Alarik was keeping you prisoner, wasn't he?" Jayne kept her voice calm, glad that at least the woman wasn't shrieking or fighting hard to get away. She didn't want to be forced to knock her out to save her life.

"Yes, but you can't help me. I made my choice a long time ago. It is what it is."

"Bullshit." Cillian shook his head, bringing up the rear. "You can choose again. He doesn't own you."

"Who are you?"

Jayne turned Deirdre out of the neighborhood and toward the bus stop. "Don't worry about him. I can protect you. I can hide you until this is all over."

"Until what is all over? Alarik will never stop. Never."

"Deirdre, you just have to trust me. I'll take you to a safe place if you let me." Jayne watched her panicked eyes and prayed hard.

Deirdre looked over her shoulder in the direction of her house. "I guess. I can't go back now. I'll never keep a straight face when he questions me about tonight. That's how he knew you'd asked about Max. He asked me and I can't lie, Jayne. I'm terrible at it."

Jayne rubbed Deirdre's back as they walked in the moonlight

to Cillian's car. "It'll be all right. I will explain everything. I have backup. Like, bigtime backup. We'll keep you safe." She really hoped she wasn't lying. Surely, even if this wasn't part of the TCO's plan, they would still protect Deirdre from her psycho husband. She was their asset, and it was their duty.

Then Jayne noticed Cillian had walked past his car and was staring at his hands.

"Hey, you okay?" What if the adrenaline rush had been too much for him? He'd seemed so confident, but he didn't have training for things like this.

He stopped, then took one more stumbling step.

"Cillian?" Worry speared her chest.

Spinning, he faced her. "Jayne. I don't...I don't feel right."

Shimmering white and gold threads of what had to be magic flowed over him. Deirdre shrieked, and Jayne shouted Cillian's name again. She left Deirdre and ran to him. The light intensified, blinding Jayne. She blinked, eyes tearing, then looked up to see not Cillian but a wolf.

A large, silver-brown wolf stood staring at her, his breath clouding in the moonlight.

The creature growled quietly, and the rumbling sounds morphed into words. "Jayne. Please tell me you know what is happening, because I sure as hell don't."

A wolf was speaking to her. Shaking, Jayne reached out a hand. "Cillian?"

The wolf came forward, hesitating before placing its snout in her palm. It hit her in a flash...Cillian was the Rogue Ruger had smelled. Her original suspicions had been spot on. But it was clear that Cillian hadn't known what his body was capable of until now.

She swallowed, fear scratching at her bones. "I think our plan just got a little more complicated." Taking a steadying breath, she spoke to both Cillian and Deirdre. "Okay. Okay. Okay. Cillian, you're what we in the magical world call a Rogue. It's a genetic thing. You might turn into a wolf sometimes. No big."

Deirdre made a terrible noise.

Jayne wiggled her fingers. They were oddly numb. "No, it's okay. He is talking to me. In my head. Yep. That just happened." Her head was getting crowded.

Deirdre gripped her robe, looking like she was going to run back to the house.

"Please don't go back to that psychopath." Jayne kept an eye on Cillian even though she was talking to Deirdre. "That would make our evening even more challenging, and I don't think I can deal with any more obstacles. Okay?"

Deirdre sniffed. She kept her eyes trained on the wolf. On Cillian.

Jayne shook her head. Unbelievable. But it'd happened right in front of her.

She checked the road. There was no one out down this way, thank all the stars in the sky. If they could figure this out before the bus came, all the better.

"Cillian. I'm assuming you can understand me right now."

He growled, and the same thing happened, the sounds tumbling into words. "Yes," he said.

"Great. Deirdre, please quit making that chipmunk noise. Cillian, I'll explain everything when we aren't so exposed. We need to get you back home. Let me think."

She and Deirdre could take the car, and Cillian could use his Rogue speed and skills to run back...but that was asking too much of him. She could sense his panic at the situation, and Deirdre was giving off fear in waves so bright it was like she had a beacon inside of her. Jayne had to get them all to safety, fast.

The Carry spell. *Bless you, Ruger.*

"Any chance you left your keys in the car? Or...is there a furry pocket in there?" She waved a hand at his new form. She had no idea how his magic worked. Where was his backpack? His clothing? Maybe in a pocket of the Torrent?

A tinkle of metal, and something hit her foot. She bent to pick up his keys.

"Good. One less thing to worry about."

Cillian growled.

"Since you're much too big to fit in the car like this, I'm going to cart you home with magic. Deirdre, you're going to have to drive. This spell wears me out, and he's huge."

"What do you mean?" Cillian's voice rumbled.

"I can do a spell that makes a cocoon of sorts for you in another dimension and take you with me. It'll make me really tired. I've never done it, so I don't know that I can drive and hold the spell."

"Fine, I'll drive," Deirdre said. "We need to get out of here.

"Yes, let's," Cillian grumbled. "Thank you, Jayne. I'm very much having a bad night, I'll be honest."

"I can't imagine."

Lights showed over the hill. Someone was coming.

She shut her eyes and found the Torrent. The green stars spun around her fingers as she imagined the woven basket of light that Ruger had shown her back in the States. The spell came forward, and she wasted no time bringing it into the world and throwing it over Cillian. He disappeared. Jayne immediately felt a weight go around her shoulders and middle like she was toting Cillian on her actual back.

"Do I look weird?" she asked Deirdre.

"No." Deirdre swallowed and looked around Jayne at the approaching bus. "You look just as you did."

"Good to go. Cillian?"

No answer.

Okay. Okay. Okay. That didn't mean she'd accidentally killed him with magic. It just meant he couldn't talk right now. Or it could be that he was dead.

Yeah. It could be.

But hopefully not.

Her fingers were numb again and her heart didn't seem to want to beat properly.

Jayne realized Deirdre was saying her name and waving her into the car. Jayne nodded and climbed in as gracefully as she could with the extra strain on her body.

Cillian was a Rogue. As a magician, was he *her* Rogue? Jayne caught herself before she laughed hysterically.

Needless to say, it was a tense ride. It was hard to give directions, and Jayne was feeling sleepier and sleepier.

And mother trucker, it was a tough climb up three flight of stairs, but they finally made it back to Cillian's place. Gods above, she was tired. Tired to her shaking bones.

Jayne waited until they reached his front door to release the spell.

One grouchy-looking wolf rolled onto the landing above the stairs.

"I'm really glad I didn't kill you."

"Same here." It was so incredibly creepy and bizarre to somehow understand growling.

"Can you change back?" Jayne asked.

"I don't even know what I am. I don't know how to do anything!" The wolf's fur bristled, and he bared his teeth.

"Easy, boy."

"Do. Not. *Boy.* Me."

Deirdre resumed the scared-chipmunk noises.

"We need to get inside, Cillian. Because we can't stay out

here. I need a safe place to make a call."

Jayne opened the door, and the three of them spilled inside.

Deirdre threw the bolt, and with the door secure, Jayne switched the TV on for ambient noise. She pulled out her phone, called Ruger, and braced herself for a storm.

CHAPTER SIXTY-THREE

Ruger said a nice, big load of very bad words. "No, seriously. This can't happen."

"It happened." Jayne glanced at Cillian in wolf form and fought back a hysterical giggle.

Sofia's werewolf romance book came to life. Crazy. Wild. No way in hell. But yeah, there he was. Mr. Hot Irish Kickboxing Dude in full fur.

Cillian settled his snout on his paws while Deirdre cried quietly on the couch.

"Are you listening to me, Officer?" Ruger's voice cut through Jayne's panic.

"Uh. Yes! Totally yes."

"That is the Rogue I was worried about. What have you told him?"

"He only knows about my magic. I have to tell him everything, Ruger. It's not fair to him otherwise. He needs to know what he is, and how he fits into our world."

Ruger was silent, and the nonsound of it made Jayne's heart race.

"Please tell me we're the good guys and you're going to let me do this," she said quietly.

She heard Ruger sigh. "I can't promise you anything. I'm not in charge. The TCO is, and I can't *not* tell them this. It's too big. They'll find out, if they haven't already. I've had people on Cillian for the better part of a week now, and it's going to be impossible to hide. It'll be better if I report this catastrophe. I can word it in a way that puts you, Deirdre, and Cillian in the best light possible."

"Thank you."

"Stay where you are. If you leave, or the others leave, this will only get worse."

"And by worse, you mean dead."

"It's an option, Jayne. I'm not joking."

She pressed her fingers into her forehead and rubbed. "I know."

"Can you mimic the wards you saw on Alarik's house?"

"I think so. I'm pretty drained from the Carry spell, but I can make something that will work."

"Good. Do it. Right now. And don't let them down until you hear from me. Stay put, stay safe. That is an order, Officer Thorne."

"Yes, sir." Ruger hung up, and Jayne put her phone away. With the little bit of energy she had left, she warded the big window and door of Cillian's flat, then dropped, exhausted, to the couch.

Cillian stood suddenly and howled.

"Don't do that!" she shushed him. "We don't need any more trouble. Are you sick?" She crouched beside him and ran a hand over his back.

He growled and shook. Light flooded the room, centering on Cillian. The strands of magic increased in size and grew too bright to look at. Jayne stepped back, shielding her eyes. The light was like a thousand SUV headlights on the highway.

When Jayne turned back around to check on Cillian the wolf, she saw instead Cillian the man. He stood, head bowed and cheeks flushed, panting.

Then he raised his eyes to her. "That was totally fooked up."

She hugged him tightly, and Deirdre whispered, "Thank God."

Under Cillian's normal soap-and-clean cotton scent, an odd perfume lingered on his neck–like moss and maybe sage. It was magic. His magic. Werewolf magic. She had to laugh. It was just too nuts.

Cillian just kept staring off into nowhere. "Do you have any idea why I am this way?"

"Give me a second." She texted Ruger. *Please? He's so confused.*

Amanda has approved you telling him. Use caution, and judgment, Jayne. We don't know that he doesn't work for them. We're sending backup. Keep your wards up.

Thank you.

Jayne settled him in the living room and gave everyone a much-needed glass of whisky.

"I don't know much about your...condition. I know you have a genetic predisposition to shift into other forms. Like my ability to do magic. Some people have it, some don't. You're very rare, and you tend to be...triggered to your baser form when you're near powerful magic. A powerful magician. You can bond to that person."

It felt weird to talk about this in front of Deirdre, but she actually seemed calmer now, so Jayne continued.

"I was told that the gene for becoming a Rogue and the one

for being an Adept are both recessive. That's why there aren't many of either of us."

"You're right," Deirdre said, her voice shaking just a tiny bit. "I've overheard enough of Alarik's conversations to glean some knowledge."

"An Adept?" Cillian asked. "That's a magical person like you?"

"Yes, that's our term for it."

"How often will I change like that? Do you know?" The fear etched into Cillian's eyes made Jayne's heart ache.

She was quick to answer. "I don't know. Deirdre?"

Deirdre swallowed and looked back and forth between them. It was pretty obvious she didn't trust either of them. "I don't know, either. I do believe you'll be able to control it, once you learn how."

Jayne took Cillian's hand for a minute. "See, that doesn't sound so bad. And I'll help you. I'm not going anywhere. My people are coming, and they'll have more answers."

Jayne felt—not heard, felt—knocking. It was against her wards. She went into a battle stance but was quickly relieved to hear her name, and her third-level code words, "Jumping River Owl." The TCO was here.

She dropped the wards, and the apartment door flew open. At the looks on the TCO officers' faces, she feared her time with Cillian might be over. She felt overwhelmingly protective of him. She stepped between the officers and Cillian.

"Don't you dare hurt him. He is my Rogue."

She didn't know if that was true or not, but they didn't seem impressed.

Jayne used Ruger's name and asked a billion questions, but the officers ignored her arguments as well as Deirdre's and Cillian's. With a professional and scary grace, they quickly, and forcibly, escorted each of them into separate black cars.

Inside the first car, Jayne twisted to see the car Cillian had been pushed into. "You all better not hurt him. None of this is his fault. And Deirdre is a victim. Alarik was going to kill her if we didn't get her away."

"Please refrain from discussing the details of this event or any further events regarding this mission," the male driver said. "You will be questioned at a secure location."

Gritting her teeth in frustration, Jayne sat back against the cold leather seat and stared at the driver and the other officer beside him. What if these weren't even TCO officers, but people posing as them? Shoot, she'd been so upset she'd forgotten. "What's your third-level code word?"

"About time you asked," the female officer in the passenger seat said. "'Chess Plate Pisces.' I'd have thought Ruger would have taught you better."

Jayne relaxed a fraction. At least the good guys had them and not Alarik. "Don't blame Ruger. That's on me. All of this is. My asset—"

"Again, Officer. When. We. Are. Secure."

They drove out of the city, and Jayne lost sight of the other two cars. She hoped Cillian wasn't flipping out too much. Or wolfing out. Again. Damn, he'd been so big.

Wiping her sweating hands on her trousers, she tried to breathe evenly. They wouldn't hurt him. Surely. Deirdre would be okay, too, right? The TCO needed Deirdre's knowledge about the Kingdom, so they'd keep her feeling well enough to answer questions. An image of waterboarding flashed through Jayne's head. No. The TCO wasn't that kind of organization.

Were they?

A red food service truck sped up, and a corner of the car Cillian was in peeked out.

"Sit still, Officer," the female in the front snapped.

Flipping her off just to vent some frustration, Jayne looked out the back window. Cillian's car and Deirdre's, too, were gone.

CHAPTER SIXTY-FOUR

Jayne's escorts pulled up to a crap row house on a very quiet street. No lights shone in any of the other houses; the whole place felt deserted. Chipped paint covered the doorframe, and the inside of the place showed similar wear and tear. They truly chose only the best of the best for safe houses.

Jayne focused on what was in front of her instead of freaking out about what might be happening with Cillian and Deirdre. She took the initiative and switched on the TV and the sink faucet as the other two TCO officers spoke into their phones and checked the street, respectively. As she watched, the lovely green mist climbed the windows and shimmered in the night sky.

Why had she never been able to see the wards before?

Your magic is changing, Master. Getting stronger.

Oh-ho! Where have you been, Medb? I could have used some help earlier. Like, I have a Rogue now. Is that important?

Silence. Gah.

"So are you going to question me?" she asked, keeping her tone light. "What's the plan here? Because I don't think my mission is going to wait around for days on end. You know. Saving the world and all that? It's kind of a twenty-four/seven gig."

They ignored her.

Jayne felts the wards shift, and Amanda walked in. Jayne was surprised at how relieved she was to see the redhead full of grouch and piss. She very nearly hugged her.

"What are you doing here?" she asked Amanda.

"Cleaning up your mess."

"Where's Ruger?"

"Ruger is detained for the time being. Now, sit. Please." Amanda motioned to the first chair and sat on the second.

"Ooh, sitting. This is serious."

"This will all go better for you if you quit with the joking around, Officer Thorne."

"I doubt it. I'm so worried about the man you took into custody I feel like I'm going to explode. The joking is keeping me from the screaming. 'Kay?"

Amanda closed her eyes for a moment as if pained, then crossed her legs, lacing her fingers together over her knee. "Take a breath. And tell me everything. Don't leave anything out, Jayne."

Jayne detailed the evening's events.

There was no point in trying to hide the fact that she'd gone off book and rescued Deirdre from Alarik or trying to hide that Cillian was a Rogue. They had Deirdre in their hands, and Cillian smelled like old magic. The TCO wasn't filled with idiots.

She did argue her own good intentions, the severity of Deirdre's situation when considered in the light of Max's murder, and the absolute certainty she had in Cillian's ignorance until he wolfed out. He hadn't intended to conceal his condition, for lack of a better word. This had been a surprise to him as much as anyone.

"We can still pull this off, Amanda. All is not lost. Alarik doesn't know we took his wife. He still believes I'm a Kingdom Initiate in heart and soul."

"How do you know he is unaware of your actions? Did he not have a camera at his front door?

"I didn't see a camera system nor any evidence of surveillance at all," Jayne said. "It was covered in wards that I removed, then reinstated."

Amanda looked duly impressed.

"But even if he did, I stayed far enough back to remain out of frame. Cillian was the one on the front step and in view of any camera. I was careful. I followed my training."

Amanda's tidy eyebrows drew together. "You believe the leader of a terrorist organization doesn't have any surveillance on his own home? Mechanical, magical, he's not stupid enough to leave his flank open. I can't imagine he didn't feel his wards come down."

"He's not the leader. There is a Head. Some woman they haven't told me much about yet."

"We are aware."

"You are?"

"Yes."

"Just what do you know? If it's more than the fact that she is a powerful Adept and scares the shit out of people who have no problem murdering a man just for asking questions, then you know more than I do. And since I'm the one dealing with the situation, being cut open and forced to heal myself at his whim, I would appreciate the courtesy of being fully informed."

Amanda's mouth pinched. "A courtesy it is. You work on

behalf of the TCO. You are not in charge of this mission. In actuality, you are off the mission completely. You have been relieved of duty temporarily while we sort this out."

Jayne stood, hands fisting, pulse rising. "And who are you going to send in there to win them over? Did you know why Alarik himself has been training me to heal? Has Ruger explained my connection to the Book of Leinster, and to Queen Medb herself? And now I have a Rogue? Come on, Amanda. You can't bench me. I'm your best chance of keeping this operation running, and you know it."

Amanda blew a hard breath out her nose and crossed her arms.

"So you do know. And you still think someone else could do my job better than me."

"You don't follow the instructions given to you. Protocols are for your protection, and for ours. You have a great talent and shocking power, but none of that means anything if you do not behave as the TCO demands. It comes down to this. I can't trust you, Jayne."

Jayne ignored how much that hurt. "You know, that's just what Alarik is asking of his people. Complete, unquestioning loyalty. Which cult leader should I listen to, huh, Amanda?"

To her credit, Amanda had the grace to look abashed.

"We're fighting against something we don't fully understand, Jayne. You have to follow the rules, or you endanger everyone, and everything, we stand for."

Amanda was a rock. "Fine. How temporarily?"

"What?"

"You said I was off the mission 'temporarily.' How long do I have to be a good girl until you let me loose so I can finish my work?"

"I didn't say that. I said you were temporarily relieved of duty."

"Semantics. This isn't helping. Can we just hide Deirdre nearby and let Cillian go? Neither of their troubles will affect my mission."

"You are no longer assigned to this mission."

"You've got to be kidding me."

"You aren't listening, Jayne. I have said it twice now. You are no longer assigned to this mission. This mission is finished. We are pulling the plug."

"No, no, no. They are going to raise the dead. They're trying to raise Medb. Didn't Ruger tell you that?"

Finally, Amanda reacted to something, going pale as the moon. She uncrossed her legs. "You will stay here tonight. Tomorrow, you will be questioned by my superiors. The director is not happy with how this operation was handled. We were wrong to bring you up so quickly. I'm sorry."

Before Jayne could say another word, Amanda was up and gone. She took the other officers with her and left Jayne alone in the dank room.

They hadn't taken her phone. That was a good sign. She held on to it like it was a prayer book. She texted Ruger.

Just checking in.

It was code for *Call me right now.*

He didn't call. For three hours, Jayne sat in that awful living room and waited and wondered and worried. He still didn't call. She had no idea what was going on with Cillian or Deirdre. Her nails were thoroughly chewed off, and she'd started gnawing at her lip. She tried accessing the Torrent, but even her magic felt stymied and sluggish, as if they'd put some sort of magical cage around it.

Finally, she barreled toward the door and banged on it. Hard.

"I'm not going to stay quiet anymore. I can't take this. I have rights!"

The door pushed open into her face. "Calm down."

A familiar face scowled down at her.

"Ruger!"

He came inside and shut the door.

"I was starting to think you were never coming back from France. I texted," she accused.

"And I came immediately. Jayne. You have caused us no end of trouble. How in the hell did you end up falling for a Rogue?" He pressed the heels of his hands against his eyes and muttered her name a few times in frustration.

"I didn't mean to! I didn't know he was one. He didn't know he was one."

"I call B.S."

"No, really. He didn't. You should've seen how scared he was when it happened. We were helping Deirdre escape—"

"Oh yes. Of course. That little side mission you decided was a good idea. You only destroyed everything we've worked toward."

"No way. Alarik has no idea it was me," Jayne said. "Cillian was the only one who showed his face in any place that might have been watched via camera or whatever. It's fine. Alarik doesn't know I'm not who he wants me to be. You need to make them let me go so I can head back to my place and get the message about where the Kingdom is meeting next. I think this is going to be the big meeting. Like, *the* meeting. And tell me what they're doing to Deirdre and Cillian. Please. I'm dying here."

Ruger touched Jayne's shoulder gently, then smiled sadly, clearly concerned about her welfare, too. "They're both fine," he said. "Our fellow officers are questioning them, but without force. I visited both of them myself. You can stop worrying. Now, it's time for you to answer some of my questions. First, at this big final meeting, did they say the Kingdom's Head would be there?"

"Yes. I have to get back in and you know it. We can't blow this just because the TCO upper crust thinks Deirdre is disposable and Cillian went all wolf on us. It's fine. It's going to work. I have their trust. My magic is growing. I'm a healer now. They are all pumped about me bonding with Medb, and I am so ready to take those assholes down for what they did to Max and Deirdre and whatever else terrible crap they have planned for the world."

"Unfortunately, Jayne, it's out of my hands. I can't open this door and watch you go. Amanda's people will detain you. You have to come up with a detailed plan of action and present it to the director's second-in-command. Joshua. He's here."

"Okay. I'd like to have a plan. But I can plan a heck of a lot better if I could get home to receive the message the Kingdom is surely going to send me. That way, I'd know where they're planning to do these spells. That should explain at least some of the ways in which they plan to work their magic."

"Relax. The TCO has another officer posing as you at your home right now."

All the breath left her, and she collapsed onto the bed. "What?"

He grinned for the first time. "Remember the spell I showed you? The layered illusion? The officer looks and talks like you. Though I doubt she has your wide-ranging array of smart-ass remarks at her disposal. Or your propensity for pie."

"Ha-ha. Won't Alarik's operatives realize it's just magic?"

"I don't think so. The scent of magic is everywhere inside your apartment already. They won't be able to tell the difference. Not for a while anyway. Since we've bought you some time, show me what you've got. We need a solid plan of action to present to the director's people. What do you have in that head of yours?"

Jayne paced the room. "I need a way to get Medb to talk to me regularly. Right now she just fades in and out like a cloud over the sun. I need her to know what is about to happen and to see what she thinks we should do about it. And I need to be sure she isn't behind this somehow, that she's as unwilling a participant as I am. She doesn't trust Alarik, though, and she's warned me against him."

A knock sounded against the door, quick and furtive. Ruger opened it, said something to someone, then shut it again. He held up a folded piece of paper. "The officer posing as you just reported a message from the Kingdom."

"So Alarik's men went to my house. They really do know where I live." She fought a shudder and lost.

"You thought they weren't trailing you since day one?"

"I knew they'd followed me now and then. That's how they got the other message to me, the one about meeting in the sea cave. But I didn't know they were aware of my address."

"Rookie guess, sport. Addresses are easy."

"I know now. I nabbed Deirdre's from Rosalind's computer tonight with no trouble at all."

"Yes. Gerard told me."

"Gerard is yours? Ours?" Jayne's mouth popped open.

"Unofficially. Jayne, have I taught you nothing? How will you explain away the break-in when your face shows up on the college security cameras?"

She smiled. "No breaking and entering. I used my ID and told the guard I forgot something inside. And then I maybe used a Charm spell to make him more amenable to my going in unescorted. Besides, if Gerard is in your pocket, won't he cover for me?"

Ruger blew out a loud breath and rubbed his chin. "A Charm spell?"

"Worked perfectly. He practically asked me out."

"Jayne. When you have all your magic, you are going to be a force to be reckoned with."

He opened the folded piece of paper, and Jayne stood on tip-toe to see the writing.

"Tomorrow. Knocknarea? Where's that?" She pulled her phone out and began googling the word.

The first search result said *Tomb of Queen Medb*.

Jayne sat on the chair, the strength sucked right out of her. She turned her phone so Ruger could read the screen. "I guess zombie time is upon us."

CHAPTER SIXTY-FIVE

Jayne couldn't believe it was happening so fast. She was going to help raise an ancient warrior queen from the dead, the one who occasionally chatted her up from inside her brain. Life had gone from strange to downright unbelievable.

The door opened, and two TCO officers brought in Deirdre. Her eyes were puffy from crying, but her face was dry now.

"You okay?" Jayne asked.

"Yes."

"Good. They've moved up the meeting. We need to hear what you know."

"I'll gladly tell you everything. But know that I don't think Alarik will be defeated easily. When he finds out I'm gone, he will come for me. He needs me. I'm his ticket into the libraries that hold the grimoires."

Ruger looked up from his computer. "The TCO has dealt with threats such as this. You're safer here with us than you are anywhere else."

"You better be serious. He won't trust me again. He'll keep me under lock and key and force me to do his bidding. I don't want to go back to that life. He is a cruel man."

Deirdre pushed up her sleeves, and Jayne noticed she wasn't wearing her wedding ring.

A shout sounded outside the door, and they all tensed.

"Get your hands off me! If I wanted to run, I could've done it already. Now, let me see her!"

It was Cillian.

They must have agreed, because the door swung wide to show him standing there, eyes flashing and fists bunched. Then Cillian met Jayne's gaze and he hurried to her.

"Are you all right?" he asked, pulling her to him. "Are you hurt?"

She smiled and touched his scruffy chin. "I'm fine. You?"

"Grand. Did they tell you?"

"Tell me what?"

Ruger looked like a bomb was about to go off. "Do we have to now?"

Cillian growled.

"Fine. It's your head," he said.

Cillian took Jayne's hand. "When you first came to Dublin, I sought you out at the behest of a…friend. I had no idea what they wanted with you, but they wanted me to get to know you, sent me to break into your flat and steal a small journal. Problem was, you were you, and I fell, hard. I'm so sorry, Jayne. I had no idea any of this was going to happen. I feel awful that I lied to you and betrayed your trust. If you want me to leave, I will, right now. But believe me when I say I'm on your side. I will never have anything to do with them again, and I've been giving the TCO all the details I can about them. They're wrong, and you're not."

Fury spiked within her, and her thoughts fractured. A setup? A break-in? A journal? That must be her father's, and Cillian taken it for those horrible, awful people?

And she'd slept with him? She was going to be sick. Blood racing, she launched herself at him.

"You bastard!" She punched him in the jaw, and he stood still for it, taking her blow. He whimpered like a dog who'd been kicked but didn't look away.

"Aye, do it again. I deserve it."

He did. She had let down her guard with him, brought him into her heart and her bed. How could he have done this? Betrayed her like this? She had told him…well, she hadn't told him the truth about who she was. She'd lied. She'd omitted. Secrets sat on her side of this as well. How could she fully blame him when she'd kept so much from him too?

The answer was that she couldn't. Her fury melted into something mellower. As livid as she was, she had to put those feelings aside. They were running out of time.

"I take it you've tested him to make sure he isn't lying?" Jayne asked Ruger coldly. Her anger at Cillian remained, but she'd have to untangle the details of it later.

"He's not lying. He means every word. He was covered in a Memory Wash spell. He didn't know what they had him do until I lifted it. The moment he remembered, he insisted on your knowing the truth, though I suggested we might leave it until another time."

Oh wow. A memory spell. Still…

"I refuse to lie to you, Jayne. I really am sorry."

An ache spread through her chest. She just wanted everything to go right and all to be happy. Was that so tough? Rubbing her temples, she looked at Cillian again and heaved in a breath.

"We will discuss this later, dog."

He had flushed a little like he might be ashamed. "I understand. Now, what is the plan? Because I need to be a part of it. I refuse to sit back and let them hurt you."

Ruger shut the laptop and came around the small side table to shake Cillian's hand. "Glad to hear it, son. That's what we think, too. Ruger Stern, TCO librarian. Welcome to the stacks."

"TCO?" Cillian asked.

"Torrent Control Office. We're the division of the CIA that deals with magic in the world. I run the Library Division, which is exactly what it sounds like. I trust you've signed all your paperwork?"

Jayne's eyebrows shot up, and Cillian grinned. "Yes, sir."

"Wait. Cillian is TCO now?" Jayne asked, completely shocked.

"He is."

"Gods help us," she said, shaking her head.

"Jayne's going to help us find a way to defeat the Kingdom, who are trying to take over the world. We'll give you the details later. Welcome to the CIA."

At the pride on his face, Jayne couldn't help it—she grinned at Cillian, who said, "You have a lot of explaining to do, lady."

"So do you. If we live through the night, I'll tell you everything, after. Now, sit."

His eyes flashing, he listened.

Ruger dismissed the other TCO officers, who said they'd stand just outside in case they were required. Jayne, just a little bit, wished they'd go to hell and not come back. After the way they'd treated her and the others, well, she thought her small team could do quite fine without them.

"Before we start—why does the Kingdom want my father's journal? And why didn't someone come for it before now? I mean, I've had it for years."

Ruger shook his massive head. "Honestly? We don't know. We don't know what's in it. We didn't know you had it, either. Cillian? Did Aaró's man tell you why he wanted the journal?"

"Only that it was vital to the cause. That without it, they couldn't succeed."

"Well, that's not ominous," Jayne said.

"I'm sorry. If I knew more..." He looked so beaten she gave him a small smile, just for comfort. Just a small one. She was still pissed at him.

"Let's not worry about it now, Jayne. Once we have Alarik in custody, we'll get all the answers we need. Now, Deirdre, what are Alarik and crew up to?"

"He's trying to collect the necromantic texts from the world's great libraries. That's why he needed me, to get him in. Though now, with Jayne on his radar...I'm probably expendable. She's got all my skills as a librarian and the power of an Adept. He's been very excited about you, Jayne. I think...well, if I'm out of the way, you can be his wife and do his dirty work in ways I never could."

"Eww. No offense, Deirdre, but he's really not my type."

Cillian squeezed her shoulder, and she didn't immediately want to break his fingers, so...progress.

"This is helpful information, Deirdre," Ruger said. "Anything else? Have you overheard anything about a plan to raise the dead?"

"Yes, but nothing concrete. He has always been very cagey when discussing operations. Just that it all focuses on Queen Medb. That's why he wanted the Book of Leinster."

Jayne mentally rifled through the spells she'd heard about at the sea cave and had seen for herself. Telepathy. Electricity. "Okay, so the necromantic text stories claim if Medb rises, she will give me something. But we don't know what that is, and we can assume the Kingdom doesn't, either. They will want to focus on something they do know they can accomplish."

Ruger nodded. "A more immediate goal."

"Yes. I think the Kingdom wants to use telepathy on Queen Medb to force her to call up some form of magical electricity."

"Jesus, Mary," Deirdre whispered.

"And Joseph, too," Cillian added, dropping to sit on the bed. He hooked one hand behind Jayne's knee like he needed the contact for some reason.

Ruger made a humming, thinking noise. "Electricity, you say. What if they downed the power grids? Alarik is an engineer. He could easily overthrow the plants close to Knocknarea and take them offline. He'll have to have a way to disable all the backup generators, as well."

Jayne snapped her fingers. "If they manage to shut down the power grids, that would certainly get the world's attention."

"But it would hardly be cause for a complete revolution."

Deirdre sat on the bed nearest the curtained windows and rubbed at the pale spot where her wedding ring used to be. "They'll do it in steps. There is little need for it to be done in one fatal swoop. That would be impossible. Alarik might be insane, but he isn't stupid. Systemic collapse serves his purposes. First the UK, then the rest of Europe, then Asia and the rest of the world. He can convert many Adepts to the cause if he shows them what they're capable of. At least, that's what he thinks."

"I agree," Jayne said. "What if Medb has the ability to magnify their Telepathy spell and use it to access someone who works at a major power center? If they could shut down power to all of Ireland and the United Kingdom, that would be something worth raising the dead."

Cillian put his head in his hands. "Listen to yourself. Crazy," he mumbled.

Jayne patted his tangled hair.

He looked up, one blue eye blazing beside the fringe of thick locks. "If you say 'good doggie,' I will be forced to take action."

A surprised laugh popped out of Jayne. Ruger rolled his eyes, and she covered her mouth.

Ruger spun his laptop so all could see. A map of the UK and Ireland took up half the screen. Black lines and multicolored dots cloaked the image like streamers and confetti.

"There is a power station in Northern Ireland that is connected to the rest of the UK. And here"—he pointed to a yellow circle on the map—"is a connector from Ireland to Northern Ireland."

"Destroy it from there, and there will be darkness across all four countries. Heck of a start." Jayne's hands were sticky, and her head had started to pound.

Deirdre put her finger over a spot not far from the stations Ruger had indicated, in a place labeled *Sligo.* "And this is where Medb rests."

Ruger met her gaze, his eyes reflecting the room's overhead light. "Plenty close enough for a Master to cast a Telepathy spell."

Cillian squinted at the laptop. "So she can chat inside some power man's head. What comes of that?"

"Telepathy can be more than idle chatting," Ruger said. "If it comes from a Master, it can be very strong. Demanding. Controlling."

"How do you know this?" Deirdre asked. "Alarik said there hadn't been a Master living in a very long time."

Ruger shot a look at Jayne, who bit her lip.

"Centuries, actually. But our organization's research team works on a combination of studying historical documents and crafting hypotheses based on current high-level Adepts and their capabilities."

"That was a canned answer if I ever heard one," Cillian said quietly.

He wasn't wrong. Jayne had been told the same exact thing during training, and it sounded a bit too tidy then, let alone now, when they were about to stare down a small army of magical terrorists.

"What do you mean exactly by *strong?*"

"Telepathy can reach into a person's will and shift it. Permanently."

Cillian went pale.

"Potentially," Ruger added. "But only if you practice and have natural power in that sense. As far as we can tell, Masters are always capable of it. Their magic is mind-blowing."

Jayne snorted. "Literally." She had to defuse this. Medb had called her a Master, but she was seriously not ready to accept it. She wasn't there yet. If she were, the magic would come to her more easily, she was almost certain. She was getting better, no doubt, more intuitive. But still.

Ruger cleared his throat. "I believe we can safely assume the Kingdom plans to raise Medb, a powerful, ancient Master, and use the Telepathy spell to influence her own Telepathy casting, with the intent to harness an electric storm over the generating stations here and here." He pointed to the map. "Their main goal here being to put Ireland and the UK in the dark. Long term."

Jayne truly wished Medb would just speak up already. "But how can they hope to control Medb's mind when she is the one with the true power?"

"This is pure speculation, but I'm guessing when a long-deceased Master is raised, they are open to influence. They won't have the shields of the living."

"I would probably be a touch foggy after being dead in the ground for that long," Cillian said.

Jayne listened for the ancient queen before continuing. "She's not technically in the ground. Buried beneath a mound of stone, Medb's body stands, in full armor, facing her enemies, even in death. Or so legend has it."

Cillian stood and began pacing. "I'm scared. I'm not afraid to admit it. This is some serious shite."

"Yes, that does sound rather intimidating, doesn't it?" Jayne said.

"How long has she been waiting on getting back into the world of war?" Cillian eyed each person in the room like they were all nuts.

Jayne shrugged. "It's debatable, but you'd be safe to assume at least two thousand years."

"Well, I think the Kingdom's plan is feasible. Hats off to the terrorists. They've cooked up a corker," Cillian said.

"You don't have to be here." She wanted to give him a way out if he needed it.

He was green around the gills, but he said, "I'm all in. When my aunt died, she was in the hospital at the end. Losing electricity and backups would've been a rough way to go. Not only that. Planes could come down. Infrastructure would collapse. Kids will die if they do this. It'll be awful. I'm in for anything I can do to help."

Ruger sighed. "And that's just the start. They want to telepathically control the entire human population. If the stories are true, and they find all the texts, and raise all five elemental Masters? They can do it. Medb would just be the first."

Deirdre was pale. She went to the tiny bathroom and shut the door. Jayne could hear her blowing her nose. Poor woman. For a second, she wondered how Alarik had been when they got together. How had he charmed her? *A spell, Jayne. Obviously.*

And then poor Deirdre had found out he was insane on a whole new level. That had to suck.

Jayne faced Ruger. "So what's the plan of attack when all the Kingdom members show up? Can I cast that Capture spell to grab them?"

"How many do you think will come to this event? Did they mention numbers at any of the meetings?"

"I've seen about fifty members so far. I'm betting all of them will be there. They're super tight and really excited about this."

"You couldn't Capture that many. It would kill you. But the TCO has several units here, and if Cillian is willing, he can shift and create a distraction. I'd say you, Jayne, could safely Capture two Adepts. More than that and your life will spill out into the Torrent. You'll be done. Burned."

"Is there a spell for making the dead dead again?" she asked.

"If there is, we don't know it," Ruger said.

Cillian raised a hand. "Um… not so sure about my role here. I don't know how to shift. That was a total accident."

"What did you feel before it happened?"

"My insides twisted up, sort of like how I feel when I look…" He trailed off thoughtfully. "Oh. I think maybe I know how to do it. Wicked!"

Ruger looked both interested and incensed at the way Cillian was now looking at Jayne, but she ignored him.

"Good. Practice that. If you can control your shifting, do it at will, we'll have a major advantage." Jayne tapped a fist on her leg, thinking. "First, we try to keep the Necromancy spell from even happening by taking out the Kingdom member stupid enough to try it."

"That person may well burn themselves to death and we'll be off the hook," Ruger said.

"Yes. But if the timing works so that we see them trying, we can Capture spell them first."

"If that doesn't immediately work, we will Spell to Kill." Ruger's voice was quiet.

Jayne's stomach twisted. Killing with magic went completely against the Torrent's will and made the magic very dangerous. It was similar to the Capture spell in that it used the caster's energy far more than other types of spells. The Torrent didn't want to end life. The caster had to force the spell into being. She'd felt that horror when she'd killed the Rogue in the Time Catch. She couldn't imagine doing it again.

"We have orders, Jayne. Prisoners are preferred, but be prepared for anything."

Jayne nodded. "Understood," she said, feeling completely ridiculous for uttering the word. She couldn't possibly truly understand. "But let's say things don't go well, and the Kingdom does indeed raise Queen Medb. I'll try to speak to her while the rest of you use the Capture spell and/or Spell to Kill against the other Kingdom members."

"Agreed."

Jayne touched Cillian's hand, and he immediately wrapped his around hers.

She couldn't believe what she'd just agreed to.

CHAPTER SIXTY-SIX

They talked over specifics, bringing in a few other TCO officers—Amanda included. Once she heard the whole story, she'd warned the director herself, and he'd given them the green light to thwart the attack. They went over what felt like a thousand plans, including studying the topography of Medb's tomb. The pictures online showed a nearly treeless area with a huge hill. On top, a pile of stones hid the Iron Age Master. It would be a very difficult place for TCO units to remain concealed as the approach to the tomb was wide open.

A slim TCO officer named Seo-joon chimed in as Ruger jotted something down on a notepad. "We'll need to use portals. I wish we didn't, because it may alert the Kingdom of our presence, but we'll have to risk it. We can't just jog up that mountain in plain sight. And if we all appear simultaneously, we'll draw attention away from Jayne and give her some time to do what she can telepathically."

"They will work at night. Under the moon. It's how they

operate," Deirdre said.

Jayne handed her a cup of tea she'd made with the house's pathetic little coffeepot. "Yeah, that's what I picked up when I was with them in the Time Catch. They like the moonlight."

"Fitting." Cillian made a second cup of tea, and Jayne happily accepted it from his warm hands. He let his palm linger over her skin and gave her an encouraging smile.

"You are handling this like a total champ," she whispered.

"So are you, and trust me, I'm still reeling. I'm just good at faking a calm demeanor."

"Oscar-winning. Truly." She sipped the orange Ceylon tea, then grinned over the lip of the mug even though she really felt like falling into the nearest bed for a very long nap with Cillian's arms wrapped tightly around her. She was still mad at him, but it was fading. She really did like him, and that was dangerous, she knew. But it felt right.

He touched her cheek gently. "Good or bad, this will be over soon."

"Can we make a date to hit your gym for some pad work? I have a feeling I'm going to need a magic break after this. If I manage to stay alive, that is."

"You can do this, Jayne. I can... This will sound strange, but...I can smell the magic on these people. And your scent is strongest by far."

"I'm not sure it works like that, but hey, I'll take it."

"There should be a Rogue Reddit thread. What is a new wolf/raven/bear/whatever to do about informing himself on his new existence? If there was a thread, I could ask if I'm on to something or not."

"You should start one," Jayne said.

Ruger took the pen he'd been chewing out of his mouth. "No internet unless you have approval."

Cillian rolled his eyes. "Yes, sir."

Ruger never even looked up from his notes. "Watch the attitude, young man."

Cillian shook his head.

"You know," Ruger started, "I can tell you a couple of theories about Rogues and their origins."

Jayne smacked Ruger's arm. "Get on with it. He's dying to know. Right, Cillian?"

"Totally."

Ruger rolled the desk chair around to face Cillian, who sat on the bed. He steepled his fingers. "No one knows for certain where the genetic divergence began. Of course, many accounts of Rogues appear in folklore from here in Ireland to Germany, and all around the world."

"I have heard mention of them in the Fionn stories as a child. Shifters, I mean," Cillian said.

"Yes. Sadly, there aren't enough primary sources to determine whether or not that was only a story or the truth," Ruger said. "The theory most researchers working with the TCO hold to is the one with roots in King Henry the Eighth's reign. That's our first direct link, though we're sure it predates this era, too."

Jayne couldn't fight a grin of excitement. With magic in the mix, history took on a whole new shade of mysterious purple sparkle wonderment. She was definitely on board for this.

"Just outside London, a group of nobles hunting found a pack of wolves dead and strangely disfigured. They burned what was left of the carcasses. All five men developed odd symptoms shortly after the event. Something like a bone density mutation. It's difficult to know for sure when our researchers are dealing with such old documents, papers that have been written in code and hidden away for so long. Three of these men conceived children while their symptoms were active. One of those children was Anne Boleyn. Most of our researchers claim she used her power as a Rogue to intimidate the king."

"Did you just tell us that Anne Boleyn was a shape-shifter?" Jayne's eyes were going to pop out of her skull.

"According to our records." Ruger shrugged.

Cillian laughed. "Well, I can't feel too bad about sharing a mutation with such a history-altering woman. At least we aren't boring, huh?"

"This is so crazy."

Just when Jayne thought life couldn't be more insane... She eyed Cillian. Rogues bonded to Masters. Would he be tempted to bond with Medb?

Or with her? She liked Cillian, a lot, but she barely knew him. As hot as he was, they were not nearly close enough for her to be comfortable with the idea of an eternal link.

Still, her curiosity got the better of her. What would happen if they did bond? Would her magic grow more powerful? How would it affect him? She longed to ask Ruger, but with Cillian here, it was...it didn't feel right. But maybe she was being an idiot. This was life or death.

"Ruger." Her voice sounded oddly far away. "What happens when a Rogue bonds to a Master?"

Cocking his head, Cillian lowered his cup and looked between them.

Jayne sipped her tea, determined to see this difficult conversation through. "Rogues can supposedly bond with a Master magician," she told him.

Ruger set his pen down and leaned back in his chair, the light glancing off his forehead and his beard. "They can. Since we've never seen it, we don't know enough about the effects. One would assume the bond increases the power and skills of both parties involved. Power tends to be the motivator in the world of magic."

"In the world, period," Cillian said.

"Will Cillian be tempted to bond with Medb?"

Cillian huffed. "I was thinking of you, lady. Not the zombie, thanks very much."

Jayne's cheeks heated. "Well, I'm not a Master."

"Not yet," Ruger said. "I think we'll have to wait and see what happens. No one alive knows enough about bonding."

This was yet again another moment when it would've been grand for Medb to speak up and lay down some wisdom. Or a warning. Anything.

Amanda finished a whispered conversation on her phone, then shut it off. She put her hands on her hips, looking from Ruger to Jayne and back again. "Okay. We're a go. It's time to share how we're going to stop Alarik and the Kingdom from raising Medb. Are we ready?"

Jayne felt a little sick. If they failed to convince their superiors that this was the way to go, the TCO might just send her packing, and she had no idea what they'd do about Cillian.

"I don't think I'll ever be ready," she said, "but it's pretty much now or never, right? This thing goes down tomorrow night. We are out of time."

Ruger brought Jayne, Amanda, and Seo-joon to the kitchen, where he prepared a portal that led to another crummy row-house. The living room of the new safe house was larger than the previous one and held two very serious-faced officers. When Jayne et al. walked in, the director's direct report, Joshua, crossed his arms and leaned against the TV table. She recognized him from training. He was the kind who cut to the quick, no wasting time with worrying about people's feelings or silly things like encouraging officers going through tough times. His associate, a woman wearing a Mrs. Weasley–looking hand-knitted

Christmas sweater (even though it was early autumn), locked the door behind the group, then stood beside Ruger.

Joshua tilted his pointy head. "Well? What do you have?"

Ruger took the lead, explaining everyone's role as well as the contingency plan.

Arms dropping, Joshua nodded his approval. "The Spell to Kill is nothing to play around with. Remember, Jayne, if you put it to use, you will endanger yourself as well as every other operative in the area. Our cover will be blown if you go for a kill."

"Or if I die trying." Jayne shivered, feeling the burn in her arms, an echo of what she'd experienced when healing.

"Yes."

"Got it."

"I will discuss this with the director. Please return to your safe house."

"But what if Alarik realizes the officer posing as me is a fake?"

"She is reading a book. It's not a tough assignment."

"Make her eat some pie."

Jayne could have sworn he almost smiled, but Amanda grabbed Jayne's arm and started her toward the door.

"And wear sweatpants! I would never wear real clothing on a quiet night at home."

"I think they have it in hand," Ruger said, helping Amanda escort Jayne out.

"If that officer is wearing a speck of makeup, we're through," Jayne said, not at all kidding. She never wore the stuff at home, and the Kingdom took details to heart. Ugh. She hated the thought of someone wearing her face and sitting on her couch. And what book had she chosen? If she'd picked up the wrong one it would blow her cover sky-high.

They returned to the safe house to discuss a few more details and to let everyone else know the jury was still out.

Jayne paced the floor, wishing she had a bag to kick.

Under orders from the TCO, Cillian left for his flat to keep up the charade that all was well. They sent Seo-joon to follow him. If the TCO didn't start trusting Cillian soon, Jayne didn't have a lot of hope for their plan.

Cillian returned in the middle of the night, and she was so glad to have him safely under her watchful eyes again. Jayne had downed three cups of tea and a cup of coffee for dessert, and her nerves had long passed stressed. She was closing in on being over all of it. There was only so much fretting one could do.

Amanda returned from a second trip outside, her eyes wide. "He approved it. We're on for tomorrow night."

An hour later, everyone had gone to bed except Ruger and Cillian. They'd taken Deirdre to another safe house to sleep and set guards in her living room—two officers who were pretending to play checkers on a flimsy table. Jayne held the door open for Ruger, who had his briefcase in hand.

"We'll get some officers for you as well. And of course, the whole place is warded. Jayne, do you want Cillian in here?"

"Absolutely. If that's okay with you?" she asked Cillian.

His blue eyes were bright in the near dark of the room. "Of course. You couldn't have dragged me away if you tried. Actually, you probably could, but let's just pretend you couldn't have. It's more fun for me."

It was Ruger's turn to roll his eyes. "Good night. See you in the morning for a final debriefing."

Jayne shut the door and hugged Cillian hard.

"You are in so much trouble, friend."

CHAPTER SIXTY-SEVEN

Sitting on the safe house's bed next to Cillian, who was watching TV, Jayne again went over what she knew about Queen Medb. The historical figure was so tangled in lore and legend that it was nigh on impossible to figure out exactly who they might be dealing with if the Necromancy actually worked.

Was she really the Queen of Fairies?

If Rogues and magicians existed, why not fairies? It wasn't the most stupid idea. And if Medb did have some sort of supernatural minions, would they also rise from their graves? Were any buried nearby? Jayne was pretty sure worrying about nefarious fae was borrowing trouble. She had plenty of it already piled high on her plate. A line of Shakespeare came into Jayne's head. *O, then, I see Queen Mab hath been with you.* The description that followed painted the warrior queen as small, with a hazelnut-shell chariot and interesting thoughts on sexual intercourse.

"I think Shakespeare had it wrong," Jayne said aloud.

"What's that?" Cillian popped a grape into his mouth. The

TV's light washed out his sharp cheekbones and thick eyebrows.

"Shakespeare said Medb was tiny. That she has this itty-bitty court of helpers and she haunts people's dreams and helps virgins have sex with their new husbands. I think he had it wrong. No way a woman who fought in a war would come back as a little, slightly frustrating, marginally helpful fairy. I think he was being an enormous jerk, honestly, belittling the historical figure."

"Maybe he thought his version made her more interesting. He was a playwright. Not a fighter like us."

Jayne hadn't thought of it that way. "You could be right. But I still think he was wrong. I think she is going to be amazing."

"You almost sound excited about the idea of our plan failing and the Kingdom raising her from the dead."

"I can't help it. I love history, and it's possible I'll see a freaking Iron Age queen tomorrow night." She pointed at the TV. "Not that reruns of *Seinfeld* aren't enjoyable."

"Tomato, toe-mah-toe." Cillian grinned.

"I'm not scared. I should be, but it hasn't hit me yet."

"Maybe that's because of all that training you've had."

"Maybe. Or I'm just in denial about the whole thing."

"Maybe you should practice your magic." He cringed at the word.

She slapped him. "You actually do think I'm a freak."

"Oh, sure. Wolf Guy is allowed an opinion on that. Definitely." A snarl ripped from Cillian's mouth.

Jayne jumped. "Jerk! Don't do that. That's scary, dude."

He tossed the remote to the end of the bed, let out another snarl, and crawled over so he was on top of Jayne, his dang fabulous arms posted out straight to hold his own weight.

Jayne acted like she was about to knee him in the balls. "Watch it, wolfie."

Laughing, he growled into her neck, where the snarling turned into kissing. She grabbed his T-shirt and tugged him closer. The scruff on his chin scratched her lips as she made her way to his mouth. She slid her hands along the waistline of his trousers, savoring the feel of his lower back muscles as he moved even closer.

His tongue teased her earlobe before he whispered, "My sexy witch."

An idea forming in her head, she accessed the Torrent, found the spell she wanted, then unleashed it, all in the space of a blink.

They were in her medieval bedroom illusion again.

Cillian froze, his hand poised over her body.

"Want me to make the magic go away?" Jayne asked. A fire snapped in the magical fireplace and coated the underside of the bed's thick brocade canopy in golden light. "Are you going to stop kissing me if I don't?"

"Not bleeding likely." He shook his head in awe. He reached for a goblet sitting beside the bed. "It's wine. Can I drink this? It looks like a nice red. Or will I really be sipping spelled water from the faucet?"

Jayne laughed and slid a leg over his knee, her toes soaking in the warmth of his thigh. "I don't know. I'll try it first if you want."

Cillian took a swallow, then smacked his lips. "It's very good. What is this, like Henry the Eighth's boudoir? If the wine is real, he might come storming in here and demand to know what we're doing in his bed."

Jayne drank from the goblet. The wine was earthy and smelled lovely. "I can always stop the old king in his tracks. After all," she said, finishing the cup, "I am a witch."

She actually felt like a gladiator the night before the big fight in the arena. Lions would go for her throat tomorrow. Blood would be spilled. There was no doubt in her head she would be in serious, real danger, but she couldn't seem to feel too worried about it yet. If the bad side of magic was going to rough them up tomorrow, then they might as well enjoy the good side of it today.

Cillian kissed her again, dragging his lips across her jaw and brushing her hair back with one hand. Waves of need crashed over her, hot and powerful.

There was a knock at the door.

Cillian growled as Jayne rose. "Who is it?" she said without opening up.

"We have your room bugged for safety, Jayne," Ruger said. "I just wanted to be sure you knew."

Jayne's face warmed, and she squeezed the bridge of her nose. "Thanks."

Cillian was in bed shaking his head. "Someday we'll be alone again."

Shrugging, Jayne readied for a tamer night, switching off the last of the lights and crawling into bed in soft pajamas. It wasn't easy to simply sleep beside him, but no one said being a TCO officer was easy.

Over a scone the next morning, Jayne found her phone while Cillian jumped into the shower. She was very glad it was the weekend and they didn't have to come up with a believable excuse for her to miss work at Trinity. Anything more out of the ordinary would've practically screamed *Jayne helped Deirdre escape!* to Alarik and his crowd.

Jayne held her phone next to her heart, wishing she could confide in Sofia. Gods above, she missed her sister. It was like a chunk of her had been carved out with a spoon so it would hurt more, à la that old *Robin Hood* movie they'd watched as kids. Jayne gave the phone one last big squeeze.

Cillian came out of the bathroom with a tiny towel wrapped around his waist.

Jayne's mouth actually watered.

He grabbed a hand towel from the counter near the sink and rubbed his hair dry. "Texting your other boyfriends a final goodbye?"

"Because we're going to die by the sword of an ancient queen tonight?"

His eyebrows lifted toward his hairline. "I was thinking because you're hopelessly in love with me." He held up his hands. "But that's grand. You go on thinking whatever you need to. I have no pride. I just want the rest of your admirers to feic off."

"Oh yes. I texted all nine of them," she joked, loving his jealousy. "Just now."

As they dressed and finished the small breakfast the TCO had brought in, Ruger showed up at the door.

Dark circles hung below his eyes and made Jayne feel bad about having a semi-great night. She should've been up worrying, too, but instead she'd slept like the dead in the arms of her wolf.

Her wolf. She had to stop thinking like this. He could bond with Medb tonight and never remember meeting her.

"Jayne, we should take today to train. And Cillian, you have work to do as well."

And so Jayne kissed Cillian goodbye and went to do just that.

To train with magic. So she could fight to the death with magical terrorists. And possibly a legendary warrior queen.

No problem.

"Rug?"

"Yes, Agnes."

"I think I need to work on a magical Xanax first."

CHAPTER SIXTY-EIGHT

Knocknarea's small collection of houses, their windows glowing, gave way to the dark, rolling countryside. Jayne had rented a car and come on her own, as instructed by the Kingdom. Cillian, Ruger, and two TCO units weren't far behind, traveling in unmarked cars and vans toward Queen Medb's tomb. She couldn't see them. The road behind her was empty.

A sign labeled *Queen Medb's Tomb Car Park* led her into a square of pavement. A red SUV and three smaller sedans were parked around the lot in no apparent order. They had to belong to the Kingdom, because who else would be up here in the middle of the night?

Teresa had sent her a message. There would be no more contact before the casting, and Jayne was to arrive at 2200 hours alone, without a phone, and unarmed, so she would be entirely committed no matter the outcome.

Teresa seemed to have hardened over the last several days. When they'd trained together in the Time Catch, she'd been quick to smile and praise, but now, there was no joy in her lean face. She looked like she needed a big, fat hug, but Jayne couldn't forgive her for not standing up to Alarik before they killed Max. It was one thing to be brainwashed into believing the Kingdom's goals were legitimate, but Max had been right there, alive and good. How did she sleep at night?

Jayne pushed her anger aside and pasted a calm, serious look on her own face. She couldn't blow this plan now. This was it. What would her epilogue look like? Tragedy, or an H.E.A. like Sofia demanded in all of her reads? Happily Ever Afters didn't usually happen in real life, and Jayne was fairly sure tonight wouldn't break that streak. Hopeful Ever Afters were as good as it got these days.

She wanted the good old-fashioned H.E.A. And with Cillian by her side. She wanted it very badly.

A bright sliver of moon shimmered through a bank of low clouds. Jayne shut the car door and began the long walk up the giant mound to the stone cairn of Medb's final (or not so final) resting place.

Thank God the moon was trying to light up the place. Jayne didn't have a flashlight, so she'd have to rely on her eyes to adjust. The wind hurried past her ears, rushing and blocking the sound of any voices or footsteps she might have otherwise detected.

Teresa had told Jayne not to portal to the grave site because it would drain some of her energy and they needed all of her, whole and brimming with power. Brimming. Yes, she'd actually used that word. As if Jayne was a nice cup of coffee for the Kingdom to down like a hungover college student.

Jayne really hoped Ruger and the rest wouldn't be too worn out portaling up here with Cillian in tow. She was going to need that backup.

And with that thought, fear finally swamped her.

Her heart shuddered, and she shoved her hands deep into her coat pockets to keep them from shaking. She'd considered trying to call Sofia again before driving here, but she'd decided she might get too emotional and could threaten the secrecy of the mission. Now, she regretted it fully. What if she died tonight? What if she never again had the chance to tell her sister that she loved her with all of her heart? She took in a breath of cold air and tried to keep the tears from coming. One escaped, and she quickly turned her mind to the task at hand. A TCO officer could not weep during a mission. Nor would a valiant Kingdom Initiate.

In the distance, pines tore a jagged line in the glowing night sky. Stones crunched under her hiking boots as the wind picked up again, and the path began to rise, growing steeper. Water glittered under the moonlight far beyond the path and fields, beautiful. Too bad she was most likely going to have to deal with a zombie right in the middle of it.

Why had Medb gone quiet? Surely the book was nearby. Their connection should be better, not worse. That worried her more than anything else.

As the stony path rose and the clouds flittered past the moon, pushed by the cool wind, Jayne whispered to herself about Medb.

"Queen Medb stood taller than most women of her time, or so the stories say."

Ancient people had walked this same path, with brightly colored shields and hunting dogs at their sides. They'd carried their powerful queen's body up this same slope. Jayne inhaled, taking in the same air they had breathed. She could almost hear their old language on the breeze, their footsteps on the rocks, their songs rising as they went to bury the great warrior.

"They say she drove a great chariot," she said to herself, "and would scream as she went into battle. There is no doubt that if the records are remotely accurate, she was a passionate and violent figure."

The wind kicked up and the grass around the path whistled. At a curve in the trail, one lone tree stood, its branches moaning slightly as the air danced through. Jayne tucked her hair behind her ears.

"Medb had many lovers. She took her warriors to bed as she pleased, as was custom in that Celtic, or rather Gaulish, culture, depending on your frame of reference. When she was finally killed, her warriors buried her standing up, in full armor, facing Ulster, the land of the king who refused to bow to her wishes and who had defeated her in battle."

The whispering continued, now off script.

"I like to think I'm similar to you in some ways, Queen Medb. Strong. Passionate. Why won't you help me now?"

Silence.

After about forty-five more minutes of incline, Jayne looked up from the path and gasped. A mound of pale stone rose, proud and immovable. In front of it, a circle of flickering torches lit a group of twenty, maybe more. She heard her name whispered on the wind and shivered.

She knew that voice. But this was impossible.

If anyone had asked her, she would've said no way she'd remember that voice. It had been too long. Too many years. And she never watched videos of her past. It had been too painful.

But when a figure came out of the shadows, hands outstretched and smile cold, and said her name again, Jayne stumbled.

"Jayne. It has been so long."

And Ruth Thorne stepped into the full light of the fire.

CHAPTER SIXTY-NINE

It must be an illusion. Alarik playing tricks on her, trying to see how she'd react.

But Ruth took her daughter's hands and gently pulled her close. Her eyes were unreadable in the dark. She smelled of iron and violets. The scent was as familiar to Jayne as her own, but not pleasant at all.

This is real this is real this is real she is real it's actually her. What the ever-loving...

Jayne yanked her hands away and braced them on her knees. She was going to pass right on out. Right here. Right now.

Mom. It was her mother.

"But you're dead. You died." Tears streamed from her eyes, and she fought to control herself.

"It was a necessary illusion. I am sorry, Jayne."

Jayne felt Ruth's hands on her back, but they did nothing to comfort her. They never had. Even when she was little, her mom had been a nasty thing. Blunt about Jayne's shortcomings and devoid of mercy when it came to childish accidents and mishaps.

Sofia. What would she say? How would Sofia process this? Terrible or not, she was still their mother.

Jayne coughed and tried to stay upright. "Please tell me what the hell is going on."

"I had to manufacture the accident to protect the cause of the Kingdom. You understand, though, don't you? After learning from Alarik and the rest how we must change the world? Tell me you understand."

"'Manufacture the accident'?" Jayne couldn't breathe. She tore her coat's zipper down and threw her head back, trying to take in air. "But Dad. What...about..." She couldn't finish the question. If she got her hopes up that her dad might not be dead...

"Your father is safe."

The world blurred.

"He lied, too? He is alive, and he hasn't talked to us?" Her heart cracked, hard and fast. She wished Sofia was here to stand beside her and help her ask these questions. Jayne didn't even know where to start.

Ruth rubbed Jayne's arm as Alarik, Teresa, and the rest looked on. "He wanted to. But we encouraged him to keep his silence."

Jayne whirled, eyes searching. "Where is he? Dad? Dad!"

Her mother's voice was surprisingly gentle, though it still cut like a razor. "He isn't here. But I will take you to him. When we are finished tonight. Let me just say, I am so pleased, proud, and wholly surprised that you are the one who shook the Torrent, that you are the Master to be, the one our organization truly needs. To think, my own child... It is fate."

"Fate? Fate that I have this power I never knew about? Fate

that you deserted us? That you've kept our father from us? What sort of fate is that?"

"All is well, daughter. You will understand soon." Ruth's arms circled Jayne's shaking body. She'd never been a hugger, and it was pretty obvious she was only doing this to calm Jayne down so that they could get down to business. Or entrap her. Which was worse, Jayne didn't know—comfort from or imprisonment in her mother's arms?

Jayne couldn't process this. There was no way she could carry on. They would have to abort. But how could she let Ruger and Cillian know about this development? She had no phone. Maybe she could use the Telepathy spell. Yes. She would manage it. Screw this. She needed a damn moment here.

Wait. Did Alarik and the others know about the TCO? Could they use the Telepathy spell to look inside her head and get the truth?

She pulled a ward from the Torrent and wrapped it around her thoughts. She couldn't jeopardize them.

Alarik smiled his creepy-ass grin. "We know you aren't Jayne Thomas. We realized you were lying when Ruth heard your description and your first name. It is understandable that you deceived us. You've been through a great deal in your young life. And you had to be careful, becoming involved with us. You are simply a careful person. We respect that."

So, no on the TCO. Phew. She tightened the ward, keeping all of them safe behind the shield.

"I don't understand, Mom. When did you join the Kingdom?" Jayne fought to keep the anger from her voice. She had to pretend to be happy about this development. It was the toughest thing she'd done, outside of attending her non-dead parents' funeral and sitting with Sofia during chemo.

"I never joined, Jayne. I *created* the Kingdom. I am the Head."

Jayne's eyes fluttered closed, and she swayed on her feet.

Her mother was the Head. The one she'd been afraid to meet.

"And," Ruth said quietly, "with the Healing skills Alarik has developed in you, you might be able to make certain Sofia no longer worries that her cancer will return."

"That would be…" She couldn't voice the hope. "I've only healed cuts. I don't think I could do more."

"It will take a long time, yes, but hopefully, tonight will go as planned and you'll have all the space and support you need to fully come into your amazing powers. I knew you were special. Even when you were little. There was just…something about you. I had hoped you had magic, but you showed no inclination toward it. And to find out not only do you have magic, but that you are this powerful? It's such a glorious surprise."

Shit. Ruth was actually rubbing her freaking hands together. Jayne finally had her TV villain. Disgusting. Ruth was only rooting Jayne on for her own purposes and was using Sofia's cancer as motivation to manipulate Jayne.

A shout of betrayal and rage crawled up Jayne's throat, but she shoved it down. She could rage another time. If she did it now, this group would just kill her, find another strong Adept, and there would be a new world coming. A dark world, full of magic-workers who didn't give a crap about anyone else. The world would lose its advances in technology, and the lives depending on such things would be lost forever. And then, they'd work to control the entire population from the inside out.

One tiny light of hope shined in this situation. They didn't seem to know anything about the TCO.

But then another shock occurred inside Jayne's head. Did the TCO already know Ruth was the Head? Did Ruger know? Did they bring her in exactly because of this?

She clutched at her coat, her heart pounding at the continued string of betrayals. No. They didn't know. They would've told her that. Surely. They would've had to know if Jayne found out like this, she'd be too rocked to operate properly.

But maybe not.

Maybe they hoped her ignorance would be a better cover. Jayne knew she wasn't fabulous at acting. Ruger knew that, too.

"Damn it all. I can't believe this." She hadn't meant to say it out loud.

Alarik stepped closer as Ruth, Teresa, and the rest looked on. "Can you continue? This is time sensitive. We need to work while the moon is full. I don't know how long we can escape notice from the locals, and we'd rather not have any outside distractions tonight."

Breathe, Jayne, she told herself. *Breathe.*

"Okay. I'm ready. I mean, I'm not. Of course I'm not. I want to see my dad. But I understand the seriousness of this night. And I'm ready."

Ruth had never given Jayne such a kind, motherly look. She was very nearly convinced her mother wasn't a monster. Nearly.

As if Ruth had felt her daughter's urge, she ran a hand over Jayne's head. "We might have to show some tough love tonight. You are fully committed to the cause, right?"

Tough love to the world? Tough love to Jayne? What, exactly, was she talking about?

"Yes. I am committed. I believe in the Kingdom's mission," Jayne lied.

"Good girl," Ruth said, making Jayne's skin scrawl. Ruth faced Alarik. "Then let us begin."

Alarik motioned to another member, who fetched a duffel bag. Jayne could see it from the dancing light thrown to the rocky ground by the torches. Ruth lifted some sort of large object from the bag's dark insides. She held it up, and the moon's glow painted it silver.

Nine long, clear crystals, bound together in copper, made a circle like a massive diadem.

"This will help us with the casting." Ruth's eyes glittered.

The man who'd brought the duffel bag wiped sweat off his head even though the air around them was freezing. "You think it will protect us? From burning?"

Ruth gave him a confident nod. "I do. And so does Alarik."

Ruth, Alarik, Teresa, bag guy, and four others came forward. Each put one hand on a crystal.

"Jayne?" Ruth glanced from Jayne to the remaining crystal.

They wanted her to take hold of the ninth spot. Of course they did. This was why they'd groomed her, why her mother had most likely kept Alarik from murdering her shortly after she'd jumped through his portal the day he'd stolen the Book of Leinster.

Suddenly, moments of childhood blinked through Jayne's mind.

Her mother singing a strange song and the sound of wind in Jayne's ears.

The Roman vase their family had given up vacation to buy and how Ruth had pressed it into Jayne's hands with an odd look, expecting something to happen that never did.

And the book of her father's that Jayne had kept, full of silly proverbs and little sayings. The book Cillian had stolen for the Kingdom.

Ah.

Now, Jayne knew why she'd seen Ruth in that book, and she now remembered what her mother had said in that vision.

"*To begin again, the world reborn.*" Jayne curled her fingers around the ninth crystal and locked eyes with Ruth.

Her mother's smile was luminous. "You remember?"

"I do."

Alarik and a few other Kingdom members had used the motto, the motto her own mother had created.

This was so messed up.

Jayne watched as each member holding the crystal diadem closed their eyes to access the Torrent. Jayne shut her own and felt the magic embrace her.

Alarik's voice echoed through the streaming green stars as he chanted. "To raise a Master. To raise the great Medb. To restore magic. To begin again, the world reborn. Raise her from her sleep. Raise her from her sleep. Raise her from her sleep."

Ruth's sharp voice joined in, then the others wove their own chants into the first.

Jayne opened her mouth to play along. "To raise…"

But the words wouldn't come out. An eerie pressure rose around her lips and tingled along her fingertips. It was almost as if the Torrent was saying, *No, Jayne. Not this spell.*

And the Torrent was right. This felt wrong. Upside down. The Torrent didn't want to work this spell, to show the shape of the magic. It was even harder than Healing or Capturing.

That was it. Her plan had to start now, with or without backup, because there was no way she was going to rebel against the Torrent like this. She would burn to cinders. She knew it as surely as she knew she loved Sofia.

Jayne would lift her hand from the crystal, then Capture Ruth and Alarik as quickly as possible. She lifted the ward from her thoughts to give her extra power. Three, two, one.

She uncurled her fingers from the cool crystal and summoned the Capture spell from the Torrent. Opening her eyes the second she had the spell in hand, she threw the woven strands of magic at her mother.

Ruth shouted as golden beams of light trapped her struggling body.

The rest of the Kingdom members dropped the diadem.

Turning from Ruth, Jayne threw the Capture spell at Alarik.

But he threw up a Block, and combined with the psychic weight of holding her mother in place, the force of it tossed Jayne to the ground.

Her spell dissipated.

Ruth stood, freed. Anger and disappointment washed over her features, the harder, meaner version of Jayne's. "Stupid girl. You always were too headstrong for your own good. I wish we could've done this without further ugliness, but you have forced our hand, Agnes Jayne. Alarik? Please bring our guests forward."

Alarik and another man disappeared into the shadows beyond the torches.

A minute later, Alarik appeared, holding a man whose hands were tied and face bloodied almost beyond recognition. It was—

"Sorry, Jayne," Cillian slurred. "My timing is usually perfection."

And the other Kingdom member dragged a woman forward.

Jayne's heart dropped. "Sofia?"

CHAPTER SEVENTY

Jayne's heart cinched, tight and painful between her ribs. "No."

She nearly fell to her knees to beg them to let them go, but she couldn't. They weren't going to give them up for any kind of begging.

She had to help them raise the dead. Maybe with Medb's mind merged with her own, she could gain the strength to get them all away safely.

Where the hell was the TCO?

Facing Ruth, she spat out her agreement. "Fine. I can't believe you'd threaten your own children, but fine. Let's do this." Grabbing the stupid diadem from the ground, Jayne gripped her crystal. She held it out to the others. "Come on. Let's do it."

Alarik cocked his head. "We didn't intend to hurt them."

Sofia's eyes were closed and her head lolled, but she didn't look beat up, no scratches or bruises marring her face or arms. She had to be drugged.

"But the Rogue," Alarik said, "he fought back."

Hell yeah, he did. That's my man.

Cillian was in bad shape, his chin on his chest and his body limp between Alarik and the bag guy. She was going to kick all their asses for this.

"We didn't realize he was a Rogue until tonight," Alarik said. "He has worked with us before, and we fully intend to free him and give him any kind of aid he wants when we finish here. We simply collected him because"—his gaze drifted to Ruth—"some worried you might back out when you realized we were going to attempt a Master-level spell."

She already knew this, but of course they'd think it was a great, nasty revelation. She played along, forcing herself to sound aghast. "He didn't work for you."

"Oh, but he did. We wiped his memory of it, but he was the one to return your father's journal to us, to your mother."

Ruth smiled. "And I thank you for that, Rogue."

Cillian slurred out a few curses. Jayne wished Sofia was awake and fighting.

Jayne, skin like ice, put all her fear into the one they could handle, the one they'd allow. "We could burn to death."

"Not with the crystals and one another's strength," Ruth said quietly.

"You're sure?" Alarik asked.

"I am willing to risk myself and my daughter. What do you think?"

Jayne thought Ruth was a psycho bitch, but that wasn't going to help here. "Okay," she forced herself to say meekly. Ugh. She really wanted to kick Ruth's teeth in. Hopefully, she'd have that chance soon enough. "Let's go."

An icy sleet began falling from the sky. It whipped through the night and lashed against Jayne's cheeks as the group gathered around the diadem again.

In the Torrent, Alarik started the chant, and the Kingdom members' voices blended to create a terrifying chorus of evil. Jayne opened her mouth to copy their words, and the pressure built against her lips. She gritted her teeth and forced the words out, her stomach turning. The Torrent did not want this.

"Raise her. Raise her up. Raise. Raise." The pressure turned into a heat like the burn of grease splattered up her arms, along her fingers, and across her forehead. She shrieked at the pain but kept on. "Raise her!"

The chanting rose in volume, filling Jayne's ears, her body, her blood. This was wrong. So, so wrong.

In the Torrent, a shape drifted toward Jayne's hand, sucking in green stars as it moved sluggishly forward. It resembled an eagle's talon, poised to pierce and take. Iridescent drops fell from the vicious points like ghostly blood.

Instinctively, Jayne knew it was the spell of Necromancy.

It didn't look like something that would bring life. It looked like a death trap. And as Jayne's body trembled, sweating in pain, burning, she knew it would indeed be hers.

A fleeting thought occurred to her. *Maybe I'll take the rest of these assholes with me when I go down, and the Kingdom will fail.*

She opened her eyes to see the Kingdom members, faces grimacing and sweating, gripping the diadem. They each held their free hand in a clawed shape, the same spell curling around their fingers. They shouted the chant into the cold rain, and at Alarik's nod, they cast the spell toward Medb's tomb.

At first, there was nothing.

Just the pain. The burning.

Jayne would never forget the smell. Her nightmares had been filled with the imagined stench of it. Now, the horrible dream was almost coming true. The searing skin. The heat on her flesh.

Jayne was burning to death.

At least she didn't have to watch her parents die as she had in the nightmare. At least she didn't have to do that.

The pain roared inside her, and she moaned.

One name echoed through her head. *Sofia.* If Jayne died here, without telling her sister anything... She choked on a sob. This would hit her sister hard. She knew it because if the same thing happened in reverse...Jayne couldn't fathom a life without her partner in crime, her shoulder to cry on, her pie-contest-loving Rock of Gibraltar.

Her hands shook, both of them, one holding the vibrating crystal, and the other left weak and lifeless from the spell's drain.

I'm sorry, Sofia.

Her stomach clenched, and her gorge rose, but she was too weak to do anything but stand there and burn. Her pulse pounded in her ears.

Another type of drumming matched its beat.

The ground was moving.

The drumming grew louder, and Ruth's eyes shone. "It's happening," she hissed, her own forehead bunched tightly as she too tried to handle the pain of burning alive from the inside out.

The torches sputtered in the pelting rain. One went black.

A stone tumbled from the top of the burial mound to the ground. It rolled all the way to Jayne's boot. She looked up to see more rocks cascading off the grave.

A shiver ripped across Jayne's back, and her vision blurred, clouded by the pain and the ice and magic sizzling through her bones. The earth under Jayne's feet hummed.

She stared toward the cairn.

A shout punched the air, and suddenly, a figure emerged from the falling stones.

She was breathtaking.

Medb—legendary Iron Age warrior, Torrent Master, queen of fae and human alike—walked out of death and into life. Dark hair fell from her elaborate high braid and over her cliff's-edge cheekbones. She looked at them each in turn, and adjusted her grip on a long, black, double-edged sword. Her voice was like ten claps of thunder at once.

"Who dares raise this queen?"

CHAPTER SEVENTY-ONE

The queen was whole, but her flesh was too pale, too blue. Her eyes were pools of light and dark, swirling and bright as she looked, unblinking, straight at Jayne. The thunderous words reverberated through her, and Jayne dropped the crystal diadem.

The burning stopped.

Medb's hips swayed under her bronze-detailed cuirass, and she pointed a long finger. More words spilled from her death-blue lips. These weren't in any language Jayne knew.

"Begin the Telepathy!" Alarik called, and everyone got a better grip on the diadem.

Jayne kept staring at the approaching queen. She felt Alarik force her hand to hold the crystal.

"Now, Jayne! Now!" Sweat poured from Alarik's face.

Medb shouted the same words again and swung her sword in a wide arc like she was warming up.

Jayne did not want to know what Medb was prepping for.

Aloud, not in Jayne's head, Medb spoke her ancient language, the rain sliding off her blue-tinted mouth.

"I—I can't understand you," Jayne stammered, fear clawing her throat.

The queen pressed her lips together and studied Jayne while the rest of the circle of casters tried to manage the Telepathy spell. Jayne had no room in her brain right now to even see if it might be working the way they'd hoped.

And then a haunting voice flowed into Jayne's mind.

I greet you with respect, Master.

Jayne froze. The queen's voice was gravel and steel. But also… familiar.

Do you not bow to queens in your age?

"I…don't. I don't know." Jayne had completely lost her ability to form a thought. She was fairly sure she was going to get her head good and cut off if she didn't bow right this second, though.

And so she did.

Jayne knelt in the wet grass and rocks, then bent her head. *And I respect you, Master and queen.*

A hand touched the back of Jayne's head. She looked up to see Medb almost smiling.

Jayne shivered hard.

What are these fools attempting here on this foul night? Medb said inside Jayne's mind. *Why have they taken me from my slumber? Do you command them?*

Jayne assumed Medb was talking about Alarik and Ruth and the rest. *I don't command them. They want you to do something for them. I am here to deter.*

Why would I help such rabble?

Then the queen paused, her eyes wide.

What was happening? *Medb!* "Medb! They're trying to control your mind!"

The queen spun on her heel, spinning through the rain, and sheathed her sword. She raised both arms to the sky.

Alarik's teeth were white in the near dark, and Ruth stared at Medb, her mouth moving.

They had done it.

They had taken control of Queen Medb's mind. With the power of eight Adepts, and the distraction of the ninth, they'd managed complete control.

Jayne took advantage of their focus on Medb. She ran to the man holding Sofia and drove her shin upward into the Kingdom member's groin. He'd been distracted, too, so the move worked, and he went down like a sack of potatoes. Sofia went down, too. Jayne gripped her arms and dragged her over the ground, aiming for a patch of thick grass. But a shout stopped her. She bent to touch Sofia's face, then ran back to find Cillian fighting with his captor.

A crack of lightning briefly blinded Jayne, and she blinked as Cillian's man fell.

Cillian's eyes—pale in the chaos of drying blood around his nose and cheeks—fixed on her.

Lightning snapped across the sky again. Jayne helped Cillian to his feet, then turned to see Medb's fingers clawing the air. Sparks zipped through her knuckles, across her palms, and then lightning exploded above the burial mound and thunder rocked the ground.

Jayne gripped Cillian's sleeve. A ball of swirling light, blue-white in the dark, formed above Medb. "Queen Medb! Please!"

The queen's palms pushed out, straight forward, aiming for something no one else could see.

Where was Ruger? Where was the TCO?

Cillian's fingers were tight on Jayne's arm. "I'll slam into the group with the crystals to shake them up a little as you try to talk to her telepathically," he said.

"It's a plan."

He rushed toward the Kingdom members, knocking both Ruth and Alarik to the ground. Cillian's face hit Ruth's elbow, and his lip split wide open, spilling blood down his torso.

Queen Medb, Jayne shouted inside her head as thunder rolled over the burial mound, *they want to use you. Don't let them sway you.*

Medb's arm jerked, but the sphere of lightning was already gone.

Alarik yanked Cillian up to stand, then held his hand up to cast some spell.

Jayne was in and out of the Torrent in a breath, holding the Spell to Kill. Ignoring the pain throbbing through her body, she threw the magic at Alarik.

He went stock-still. Then fell dead to the ground.

Ruth was at Jayne's side in the blink of an eye. Jayne's energy dropped, and unthinking, she grabbed for Ruth, the knee-jerk reaction of a daughter needing help from her mother.

"You killed him!" Ruth slapped Jayne hard across the cheek, and Jayne fell, rolling to land beside Alarik's body.

The slap felt worse than any kind of magical drain or burn. Her mother truly was a monster.

Jayne had to kill her, too.

Cillian called Jayne's name, but another three Kingdom members had grabbed him, and his words dissolved in the thunder before Jayne could untangle them.

Ruth shouted something, and the rest of the Kingdom members rushed toward Medb—to do what, Jayne didn't know.

Teresa held up what looked like a small box. "The first stations are out. We hit Northern Ireland!"

A cheer went up and Medb glared, looking for all the world like a cornered and darted lion.

Master Mage, Medb said to Jayne. *I have a gift.*

And then the world went black.

CHAPTER SEVENTY-TWO

Jayne opened her eyes to see Cillian's face and stars above. So. Many. Stars.

"Thank Jesus, woman. I thought you'd died." Cillian helped her to stand., hugging her tight to his side.

Medb stood watching them, a Mona Lisa smile on her mouth. She still wore her armor, but her flesh was rosy and whole. "Come."

Then Jayne realized that not only was the sky filled with sparkling starlight, but that the air showed plumes of bright Torrent stars as well.

Turning, Medb walked toward a pillar of smoke rising into the night sky. Men and women in patterned cloaks circled the fire, humming, eyes on the fire.

"Where are we? What happened?" Jayne tasted charcoal on her tongue.

"You're asking the wrong person." Cillian kept her arm linked through his, large fingers lightly perched on her wrist.

A scent drifted through the smoky air—something floral. Roses and woodsmoke. She jerked to a stop. "That's the scent of my magic."

Medb eyed her over a shoulder. "Our magic. Here, in the past, such power as ours flowed in and out, all around. Breathing."

"The past?" Jayne's stomach turned.

"I crafted a passage of protected moments for this event. This is my age. Before the humans savaged the world with their vibrations."

"Does she mean technology? Like frequencies?" Cillian asked.

"I guess so."

Medb ignored their musings. A cluster of stone structures roofed with earth or thatched surrounded a fortress. Stone walls supported by large wooden beams cast shadows over the town. *The Iron Age town,* Jayne realized, her mouth dropping open and her history-adoring eyes soaking as much in as they could.

"Master Mage," Medb said, "we were meant to cross paths. You, me, and your Candle."

"My Candle?"

"Cillian draws power from the Earth in a way we mages cannot. Then he feeds you. Together, you are stronger." She pronounced his name just a bit differently, with a strange *shh* and clip of the tongue in the middle.

Jayne frowned. "But we aren't bound."

Medb unsheathed her sword. "You are."

Cillian pressed his hand into Jayne's. "No offense, ladies, but I belong to no one. Not until I say it."

Medb laughed, a deep, husky sound that echoed in the ground under Jayne's feet. "Men."

Jayne started to say something—anything—to Cillian, but they'd arrived at a stand of enormous oak trees, and Medb held up her sword like she wanted silence. Jayne wasn't about to rebel.

A noose hung from the first oak's branches, and a pale robe sat folded at its roots.

"First, Master Mage, you must show sacrifice."

A line of men and women in white woolen robes streamed from the fortress toward the oak. The wind stirred their long hair and the fire of the torches they held as they gathered around Medb.

"These are my learned ones," the queen said.

Jayne's fear subsided under the academic thrill of seeing actual druids. "Yeah. I thought maybe that's what they were. But... I'm not sure I understand." It wasn't as if Iron Age queens spoke English. This was all magic, and perhaps the translation was muddied. *Please, please let it be muddied,* she thought. The muscles in her legs shook as she tried to stand tall instead of crumpling to the ground.

The druids began to hum, their voices combining to create a haunting tune that rose and fell with the flickering light.

Medb pointed her sword at the noose. "A sacrifice must be made to show your wolf heart, Master. You will show us you are worthy of my gift."

The. Hell. "If I hang myself, then giving me something seems rather ridiculous, doesn't it?"

Medb lowered her head, keeping her gaze on Jayne. Her dark eyes reflected the fingers of torchlight and the glow of the Torrent stars drifting through the air. "Trust me, your fellow Master."

Cillian shoved Jayne backward, took three steps, and placed his head in the noose. "If you demand a death here, I'm sure as hell not watching her die."

A shiver rocked Jayne, and she took a step toward the queen.

"I won't sacrifice myself or Cillian this way."

"Hmm." Medb flipped her sword and pointed the tip at Jayne's throat.

Jayne summoned every ounce of courage burning in her cold veins. "You won't kill me. You said you had a gift."

Standing her ground against the ancient queen, Jayne refused to allow her legs to shake or her eyes to lose focus on Medb.

"How little they teach mages in your time... But I see the wolf heart in you." Medb ran the sword through Jayne's neck.

Mind on fire, Cillian ripped the noose out of the tree and lunged for the queen as leaves fluttered to the ground where Jayne had fallen. "She trusted you!" He tore the noose from his neck, fury rushing through him.

Medb whispered words Cillian couldn't understand, her sword dripping, and then he was tossed against the tree trunk. Invisible hands pinned him to the bark, and a crack sounded from his side. He cried out in every kind of pain, watching Jayne's blood pour from her wound, her eyes gone wide and lifeless.

"And you should trust me as well, Candle Flame." Medb held out her sword. A druid handed his torch to the man beside him, then cleaned the queen's sword on a strip of cloth. Medb sheathed the weapon, then knelt by Jayne, the cloth in her hand.

The sick freak. "Get the hell away from her," Cillian croaked, his side burning with pain.

Jayne coughed, and Cillian's breath caught as she sat up, alive.

Jayne blinked. Anger rushed through her, and she gripped Medb by the throat. "You're going to tell me what is going on. Right. Now."

More and more Torrent stars spun around Jayne's hand and in the air around Medb, the magic making Jayne feel drunk. Her brain couldn't catch up with what had happened. It was impossible.

"You had to die so you could live. I had to kill your fear." Medb stepped back, flicked a hand at Cillian. He dropped from where she'd obviously pinned him. Then the queen helped Jayne to rise, her grip like steel.

Jayne touched her own neck, where the sword had gone through, and only felt the bump of a scar. "You healed me?"

"Yes, but that is not my gift for you."

Cillian came close, and Jayne could see his hands shaking. "It had better not be, considering you're the one who wounded her."

Medb faced a female druid with braided silver hair. "The gift."

The druid, the only one not holding a torch, drew something from the folds of her robe. Stone-faced, she handed it to the queen.

It was a small box carved with curling symbols often seen in La Tène artifacts. Medb held the cloth above the box and squeezed it tightly. Blood dripped on the latch—Jayne's blood—and the ancient Iron Age lock creaked open. She lifted the ornate lid and removed a shining stone.

In her large, warrior's hand, the stone looked like a massive opal, but with more flecks of green. As Jayne watched Medb lift the stone to show it off, visions soared through her mind. Rolling hills of emerald. Mossy stones carved with spiraling designs. Roots churning under the jade growth of tall grasses.

"Earth," Medb said, her voice like thunder echoing in Jayne's bones. She pressed the stone against Jayne's forehead, and the visions grew brighter. Jayne's fingertips tingled and she couldn't catch her breath and then Medb stepped back. "With my blessing and the blessings of those present, you now possess the elemental power of the Earth."

Jayne touched the place where Medb had held the stone.

"It's shining." Cillian's words lifted barely above a whisper. "It's...the stone is...part of you, Jayne."

It should've been horrifying that a stone was now embedded in her skull, but elation spread through her chest. She felt stronger than ever. More powerful than anyone. And at the same time, peaceful. Like this was right.

Medb placed her hand over Jayne's newly crowned forehead—because that's what the stone felt like, a crown—and smiled like a proud mother. "Go now, and lead them."

Once again, the world faded to black.

CHAPTER SEVENTY-THREE

Jayne and Cillian returned to the present, and it was as if they'd never left. Medb was not the Medb from the past; this one was corpse-gray and even more frightening as she swung her sword and cast wild spells that tore the ground and ripped the sky with lightning.

Five distinct pops sounded. Portals opened up everywhere.

Finally!

Ruger, Amanda, Seo-joon, and the TCO units poured out, taking up stations between Kingdom members. Magic flew like bullets. Teresa was hit, went white, and fell. Ruth dodged a spell from Ruger, then dropped behind a small group of Kingdom men who were throwing Capture spells at the TCO.

Jayne drew on her new magical energy, the stone above her eyes pulsing with tingling power.

Cillian shouted, then shifted into a wolf to stand snarling beside her. Energy poured from his presence and rushed through Jayne's skin like sunlight. Her *Candle*, Medb had called him.

As Jayne sifted energy from Cillian, herself, and the ground—this had to be a magnetic field, like Max had shown her—she tried to speak telepathically with this Medb.

It's over. Please stop! You may rest again, great queen!

But there was no answer or any indication that Medb had heard Jayne.

Hear me, please. Master to Master. You can feel the foul souls inside these Adepts. Help me stop them.

Then finally, her voice rose inside Jayne's mind. But she sounded so different from when they were in the past or even the person she'd been in Jayne's mind earlier.

And what do you suppose I should do with these bent ones? Medb said.

You are the only royal here. You must decide what is just.

Wise woman. Wise Master. I wish you had been in my court during my reign. Tell them never to disturb me again.

Medb shouted, a battle cry, as if she might strike wildly in the middle of the spells bounding from TCO officers to Kingdom members and back again. The world was lit in blazing green and bright white. Surely, Medb wouldn't kill them all. After what they'd survived, to die now…

Sofia still lay inert on the ground. Ruger was there. And as she watched in horror, Cillian stumbled into a run and rushed headlong into the fight, still in his wolf form.

"Cillian!" Jayne flew after him.

Medb raised her sword high. Lightning flashed over her fierce eyes, parted blue lips, and smooth-edged armor. The crackling light gathered and spilled into the tip of her black iron weapon.

Ruth must have regained control of Medb's mind. All of Ireland was already suffering from the power outage. Now, Medb would hit the power stations that connected the island to the rest of the UK

The world would begin its descent into darkness, and chaos would follow on its heels.

Jayne had no plan in her head except to do something, anything. No matter what power now resided in her, she was no match for Medb while she was controlled by Ruth.

Cillian's snarls broke through the sounds of the fight and the sky. He went for a Kingdom member's throat, bright fangs flashing.

Medb lowered her sword and pointed it at the battling Adepts.

Jayne shouted, "TCO, Block!" They didn't hear her. They didn't move into defensive positions.

And Cillian had nothing to protect himself, either, save tooth and claw and a blind will mostly out of his control.

Please.

Medb's lightning blasted across the stony ground and connected with every Kingdom member left standing. The air clouded with power and light and sparkling magic, and Jayne clutched her chest, unable to breathe.

Jayne willed the TCO officers to move, to Block themselves. Sweat trickling down her temples, tears burning her eyes as much as the magic, she divided all her remaining energy between the desire to put Medb to rest and the fear for their lives. Dozens of spells that Jayne intrinsically understood wrapped around her fingers like rings and her wrists like bracelets, cold and ringing as they pealed from her in rippling sound and light.

At the last possible second, Ruger and the rest of her cohorts raised their arms in a massive Block spell.

The clash of the spells colliding was blindingly bright, and loud as a thunderclap. The battleground burst into daylight, and just as suddenly, plunged back into darkness.

When the crackling ceased, Medb was gone.

Her tomb looked as it had before the spell work. Every stone stacked in its place.

All the Kingdom members lay on the ground, dead.

But the TCO officers were unharmed.

Heart pounding, Jayne scanned the battlefield. Cillian stood, transformed back into a human, held up by Ruger. Sofia. Where was Sofia?

Jayne rushed toward where she'd laid her sister. Under a coating of ash and dirt, Sofia stirred. Jayne put a gentle arm under her head while Ruger and the rest shouted orders for which she had no time.

"Sofia?" Her sister was limp in her arms, and her bones felt thinner, like they had when she'd been sick.

Sofia's large eyes blinked open, then her face crumpled and she began to sob. "Jayne. I should've told you everything. About Mom and Dad. About our magic."

"You have magic too?"

"Not like you. Nothing like yours. But a little. And I didn't want it. I pushed it out of my mind. Alarik said that's what caused my cancer, me fighting to rein it in. That's what your migraines were, too. I know it now that I've let my magic out again. You wouldn't know it to look at me right now, but I feel better than I have in years." She broke into crying, her words unintelligible except for one phrase: "...and Dad is alive and..."

The truth was simple. Sofia's repression of her magic had forced her body to attack itself. It made so much sense. Jayne just held her and cried, too. For their father, held by their monster of a mother. For all the lies and fear. For what could've have been.

Jayne helped Sofia stand.

"They drugged me. The Kingdom. And Mom knew about it. All of it. I just can't believe she is so horrible. I can, but I just..." Sofia coughed and leaned on Jayne.

Jayne kissed the top of her sister's head. "I know. But we have one another. It'll be better from now on. We will find Dad, and we will end this." A heat like spreading wildfire surged through her veins, her magic responding to her determination.

Sofia's gaze drifted to the Earth stone on Jayne's brow.

"I have a lot to tell you about, Sofia. But for now, let's get you out of here. Cillian? You all right?"

He walked over, a slight limp in his step, and pressed a fast kiss on Jayne's mouth.

"Sofia, meet Cillian. He is sometimes a wolf."

Sofia laughed through her tears, but then her expression turned grim. "Is Mom gone?" Jayne knew Sofia didn't mean whether Ruth had left. She was asking if their mother was dead.

They began searching the dark ground.

Jayne's stomach clenched when they came to Teresa's body. She lay sprawled, eyes wide. Half her face was black from the queen's strike. A man with a white beard had fallen partially on top of her, his glasses twisted and hanging from one scorched ear. Smoke rose from his clothing. Everywhere Jayne looked, there were bodies.

Where was Ruth's?

Jayne searched the dead again, Cillian and Sofia at her side. None of the bodies had Ruth's shape or coloring. Not that it was easy to see in just the moonlight. But no, Ruth's body—the one Jayne had watched burn over and over during her nightmares—was nowhere to be found.

"She's not here, Ruger." Jayne felt him take her hand like a father would. "Ruth is gone. Did she portal out? Did you see her?"

"There was a flash, moments before the queen's hit. She must have portaled out. And she took your father's journal with her." He pointed to Alarik's body. "He doesn't have it anymore."

"Damn." Jayne looked up at him. "Tell me you didn't know my mother was the Head of the Kingdom."

He wouldn't meet her eyes. "We didn't know for sure. Originally, the TCO believed her dead. But some had a guess based on some chatter we picked up along the coast a few months ago. I am so sorry, Jayne. I was under orders. You must understand that."

But Jayne didn't. She dropped his hand. "Where is my father? Ruth said he wasn't dead. And she escaped. She has to be going to where he is."

"I doubt it. Why would she lead us there? She has to know we already have someone tailing her. Trying to tail her, at least."

"But we have to try!" Jayne shoved Ruger, her heart on fire.

"Jayne." Sofia's voice was a plea.

Ruger grabbed Jayne's hands, put his heavy fingers over hers. "We will. But we will do it in a way that doesn't get him, and you, killed."

She pulled away to stand beside Sofia and Cillian. "How am I ever supposed to trust you and the TCO again?"

"I am your mentor. I can't always give you what will make your heart lighter. I must make you stronger and shape you into the powerful TCO officer I know you can be."

"She is already kicking a lot of ass, I'd say," Cillian choked out, his anger simmering between them. Jayne was glad to see it.

"Yes, she is," Ruger said. "But she can do more. We will go after your father. As soon as you have some recovery time. We're tracking everything. Ruth won't get far. We'll find her, and then we'll find Henry."

"I don't know if *you* will," Jayne snapped, "but I will. I swear it. And the TCO better not get in my way."

Her fear of the organization had faded.

"Please try to understand why we did what we did, Jayne. Why I did what I did," Ruger said, his voice sad.

"I don't understand anything, Ruger. Our lives"—she looked at Sofia and Cillian—"are filled with lies." It was insane to think of how the Kingdom had wiped Cillian's memories and how he'd been used.

Jayne started to walk away, but at the first steps, Cillian crumpled to the ground, a garbled word coming from him as he hit the earth.

Panic cut Jayne's chest. She knelt and grabbed his arm. "Cillian? What's wrong?"

His eyes rolled back in his head and he started to shake. There had to be another, more severe wound that she hadn't noticed.

Ruger dropped to his knees and pulled Cillian's shirt aside. They searched his body, seeing nothing on his torso. Jayne rolled Cillian toward her and saw it, a deep, ragged cut in the back of his shoulder. It must have struck a lung, too; he was wheezing, gasping for breath. Blood flowed from the wound in slow, dark pulses. Jayne met Sofia's gaze, then Ruger's as he touched Cillian's pale forehead, felt his pulse.

"The wound is mortal, Jayne."

Sofia gripped Jayne's arm, a silent support. But Jayne was having none of this. Fury flowed through her veins. No, Cillian was not allowed to die. Not after all they'd accomplished today. The world needed more men like Cillian, not fewer.

Jayne needed him.

A steely cold slid over Jayne's body. She had to try to heal him.

"Ruger, Sofia, stand back. Give me some space."

"Jayne. No. You can't heal this. It's a magical wound..." He looked down at Cillian, misery etched across his granite features. "I'm sorry."

"You can do this, Jayne," Sofia said, surprising Jayne.

If Sofia believed in her...

Sofia stepped away, and Amanda joined her, asking quiet questions.

"Back up, Ruger," Jayne said. He just shook his head. Fine. She'd warned him, so it was on him if he went up in flames with her. Every one of Jayne's lifelong nightmares of fire and screaming tore through her mind. But she had to try. She wouldn't be able to live with herself if she didn't at least try.

She plunged into the Torrent without thought, and the twinkling, green lights chilled her forearms and the back of her neck. Envisioning Cillian's deep gash, she searched the Torrent for the Healing spell. How much time did he have? Would he be dead by the time she located the spell? What would happen if she tried a Healing spell on him then, if her timing was wrong?

The spell materialized in front of her face, bone-white, glistening, humming with dangerous power. She moved her hands to encircle the spell, then ripped it from the Torrent, bringing it back into the physical world. She didn't notice the stars surrounding her as they leaked from the magical realm into the physical, slipping out the rift she'd created. Focusing on Cillian's wound, floating the spell an inch above the bleeding gash, she poured herself into the magic.

"*Heal!*" she commanded, not recognizing her own voice.

"Jayne! No!" Ruger was moving in her periphery, but she ignored him.

Her fingers felt like wax-soaked wicks catching fire, and her forearms sizzled. The scent of flesh burning rose into the air around her sweating face. The pain of powerful, Master-level magic flamed up Jayne's toes, into her legs, her torso, her chest until she thought she would scream in agony. But she stayed focused, pouring all her energy into Cillian's wound.

Please work. Please, please, please.

Then the river of stars flowed through her, the wake of their essence cooling her blood. Her magic faded; the burning of her flesh ceased.

And Cillian took a deep, unimpeded breath and opened his beautiful blue eyes.

"Jayne?"

"Thank you, thank you, thank you."

She didn't know if she was thanking Medb, or the Torrent, or the universe itself.

"You're welcome?" Cillian's eyebrows knitted.

Jayne exhaled and braced a hand on the damp ground beside Cillian's arm. The wound was puckered and red, but fully closed. She touched his neck, and his pulse beat sluggishly under her fingertip.

"Had to get a bit of attention, didn't you?"

"What happened?" he asked.

Ruger gripped Jayne's shoulder, praising her skills and talking about future plans, but Jayne had no ears for it. She leaned forward and pressed a kiss to Cillian's soft lips.

"You tried to die on me, you idiot. Don't do that again."

"Yeah, please don't," Sofia added. "I like how my sister looks when she smiles at you."

Cillian grinned against Jayne's mouth. "I only wanted to help you show off your muscle. You healed me, Jayne. I felt your magic move through me, and then all the pain stopped. Amazing."

"Can you get up?"

"I can try." Smiling, she helped him to his feet as TCO officers scurried this way and that, throwing out congratulations to Jayne on her proficiency and whispering with one another, glancing with awe. There was a Master in their midst.

Ruger, too, was staring at them in admiration, or fury, she couldn't figure out which.

"Hey, want to portal us home? I couldn't replace all his lost blood, and I need a nap. And pie. Immediately."

Before Ruger could act, two officers jumped to do her bidding, working magic in spurts of movement and flashes of blinding light.

"Portal is ready, ma'am."

"Let's go home." Jayne took Cillian's arm, and they started down the hill toward the shimmering portal in silence, passing the twisted bodies of the Kingdom members as they went.

Thank you, Medb, Jayne thought, and was astonished to feel the whisper of the breeze gathering around her body, a sound that seemed to say, "Thank *you,* Master."

CHAPTER SEVENTY-FOUR

Jayne opened the door to Sofia's new apartment, and the cinnamon and brown sugar scent of sweet potato casserole wafted right into her face.

Cillian sniffed noisily. "I could get used to this dessert-heavy treatment you Thorne girls dish out."

Jayne tried to smile, the spell to mask the Earth stone on her brow tingling. It wasn't easy to grin or laugh, knowing her dad was out there, somewhere. Her mother, too. But there was work to be done and a lead to follow. Though she hadn't outright quit the TCO, she had many, many thoughts of doing just that. They lied to her, kept secret the fact that her parents were alive. Not cool.

Cillian squeezed Jayne's hand briefly. They'd talked vaguely about it on the plane ride over after their final debriefing with Ruger. Thankfully, Cillian supported her, no matter what she chose to do. To lighten the last leg of their trip, Jayne had given Cillian Sofia's werewolf romance book. *A guidebook to the new you,* she'd joked.

Now, with his duffel thrown over one shoulder, Cillian held the beat-up paperback, ready to return it and enjoy some cheeky discussion of the details with Jayne's sister.

The paperback made Jayne think of Gerard. Before she and Cillian had left Ireland, Jayne had sent a written letter to Rosalind, Gerard, and even Deirdre, because Jayne had to pretend she didn't know Deirdre wasn't coming back. She'd thanked them for welcoming her in, mentioning the joy of working under someone as dedicated and intelligent as Rosalind as well as the fun she'd had in verbal sparring with Gerard—a worthy adversary in the art of insults. She had turned in a leave of absence, claiming personal issues, knowing Gerard would go along with the ruse to keep Rosalind ignorant and protected.

Jayne shook her head. Personal leave. Sure. Just the fate of the world. No big.

The whole scenario remained nearly too much for Jayne to take in. Since Ruth had gotten away with Henry's journal, no doubt the Kingdom would rise again, with her horrible mother leading the way, and they would come for her and that stone she'd been given. They wanted to control nonmagical humans, and now that Jayne possessed the first of the five elemental gifts needed to unlock the ability to do just that, the Kingdom would come and she'd have another terrible war to fight.

But she would never feel like Officer Jayne Thorne, TCO Magician and Master of the Torrent. Conqueror of Zombies and Taker-Downer of Magical Terrorists. Nope. She was still just Agnes Jayne Thorne, book nerd. She was just a gal who wanted a good read, a bucket of tea, and a pie the size of her face. And of course, the hot wolf by her side.

Sofia came happily screaming down the hallway, arms outstretched and red lipstick highlighting her open mouth.

Jayne collided with her into the hug of a century.

Sofia squealed into Jayne's ear. "Can you smell the awesomeness? I cooked all your favorites!" She shoved Jayne back and stared at Cillian, wiping buttered hands on her apron. "Nice to see you again, Cillian. It'll be a while until dinner is ready. Take your things to the first door on the left." Sofia pointed up a set of narrow stairs and grinned. "I'll just be in the kitchen." She turned, putting her earbuds back in. Her music was so loud they could hear it from two feet away.

Upstairs in the guest room, Cillian tossed his duffel on the floor and bounced on the bed. "Cozy."

"Do you want me in here, or should I give you some space?" Jayne was truly okay either way. It had been a tiring flight and drive here, and she wouldn't blame him if he needed some peace in all this strangeness. "I can totally stay in Sofia's room."

Cillian stretched out on the bed and put his arms behind his head. He wiggled his eyebrows and thrust his hips teasingly. "What do you think?"

Jayne laughed. "Not until after I have had a shower, sir. I feel disgusting."

"A shower? Yes, that does sound nice." Standing, he pulled his shirt over his head.

"I wonder…are all Rogues so hot?"

"Sofia's book leads me to believe that's a *yes*. And thank you. Although I'd say you are the hotter one."

"No way. I'm the bookish one."

He moved to her and peeled her shirt off slowly, kissing her ribs and neck. "Any chance time with me might manage at least second place to books?"

"I doubt it." Delicious chills spread over her skin as his hands moved expertly about their business. "But I think you should definitely give it the old college try."

"As you wish, my lovely librarian."

Jayne pulled away, stunned with delight. "Did you just sort of quote *The Princess Bride*?"

Cillian gave her a sly look. "Perhaps."

Before things got totally out of hand, Jayne's phone rumbled to life on the bedside table. She groaned when she saw Amanda's number on the screen.

"Duty calls?" Cillian asked.

"Duty can kiss my ass."

Cillian hooted a laugh. "An intriguing visual."

As she silenced her phone and started the water, Cillian set to kissing her throat, his scent and warmth as intoxicating as the dirtiest of martinis. She gripped his waist, pulled him to her. He kissed every finger, then blew warm air along her arm, his breath fanning across her skin, before he nipped at her neck. Steam rose around them. She was going to lose her mind. At last, they were somewhat safe, secrets bared, ready to enjoy one another in full.

Later, hair still damp from their extended time in the shower, Jayne extricated herself from his arms and picked up the phone. Seven missed calls. Uh-oh. The phone wriggled in her hand with call number eight. Jayne recognized the number.

"Yes, Amanda?"

"Jayne, thank the Goddess you finally answered. We have a problem. Ruger has gone off the radar. He's been in Paris following up on some of Alarik's previous book inquiries. There's a grimoire we think Ruth might be after. We haven't been able to make contact with Ruger for three days. You're needed, Jayne. We're preparing a portal. Get back to your apartment in Nashville and await instructions. And bring your Rogue. He may be needed as well."

Amanda hung up without getting a reply. Jayne swung off the bed, put her feet on the floor.

Ruger. Damn.

"What's the matter?" Cillian asked, a hand on her thigh.

Jayne sighed. "There's a disturbance in the force. Have you ever been to Paris?"

ACKNOWLEDGMENTS

Thanks to the following fabulous people and institutions for
their help in developing the world of
Jayne Thorne, CIA Librarian

Brandee Crisp, Park Ridge Public Library
Teresa Gray, Special Collections and University Archives,
Jean & Alexander Heard Libraries, Vanderbilt University
The Nashville Public Library Archives
The Library of Trinity College Dublin
Amy Kerr
Laura Blake Peterson
Kim Killion
Phyllis DeBlanche
Leigh Kramer
Joss Walker's Readers and Rogues
Our families
And the Knights in Shining Armor, with love
Randy Ellison and Daniel Klapheke

Look for *New York Times* Bestselling Author
JOSS WALKER'S
next book in the Jayne Thorne,
CIA Librarian adventure series

THE MASTER OF SHADOWS

Coming soon

CONNECT WITH JOSS

Website: www.josswalker.com
Newsletter: www.josswalker.com/newsletter
Instagram: @josswalkerbooks
Twitter: @josswalkerbooks
Facebook: @josswalkerbooks

LOOK FOR MORE TITLES FROM TWO TALES PRESS

ABOUT THE AUTHOR

JOSS WALKER is the fantasy pen name for *New York Times* bestselling thriller author J.T. Ellison, where she explores her love of the fantasy genre and extraordinary women discovering their power in the world. With Jayne Thorne, CIA Librarian, Joss has created a brilliant new lighthearted urban fantasy series perfect for lovers of books, libraries, romance, and of course, magic.

The first novel in the series, *Tomb of the Queen*, was co-written with Alisha Klapheke.

ABOUT J.T. ELLISON

J.T. ELLISON is the *New York Times* and *USA Today* bestselling author of more than 25 novels, and the EMMY® award winning co-host of the literary TV show A WORD ON WORDS. With millions of books in print, her work has won critical acclaim, prestigious awards, has been optioned for tele-vision, and has been published in 28 countries. Ellison lives in Nashville with her husband and twin kittens.

ABOUT ALISHA KLAPHEKE

ALISHA KLAPHEKE, a *USA Today* bestselling fantasy author, wants to infuse readers' lives with unique magic, far-flung fantasy settings, and romance. Her inspiration springs from an obsession with history, years of world travel, and the fantasy she grew up reading when she was supposed to be doing her math homework.

CPSIA information can be obtained
at www.ICGtesting.com
Printed in the USA
LVHW112003090821
694928LV00004B/6/J